Welcome to the Working Week

Welcome
to the
Working Week

Paul Vlitos

First published in Great Britain in 2007 by Orion Books,
an imprint of The Orion Publishing Group Ltd
Orion House, 5 Upper Saint Martin's Lane
London, WC2H 9EA
An Hachette Livre UK Company

10 9 8 7 6 5 4 3 2 1

A CIP catalogue record for this book is available
from the British Library.

ISBN (Hardback): 978 0 7528 8511 7
ISBN (Trade paperback): 978 0 7528 8512 4

Typeset by Deltatype Ltd, Birkenhead, Merseyside

Printed and bound at Mackays of Chatham plc,
Chatham, Kent

The Orion Publishing Group's policy is to use papers that
are natural, renewable and recyclable products and made
from wood grown in sustainable forests. The logging and
manufacturing processes are expected to conform to the
environmental regulations of the country of origin.

www.orionbooks.co.uk

Acknowledgements

For their advice and encouragement at various points I'd like to thank Cara Jennings, Katy Vlitos, my parents, Jenny McGrath, Julia Jordan, David McAllister, Alex von Tunzelmann, Claire Sargent, Heather Tilley, Nick Jones, Louise Joy, James Martin and Oliver Seares.

Very special thanks also to my agent Gráinne Fox, and to Genevieve Pegg, Jon Wood and the team at Orion Books.

Part One
The Offer of a Lifetime

Batsard

On Sunday at 18:56 Kate Staple wrote:

Dear Martin the Batsard,
I am sending you this at your work account because I know your bitch girlfriend reads your hotmail one and unlike some people I have dignity. I just got your answering phone message. HOW DARE YOU? I knew you were a coward but I never knew how much of a coward you were until now (when I got your message). I am disgusted with you and with myself. Martin you make me sick.
REPLY TO ME.
Love, Kate

p.s. I think I have a disease and I sincerely hope you (and your girlfriend) have it too.
p.p.s. By the way, I did assume you were gay when I met you. So did my friends.

On Monday at 10:07 Kate Staple wrote:

Dear Martin,
Why have you not replied to me? Are you REALLY such a coward? I haven't slept at all (well one hour). I am very upset with you. I'm sorry about what I wrote about your girlfriend. I really need to hear from you. I'm at work now, but I'm checking my hotmail. Please reply to me.
Love, Kate

On Monday at 10:34 Martin Sargent replied:

Dear Kate

Sorry not to reply to you sooner, I was a little late into work this morning due to a bomb scare at Baker Street. I've just got round to reading your messages. I think you meant to send them to Martin Sergeant, who works in the IT department. His email is ms23@mediasolutions.com. I am the other Martin Sargent, ms24@mediasolutions.com. It is a common mistake! Please don't worry about it. I hope you and Martin reach an amicable agreement.

Best Wishes

Martin Sargent

P.S. I'm sorry to hear about your disease.

P.P.S. We all assumed Martin was gay at first as well. I think it's those glasses.

Offer of a Lifetime

On Monday at 13:32 Martin Sargent wrote:

Hello all

Due to an unforeseen domestic rearrangement, there is a room available to rent if anyone is interested. If you are looking for a place to live (or know someone who is) please get in touch. This should not be taken as an excuse to offload your undesirable flatmate/lover on me. The details are as follows:

The flat: damp, mysterious odour, dark. Close to train line. Enigmatic boiler provides tepid water almost on demand.

The location: Kensal Green, NW 11 (Zone 2)

Why not take advantage of a limited period offer to experience this part of London before it's gentrified?

A twenty-minute walk to the tube takes you past the local amenities: closed public baths, semi-closed library (wide selection of work-out DVDs and large-print books), over-priced 24-hour shop, crap video shop, one halal butcher's, two dodgy pubs, one shiny new curry palace, 4 posters about gun crime, 3 appeals for witnesses.

Experience the vibrant multiculturalism of contemporary London at first hand. Listen as the schoolkids banter playfully with Mr Singh, our local shopkeeper. See them pocket Twix bars when he isn't looking. Shrug as they stare you out. Hear domestic disputes in five mellifluous languages. Smile with pride as our local lads comment appreciatively on your bike. Meet our fashionably diverse local crew of derelicts. There is also some brilliant if baffling graffiti: 'Love is for Suckers', 'I Hate Your Dog' and 'Sit on it' are my personal favourites.

Celebrity local residents include Isambard Kingdom Brunel, celebrity chef Alexis Soyer and Anthony Trollope. Apart from the world-famous cemetery, Kensal Green shops also boasts one of London's few surviving Victorian public toilets, featuring elegant tiling and a tasteful pseudo-classical portico. Make use of it now before it is converted into a desirable flat.

Don't delay. Every month the health-food shops and gastropubs of Queen's Park are creeping west. The first skips of spring have appeared in the road already. Soon the sights, smells, and noises of this lively part of London will be transformed for ever.

The occupant: moody, newly single smoker, 25. Dislikes job. No hobbies. Casual about housework. But not too casual…

Should interest: sociologist looking for area-study; exiled dictator looking for somewhere quiet to hide out; language student; trainspotter; graffitologist.

Please do not apply if any of the following words describes you: zany; bubbly; fussy; spiritual; kleptomaniac.

Rent: extortionate.

I anticipate great demand, so please pass the word around without delay.

Martin

A Jesus-shaped Hole

On Monday at 13:05 Martin Sargent wrote:

Hi Mum

Writing to say thanks for the parcel. I think the jumper is actually Dad's, but tell him I'll take good care of it. The book looks very interesting, and I look forward to getting the chance to read it. Hope is all well with you. I'm not sure about the weekend yet.
Lots of Love
Martin

On Monday at 13:10 Martin Sargent wrote:

Hey Sis

Hope term is going OK, and that life in Hall is still treating you well. I take it you're getting leaned on to go home this weekend as well? On the subject of which, I got the most extraordinary parcel from the Mum this morning. She sent me one of Dad's jumpers (that piece of foolery with the leather elbow-pads that makes him look like a retired general) under the insane misapprehension that it belongs to me. I also got a book titled *Is There a Jesus-shaped Hole in Your Life?*. I wasn't aware of it, though I am strongly conscious of a Sally-shaped hole in my love-life and a TV-and-video-shaped hole in my living room. On which note, do mention to that next-door neighbour of yours that I am now single. Speak tonight about weekend?
Love
Martin

P.S. I'm thinking of growing a moustache. Any suggestions for shape?

On Tuesday at 00:25 Lucy Sargent replied:

Hi, Martin,
In computer room at college, checking messages after night out. Mmm, chips are good. Very sorry again to hear about you and Sally (and about your TV). Next-door neighbour is here (her name is Miriam, by the way) and says Hi, but I think she has a boyfriend. Also, don't be a perve. Thought you were supposed to be heartbroken?
So I guess we won't speak tonight about weekend, but I think I may make an appearance on Sunday. Surprising how fast an allowance can go, isn't it? Last time I saw that jumper Lady was sleeping on it, so I would give it a wash if I was you.
Love,
Lucy

PS: I would advise against moustache of any description. Miriam agrees. How about a Jesus-shaped beard? (Shape of Jesus' beard, not beard in shape of Messiah obviously.) Will await further developments, and maybe see you at weekend?

On Thursday at 13:57 Martin Sargent wrote:

Hi Sis
Dad rang last night, so clearly there is a three-line whip as regards Sunday's family festivities. I'm still not quite clear why this weekend of all possible weekends we have to gather the clan. It's not that I have anything better lined up, more that almost anything else I can think of to do would be more fun than being at home. Apparently there's a big pile of my old shirts waiting for me to go through them and decide which ones I want to keep and which ones can go to the jumble. To be perfectly honest,

since I haven't worn a single one of those shirts for almost a decade, I probably wouldn't have missed any of them. I'm also unconvinced that it's a giant parental vote of confidence in me that they have kept my Sainsbury's uniform 'in case I need it again'.

I told Dad I'll be down Saturday morning, but I'll have to get away sharpish after lunch on Sunday. Sally's coming round Sunday evening to return some things she has decided she doesn't want and to steal some more of my stuff. I hope you've recovered from Monday night, and I'm sorry to hear that Miriam has a boyfriend. Is he better-looking than me? Is he taller? Is he tougher?

Wow, that book Mum gave me has really changed my life. I will give it to you at the weekend. I have abandoned the moustache idea and decided to give my life to God. As most of my worldly possessions are now in Sally's new flat, I'm already at an advantage as regards renouncing them. I have decided to forgive everyone. Can't wait to tell Mum the good news.
Love
Martin

On Friday at 16:52 Lucy Sargent replied:

Dear St Martin,
Yeah, right, you gaylord.

By the way, I met Miriam's boyfriend Frank last night (and over breakfast). As he is a large rugby-playing man, I would avoid tangling with him. Although, interestingly, he has a beard. The shape of it defies description somewhat, as it's hard to tell where the beard ends and the neck acne begins. Rather perverse I would have thought to have a beard AND shaving rash. Not a look I recommend you go for.

See you Saturday – presumably this means you'll be accompanying Mum to church on Sunday?
Love,
Lucy

David

On Monday at 11:35 Martin Sargent wrote:

Hi Lucy

Good to see you at the weekend. Very kind of you to suggest I wear my 'new' jumper to church on Sunday. And I still maintain the vicar was sniggering at my stupid elbow-pads. Possibly because I kept slipping off the communion rail.

Well, the plot thickens with Sally. As expected she turned up to pick up a few (more) things - she rather absurdly accused me of hoarding some of her underwear (which I hadn't, of course).

Not that she turned up alone. Her friend David gave her a lift over. Very kind of him. You may remember him from Sally's and my last party (which I didn't realise at the time would be our *last* party). He was ambushing people in the hall and handing out flyers for his play. As I recall he was outfitted in tapered combat trousers, a white shirt and a waistcoat Ali Baba would have rejected as being a bit 'busy'. He ends, abruptly, about five feet from the ground, in an explosion of ginger hair. Like a rather disappointing firework. I didn't see his car, but I imagine it looking like the Noddymobile.

This is NOT how it happens. I don't get dumped for David. David is the guy who gets dumped at the end when Sally realises who she really loves. He ends up falling in a duck-pond or getting a ton of manure dumped on him. He could be played by Tom Hollander in a ginger wig.

Mild revenge: I managed to slip *Is There a Jesus-Shaped Hole in Your Life?* into a box of books I was helping pack for Sally.

She sends her love, by the way.

Love
Martin

Poor Martin!

So sorry to hear about all that. I do recall David. Physically, he's more how Mackenzie Crook would look playing Malcolm McLaren. But that's not his fault. We discussed his life and works at length in the hall while he tried to peer down my top. Alas for him he was too short and he's not really my type. On the subject of casting, he told me I had the perfect face to play Lizzie Bennet in *Pride and Prejudice*. He'd make a great Mr Collins. Are you sure Sally and he are a thing? Perhaps he has hypnotic powers. Or perhaps you really pissed her off ...

The jumper looked pretty good, actually. We discovered you had accidentally left it after I dropped you at the station. In fact, you'd left it right at the back of your cupboard, stuffed behind a bag full of plastic dinosaurs. It was very lucky for you that Mum found it. Auntie Jean came round and we were looking for your school photo.

Take care of yourself, and for god's sake shave that monstrosity on your top lip off before you see Sally again. Send her my regards when you see her.

Love,
Lucy

PS: Someone was insisting to me the other day that ginger is the new blonde. I can't remember who it was now. Possibly Mick Hucknall.

Moustache

Hi, Martin,

Hope things went well (or at least as well as they could in the circumstances) with Sally last night. We found after you had gone that you had left your jumper! Will send it on. I don't suppose you want your old plastic dinosaurs. By the way, whatever happened to your old school photo? I wanted to show it to Auntie Jean. I'll look forward to hearing what you *really* thought of the book. Make sure to look after yourself. Life goes on, you know.

Love,

Mum

PS: Sorry to have to tell you but Lady has cancer again.

PPS: Darling, you know that wherever you go and whatever you do your father and I will always love and support you. But we do think that moustache is something of an error.

12

Offer of a Lifetime

On Tuesday at 9:54 Barney wrote:

Alright mate,

Long time and all that. Got your email about the flat. Afraid I am already installed with Uni mates in Balham. Not sure if you knew I was in London? Quite a few of the guys from school live around here actually. Shall I see if any of them are looking to move? Flat sounds pretty attractive. As for the company... That's you, right? Doesn't sound like you have changed much from school (except you weren't 25 at school). By the way, it might be worth thinking about making the advert more positive if you are serious about getting someone to move in.

It would be good to meet up, wouldn't it? Give me a ring (mobile still the same) if you are free over the weekend.

By the way, if you are free Saturday, I'm DJing in a bar up your way. I'll put you on the guestlist if you fancy it. Would be good to get a few friendly faces in the crowd... (Details attached)
Laters, Maters,
Barney

Saturdays @ Bar Loco
'It's Loco Time!'
15 Victoria Street
Tube: Royal Oak/Warwick Avenue
Pitchers £7.50 till 10   Shooters £3
After 7.30: £5 on the door; £4 w/flyer
No Trainers
Sounds by DJ Barney

On Tuesday at 10:15 Sally wrote:

Dear Martin,

I don't think you meant to include me on that mailing-list? Good luck with finding someone quickly. I have put the cheque for last month's electricity in the post. It was nice to see you the other day. Hope things OK with you. Speak soon, Perhaps we could go out for a drink sometime?

Warmest regards,

Sally

On Tuesday at 10:17 Martin wrote:

Dear Sally

No, I meant to put you on the list. Thanks for sending the cheque on. I miss you. As regards that pint, an old mate is DJing at a bar not far from me on Saturday - he's offered to put us on the guestlist. It's Barney from school, but the bar's alright.

Love

Martin

P.S. 'Warmest regards'?!?!?

At 16:59 on Tuesday Sally replied:

Dear Martin,

Sounds great! I'll have to come straight from rehearsal. Do you think you could put David on the list as well? I'm glad things are cool between us. See you then.

Lots of love

Sally

PS - By the way, David really likes the moustache. If that's what that thing is supposed to be.

Re: Offer of a Lifetime

Dear Martin (!),

Hi, this is Martin Sergeant (in IT). Rumour has it you're looking for a flatmate? I was wondering if you could send me the details? I've recently started looking for somewhere to live myself, so perhaps if I catch you at lunch we could discuss it?

Best,

Martin Sergeant (not you!!!)

At 11:37 on Friday Martin Sargent replied:

Hi Martin

Not sure yet, but I think the room might be taken. Thanks for your interest, look forward to discussing it with you.

See you at lunch

Martin

At 11:40 on Friday Martin Sargent wrote:

Hi Laura

How's things down in production? Don't suppose you know who's been spreading the word that I'm looking for a housemate? More to the point, how does Martin Sargent know about it? I just wondered if you had mentioned it. Otherwise, I wonder whether he is monitoring my emails? In which case, 'Hi Martin'. Want to go out (for sandwiches) this lunchtime?

Still no luck finding anyone to move in, by the way...

Let me know about lunch.
Martin

Martin,
No idea how the other MS heard about it, since I hadn't heard.
Slightly hurt, in fact, that you didn't ask me. I have a 'working'
'lunch', so looks like fish and chips with your namesake for you.
By the way, if you're so desperate for a housemate, what's wrong
with Martin? I trust it's not prejudice.
  Soon,

                              Laura

Laura
You will note I topped your flirty 12-minute response time
with a nonchalant 14 minutes. My reasons for not wanting
to live with Martin have nothing to do with his orientation
(he's not, by the way). Firstly, I have it on good authority he
is a batsard, and may well be diseased (in an unspecific but
unpleasant way). Second, I don't want to live with anyone from
work. Third, he is the kind of person who reads magazines. And
not on the train.
  Of course, I thought of you as a flatmate immediately. But: 1)
See reason two above, and 2) I may have other plans for you.
How soon?
Martin

Martin,
Two hours and forty-one minutes. Beat that! Look forward to

hearing about your battered cod with Martin. Also about your surprising grasp of his medical history.

'Other plans' sounds a bit sinister. Free this weekend.

Laura

At 16:55 on Friday Martin replied:

Laura
Only two hours ten, but it's time to go home. Genuinely busy this weekend. You're obviously a popular girl.
Have a good one.
Martin

P.S. I'm very heartbroken and vulnerable at the moment.

At 16:59 on Friday Laura replied:

Yes, I heard about the break-up. I'm sorry about that, and it's obviously very sad, but can I ask one question? Were her parting words 'Either me or that moustache has to go?' If they were I'm afraid to say I think you may have made the wrong choice.

At 17:02 on Friday Martin replied:

OK, OK, I get the message. I fact I got the message last night when a gang of kids behind me on the bus started singing 'macho, macho man.' I suspect they were being ironic.

Re: David

Alright Mate,

Thanks for coming last night. I hope you had a good time. It was good of so many people to turn up. Sorry about the muck-up with the guestlist. I'd love to know what you thought of my set. They cut me a bit short, actually, and they were a bit funny about some of the stuff I played, but everyone I spoke to was really encouraging.

I was wondering if you could let me have your mate David's email? We were talking about my maybe doing the music for a play he's directing, and I wanted to follow it up. He seems like a really chilled guy.

Cheers, Ears,

Barney

Jumper

On Tuesday at 11:15 Martin wrote:

Hey Luce

It turns out the joke is on me. I went to see Barney from school DJing at a bar on Saturday and about three people were wearing the exact same jumper as the one Mum keeps sending me. It seems to be some Paddy-Ashdown-chic thing.

You probably remember Barney (Mark Barnwell). He used to have a floppy fringe and wear a pinstriped jacket to parties. He's about eight feet high with a chin like the prow of a trireme. Well, if you want to hear some crap music ineptly cued, book him for an event. I will never be able to erase from my memory the image of him pumping his fist in the air, with a grin on his face as if he is jamming onstage with Miles Davis, when he's actually playing a mix of ironic hits to a bunch of idiots from school in a bar with no dancefloor. Not one of the greatest evenings ever. Although, having said that, David obviously enjoyed it. Indeed, they are thinking of an artistic collaboration. In a better-organised society those two would be stoned to the edge of town and banished into the desert.

Various schoolies were lurking around appraising each other. I had an extraordinary conversation with one Philip Hayward. In a brief pause in the music (Barney managed to unplug himself by dancing around behind the decks) Hayward managed to drop into conversation three times that he was 'not academically brilliant'. He emphasised the 'academically', and there wasn't much I could do except nod politely and clutch my five-quid pint to my chest to avoid it being bashed out of my hands by the coke-fuelled harpies and posh thugs struggling to get to the bar. I got the strong impression, though, that I was being asked to vouch for having recognised some special quality in him, even as a boy. The whole thing was a bit baffling.

He used to be in my history set, and I don't remember him being spectacularly stupid, but then I don't remember much about him at all, except that he fell in a river on the last day of school (or was he pushed?). Anyway, it was clearly his impression that I spend a great deal of time lying awake and thinking about how stupid he was (or is). I didn't quite catch in what way he was hinting that he was so very brilliant that society had neglected to notice. I kept expecting him to tell me he knew how to make a boat, or a pot, but he didn't. He hasn't made a million since school, or invented a cure for anything, or done much of anything I can tell except go to university and move to Clapham to live with old schoolfriends. He doesn't make clothes, or music, or even jokes. So in what way his implicit brilliance might ever be measured is hard to tell. I think he reviews restaurants online. And he was wearing Dad's jumper. All of which reminds me why I ceremonially set fire to my school photo before going off to uni. I won't tell you how I put it out.

Anyway, too long already this email, so I will say goodbye. Hope all well with you.
Love
Martin

P.S. Philip did mention, though, that he has a mate from college called Ross who is looking for somewhere to live, and he has promised to put us in touch. The mind boggles at what I'm letting myself in for there...

On Wednesday at 12:15 Lucy replied:

Hi, Martin,
Sounds pretty ghastly. Of course I remember Barney. I used to think he was pretty fit, actually, although I see what you mean about the trireme chin. Didn't quite follow for a minute and

thought you meant he has enormous painted eyes on the side of his head (has he?).

I don't suppose your irritation with Philip Hayward has anything to do with your email's conspicuous failure to mention Sally?

How is the work flirtation coming on?

Love,

Lucy

PS: Oh *that* was why you burned the school photo. I'd forgotten that. But then I was under the impression you burned it because it you looked like a freak in it.

PPS: To be fair, you did look like a freak in it.

On Wednesday at 14:15 Martin replied:

Hey Luce

I had lunch with the divine Laura today, as it happens. I doubt it will go anywhere, but it's certainly better than having lunch with Martin Sergeant (don't ask). I was enthralled to learn that she doesn't write, or paint, or act, or DJ. She will no doubt turn out to do all of the above.

As for Sally, she of course looked stunning on Saturday and was polite and charming and generally winning. She even found ways to compliment Barney (I was cornered and made to confess my opinion too: I managed 'interesting'). Which left me in an undefined and generally foul mood, which the next day drifted seamlessly into a hideous hangover. I paid a man in the loos a quid for watching me have a slash and dispensing some soap. At first I felt noble, then I felt exploited, then I realised how much the cab home alone would be and almost asked for my money back. I believe I made a drunken effort to persuade Sally to come back with me, which largely consisted of saying things like 'You're amazing; the flat is a mess without you.' I was under the impression I had said 'My life is a mess.' Needless to say, she left with David.

By the way, I notice you are cultivating an undergraduate attitude of barbed insight. Very impressive, but I do miss the old air of unqualified admiration.

Love

Martin

P.S. Too late, I realise that I should have told Barney his set reminded me of seeing Fatboy Slim play Brighton Beach. He would have been thrilled, and I wouldn't have mentioned that the specific aspect of that experience which came to mind was point at which to my horror I saw a middle-aged raver taking a crap in the sea. There was something about Barney DJing that reminded me of the mixture of pleasure and anxiety on that man's face.

P.P.S. I only looked like a freak in the school picture because they made us line up alphabetically, and I was stuck between Mark 'Basher' Townsend and Andreas 'Andy the Dandy' Sedgeworth. I looked like the middle figure in the ascent of man. Or a composite photograph out of a Victorian study of degenerate types.

On Wednesday at 16:42 Lucy replied:

Oh dear, sounds like you played it pretty uncool with Sally. As for 'unqualified admiration', that may have always been in your head, I'm afraid.

Love,

Lucy

PS: Whatever happened to 'Andy the Dandy'? He was a living legend at my school. Girls used to weep openly at the thought of his perfect centre parting.

On Wednesday at 16:45 Martin replied:

Yes, Andy used to use a ruler for that. It took him hours. Tragically, it turned out not to be a transferable skill. He was back living at home, the last I heard. However, I believe he is still a living legend at your school. No doubt the police are gathering a dossier as we speak.

On Wednesday at 16:46 Lucy replied:

'Here, Sarge, we've managed to dig out the suspect's old school photo. Christ, look at this geezer next to him. Looks like the love-child of Mr Bean and Sawney Bean. Do you think it's a ring? Let's drag him in and see what he has to say for himself.'

Take care, and let me know how things go with the mysterious Laura. By the way, we haven't heard much about your book recently ...

Re: Re: Offer of a Lifetime

On Sunday at 19:27 Crazylegs75 wrote:

Hi Martin,
A friend of yours forwarded your message to me. Are you still
looking for a housemate?
I am: fun, flirty female twenty-something (just!).
I love: dancing, clubs, music.
Sounds like you're spending too much time in the flat alone. If
you pick me as your new housemate I promise to make your life
200 percent more fun. I'm not too fussy about housework either.
Working in boring job at the moment, but do a bit of dancing
as well (club, and a bit of freelance pole/lap).
Look forward to hearing from you
Love
Susan.

On Monday at 15:45 Martin replied:

Dear 'Crazylegs'
Sorry for the delay in getting back to you. I'm afraid my
account dumped your message in with the junkmail. Thank
you very much for your kind offer to increase my fun levels by
200 %. I take it the friend who gave you my email address was
Barney? I am afraid that the room is already taken.
Regretfully
Martin

On Tuesday at 12:30 Barney wrote:

Hey Mate,

I'm following up on my request for David's email? Sorry to bother you again, but it would be great to contact him before the end of the day.

By the way, did my mate Suzie email you? If you're looking for a flatmate she's incredible. Really amazing energy levels - and not only on the dancefloor!!! Seriously though, she'd be pretty great to live with, if you think you could handle it. She'd transform your flat into party central, mate! Let me know what you think of the idea...

Cheers in advance for David's email address,

See Ya Soon, Loon,

Barney

On Tuesday at 12:40 Martin replied:

Barney

I don't have David's email. Why don't you see if it's on his webpage. If you google 'theatre' + 'London' + 'loathsome pretentious diminutive girlfriend thief' you'll probably find his site. It lists every possible way of contacting him. No doubt he's also on MySpace. I think you'd make a very good team, so would advise you to go for it.

As regards your mate Crazylegs75, I got a very excitable email from her enquiring about the place. Not entirely sure we're temperamentally compatible, I'm afraid. As I mentioned to her, I think I have someone ready to take the room, and I don't really want to muck them about etc. etc. I'm sure you'll pass on my apologies. If she's looking for a place to live, perhaps suggest the Big Brother house...

But thanks for passing the word around. As I mentioned, I think the place is taken, so no need to go to any more effort. Cheers though.

Martin

On Tuesday at 20:52 MadMan22 wrote:

Hi, Mart,

Barney passed on the word that you have a room. Any space for another 'smoker'? I have some cutlery and other accessories. Working in a tattoo parlour in Camden at the moment. Could arrange a deal if you need anything inked or pierced. How convenient are you for the Northern Line? Barney was telling me some good things about you, mate. Think this could be the start of something wicked …

Let me know about the room,

Adrian

On Wednesday at 9:28 Martin replied:

Hello Adrian

Thanks for yours. Very inconvenient for the Northern Line, I'm afraid. Also, I have someone interested in the room. Sorry about that.

Good luck with the room-search.

Martin

On Wednesday at 9:45 Sam Hucks wrote:

Martin,

Huckster here. Need accommodation. I been away for a while. Questions: Do you cook? Do you clean? Are you flexible about rent?

If so, I'll take it.

THE HUCKSTER

On Wednesday at 10:00 Martin replied:

No, No, No, and No you won't.
Martin

On Wednesday at 10:17 LadySpank wrote:

Hi Martin,
Word is you have a room. I'd love to take it. I hope the room
is still available. I heard about you and the housework. Sounds
like you are a pretty dirty boy. I warn you, as housemates go I
am pretty dominant! I hope you don't mind me working from
home at the weekends.
Love
    Lady Spank

On Wednesday at 10:19 Martin replied:

Oh sod off, Barney. Haven't you got anything better to do?
Warm Regards
Martin

Blocking Unwanted Email

On Wednesday at 14:03 Martin Sargent wrote:

Hi Martin
Nice to see you for lunch the other day. Hope we can do it again soon, and I hope you find somewhere to live soon too. This is a work-related email (for once!): Is it possible to block email from the same sender, if they are using different names?
Many thanks
Martin

On Wednesday at 16:57 Martin Sergeant wrote:

Hi, mate
Yeah, no problem. In fact, there's a few things we can do to improve your email set-up generally. I'll pop up tomorrow morning. Most people are using the newer, much improved system we've been installing around the building, so I'll set you up with that at the same time. It's a lot more streamlined and about 150% faster, as well as giving you a much wider range of available functions.
                    Martin

On Wednesday at 17:02 Martin Sargent wrote:

Cheers, mate
Really appreciate the rapid response, by the way. If it's all the same, I'm quite happy with the rest of the computer as it is, but

appreciate your offer. See you tomorrow.
Martin

On Thursday at 11:56 Martin Sargent wrote:

Dear Martin@helpdesk
Sorry to bother you again, but it seems like I've been blocked
from getting online entirely. Would be great if you could have a
look at my account.
Cheers
Martin

On Thursday at 12:01 Martin Sargent wrote:

Bloody IT! I asked Martin to do one little thing, but he
insisted on rejigging the whole computer brain and now it's gone
mental (technical terms). Are you using this allegedly 'improved'
system? It lets me do a million new things I don't want to do, but
it won't let me send external email or go online. I can't even find
my inbox any more. I am sending this out in the vague hope it
will get to you... Not holding my breath.

On Thursday at 12:10 Laura replied:

Got it! You see, it does work. I can't believe you were still on
the old system. Wasn't it really slow?

On Thursday at 12:15 Martin replied:

It was slow, but at least I knew how to use it. This is
ridiculous. If I don't get the internet back soon I will have to
do some work. Why does IT always do that? I don't need to
downline movies or upstream an ipod, I just want to be able to

find emails people have sent me. It's like you go to the garage to get your wing-mirror fixed and they install a rocket engine. One that doesn't work. Better go, this is turning into bad stand-up.

Shall I download sandwiches for two in about an hour?

\-

On Thursday at 16:58 Martin Sargent wrote:

Dear Martin@helpdesk
Sorry, it's me again. Any chance of getting my external email/internet access back?
Thanks again
Martin

\-

On Friday at 9:24 Martin Sargent wrote:

Dear Martin@helpdesk
Help! I think the entire internet has disappeared. Perhaps it has been kidnapped and is being held to ransom. Either that, or you have buggered up something on my computer. In either case, please sort it out when you get a chance.
Cheers
Martin

P.S. Although I am really starting to get into solitaire.

\-

On Friday at 10:11 Martin Sargent wrote:

Hi Martin@'help'desk
I know you're really busy, but I kind of need my external email to do any work. Any possibility of getting it back today?
Thanks and sorry again
Martin

\-

On Friday at 12:15 Martin Sargent wrote:

Dear Martin@helpdesk

I have some questions I hope you can help me with:

- Is it acceptable to wear brown shoes at a formal event?

- I occasionally suffer mild irritation when I shave. Should I change my moisturising routine?

- Whose coronation is celebrated by the coronation chicken sandwich? And why do they have those horrible puffy raisins in them?

- Can you suggest any healthy alternatives to dairy?

- Why is it called Echo Beach, if waves make the only sound?

I'm asking on the off chance that for all this time I have fundamentally misunderstood the kind of 'help' your 'desk' is supposed to provide.

Oh, also I am having trouble with my computer.

Martin

On Friday at 15:45 Martin Sargent wrote:

Checking on the email/internet situation again. Any chance of getting it fixed over the weekend?

Have a good one.

Martin

On Monday at 9:13 Martin Sargent wrote:

Hi Laura

I've finally got the internet back. I think I am the object of a vendetta. Martin S isn't replying to me and I had to go to the IT cave four times before I got someone to come up. And he keeps giving me the thousand-yard stare when I see him in the corridor. I think he's really pissed off about the flat. Hope you had a good weekend?

Martin

On Monday at 9:16 Laura replied:

Hi, Martin,

It may be to do with the fact that I let slip to a few people that he is a cheating 'batsard'. Oops! Unless he really is reading your emails. Weekend dreary.

Laura

On Monday at 9:19 Martin replied:

Oh, well that explains it. I just got a stern email from the IT department about proper use of the internet - cruel irony, since for about a week I have been unable to access it due to their pointless overcompetence. Now I have a stupid backlog of work to catch up with. Lunch tomorrow instead?
Martin

On Monday at 10:12 Ross wrote:

Hi Martin,

I've tried this address a couple of times, but things keep getting returned. Are you having trouble with your email? Philip Hayward mentioned to me that you have a spare room and are looking for someone to fill it. If it's still available it would be great if you could get back to me and we could discuss rent etc. I'd be looking to move in as soon as is convenient for you. Let me know if there's a good time this week for me to pop over and have a look at the flat - and at the same time we can establish that neither of us is a total freak.
Best,

Ross

Re: Re: David

Hello, Martin,

I hope all is well with you. I don't think you are going to be pleased to hear this, but anyway ... Since I've been working with David we've got really close, and it seems silly that since we're spending so much time together rehearsing we are living at other ends of town. Since we're both looking for a place, we are going to move in together at the end of next week. Please don't jump to any conclusions, and don't take things personally (as always). It's a purely practical thing. I've been talking to David a lot about you, and you may be surprised to hear it, but he has been taking your side a lot. As he says, though, sometimes people do simply grow apart, and I think that is what happened between us. I wish you all the best with your writing, of which I have always been tremendously supportive. I still love you a great deal, I am just not in love with you. I hope you are not too hurt, and that you find someone to move into the spare room quickly.

Lots of love,
Sally

On Tuesday at 9:01 Martin replied:

Sally

Thanks for yours. As it happens I have had heaps of interest in the flat, thanks for asking. Good luck with your move. I haven't been writing much, because you took all the pens. I'm never quite sure what people mean by the 'love you/ in love'

divide, but it was nice of you to express concern that I am not 'too' hurt. I suppose a mild amount of pain is acceptable.
See you soon.
Martin

Lady

Dear Martin,
Glad to be able to tell you that Lady seems not to be suffering, although it looks like this time she will have to be put down. By the way, I haven't heard what you thought about the book yet.
Love,

Mum

Part Two
A Face to Watch

Martin Mortified

The Mysteries of Ross

The Picnic

Barney Invents a New Dance

Local Paper Hypes Local Mediocrity

Minxy

What the Hell is a Goth Barbecue?

Invitation

On Saturday at 14:23 Frequent Flyer Promotions wrote:

Dear All,

Frequent Flyer Promotions presents

The LADY of SHALOTT

Written, Directed and Produced by David Fauntleroy

Starring
Sally Kendle as The Lady of Shalott/Sarah
Mark Thornhill as Lancelot/Lance
Sebastian Tilly as The Mirror/Narrator

Inspired by the poem by Alfred, Lord Tennyson
Soundscapes by DJ Barney.
At The New Place (Over the Two Tuns Inn, SW1)

Brought radically up-to-date, this is an in-your-face 21st century version of the classic Victorian poem. 'Camelot' is the city's hottest nightclub, 'The Lady' is Sarah, a girl coming of age fast in a world of slippery values, who hears from afar about 'Lance', the city's hottest new DJ. Based partly on improvisations developed by the cast and its noted young director, The LADY of SHALOTT will guarantee that you will never think the same way about Victorian love poetry again. Sumptuously staged in the intimate surroundings of The New Place, The LADY of SHALOTT features a mixture of classical music and the latest underground sounds from DJ Barney.

About The Director

David Fauntleroy is fast acquiring a reputation for daring reinterpretations of classic texts. Last year his drum'n'bass *Tristan and Isolde* was acclaimed at the Edinburgh Fringe. While still at university the *Cambridge Evening Post* included him as one of its 'Young Faces to Watch'. With his emphasis on improvisation and reckless experimentation, David Fauntleroy is fast gaining a reputation as one of the most daring new directors now working.

On Monday at 9:15 Martin wrote:

Dear Sally
I got the flyer for the new play. It sounds very interesting. I hope the rehearsals are going well. Look forward to seeing it. Hope you are well.
Martin

On Monday at 9:27 Martin wrote:

Hey Luce
Oh my goddy god. I've attached the flyer for this thing Sally and David have dreamed up. David's surname is Fauntleroy. I believe the idiocies of the play speak for themselves, but may I draw your attention to the following? I like the bit where David claims to have written *The Lady of Shalott*. 'Noted' 'young' director - noted by the *Cambridge Evening Post*, and a 'young' 36. The most 'daring' director now working? I think that is a misspelling for 'shameless'. Unless 'daring' means 'utterly lacking in a sense of the ridiculous and willing to crucify acquaintances with boredom to enhance his own self-esteem'. I notice the blurb fails to mention his shit hair. I'm sorry to have missed the drum'n'bass *Tristan and Isolde*. No doubt the 'Skiffle *Two Gentlemen of Verona*' and the 'Punk *Three Men in a Boat*' were considered pretty radical in their day too. But really, what is the fucking point? I have no doubt theatre can offer a genuinely

moving and exciting experience. But not for the audience. 'Soundscapes by DJ Barney'? Sweet Jesus. I bet you my kidneys that the Classical is a bit of swirly strings when Sally prances around, and the 'edgy' urban music (i.e. something by Roni Size from about 1997) is played by Barney during the interval to drown out the sound of the audience walking out. I have been to The New Place (founded 1977) before, and intimate is the word. You have to duck and sprint across the back of the stage if you need a pee during the show. I imagine 'sumptuous' means they've hung up a bit of velvet curtain and will keep the lights low. Don't suppose I can lure you to this? The only thing more horrifying than the thought of the show is the thought of the audience. If anyone deserves to suffer through this, it's people who like and admire David Fauntleroy. I don't mean to sound smug and snotty about this, but I am, so I do.
Aghast
Martin

P.S. Loud spinning noises coming from direction of the cemetery. Wonder what that is? And I don't even like Tennyson …
P.P.S. I am still hoping the reference to Barney as 'underground' is an attempt at humour. His dad, for God's sake, owns a very expensive boat club in Henley. They live in a glass-fronted barn with a tennis court.

On Monday at 15:23 Martin wrote:

No reply? We better move fast if you want tickets.

On Monday at 16:04 Lucy wrote:

Hi, Martin,
Sorry? I think I missed an email somewhere. Hope it was nothing important.
Lots of love,
Lucy

On Monday at 16:05 Martin wrote:

Oh shit! You won't believe what I think I've done...

On Tuesday at 11:13 Sally wrote:

Dear Martin,
Thanks for your emails. Nice to get your real opinion for once. I think you will be pleasantly surprised by the play. There is, of course, no pressure to come. In fact, if this is your real attitude, don't bother. Why do you have to be so negative about everything?
Sally

Mortified

On Tuesday at 11:15 Martin wrote:

Sally
I am so sorry. What can I say? I was having fun with the flyer, not the play. I'm really looking forward to it. Genuinely. I couldn't feel worse.
Martin

P.S. I'm not negative about everything. I just feel very positive about expressing my negative feelings.

On Wednesday at 11:56 Sally replied:

Martin,
I prefer it when you're at least being honest. Even if your attempts at humour do reveal a nervous, rather insecure little man. It's easy to criticise when you're a sarcastic observer. How is the book coming, by the way? Or do you only write snotty emails nowadays?
Sally x

Still Mortified

On Thursday at 9:11 Martin wrote:

I'm still really sorry.

On Thursday at 12:15 Martin wrote:

Sally
Writing to apologise again. I am embarrassed and ashamed
of myself. I'm really looking forward to the play, and I'm sure
you in particular will be excellent. There is nothing funny about
David's surname. Tennyson needed updating. Barney is very
underground.
Sorry
Martin

P.S. I don't suppose we're all still on for the picnic on Sunday?
I promise to bring loads of stuff. And it will be a chance to meet
the new housemate...

On Friday at 11:22 Sally wrote:

Take it back about the hair, and you can come.

On Friday at 11:27 Martin wrote:

Glad you're being big about this. By the way, it's a free
country, and you can't stop me going to the park.

On Friday at 11:32 Sally wrote:

Not time for you to stop grovelling yet. David's hair is ...

On Friday at 13:46 Martin wrote:

David's hair is nice and fuzzy and keeps his head warm.
It also adds a welcome three inches to his height. I like it. In
no way does he resemble nightmarish children's entertainer
Pennywise the Clown. I said NO WAY.
See you Sunday.
Martin

P.S. Fauntleroy???

On Friday at 15:34 Sally wrote:

Good enough. I wish you hadn't said that about Pennywise
shudders. See you Sunday. Will call to confirm. I will expect
an excellent array of sandwiches and refreshments from you,
Sargent.
      Sally

On Friday at 16:02 Martin wrote:

Great, I'm looking forward to seeing David again too. I have
a project to discus with him. Fancy being in my Garage/Two-
Step version of *The Pickwick Papers*? Mr Pickwick's brother has
been killed by paedophile drugs dealers (led by the sinister Mr
Winkle), and he gets together a gang of vigilantes ('The Pickwick
Club') to mete out bloody yet picaresque revenge...

On Friday at 16:03 Sally wrote:

Don't push it, Martin Sargent.

Ross

Hey, Brother,

Hope you got things sorted out with Sally. Again. Your subconscious seems to be doing a very good job of sabotaging your attempts to get back together. I'm not sure whether I'll be able to make it to the play, sorry about that.

How's the new flatmate?

Lots of love,

Lucy

Hi Luce

Things going well with Ross thus far. He moved his stuff in yesterday and hasn't manifested any obvious signs of freakishness. I was a little perturbed when he brought out a samurai sword and wanted to hang it over the TV, but at least we now have a TV to hang it over. He cooks too! We established fairly swiftly that Philip Hayward is a mutual acquaintance, rather than an actual mate. Ross was at uni with him, but claims to have been trying to shake him since more or less the second half of Freshers' Week 1997. I did wonder if Ross would be able to shed any light on the mystery of what Philip is or does that makes him think he's so terribly special. Unfortunately, he is as puzzled about that as I am. As far as either of us can tell the chief ingredients of Philip's personality seem to be a very loud voice and a total immunity from self-doubt. Worryingly, though, Ross does approve of his taste in jumpers

47

It would be great if you could come to the play. I'm sure Sally would love to see you. Perhaps you could have a quiet word with her about David.

Love

Martin

On Saturday at 11:26 Lucy replied:

Raining here, so checking my timetable online and waiting for CD:UK to come on. I'll see about the play. Samurai sword?

On Saturday at 12:01 Martin replied:

Ross is still asleep, and I decided to help him unpack by putting his books on the shelf in the living room. I think I have made a terrible discovery. The clues: Haruki Murakami, Yukio Mishima, Milan Kundera, Hunter S. Thompson, biography of Serge Gainsbourg. Opinion?

On Saturday at 12:33 Lucy replied:

Sorry, couldn't respond until I'd seen the backstage report from the Westlife show at Wembley and caught up with U2 on tour in Japan. Charts rotten. Another hour wasted.

Don't get it. What's wrong with Ross's books? *nervously checking bookshelves*

On Saturday at 12:35 Martin replied:

Well, ONE interpretation is that late-sleeping Ross is a broad-minded hipster with varied literary tastes and an interest in hard-living French crooners.

On Saturday at 12:37 Lucy wrote:

Is that not a good thing? What is the other possibility?

On Saturday at 12:39 Martin wrote:

The other possibility is that he buys all his books in HMV.

On Saturday at 12:40 Lucy wrote:

Horrors!

Mortified Again

On Monday at 9:10 Martin wrote:

Sally

I'm so sorry. What can I say, except that it was a genuine accident. Ross is completely embarrassed, and so am I. Other than that one incident, I thought the picnic was lovely. I hope the wait at A and E wasn't too long, and that David is feeling OK.

Sorry, sorry, sorry

Martin

On Monday at 10:05 Sally replied:

I'm not very impressed with you, but it wasn't entirely your fault, so there's no need to over-apologise. David's not feeling too great, actually. He has two black eyes and a broken nose, and he's being interviewed about the play today.

Sally

On Monday at 10:10 Martin wrote:

Hi David

Writing to say I hope you are feeling a little better today, and good luck with the interview. It was good to see you and Sally yesterday, and I really enjoyed the day, apart from the unfortunate incident. I can't apologise enough for what happened, and I can only assure you that it was a genuine accident, and that Ross was only trying to help. It was a very stupid idea of me to bring the football.

Really looking forward to seeing the play.

Get well soon.

Martin

On Monday at 10:18 Martin wrote:

Hi Ross

Sally's email is s_kendle@demon.com, if you have a moment to email today. David can be contacted via his website or frequentflyer@hotmail.com. Apparently his nose is broken and he has two black eyes. I've already dropped them a line, and I think they would appreciate it if you did too.

By the way, there wasn't any milk this morning. If you're around the flat today, it would be great if you could pick some more up.

Cheers

Martin

Clash of Personalities

On Monday at 11:31 Lucy wrote:

So how was the picnic? Did you dazzle and outshine Dreadful David? Was Ross a hit?

On Monday at 13:45 Martin replied:

Ross was a hit all right. We managed to send David to casualty with a broken nose and two black eyes.

On Monday at 14:14 Lucy replied:

What, intentionally?

On Monday at 14:16 Martin replied:

Unfortunately not.

It was all going fine: lovely day, excellent spread from M&S, decent bottle of sparkling wine. Ross was telling us about his last flatmate, who he reckons was an undiagnosed obsessive-compulsive. Ross is a pretty funny bloke, full of plans and ideas. I got a few good lines in, too. Even David wasn't being too dastardly, although he did insist on hand-feeding Sally grapes. Then I decided to tempt the gods by getting the football out and suggesting a kick-around. The rest, in true sitcom style, is perfectly predictable. We were all a bit drunk and lively, and some of us (I admit) may have been feeling a bit over-competitive.

To cut a long story short: we were one-nil down, the ball was in the air, David, Ross and I all went for it. I managed to slam into David from behind, and then Ross, going for the header, managed to connect forehead to nose with David. He went down. Recriminations were thrown.

Which was when Ross did the unthinkable. David was having a sit-down, with Sally fussing around with towels and ice. He reckoned his nose was broken, so we all had a look at it, and it was definitely a bit swollen. Ross, having taken a look at it, asks whether David had heard a crack when they collided. David thought that he had. With no further ado Ross reaches over and twists David's nose, hard, to the right. There is definitely a crack this time.

David, understandably, gets in a right old sulk. Exit David and Sally to casualty, David threatening to sue us for assault. Ross and I did offer to come with them and explain what had happened, but we were informed our presence would be surplus to requirements.

So David gets nursed and fussed over by Sally, while I get accused of having encouraged Ross to assault him. A disappointing result.

Hope things going better with you.

Lots of Love

Martin

Do the Crunch

On Wednesday at 14:45 Barney wrote:

Hi Mart,
I heard about Sunday's antics. Guess you aren't over Sally yet, eh? I've composed a little track in honour of the occasion (see attached file). I think (humbly) it's pretty good. It's a kind of punk-dance thing. Dunce, if you will. Let me know what you think.
Regards, Pards,
Barney

On Thursday at 11:16 Martin replied:

Cheers for this, Barney. Very sensitive of you. Have you sent it to David?
I thought it was quite funny, but I'm not sure it's actually legal to have a record which instructs its readers to 'take your partner by the hand', 'hold them close' and 'headbutt them on the nose'. There may also be health and safety objections to having everyone 'form a circle, turn around, punch a stranger to the ground'. I would very much like to be there if you play it at your next night. I should add, of course, that I would be sitting that particularly tune out at the bar.
Martin

The *Chalk Farm Gazette*

On Wednesday at 12:45 Martin wrote:

Hi Sally

I've just seen the *Chalk Farm Gazette*. Nice interview with David, very probing and not at all adulatory. Who wrote it? His auntie?

I was a bit surprised to learn from the article that you and David are officially an item now. Is this a serious thing or a publicity stunt?

Good photo of David. I think the black eyes suit him. I hope he's recovering, anyway.

Regards

Martin

On Wednesday at 13:34 Sally replied:

Hello, Martin,

No, the article wasn't written by his auntie. Yes, David and I are 'officially' an item now, and no, it isn't a publicity stunt.

Lots of people have been in touch to say they've seen the article, and to enquire about poor David's eyes. He's doing well - the swelling's going down, and has gone from red and black to iridescent green and bright yellow, which is apparently normal. I shall be quite glad when he has recovered - he's being a bit 'dramatic' about the whole thing. Apparently a few friends weren't taken in by the version of events in the article, and have been in touch with David to see if I've been beating him. Please thank Ross again for the flowers and chocolates.

Love,
    Sally

On Wednesday at 13:42 Martin wrote:

Hi Ross

Hope you're having a productive day. I sent David and Sally the flowers/chocolate as we discussed. If you want to split it, it came to about a fiver each.

By the way, sorry to be boring, but I think the gas bill is a bit overdue. I put a cheque in the envelope on the kitchen table. It would be great if we could get that sent off today.

Cheers
Martin

On Wednesday at 13:46 Martin wrote:

Hi Luce

I'm forwarding you the latest email from Sally. Please note that she has started signing off with 'love' again. That probably means there is still hope, right?

Martin

On Thursday at 14:23 Lucy wrote:

Thanks for sending me the latest from Sally. Yes, Martin, that is a very exciting development. I would draw your attention to the rest of the email, however, i.e. the bit about her having a new boyfriend.

Tell me more about the article, though.

Love,
Lucy

On Thursday at 19:14 Martin replied:

Hey Luce
You're right. I think in retrospect that I got a bit over-excited

about Sally's sign-off. I'm writing from the flat. I'm not sure where Ross is. He was supposed to be writing at home today - apparently there's a producer interested in his idea for a sitcom about the romantic entanglements of a group of G8 protestors - but there's no sign of him. Gas bill not paid - grrr. Also no milk again. Perhaps he got kidnapped as he was about to clean all his stuff out of the living room. Or perhaps he decided to have a go at cleaning the loo, and it got him before he got it. The bathroom's a bit of a shocker too at the moment - I found a three-inch-high mushroom growing under the sink yesterday, and I'm not sure whether to clean the bath or shave it (yuck, sorry).

I'll save the article about David for you, but here are some edited 'highlights', courtesy of Rachel Farnaby of the *Chalk Farm Gazette*:

*

I'm surprised when David Fauntleroy, whose radical reworking of Tennyson's 'The Lady of Shalott' starts next week at the New Place, enters the café where our interview is to take place. I'm not surprised by the fact he is talking excitedly on his mobile - after all, he is a busy man these days, with the final rehearsals under way for the play (and as I discover he has plenty more ideas buzzing around his fertile brain for future projects). Nor by the way he greets me - a howl of recognition that turns heads, followed by a kiss on both cheeks. Nor am I surprised (although I was a little disappointed) that he is accompanied by a gorgeous creature called Sally - his current leading lady - who obviously dotes on him. Nor am I surprised at his outfit: standard director's uniform, although with a personal twist: long college-style scarf, corduroy combats, and a military-style jumper, set off with a heavy belt with a crescent-moon-shaped silver buckle. I am surprised to see one of London's most talked-about young directors sporting a magnificent pair of black eyes.

I ask where he got the shiners. He is properly modest, but it turns out he was forced to defend someone's honour. Sally, who is an elegant blonde, blushes. He doesn't want to talk about it, he says: 'It's nothing Dr Theatre can't take care of.'

When I ask whether it's a case of 'You should have seen the other guy' he merely gives me a charming smile. 'Guys, plural,' he admits, before asking if he can get me anything to eat. 'The strawberry shortcake here is a little miracle,' he tells me, changing the subject.

He's modest about his background. 'It's all very boring,' he says. 'Like most people I did English at Cambridge.'

I ask Sally whether she worried what people would think about her stepping out with the director. After all, it's on page one of the book of theatrical clichés.

David jumps in. 'I don't think anyone who knows Sally and I would question the sincerity and solidity of our relationship,' he says. He pauses, thoughtfully, and squeezes her hand. 'I know it sounds corny, but we really are soul-mates.'

There's something in the way he says it that reinvigorates the old-fashioned sentiment. Yours truly admits to feeling, at that moment, a little stab of jealousy.

I end by asking what's next for Sally and David.

'Professionally?' he asks 'Or personally?'

His meteoric rise is not likely to stop any time soon. He's already working on a TV project (with a big-name actor I've been sworn to keep a secret, because they haven't yet committed), and has a play he is hoping to unveil at next year's Edinburgh Festival.

'It's really very early stages,' he explains 'But I can reveal it's a little bit political, and deals with contemporary issues of race, gender, religion and sexuality.'

And will Sally be starring in it?

'You'll have to ask her,' he says, with a twinkle in his eye. 'I certainly hope so.'

It's impossible, meeting this charming couple, to wish them anything but the greatest of success together.

As we are leaving, ever the gentleman, David helps me into my coat. I notice he smells delicious, a little like freshly baked bread. 'I was making some scones for Sally this morning,' he reveals, when I comment.

'Don't make too much of the eye thing,' he smiles. 'It's not what I want people to focus on. It's really the play that matters, not anything personal about me. It's my work that I want to be remembered by. I hate all this culture of celebrity nowadays. All I want is for people to enjoy my plays, and, if it doesn't sound too arrogant, to change people's lives. After all, I think that's what theatre, real theatre, is there for.'

From anyone else this might indeed sound a little arrogant. But in the case of David Fauntleroy, I think he's being much too modest.

***

The photo's a stinker, too: they've got David posing like a boxer in front of a poster for his play, with his shiners on display. He looks like a pugnacious panda, or perhaps like something the NSPCC should know about.

I can confirm that it is certainly not 'impossible' to wish this charming couple anything but the greatest success.

Lots of Love

Martin

Solidarity

On Friday at 11:30 Martin wrote:

Dear Ella/Mike/Chris (and Emily)

Apologies for the group email. Writing to let you know about Sally's play next week (see attached flyer). I know Thursday nights are a pain, but I'm sure she'd really appreciate a show of support. I'm going to be there, and it would be great to have some backup. Apparently the cast and crew are going on for karaoke after, and we are also invited. Hope you are all well.

Best

Martin

On Friday at 11:35 Martin wrote:

Hey Laura

End of the week at last! Sending you the attached on the off-chance you are free next week. Getting a bunch of people together to go, so let me know if you fancy it.

Martin

On Friday at 11:41 Ella wrote:

Hey, Martin

Thanks for the invite. I'm afraid I can't make it. I'm writing an article for G2 about what it's like to avoid all cultural stimulation for a week. Would be great to see you soon, though, and give my best to Sally.

Lots of love, Ella

On Friday at 12:05 Martin replied:

Really? Good luck with the article. How long have you been planning this little experiment?

On Friday at 12:11 Ella replied:

I just came up with the idea, actually. See you soon. Hope you're taking good care of yourself.

On Friday at 12:34 Mike wrote:

Hi, Martin,
Thanks for the invitation. Play sounds great, but not sure what I'm doing. I often have work things on Thursday, but I'll let you know next week.
Best,
Mike

On Friday at 13:06 Chris replied:

Hey, Martin,
Thanks for the invite. I don't want to come, because the play sounds rubbish. Not being funny, but you've broken up with Sally, which means you no longer have to do things like this. I'd love to come and be supportive, but I'm not willing to pay £7.50. Sorry not to think up an excuse. No doubt Emily will be bothered to think one up - can we assume it counts for me (too)? By the way, she's going to be a bit upset about being put in brackets.

Mate, over the last year you have invited us to come and see: a punk band covering Bulgarian folksongs; two poetry readings; a showcase for new ventriloquists at something called the Giggle Club; and an exhibition on the meaning of Frenchness despite the fact we're not French. Can we not simply go for a pint sometime?

Saw the *Chalk Farm Gazette*, and very sorry to hear about Sally.

Chris

On Friday at 13:42 Martin replied:

Cheers for your honesty, mate. How about a pint next week, then? There's an old coaching inn in the East End that has a Dickens theme and serves Victorian drinks. How about an evening getting uncommon lushey on shrub or half-and-half?

On Friday at 15:07 Chris replied:

Yes, that would be an option. Alternatively there's a contemporary-themed pub on the high street near me that serves contemporary-themed drinks. Why not experiment with that?

On Friday at 15:11 Emily wrote:

Hi Martin

Chris and I were saying only last night how much we'd love to see you. I'm afraid I think we have a dinner party (snore snore) that evening, otherwise it would be lovely. Send my love to Sally.

Hope you are well, and thinking of you,

Emily

(PS. Why am I in brackets?)

On Friday at 15:14 Martin replied:

Dear (Emily)
Sorry about the brackets. Actually I've already heard back from Chris. He didn't mention the dinner party, but we said we'd meet for a pint soon. Just a pint, no New Iranian Cinema or Czech Animation. I'll give your best to Sally, and try to think up a decent excuse why you're not there. You guys should co-ordinate your excuses better.
Lots of Love
Martin

On Friday at 15:23 Emily replied:

Oops. Well, I guess that makes us even for the brackets thing. See you soon,
                    Emily

On Friday at 16:45 Laura wrote:

The play sounds like it should be interesting. Count me in. Have a good weekend, and looking forward to next week.
    Lots of love,
                    Laura

Lack of Solidarity

On Monday at 10:03 Martin wrote:

> Hi Lucy
> Any chance at all you can make it on Thursday? I'm willing to reimburse your train fare etc. Only £5 on door for students. I'd really appreciate it. I was trying to get a gang of people together but everyone's ducking out, with the exception of Laura.
> Hope all going well.
> Martin

On Monday at 11:34 Lucy replied:

> Hi, Martin,
> Really don't think I can make it. Miriam's having a dinner party and I already said I'd go. Why not just go with the lovely Laura?
> > Sorry to be crap,
> > Lucy

On Monday at 14:02 Martin replied:

> Hi Lucy
> I don't suppose the dinner party is a scheme you've devised to entrap this Sam guy you mentioned on the phone?
> I had lunch with Laura today, and despite my attempts to suggest an alternate plan, she is definitely up for coming. The problem, as I see it, is now twofold:
> 1) I promised mates, and have come up with none. Thus to

Laura I am going to look like a right Billy.

2) This also lends a creepy vibe to the fact I am going to Sally's play with her, and makes it look like I am doing it because Sally is going out with Bilbo the ginger theatre hobbit.

But if I don't go, it will look like I am a) upset about the article and about Sally moving on and b) not interested in Laura.

Suggestions?

Love

Martin

On Monday at 14:04 Lucy replied:

Why not take Mum?

On Monday at 14:14 Martin replied:

Great. Thanks a lot for that brilliant suggestion. Good luck with Sam on Thursday. After all I've done for you...

On Monday at 14:59 Lucy replied:

Not my fault you got no mates. Perhaps if you stopped insisting people come to evenings of satirical puppetry and Belgian chanson ...

Only joking, and sorry not to be able to make it. As you guessed, the dinner party is a fiendish scheme to ensnare the lovely Sam from down the corridor. He doesn't stand a chance against my seafood risotto and little black dress.

Let me know how it goes on Thursday, and good luck,

Lucy

PS: Not quite sure what you meant by 'all you have done for me'. To which of the following incidents are you referring?

1. When I was four and you told me Mum and Dad got me at

the Spastics shop?

2. When I was six and you told me you'd overheard them saying they wanted to take me back 'cos I was defective, but they'd lost the receipt?

3. The numerous times you asked me to play hide-and-seek with you and your friends, only after about an hour I realised no one was looking for me?

4. The time when I was eight and you told Mum and Dad I was sleeping in the back seat of the car, and they left me for two hours at a French service-station?

5. The time when Michael came to take me to see *American Pie* and you told him I was 'upstairs having a shave'?

6. Or perhaps the time I stayed with you at college and you did the 'Bombardiez gag' on me? That joke is so lame, by the way.

On Monday at 15:02 Martin replied:

Bitter?

On Monday at 15:14 Martin wrote:

Hi Ross

Sending you the flyer for Sally's play. I'm sure you'd be very welcome.

Martin

P.S. By the way, I hope you're not dead. Didn't see you all weekend and there's a bit of an odd smell in the flat. If you are, no need to come on Thursday.

On Monday at 15:58 Martin wrote:

Hi Martin-in-IT

It's the other Martin here. Don't suppose you are interested in coming to a play on Thursday? Ask other people too, if you'd like.

Martin Sargent

On Tuesday at 9:05 Martin wrote:

Hey Luce

Bollocks. I think in desperation I may have made a major tactical error. I suspect what you always say is right, and at some subconscious level I wish myself serious ill. Possibly guilt over my childhood treatment of you? I know it means nothing to you, but if you talk to Mum please ask her to send up a quick prayer for Martin Sergeant to be busy on Thursday.

On the other hand, I should add that I hold you personally responsible for this predicament. I regret ever having told Mum and Dad you weren't in the back seat. You should thank me - if I hadn't mentioned it you'd now be living off discarded croques messieurs and flat Orangina and sleeping in a unisex public toilet outside Calais.

Cheers

Martin

What the Hell is a Goth Barbecue?

On Wednesday at 10:58 Lucy wrote:

It must be Karma. Without consulting me Miriam has
decided to make the dinner party fancy dress. Not only that,
the theme is Goth. Brilliant. Now not only will I be dressed as
Morticia Adams but Sam will be wearing eyeliner and white
makeup. Drat. Well, it may be worth it to see what Miriam's
boyfriend wears. I bet you it's either drag or his old lab coat. Any
suggestions for a sexy Goth costume? (Imagine I am not your
sister.) Don't say big white sheet.

On Wednesday at 11:14 Martin wrote:

Why not be a sexy cat? Everyone loves a sexy cat.

On Wednesday at 12:05 Lucy wrote:

Thanks. Of course I'd already thought of that, but Miriam has
explicitly vetoed sexy cats, horny devils and mad scientists. Is
there such a thing as a sexy zombie? I got a worrying text from
Sam a minute ago asking if I have any black nail varnish.

On Wednesday at 12:32 Lucy wrote:

Better and better. Now it's not a dinner party in my kitchen,
it's a barbecue in Christine's garden. A Goth barbecue. Surely
that's a contradiction in terms? AND the weather forecast

is rain. I bet the whole fiasco is Miriam trying to get in with Christine and the pink-shirt gang on the third floor. I can't sum up Christine better than by reporting that she spent the first term trying to get everyone to call her 'Minxy' and claiming it was her family nickname. I bet you anything it's not.

Then she claimed everyone on her corridor was ignoring her and got her parents to buy her a flat. Her unpopularity may have been to do with a series of her horse-faced one-night-stands puking in the kitchen and showers and the fact that she reported us all to the warden for using her Maldon Sea Salt. She's not even properly posh! She can't get her collar to stay turned up and has a weird ruddy face like bacon. I don't like her very much. I've texted Miriam suggesting we make it a crap Sloane party, but haven't got a reply yet.

By the way, who is Martin Sergeant? Have you developed an alter-ego? If you're creating a secret identity to fight crime may I suggest that you go a bit further than merely changing the spelling of our surname?

Just a thought,

Lucy

Thursday Night

On Wednesday at 12:40 Mike wrote:

Alright, Chum,
Sorry to say that it turns out I'd forgotten I have a do
with work people tomorrow night. Sorry about that. Let's do
something soon. Not this weekend, I have paintballing with the
gang from the office. By the way, how's your sister?
Mike

On Wednesday at 12:45 Martin wrote:

Mike, you had 24 hours to come up with an excuse and that's
all you could think of? Also: paintballing? You are so corporate.
'Oh no, you got me again, boss. Wow, you're really good at this.
Ooh, I missed. Ooh, I missed again.' I hope you get thoroughly
splattered. Stay away from my sister, you slimy suit. How's your
mum?
Martin

On Wednesday at 12:47 Mike wrote:

My mum has cancer, and I really do have a work thing
tomorrow.

On Wednesday at 13:03 Martin wrote:

Mate, I am so sorry, I hadn't heard. Please give your mum my

best and let her know I'm thinking of her. It must be incredibly tough - if you want to meet up for a chat, give me a bell. Really sorry about that. I'm wigging a bit about tomorrow night, if that's any excuse. Long story.
Best Wishes
Martin

On Wednesday at 13:05 Mike wrote:

Ha ha.
Wow, you are such a sensitive guy. You deal with serious issues really well, you know that? My mum is fine, but I'll let her know you're 'thinking of her'. Be careful when and where you do so, freakzone.
'Best Wishes' is such a dipstick way to sign off, by the way.
Mike

PS 'corporate'? 'you slimy suit'? Kurt's dead, man, Kurt's dead.

On Wednesday at 16:29 Martin Sergeant wrote:

Hi, Other Martin,
Thank you for the invite. I'm not going to be able to make it. I've got back together with my ex, so I'm moving my stuff back in. Which isn't a euphemism.
Best wishes,
Martin

Part Three
Special Friends

The Fear

The Ballad of Martin Sargent

The 'Bombardiez' Gag Explained

The Play

Aftermath

On Friday at 7:15 Elizabeth Sargent wrote:

Hello, Martin,

How was the play? I heard you took a 'special friend'. Ooh, very exciting. Can't wait to hear all about it. And have you heard anything about Lucy's barbecue? Dad sends his love.

Love,

Mum

PS: I did the prayers last Sunday and slipped in one for Lady. She doesn't seem to be suffering much, but is getting very slow and sleepy. Taking her to the vet tomorrow. I said one for you as well – I hope you don't mind.

On Friday at 9:42 Martin replied:

Hi Mum

Sorry again to hear about Lady, and thanks for thinking of me too. Had a good time last night - we ended up going on to karaoke after the show. Play wasn't much cop, but a good time was had by all. Haven't heard about Lucy's barbecue yet - it being 9:42 in the morning. Speak at weekend.

Love

Martin

P.S. I wish you wouldn't use the phrase 'special friend' - her name is Laura, and she isn't retarded.

On Friday at 9:44 Martin wrote:

Hi Lucy

Hope the Goth barbecue went well. I had an email from
Mum asking about last night. Just got into work, and still a bit
shaky. Very hazy recollections of last night, although it definitely
involved karaoke later on. There was a taxi, too. Woke up with
Leonard Cohen on my ipod, which is never a good sign, but as
far as I can recall I behaved myself. Don't think there was a snog.
Lots of Love
Martin

P.S. Apparently Mum mentioned me in her prayers on Sunday.
God knows what she said. Ha ha, I reread that. Still a bit drunk,
to tell the truth.

On Friday at 9:46 Martin wrote:

Hi Laura

Hope you had a good time last night (and aren't suffering
as much as I am this morning). Fancy meeting later for (light)
lunch and to try to piece together what actually happened?
Martin

On Friday at 9:52 Martin wrote:

Hi Ross

Hope I didn't wake you up banging around this morning. I'm
a bit of a state still. Thanks for coming - I hope it wasn't too
awful. I remember us doing karaoke together and there being a
bit of kerfuffle with someone about the tambourine we hired. Let
me know if you recall any more.
Martin

On Friday at 9:55 Martin wrote:

Hi Sally

I wanted to say (although I'm sure I said so last night) how much I enjoyed the play (and thanks for inviting us to the karaoke). Hope it wasn't weird to bring Laura. Not quite sure about the sequence of events, so would be great if you could help me putting the pieces together. Better go and get on with some work at last.

Lots of Love

Martin

P.S. Have just remembered that you helped put me in the taxi, I think. Cheers. Not quite sure how I ended up getting so wasted. I seem to recall some shots of tequila - hope you feel less dreadful than me! Congratulations again on the show.

P.P.S. Do I owe you money for the karaoke?

On Friday at 10:02 Martin wrote:

All right Barney

Well done for last night. What happened? Starting to sober up, and feeling the fear coming on.

Martin

The Dark Side

hy mutton, bswv ciou chuihnwoic cxniowuec. cuiwnwicu. yghyubuin. ucnhuiwhcuiw cuionwoc ichnuiwe coihjweo. fhyfhiw. yhtrnendi. biewhbic. ncuiewncwei. ugh. urrrgh. aaargh. feel shit. yours truly, ross. p.s. i woke up with the tambourine. who paid for the taxi?

On Friday at 12:06 Barney wrote:

Alright Chief,
Bloody hell, wouldn't want to be you this morning, wild man. Not sure those tequilas agreed with you. I think you went to the dark side a little bit. Bloody good night, though. Do you remember the karaoke? I have to say you were the evening's star turn. Not sure your bird was too impressed, though.
Rock on, Obi Wan,
Barney

PS cheers for the suggestions for a DJ name. Hope you don't mind me using them.

On Friday at 12:13 Martin replied:

Barney
Seriously, is this a wind-up? Did I piss Sally off? Is it something to do with the tambourine?
Martin

On Friday at 12:17 Barney replied:

No wind-up, but don't worry about it. You were a bit lively, that's all. What I want to know is what you said to David at the urinal. It was after you accused him of hogging the tambourine and tried to pour beer on him, and before you fell off the table. He looked pretty weirded out, and Laura didn't look too impressed. Sally was, I would say, more resigned about the whole thing. By the way, I didn't know you speak Japanese.

On Friday at 12:20 Martin replied:

Urinal? Bloody hell, I'd like to know too. Did he say anything about it to you? Also: Why was I on the table in order to fall off it?

I don't speak Japanese.

On Friday at 12:30 Barney replied:

Well, you were on the table to demonstrate your Jagger dance. You'd just got everyone's attention when you went over and took all the drinks with you. That was when you managed to whack Laura in the contact lens. So we were all looking for it and I thought you were too, but it turned out that you were looking for the slice of lemon peel you 'slipped' on, in order to prove you weren't drunk.

You were certainly claiming to be able to speak Japanese last night. You went off to find the management at one point in order to tell them we wanted another hour, and claimed you would negotiate a discount with your mastery of the language. Bit odd since the people at the desk weren't actually Japanese.

We went to look for you after about forty minutes and you were doing 'Ghostbusters' in someone else's booth. They looked pretty unimpressed, even when you explained that your dad knew Ray Parker Jr.

That, I think, was when the management asked you to leave.

No idea what role the tambourine played in the evening's events.

Does your dad really know Ray Parker Jr?

\----------------------------

On Friday at 12:32 Martin replied:

Of course my dad doesn't know Ray Parker Jr. Things are coming back to me now. Let me know if you remember anything else - I'm going to the loo for a cry and then I'm going to find Laura and apologise.

\----------------------------

On Friday at 13:34 Martin wrote:

Ross

Memories from last night keep lurching out of the brain-fog like zombie pirates, and they ain't pretty. No sign of Laura at work today. I need you to tell me all you remember. In particular: Do you know what I said to David at the urinal? Did Laura find her contact? Was she pissed off? What is the full story of the tambourine? Were we thrown out because of me? Do you think it was me who paid for the taxi?

Martin

\----------------------------

On Friday at 13:45 Martin wrote:

Dear Laura

I am so sorry about last night. The evening didn't quite turn out as anticipated. I hope you are feeling OK. I feel extremely bad, in all senses of the word.

Yours Sincerely

Martin

\----------------------------

On Friday at 13:48 Martin wrote:

Oh shit. The girl who sits opposite Laura just walked past and gave me an absolutely filthy look. Filthy in the sense of 'you twat', I mean. Ross, I think I have done bad and foolish things.

On Friday at 14:30 Ross replied:

Still drunk, and have a tingle all down one arm. In answer to your previous questions: Yes, I do know what you said to David at the urinal. You explained it to me and the taxi driver on the way home. Sally gave you twenty quid to pay for the taxi, I think, and you gave the driver a fiver of your own. That was after we were asked to leave, and you tried to hide in someone else's booth. You gave your position away by singing the *Ghostbusters* theme tune, and then declared they couldn't throw you out because you were a family friend of Ray Parker Jr. Surprisingly, that didn't work.

Laura didn't find her contact lens, and declined your invitation for a nightcap. I think Sally and David gave her a lift home. I'm not an expert on feminine psychology, but I believe that she was indeed rather pissed off.

The tale of the tambourine is as follows. You wanted us all to hire them, but there turned out to be a four quid deposit, so only you got one, but promised to share it around. Then you had a row with David because you accused him of hogging it, and you poured beer on him. I believe David had taken the tambourine into safe-keeping because you'd been hitting him on the head with it. After we were thrown out you declared moral victory because you had hidden the tambourine under your shirt. Then you did a little dance on the pavement and made up a song about it, which you sang at the bouncer. Which was when Sally put you in the taxi. So in effect you bought a tambourine for four quid. When we got home you conferred it on me, quite tearfully, as a solemn symbol of our mateship.

Hope this helps.

On Friday at 14:40 Martin replied:

Oh God! But how come Sally and David were driving?

On Friday at 14:43 Ross replied:

Because they weren't drinking all night. Which is why you had their tequilas. I forgot to tell you your account of what you said to David at the urinal. You rushed out and followed him when he went to the loo. Then, apparently, you stood next to him and said 'Massive cock.' He replied 'Thanks', and you said 'No, I don't mean you *have* a massive cock, I mean you *are* a massive cock.' Class. The taxi driver thought it was hilarious, which I think was why you over-tipped him.

On Friday at 14:47 Martin replied:

Bloody hell. Although I shudder to ask, do you remember me making suggestions of a DJ name for Barney? When was that?

On Friday at 14:49 Ross replied:

I certainly do. It was when we were walking from the pub to the karaoke and you were beginning to go to the bad. He wanted to know whether we preferred DJ Asbo or DJ Anarchitect. Laura came up with DJ Dinner Jacket, and I had DJ Mike Hunt. You suggested DJ Taylor, then declared you had a 'genius one', but were laughing too much to tell us. You prefaced it by saying it was a reference to Dostoyevsky and Iggy Pop.

On Friday at 14:51 Martin replied:

Don't muck about. What was it?

On Friday at 14:54 Ross replied:

DJ Idiot. He seemed pretty taken with the idea, actually.

On Friday at 14:55 Martin replied:

Please tell me I didn't do the 'Bombardiez' gag on anyone.

On Friday at 14:57 Ross replied:

That depends what the 'Bombardiez' gag is.

On Friday at 15:00 Martin replied:

Don't worry. You'd remember if I'd done it.

On Friday at 15:06 Martin wrote:

Dear Sally
I am so sorry. Again. From what I've pieced together I made a complete idiot of myself. I can only hope I didn't entirely spoil your night. Please pass on my apologies to David for what I said in the urinal. And for knocking all the drinks over. And for getting us thrown out. I owe you twenty quid. I couldn't possibly feel any worse. Thank you so much for taking Laura home. I doubt she was very impressed. Did she say anything to you? Congratulations on the play, as well. It was a very pleasant surprise.
Wretchedly
Martin

On Friday at 15:04 Sally replied:

I can only suppose you're under the impression that you did the 'massive cock' joke on David. In fact, you said 'You have a massive cock', waited for a response and didn't get one, and then said 'No, you *have* a massive cock' again and collapsed in hysterics. He wasn't upset, but he was a bit bewildered. I don't think he much appreciated being referred to as 'Garfunkel' all night, though. Or being repeatedly told to sing something by Simply Red. I take it the 'new blonde' thing has totally passed you by?

Laura seems like a very nice girl. I have to say she didn't appear to be blown away with your charm last night. We got her home safe. I think you owe her an apology too. Or here's a better idea - instead of continually having to apologise to people, why don't you try not being a complete prat?

I take it you don't remember what you sang? Don't bother apologising when you remember. It's very tedious being apologised to all the time, and it puts me in the awkward position of having to either forgive you or act like I'm more upset than I am. You made an idiot of yourself, and I don't think, deep down, that you actually are an idiot, or I wouldn't have gone out with you in the first place. But once again you've managed to make everything all about you.

Get in touch when you're prepared to behave like a human being.

Sally

PS - David and I thanked Ross for the flowers etc and he looked completely blank. I did assume it was all your idea, but you could at least have mentioned to Ross that you were sucking up on his behalf.

PPS - At least you didn't do that stupid 'Bombardiez' gag. Which shows what small mercies I'm nowadays grateful for.

On Friday at 15:07 Martin wrote:

Barney/Ross
For the love of God rack your memories. What did I sing? Something I sang really rubbed Sally up the wrong way. Martin

----

On Friday at 15:09 Ross wrote:

Well, you did a duet with Laura to start. Could that have been it? I think it was 'Close to You'.

On Friday at 15:11 Martin replied:

No, that would merely have been grossly inappropriate given the circumstances. To piss Sally off I'd have had to have chosen something truly awful. Think, boys, think.

On Friday at 15:15 Barney replied:

Well, next you discovered they had Leonard Nimoy's 'The Ballad of Bilbo Baggins', which you insisted on crooning at David.

On Friday at 15:17 Martin replied:

That's bad, but I must have done something worse than that. P.S. Surprised they had Leonard Nimoy. Usually people prefer his acting.

On Friday at 15:19 Barney replied:

I was very impressed you knew the words, actually. Then you did 'Love Will Tear Us Apart' and 'You Were Always on My Mind', which were directed at Sally.

On Friday at 15:21 Martin replied:

That's not good either, but there must be worse.

On Friday at 15:23 Barney replied:

Then you and Ross did 'This Town Ain't Big Enough for the Both of Us', while hitting David with the tambourine. Nice falsetto, by the way.

On Friday at 15:24 Martin replied:

Bad, bad, bad. Was that it?

On Friday at 15:25 Barney replied:

As far as I remember. You managed about half of 'Let's Spend the Night Together' before the table attacked you.

On Friday at 15:27 Ross wrote:

That's all I can remember. Except you did 'Fill Your Heart' by David Bowie at one point.

On Friday at 15:28 Martin replied:

That would be it.

On Friday at 15:30 Barney wrote:

In fact not many people who listen to *Hunky Dory* realise that song is not actually a Bowie original - it's a cover of a song by Biff Rose and Paul Williams.

On Friday at 15:32 Ross wrote:

I knew that.

On Friday at 15:35 Barney wrote:

I have a slightly creepy ukulele-and-falsetto version of it recorded by Tiny Tim if you want me to send it to you – it was the B-side to 'Tiptoe Thru the Tulips' and appears on the 1968 album *God Bless Tiny Tim*. I sometimes throw it into my set at the end of a night, and it's never failed to clear the dancefloor yet.

On Friday at 15:37 Martin replied:

That's great, Barney, although a bit beside the point. That was the song Sally and I listened to over and over when we went to Cyprus, thus a deliberately painful thing for me to sing. That was rather evil and stupid of me. No wonder she's upset.

On Friday at 15:39 Ross wrote:

That song's *rubbish*.

On Friday at 15:42 Martin wrote:

Still, if you could send me the Tiny Tim version I'd love to hear it. Cheers, Barney.

The 'Bombardiez' Gag

On Friday at 15:50 Ross wrote:

OK OK, the suspense is killing me. What is the 'Bombardiez' gag?

On Friday at 15:52 Martin replied:

It only works in a pub that serves Bombadier bitter. You wait till someone is getting a round in, then ask for a pint of 'Bombardiez'. They go up and order it, and all the old men at the bar laugh at them.

On Friday at 15:54 Ross replied:

Because it's really pronounced Bombadier?

On Friday at 15:56 Martin replied:

Yeah. Actually, it's not the greatest joke ever.

On Friday at 15:59 Ross replied:

No shit. But what happens if the person getting the round just looks at you oddly and says 'I think you'll find it's pronounced "Bombadier"'?

On Friday at 16:02 Martin replied:

Yes, that's the flaw in the 'Bombardiez' gag.

On Friday at 16:03 Ross replied:

To be honest, mate, I think there's more than one flaw in the 'Bombardiez' gag.

On Friday at 16:11 Martin wrote:

Hello All
The girl who works opposite Laura has just walked past again, whistling the *Ghostbusters* theme tune.
Yours Sincerely
Mud in the Office

P.S. I don't suppose anyone fancies phoning in a bomb scare?

Success!

On Friday at 18:35 Lucy wrote:

Hi, Martin,

Sorry not to get back to you sooner. In fact, I only got home about an hour ago. From which you may draw the conclusion that the Goth barbecue was a success (as far as I was concerned, anyway). Went back to Sam's, and made the (I think in retrospect wise) decision not to go straight to lectures in a black dress with little spiders stuck all over it, and with my hair backcombed and hair-sprayed. God, if I can pull in that get-up ...

Obviously none of Christine's mates made any effort at fancy dress, and it seems she hadn't even told them about it, so it was only me and Miriam dressed like idiots when we first turned up. Felt more casual about this as the night went on. Miriam's boyfriend, Frank, was Frankenstein, and had gone to a lot of effort – perhaps too much effort. It was quite unnerving, in fact. Miriam spent most of the evening wandering around with smears of green all over her. He departed about 4 a.m., still in costume, to get the London train, as he was working this morning.

Sam got the balance pretty right – he was a rather dashing Dracula. Of course, that started a long semi-playful argument with Christine (who was, despite the warning, a sexy cat) about the difference between a Goth party and a Halloween party. It ended with a compromise, with Frank saying he was a Goth dressed up for a Halloween party, and Sam agreeing that he was actually being Dave Vanian out of The Damned. I don't *think* Christine heard me asking loudly whether she had come as a fat cat. Of course we got the usual crowd of randoms (someone had invited a vet, and that was taken as a general declaration we wanted every vet who could be mustered to turn up when the pubs closed. So until they all paired up, passed out or pissed off, you couldn't move without being 'regaled' with gross stories about calving and horseshit told by very drunk and ugly boys wearing lab coats. Twats. But at least it wasn't the dental students). Felt a bit sorry for one of them - he'd obviously and rather sweetly (despite not knowing any of us) given the theme a lot of thought, and was wearing a horned helmet. Then he had to spend the whole evening explaining he wasn't a Viking. He pulled Christine, and the last thing I heard as we left this morning was his voice through the bedroom door explaining about the end of the Roman Empire. I'm not sure whether she knew, but he'd puked profusely in the cloakroom earlier. 'There's bits of chewed-up pasta on my pashmina' was perhaps my favourite quote of the evening.

After Frank(enstein) lumbered off to the train station, Miriam started cracking on to the remaining male at the party, a sinister red-eyed creature called Rupert who may have been asleep. Not impressed with that young lady.

Anyway, on the walk of shame back to Sam's, past smirking milkmen etc etc, he revealed that he's Christine's cousin, so I've been racking my brains all day to see if I said anything indiscreet. Sam offered to walk me back to mine but somehow we ended up getting diverted by the all-night garage and going back to his, despite the fact it's further (he is really sweet, so don't get all faux-protective. Also he could whup your ass). Nice flat, too. But even better the great (if not unexpected) revelation: no one in the family as far as Sam knows has ever called Christine 'Minxy'. In fact (until she went a bit bulimic in the sixth form) her family nickname was 'Chubby Chris'. Brilliant.

So, how was the play? As bad as expected? And more importantly, how did things go with Laura? Was Sally eaten up with envy?

Lots of love,
Lucy

PS: Or do I mean eaten up with jealousy? What is the difference?

Not sure of the difference between envy and jealousy, but I think it's fair to say Sally wasn't exactly eaten up with either.

Laura's not responding to my emails. Either she's playing hard to get or I've managed to fuck things up. I suspect the latter. I managed to knock out one of her contact lenses. Although I think it turned out that it had in fact slid round behind her eyeball. Not sure if that's better or worse.

Going to crawl into bed now and reflect on my sins. Flat an absolute state and no sign of Ross (another participant in last night's fiasco). I was shocked and awed when I saw the hoover in the hall, but I think it simply means that the gasman came and had to get at the meter. Still, at least Ross knows where it is now. Perhaps curiosity will compel him to try to turn it on. I'll leave it there to see. I don't think he has figured out that the little letters with the plastic window and the red writing on have bills inside.

Will call over weekend. Congratulations about the party. I hope you are being sensible etc etc.

Lots of Love

Martin

The Play

Hi, Martin

Had a late breakfast at The Eagle with David and Sally. He really is ghastly, isn't he? He invited me to come round and try his crumpets sometime. Fuck Off! Seriously. It must be quite upsetting that Sally prefers him to you. Heard about your antics on Thursday, and was most amused. It doesn't look like I'm going to be able to avoid this play after all - I'm kicking myself for not having given up culture for a month. Is it as atrocious as I suspect it will be?

Ella

On Saturday at 14:35 Martin replied:

Hey Ella

Yes, it is pretty upsetting that Sally prefers David to me, although I had hitherto avoided putting it to myself quite so bleakly. I wonder if he's giving her drugged bread? All other options are too painful to contemplate.

As for the play, it depends how low your expectations are. Sally, I have to say, is pretty good. The bits with someone pretending to be a mirror and Sally 'looking into him' were pretty amusing. I only found myself thinking longingly about my own death about three times, which is pretty good for pub theatre. The first time was when someone mentioned the 'round table' and they projected a picture of a set of decks onto the back wall. I'd almost recovered from choking on that particular slice of idiot pie when 'DJ Lance' played 'Ghost Town' by The Specials.

94

Why he did that God only knows, except that all plays with some faint claim to social relevance apparently have to feature it. It's like the third rule of theatre, after 'Make your entrances and exits quick' and 'Never act in anything based on the works of C. S. Lewis or Jerome K. Jerome'. Surely 'Almost Medieval' by the Human League would have been a more logical choice?

Anyway, the sight of the cast faux-skanking around in medieval dress to a song about the plight of the inner cities under Thatcher was fairly unforgettable. Although the man dressed up as a jester who was dancing like Bez may or may not have made a pretty telling point about contemporary culture. That could have been accidental. After that I was sure I could handle anything. Boy, was I wrong. They only went and did 'mime horses'. Although by that time my eyes had rolled back into my head in embarrassment and my toes had retracted into my feet, I think the idea was that Lancelot was riding to save The Lady ('Shally'?). On another actor. She OD'd (or perhaps died of shame) stage right, and he 'galloped' past her on a man in a black polo neck three times. I think that was meant to convey the distance he had to go. Not a dry eye in the house, I tell you. Alas, they didn't play 'Crazy Horses' by the Osmonds. God, it made me realise how much I love television.

Anyway, it's the kind of magic that can only be generated when a paying audience and a team of actors come face to face to waste each other's time in person. I will be laying flowers at the feet on the nearest statue of Oliver Cromwell later on today.

Almost forgot the best bit. Halfway through one of the dance numbers (there were several, but let's not go there. Let's just say that at one point the Lady of Shalott's woe was illustrated by a weeping willow dance to the contemporary club sounds of... Portishead) the door opened and someone in a leather waistcoat wandered onstage from the horrible 90s ciderpunk pub below. Looking a bit bewildered, understandably, he delivered the immortal line 'cigarette machine?' before wandering off again. I don't imagine for a minute I was the only person considering taking advantage of the intrusion to bolt across the stage and escape. Possibly covering my exit by pretending to be a ska-loving medieval peasant who is thoroughly disgruntled with Thatcherite employment policy. That, as David might put it, is the kind of unpredictability and energy you only get with theatre.

But that's only my opinion. You might like it. Anyway, definitely go and show your support. The flyer was certainly right in one respect: I won't ever think about Victorian love poetry in the same way again.
Martin

On Saturday at 14:42 Ella replied:

Thank you for the warning. I guess from the fact you are lurking online on a Saturday afternoon that you haven't heard from this Laura girl since your memorable evening? Pint soon?
Ella

PS It may not be drugged bread. Perhaps David's simply a better lover than you.

On Saturday at 14:45 Martin replied:

Oh THAT was the image I've been frantically repressing for the last few weeks. Cheers, Ella. I disliked David quite enough already without needing to picture him as a nimble-fingered sex wizard.

On Saturday at 14:49 Ella replied:

Let's not go overboard here. I only speculated that he might be better than you.

On Saturday at 14:52 Martin replied:

I'm not even going to ask what Sally's been telling you. Thanks for getting in touch, though. You've really put the finishing boot into my day.

Thursday Night (Again)

On Sunday at 10:15 Martin wrote:

Hi Laura
Sorry to bother you again. Writing to apologise again for my ridiculous and idiotic behaviour on Thursday night. Also, I probably should also have mentioned that Sally was my ex. Hope things aren't going to be weird now. I would be very grateful if we could forget the whole thing ever happened. Anyway, hope you're having a good weekend.
Martin

On Sunday at 18:23 Laura wrote:

Hi, Martin,
No problem, for goodness sake. Sorry not to get back to you sooner. An old friend appeared unexpectedly for the weekend, so I haven't been checking my mail. If you want to forget Thursday - and I'm surprised you can remember it - that's fine. There are a few little images it will be hard to erase from the memory, though - not least your version of 'The Ballad of Bilbo Baggins', and the spectacular moment you declared 'Oh my God I'm channelling Mick' before capsizing the table. And poking me in the eye. Anyway, no harm done. No permanent harm, at least. By the way, I managed to record a snippet of you singing 'You Were Always on My Mind' on my phone. Stirring stuff.

I'm a bit bewildered by your encounter with David in the toilets, though. As indeed was he. Is it really Sally you're upset about, or is there something you aren't admitting to yourself?

If it would make you feel any better, you can give me the

tambourine. See you tomorrow, and you can buy me lunch if you still feel bad. But there's really no need. I like you - but don't let it go to your head. Most people I like turn out to be complete idiots.

Lots of love,

Laura

PS. But please don't invite me to the theatre again. What was with that dancing jester? Sally and David were asking what I thought about the play on the way back. I said it was 'interesting' and 'thought-provoking'. I didn't reveal that the thought it mostly provoked was 'I hope the fire alarm goes off.' By the way, I've met them both before.

Part Four
Rock and Roll Heart

A Disciplinary Matter

The Ross Mystery Deepens

Betrayal • Underwear • Fork

A Disciplinary Matter

On Monday at 9:01 Martin Sergeant wrote:

Dear Martin Sargent,
We would appreciate it if you could come to room 13b at 13:00 today. I will be there with Mr Simon Tapper from Security. Please feel free to bring a colleague to act as a witness. This is in relation to a security matter. I have copied this email to Mr Tapper.
Yours sincerely,
Martin Sergeant, IT

On Monday at 9:04 Martin Sargent replied:

Right. And what's going to be in room 13b? A CD player with 'Ghostbusters' on it?

On Monday at 9:08 Martin Sergeant replied:

Dear Martin Sargent,
Our email monitoring system has detected an inappropriate message sent from your work account, and we would like to discuss it with you. Please be on time.
Yours sincerely,
Martin Sergeant, IT

On Monday at 9:12 Martin Sargent replied:

If this is about an email entitled 'Bosom Buddies', that was sent to me uninvited by a friend from school and I was forwarding it to show my disapproval.

On Monday at 9:15 Martin Sergeant replied:

Dear Mr Sargent,
We are aware of that correspondence, but this meeting is in relation to a separate and unrelated matter. As a general point the IT Department would like to underscore the point that work email should be used for work purposes only. We look forward to seeing you at 13:00.
Yours sincerely,
Martin Sergeant, IT

On Monday at 9:22 Martin Sargent wrote:

Barney (and whoever else is reading this)
Don't send me any more crap 'jokes' over the internet. I am in trouble at work about something to do with email misuse. Seriously.
Martin

On Monday at 9:33 Martin Sargent wrote:

Hi Laura
Thanks for your lovely email yesterday. I am afraid I may have to skip lunch today - see the attached from Martin Sergeant. He really does read our emails! Perhaps it's to do with my not wanting to live with him? God knows what all this is about. Tell you over lunch tomorrow? When you can also reveal how you've met David and Sally before.

Lots of Love
Martin

On Monday at 9:45 Laura replied:

Hi, Martin,

What have you been emailing? It wasn't that stupid 'Bosom Buddies' email, was it? You're in trouble with Martin Sergeant! Do you want me to get in touch with the union rep? I hear Martin can be a right batsard. Lunch tomorrow sounds fine - if you're still employed by this company by then.

Lots of love,

Laura

PS. I've checked who your union rep is - it's only Charlotte Greely. Things could get pretty messy in there. She threw Martin out of the flat again over the weekend.

On Monday at 9:48 Martin Sargent replied:

Again? Never realised the girlfriend was Charlotte 'the party at the Brewery is cancelled' Greely. Oh God, if she's thrown him out he's bound to be in a great mood today. And an even better one if he's reading this. I would like to make clear that I never thought he was gay, I like his glasses, and he is a fine young man. Why did his girlfriend throw him out (again)?

On Monday at 10:15 Laura replied:

Dunno. Perhaps because she found out that everyone in the office knew he'd been cheating on her with Kate Staple (again)? Good luck later - do you want me to come along?

On Monday at 10:20 Martin Sargent replied:

I think I can handle it alone. If I'm in there for more than about an hour, set off the fire alarm. Who is Simon Tapper?

On Monday at 10:22 Laura replied:

The grumpy little Security guy.

On Monday at 10:25 Martin Sargent replied:

Not that little guy who lurks around the lobby and shouts into his walkie-talkie? The one whose attitude screams 'three inches too short to get into the Prison Service'? We used to call him 'Ming the Merciless's little henchman'. He bloody hates me.

On Monday at 10:27 Laura replied:

Paranoid. Why would he hate you?

On Monday at 10:28 Martin Sargent replied:

Because he heard me refer to him as 'Ming the Merciless's little henchman'.

On Monday at 10:34 Laura replied:

Careful, I hear he has a bit of a short fuse. He's not inclined to be big about things like that. He thinks we all look down on him. He wants to do something more high-powered. He keeps his ear close to the ground. It's only a low-paid job, but he aspires to reach the heights of his profession.

On Monday at 10:35 Martin Sargent replied:

Does he feel dwarfed by his responsibilities?

On Monday at 10:36 Laura replied:

Yes, but luckily he's got a great team working with him. Dorothy, the Tin Man, a Scarecrow, the Cowardly Lion, all the other Lollipop Men ...

On Monday at 10:48 Martin Sargent replied:

Sorry for slow response. I had an email about work. I believe if things get really bad he can also call for back-up from Gandalf, Gimli and Galadriel.

On Monday at 10:52 Laura replied:

So THAT'S why MediaSolutions has never been invaded by Orcs.

On Monday at 10:53 Martin Sargent replied:

Yeah, and if things get really bad he can always get help from Val Kilmer.

On Monday at 10:57 Laura replied:

?????

On Monday at 10:58 Martin Sargent wrote:

Willow gag. With the sledge? And the pig?

On Monday at 11:05 Laura replied:

I think this has gone far enough. Please allow me to do some work, or I will report you to IT for misusing email. Good luck later. Word of advice: don't wear shoes with stacked heels.

On Monday at 12:38 Martin Sergeant wrote:

Dear Mr Sargent,
We would like to advise that a second disciplinary matter related to the misuse of email has now arisen, and will be discussed at our meeting today. Please be on time. Mr Tapper and I will see you in twenty minutes. Please wait outside room 13b until we call you in.
Yours sincerely,
Martin Sergeant, IT

On Monday at 12:40 Martin Sargent replied:

Yes, yes, I'll be there shortly.

Jokes about Bombs

Dear Mr Sargent,

Further to our meeting at 13:00 today in room 13b I am putting the following disciplinary complaints in written form, with the agreement of Mr Simon Tapper (Head of Security). Please print and retain a copy of this FORMAL WARNING. As you know the complaints are related to the misuse of MediaSolutions email and are as follows:

1) Using company email to encourage others to submit false bomb threats.

2) Using company email to encourage other to misuse fire alarms.

These are serious offences, and Mr Tapper and myself have made it clear that further violations will result in higher-level disciplinary proceedings. If you have any complaints regarding this procedure, please raise them with your union representative, Ms Charlotte Greely. At the present time Mr Tapper and I have decided against adding these infractions to your permanent record.

Jokes About Bombs Are Not Jokes.

        Martin Sergeant, IT Department

        Simon Tapper, Head of Security

On Monday at 14:31 Martin Sargent wrote:

Hi Laura

Have attached my warning from Tapper and Sergeant. Note their final comment. Surely that doesn't quite work? Surely

'Jokes About Bombs are Not Funny' or 'Jokes About Bombs Are No Joke' would be better?

I kept an admirably straight face when Tapper told me he'd have liked to 'take the matter higher'. Apparently (allegedly) it wasn't just Martin reading my emails: I used one of the 'trigger-words' that automatically raise an alert. I think a red light starts spinning on a computer in the IT room and a painting slides to one side to reveal a map of London with little flashing lights on. Then Martin uses a stick to push little(r) models of the security personnel around a big map on the table.

Jokes about Cub Scout's Woggles are Knot Jokes.
Martin

On Monday at 14:36 Laura wrote:

> Al-Qaeda, jihad, George Bush
> Martin Sergeant is a tool

On Monday at 14:37 Laura wrote:

> Terror, Saudi link, mad mullah
Just testing, Martin.

On Monday at 14:40 Laura wrote:

> It does work! I have to see Sergeant and Tapper tomorrow at lunch. Sandwiches on Wednesday?
> Laura

PS. Hijack, Bliar, martyr
Martin Sergeant is a cheating batsard

George's Bush

On Monday at 16:23 Martin Sargent wrote:

Barney, you buttoncock, I'm not even going to open whatever crap it is you've sent me now. I have no interest in a jpeg entitled 'George's Bush'. Send it to my hotmail. This account is for work only.
Martin

P.S. Clash of civilisations, Rumsfeld, oil
Martin Sergeant sleeps under his desk in the office
P.P.S. Will explain when I next see you.

Bit of Consideration

On Monday at 16:44 Ross wrote:

Hi Martin,
Not being funny, mate, but did you leave the vacuum cleaner out? I tripped over it this morning and nearly broke my neck on the stairs. If you're looking for it later it's in my room because I was hoovering in there earlier - feel free to go in and get it.
Ross

PS Would be great if you could pick up some milk for the morning on your way back from work. I'll probably be back late.

The Inner Sanctum

On Monday at 20:34 Martin wrote:

Hi Lucy

Today gets odder and odder. I've just been inside Ross's room for the first time since he moved in. I wasn't spying, I went in to get the hoover (to quote Mum). Well, that clears up where the smell was coming from. And where all the cutlery went to. Christ, not even a badger fouls its own lair. I went to let some air in and there was a pubic hair stuck right to the middle of the window. How? Why? I trod in a bloody tuna sandwich in bare feet as well. I swear to God there was a dried-out slice of cucumber on Ross's pillow. Perhaps he was saving it for the morning? A touch of class: he claims to have vacuumed in there today, but the floor is still covered in clothes. Conclusion? He did the bachelor classic of hovering *round* the piles of crapola on the floor. The whole room smelled like when you leave damp sports kit in the hall all holidays and open it the day before the start of term to find it's grown mushrooms. No wonder he's always out. That's another thing - where does he go? Not buying milk, that's for damn sure. And if he's really serious about being a writer, where is his *Writers' and Artists' Yearbook*?

Lots of Love

Martin

On Tuesday at 11:20 Lucy replied:

Gross. That's really helped my hangover. Must go and puke now before lectures. Speak soon.

Re: A Disciplinary Matter

On Tuesday at 12:00 Laura wrote:

Why is the union so utterly useless? Bloody Charlotte
Greely has got back to me to say she can't come with me to my
disciplinary meeting. No excuse offered. Not even: I don't want
to see my on-off boyfriend and so I am being wet. Then again
you have to wonder about someone who volunteers to be union
rep anyway. The rumour is she went for it because she was
pissed off that Julie was made First Aid Officer. And she wasn't
made milk monitor at school and that still stings.

On Tuesday at 12:32 Martin replied:

I'll come along to support if you want. I hope you're not
wearing high heels. I think Petty Officer Tapper is actually
shrinking.

On Tuesday at 12:41 Laura replied:

He's being eaten up with rage. Perhaps he thinks we all look
down our noses at him?

On Tuesday at 12:42 Martin replied:

Oh God, don't start that again. He'll never reach the top with
that kind of altitude. Sorry, that should read 'attitude'.
On a related note, do you know Craig, otherwise known as

the nice security guard? i.e. the one who will actually hold a door if you are carrying a box of stationery, and who smiles when you come in, and doesn't generally act as if his job would be a lot easier if people didn't insist on getting in the way by trying to use the building as an office? He came up to me this morning and said he'd heard I'd had a run-in with 'Toulouse-la-twat'. Apparently all the cleaning staff hate him too. He asked Benita why she didn't wear a burqa. Ummm, is it because she's Peruvian? But under what possible combination of circumstances would you ask someone that, anyway? She's the coolest cleaner by a long way. Have you noticed she NEVER takes her rings off ever?

Why didn't you volunteer to be union rep? People actually like and respect you...

On Tuesday at 12:45 Laura replied:

Sweet of you to say, but I do know that. I bloody should be union rep. WHY is the coffee machine still broken? And how come all the best magazines end up in the smoking room? And which practical joker hired the receptionist with the speech impediment?

Come along at one - it's in room 13b again. Otherwise known as the Security sandwich room. That's why the meeting can't go on beyond one thirty - they all want to come in and have their lunch.

On Tuesday at 12:46 Martin replied:

I don't think it's a speech impediment. I think she talks like that because she's deaf. See you at the sandwich room. I mean anti-terror nerve centre.

Judas

On Tuesday at 14:02 Laura wrote:

Tee hee no written warning for me.

On Tuesday at 14:03 Martin replied:

I can't believe you sold me out.

On Tuesday at 14:12 Laura replied:

Well, you have been getting a bit smug. I said the contact lens incident was forgotten, not forgiven.

On Tuesday at 14:15 Martin replied:

I'm going to complain to the union.

On Tuesday at 14:18 Laura replied:

Well, how do you know I wasn't telling the truth? I might have got the spellings of your surnames mixed up and been calling you a tool. The look of triumph on Tapper's face when I said that. I made his day.

On Tuesday at 14:19 Martin replied:

You made his life. As for the implication that you were acting as an agent provocateur and trying to trick me into revealing my terrorist sympathies...

On Tuesday at 14:25 Laura replied:

Yes, I wondered if that was over-egging it. I got a very strange look from Martin when I said 'agent provocateur'. The thought of Charlotte Greely in expensive lingerie is a bit much for a Tuesday lunchtime, I must say.

On Tuesday at 14:26 Martin replied:

Tomorrow for the long-delayed lunch, then? Of course, that's provided they let me back into the building...

By the way, the best magazines end up in the smoking room because that's where the cool kids hang out. You should come on down sometime and join the emphasemic bitching. You've not lived until you've heard Benita dissect a copy of *Hello!* over a Rothman's: ' 'e is a gay' (turns page), 'e is a gay (turns page), I can't believe she is marryin' 'im, 'e is a gay and all (throws paper down in disgust, lights up again).' She literally never makes any other comment. She was next to me the other day, and she pointed at a picture of Elton, and said, 'An' 'e is the biggest gay of the lot.' I couldn't think of an adequate response.

On Tuesday at 14:31 Laura replied:

Did she mean by campitude or by sheer body mass, I wonder. Or perhaps she's trying to tell you something?

PS. You're the one to be funny about other people's accents. Your voice goes really posh when you're plastered. 'Hands orf my tambourine'.

Simple Maths

Hey Ella

I had a very interesting conversation over lunch with someone who saw David and Sally snogging outrageously at a party nine weeks ago. Apparently they almost fell out of a window. Apparently they didn't even stop kissing to drink, and were pouring white wine out of a single glass into the gap left between their two sets of slobbering lips. Apparently Sally was sitting on his lap with her skirt rolling up and ruffling his horrible orange hair. Apparently no one could get to their coats at the end of the evening, because they'd locked themselves in the cloakroom. I don't have orange hair, and I don't drink white wine, so I don't think it's a case of mistaken identity. Now I'm not Carol Vorderman, but nine weeks ago Sally still lived with me. In fact, nine weeks ago I was at a stag weekend in Wales. Now I was a bit sleepy when I got back, but I think I would have remembered if Sally mentioned snogging someone. Particularly if she'd told me she almost rolled out of a window doing so.

I can only assume that you knew about this? Does everyone? I'd appreciate it if you would put me out of my misery.
Martin

P.S. And it was a shit stag weekend. Since when did people start going go-karting and sleeping out in tents to celebrate the end of their bachelorhood?

Hi, Martin

By 'put you out of your misery', I guess you mean tell you what I know about Sally and David. As opposed to shooting you like a broken pony. I assumed Sally told you when she moved out. That was why I wanted to avoid being at the first night of the play. But if you didn't know why have you been making such a total cocksneeze of yourself? Jesus - you broke his nose and you didn't know he'd been shagging Sally behind your back?

Well, yes, that party was the first time they got together. If you think it's been tough on you, I've had to hear Sally dripping on about it for nine weeks in the way only actresses can. She's been very confused, she had strong feelings for both of you, David was overwhelmingly attractive and brilliant, the sex was amazing, etc, etc. Imagine my surprise when I first met this astonishing prodigy and found he was a loathsome little goblin. Obviously I feel pretty bad about not telling you, but then I'm Sally's mate too and I hoped it wouldn't come to this. She didn't mention his hideous tapered combat trousers, otherwise I would have been much firmer about telling her to stick with you.

Did 'everyone' know? No. I knew, all Sally's other friends knew, and a sizeable selection of yours as well. But the vast majority of the world went on with their daily routine unaware of the seismic events unfolding in north-west London. I know it's a shock and all, but please keep it in proportion. After all, you knew they're together now, so is it really such a big deal that they got together then? It could have been one of those things that make someone realise how much they treasure what they have. Unfortunately, it wasn't. So yes, we knew, but we didn't go dancing around with models of you with horns, shouting 'cuckoo', 'cuckoo'. Well, we did actually, but that was for kicks, not out of malice. No one refers to you as 'Martin the Cuckold'. Possibly because we don't know any other Martins.

In fact, had one of your friends come to you under similar circumstances, you would have done exactly the same thing. I'd say it's a chance for you both to grow and move on in your lives,

120

but let's be honest, the whole thing will probably gnaw at you in the night for years and shrivel you up inside 'til you're a wizened drunk muttering about never trusting women in a pub that you haven't noticed has been remodelled as a theme bar. Or you end up wandering around Oxford Circus asking people if they're a winner or a sinner.

Let's face it, when the sex goes you're just friends. And friends who bicker all the time aren't very good for each other. Hope this helps.

Ella

PS (In response to your PS) I don't know when that happened. Moreover, I don't care. Blame it on feminism and get your own opinion column in the *Daily Mail*.
PPS I was alarmed to see that Carol Vorderman is the only mathematician you know the name of.

On Wednesday at 14:40 Martin replied:

Thanks, Ella, for your borderline-autistic candour. And thanks for the revelation that they were actually having sex, too. I thought I was upset when I was just imagining heavy petting.

I don't follow your argument about the timing. That's like saying 'well, yes, it was murder, but the victim's dead now anyway, so it doesn't really matter.'

And, by the way, the sex hadn't gone.
Martin

On Wednesday at 14:42 Ella replied:

Umm, I think when you turn down the offer of lovemaking with your partner in order to watch a documentary about Lou Reed, the sex has gone.

On Wednesday at 14:43 Martin replied:

Oh come on! I can't believe she told you that. They hardly ever show *Rock and Roll Heart*, and I offered to put a video in.

On Wednesday at 14:46 Ella replied:

When you turn down sex with your beautiful and sexy partner to watch someone with a mullet and no end on his guitar doing songs from *Magic and Loss*, while one of Penn and Teller talks about how much the *New York* album means to him, the sparkle has left the bedroom. And for God's sake, you don't say 'Let's do it on the counter' when someone is trying to cook lunch for your parents.

God it feels good to finally be able to tell you these things.

On Wednesday at 14:48 Martin replied:

You are a cold cold person, Ella.

On Wednesday at 14:52 Ella replied:

Yes I am. But for fuck's sake I can't stand all this moping and mewling about. And that goes for the pair of you, but particularly you. Why act as if you're going to challenge David to a duel when the worst it will ever come to is you giving his plays anonymous bad reviews online? A couple of tearful wanks and you'll be fine.

And for goodness' sake if you're going to liven things up by having sex in the woods a) at least one of you should preferably be wearing a skirt and b) make sure you tie the dog up securely. I'd love to have been a fly on the wall that weekend: 'So how did Digger get loose in the first place, Martin?' 'Well, the thing was, Mr Kendle, I was trying to boff your daughter and we couldn't work out what to do with her jeans.' 'One leg off, boy, one leg off.'

I think you should give Sally her underwear back, too.

Warm regards, Ella

On Wednesday at 15:03 Martin replied:

Trust me, she wouldn't want it back now. By the way, this may be totally inappropriate, but I'm sure I could recover a lot of my sex confidence if I was to practise with someone who I didn't feel too strongly about and who I knew wasn't going to get all hung up on me.

Martin

On Wednesday at 15:04 Ella replied:

You couldn't begin to handle me, Sargent.

Just a Pint

On Wednesday at 20:15 Martin wrote:

By the way I was joking about the underwear.

On Thursday at 10:10 Ella replied:

So I assumed. Until I got this email.

On Thursday at 10:11 Martin replied:

I was joking about the other thing, too.

On Thursday at 10:15 Ella replied:

Oh damn. But wasn't it Freud who said there's no such thing as a joke?

On Thursday at 10:16 Martin replied:

I think he said there's no such thing as an accident, actually.

On Thursday at 10:18 Ella replied:

Nice try, though. Pint next week?

On Thursday at 10:22 Martin replied:

Ah, but surely there's no such thing as a pint...

Yesterday

Dear Martin,

I'm really sorry if what I told you upset you yesterday. I guess that story's a lot less funny if one of the people involved is your ex. It was very inconsiderate of me.

I don't know if I should mention this, but it seems relevant that the person who turned up at mine unannounced last weekend was Gwyn, my ex. He unloaded a lot of stuff on me (emotional stuff) and is in quite a bad way, so I'm not really sure what to do about that at the moment. Anyway, doubt it makes much difference, but I wanted you to know.

Lots of love

Laura

On Thursday at 10:50 Martin replied:

The ex in the band?

On Thursday at 11:15 Laura replied:

Yeah, but they've broken up. That was part of what he was so upset about. Except they haven't actually broken up. They told him they had, and then he rang the drummer up for a pint and found they were on tour in Belgium and Germany with a new singer. He was talking about getting back together, which has taken me a bit by surprise. (Getting back together with me, not with Fork).

126

On Thursday at 11:22 Martin replied:

Your ex's band is called Fork? That's aggressively bland. I suppose Spoon was already taken. I can imagine the scene: they were all at dinner, trying to choose a name... May I hazard a guess they are a knock-kneed indie guitar band? Does he wear a jacket with badges on the lapels?

On Thursday at 11:32 Laura replied:

Afraid so. They used to be called The Romantic Movement, so Fork is an improvement.

He was in a state, actually, so I kind of felt I had to let him stay for a bit. He's being quite sweet - he's written some really good new songs about how things have been for him.

On Thursday at 11:35 Martin replied:

How nice of him. This is the boyfriend who owes you money?

On Thursday at 11:52 Laura replied:

Not very much money.

On Thursday at 11:53 Martin replied:

This is the ex-boyfriend, to be clear, who has the attractive habits of scratching his crotch and blowing his nose into his palm and then chucking it?

On Thursday at 11:55 Laura replied:

Look, I was very upset when I told you that. I don't think you should judge until you've met him.

On Thursday at 11:57 Martin replied:

I can't wait. This is the guy who your friends refused to let in the house after he threatened your neighbour with a hammer?

On Thursday at 12:00 Laura replied:

Well, he's very protective, and the neighbour used to peer in the windows.

On Thursday at 12:01 Martin replied:

There's such a fine line between psychotic and protective. Oh, wait a minute, actually there isn't. You said the neighbour was about 80.

On Thursday at 12:05 Laura replied:

Not more than 60. Besides, Gwyn was going through a stormy patch with the label.

On Thursday at 12:06 Martin replied:

I don't suppose it's any of my business. What's he going to do now? Start up a hardware shop?

On Thursday at 12:17 Laura replied:

Well, for the moment he's staying at mine.

On Thursday at 12:20 Martin wrote:

Hi Lucy
How are you? Aaaaaaaaaaaaaaaaaaaaaargh! Bollocks! Women are idiots! Men are idiots! Hope things are going well with the boy Sam. Speak soon.
Lots of Love
Martin

On Thursday at 12:58 Lucy replied:

Feel better, mate? Of course they are. Otherwise no one would ever get together and the race would die out. Everything going well with Laura?
Lots of love,
Lucy
PS: Going to the pictures tonight, but speak at weekend.

On Thursday at 13:03 Martin wrote:

Hey Laura
Hope that works out. Do you fancy a spot of lunch in a mo?
Martin

On Thursday at 14:23 Laura replied:

Hi Martin,
Sorry I missed your email. Had to meet Gwyn for sandwiches and to look at some instruments. Took a bit longer than expected

and only just snuck back in. Hope you didn't have a lonely lunchbreak!

Lots of love,

Laura

Part Five
DJ Idiot and the Adventures
of the Dialectic

If I Had a Hammer ...

On Thursday at 14:45 Martin wrote:

Hi Barney

Thanks for your help piecing together the shattered fragments of last Thursday night. No one seems inclined to prosecute, thank god. Ross and I are in negotiations over who gets custody of the tambourine, so I can't comment on that at the moment. Could I ask you a favour? I'm putting together a themed collection of songs for someone - do you have any of the following?: 'If I had a Hammer', 'Maxwell's Silver Hammer', anything by MC Hammer; any Hammer Horror themes...

Cheers

Martin

On Thursday at 15:20 Barney replied:

Alright squire,

I've got a bootleg which mixes 'Hammer Time' with 'Don't Stop' by Fleetwood Mac. Any good to you?

Keep it loose, Bruce,

Barney

On Thursday at 15:23 Martin replied:

That's perfect. Presumably it's called 'Don't Stop Thinking about Hammer Time'?

On Thursday at 15:33 Barney replied:

Nah - 'Hammer Time'll Soon Be Here'. Actually, I'm making one that mixes 'Hammer Time' with 'Immigrant Song' by Led Zeppelin.

On Thursday at 15:34 Martin replied:

'Hammer Time of the Gods?'
By the way, surely you're meant to be at work?
Hope all well.

On Thursday at 15:40 Barney replied:

I am at work. I'm smiling at one of the partners across the office as we speak. I'm an artist, Martin. I can't just turn it off. Titlewise, I was thinking of 'Led Zep please don't hurt 'em'.
All going extremely well with me - hooked up with someone after the gallery party. I believe you know her, a girl called Ella? We had a long chat about you, in fact.

On Thursday at 15:42 Martin replied:

I can imagine exactly what you were discussing.
Stop.
Hammer Time.
You hooked up with Ella Tvertko?

On Thursday at 15:43 Martin wrote:

Sorry, I forgot that emails don't always convey the proper emphasis: *You* hooked up with *Ella Tvertko*? She whose icy beauty freezes Evian at twenty paces?

134

On Thursday at 15:47 Barney replied:

Yes, *I* hooked up with (i.e. spent the night with (i.e. to put it bluntly, shagged)) Ella Tvertko. Seeing her again tonight in fact, after the play. Shall I send my regards?

On Thursday at 15:48 Martin replied:

Send my outraged jealousy. You shagged Ella Tvertko. But how?

On Thursday at 15:49 Martin wrote:

To clarify that last bit: how did you end up pulling her?

On Thursday at 15:51 Barney replied:

Actually, she pulled me. Like I said, it's not something I can turn off. Oh and by the way, it was astonishing. Sorry, that should read *astonishing*.

On Thursday at 15:53 Martin replied:

Well, farewell, Old Mate. She will devour you. There will be nothing left of you but a pair of headphones and an 'ironic' wristband. And perhaps the lingering whiff of unutterable smugness.

On Thursday at 15:54 Barney replied:

Counting on it, mate, counting on it. Jealous much?

On Thursday at 15:55 Martin wrote:

Hi Laura

Don't suppose you saw a cheap pair of record decks for sale when you were out at lunchtime? It seems the years I have spent trying to attract girls by transforming myself into a sensitive, charming, well-informed and fully rounded human being have been a total waste of time. What I really should have been doing is practising how to play two records at once while wearing a silly pair of sunglasses.

Martin

Re: DJ Idiot

On Thursday at 16:04 Martin wrote:

Well, well, Ella. I hear you hooked up with DJ Idiot last night. One question: why? Free drink, was it? Oh sorry, two questions. Yours in disbelief
Martin

On Thursday at 16:45 Ella wrote:

Hey, Martin
Simple answer: He's sexy. Nice strong chin. Getting ready to see him later. Lucky boy. Should give me something to think about during this bloody play, anyhow. Nice to see what loyal mates Mark has.
Ella

On Thursday at 16:47 Martin replied:

I know he's my mate, but he's also a complete foolio. He makes Dr Fox look like Merleau-Ponty. And he's rubbish at DJing. He's totally undeserving.
Martin

On Thursday at 16:52 Ella replied:

Poor sweet Martin,
It's got nothing to do with being deserving - it doesn't work

like AirMiles, you know. Do I really have to explain this to you?
I'm not putting together a pub quiz team.

On Thursday at 16:53 Martin replied:

Just as well. He once told me: 'You can knock Cathy Dennis
all you want, but she did write "Waterloo Sunset"'.

On Thursday at 16:57 Ella replied:

So what?

On Thursday at 16:58 Martin replied:

So it's by Ray Davies. Everyone knows that! It was a
wretched cover version as well.

On Thursday at 17:02 Ella replied:

Well done. You've proved whatever minor point you wanted
to make. By the way, this is all a bit creepy of you. It's really
none of your business, panty-hoarder.
On which note, you know Mark pretty well: thong or
something more sensible?

On Thursday at 17:05 Martin replied:

Point taken, point taken. As for the pants, I don't care and I
never want to know. Just don't break him - he's my idiot and he
has sentimental value.

Big News

On Thursday at 18:22 Emily wrote:

Hi Martin

Hope the play was good. Sorry we missed it (No we're not - Chris. Oops and we missed it again last night as well. Sorry, Sally). Apologies, Chris is reading this over my shoulder. How about a good, honest pint on Friday? We've got big news!
Emily (and Chris)

PS. To make things clear, Chris and I have discussed this and are in total agreement. We will meet in a pub. A normal pub. To drink pints or perhaps a glass or two of wine. Like normal people. At no point in the evening will you reveal that you have taken us to the most haunted pub in London, or Lord Lucan's old local, or anything involving bloody Dickens. If we're hungry we may order Twiglets or a bag of crinkle-cut crisps. There will be no eels, no roasted trotters and certainly no winkles. And if you use the word 'psychogeography' or let slip that we are drinking in an establishment built on the site of Pepys's old house or Black Bess's stable or a plague pit, I will glass you myself. Or should I say, invite you to partake in the timeless violence of this most unpredictable of cities ...

On Thursday at 18:45 Martin replied:

Can't interest you in a night of avant-garde burlesque in Clapham?

Hi Martin,

Chris here. Using Emily's email account in a spirit of transgressive subversion of which I trust you will approve. We have thought seriously about your offer of a night in Clapham watching burlesque, and have decided against. Instead, I am going to soak my balls in white spirit and then Emily is going to flick matches at me. I hope this answers your question. Come for a pint. Will text to arrange shortly. Don't make any more suggestions that we all do something else 'cultural' and tedious or I will kill you. I'm not joking.

Chris

Fork Is Genius!

On Thursday at 21:25 Johannes wrote:

Dear Gwyn

I can't believe I am writing to you. I am biggest fan of Fork from Dusseldorf. Before I liked The Doors and Pink Floyd but now Fork is my favourite. You are so great! I have all your record and even poster and my mother made me T-shirt with Fork on. But when I wear it to your gig last night I am so disappointed because there was new singer. He is not so great! I want you to rejoin band. You are the best singer. I write to band as well, and tell them new singer 'sucks'. You should rejoin Fork and make more brilliant indie guitar music with them. Perhaps you should tour Australia and the Far East for a long time.

Yours truly

Johannes Jester

Your Idiot

On Friday at 12:06 Barney wrote:

Who is Merlot-Poncy?

On Friday at 12:23 Martin wrote:

Maurice Merleau-Ponty (1908-1961)

A key figure in post-war French philosophy. Merleau-Ponty served in the infantry during the Second World War, and in 1949 was appointed to the chair of Child Psychology at the Sorbonne. In 1952 he became the youngest person ever appointed to the chair of Philosophy at the College de France. In 1945 he co-founded with Jean-Paul Sartre and Simone de Beauvoir the influential political, literary and philosophical journal *Les Temps modernes*. Like Sartre and de Beauvoir, Merleau-Ponty is usually associated with the existentialist movement, although he remained sceptical of some of the movement's more extreme accounts of personal freedom and responsibility. Indeed, Merleau-Ponty extensively critiqued many of Sartre's positions, not least what he saw as the privileging of subject-object relations in Sartre's version of phenomenology. Merleau-Ponty's disagreements with many of Sartre's political positions was also a key factor in the somewhat bitter ending of their friendship. Merleau-Ponty gave his assessment of their differences in *Adventures of the Dialectic*, while Sartre's version of events is recounted in *Situations*. Merleau-Ponty died before completing his final work, *The Visible and the Invisible*, which was to have been both a rethinking and an extension of his attempts throughout his philosophical career to break down the traditional dualisms between sensibility and understanding, activity and passivity, mind and body.

<u>Dr Fox (1961-)</u>

Actual name: Neil Fox. Also known as 'Foxy'. Should not be confused with Dr Liam Fox, Conservative MP.

Dr Fox began his radio career as a student, broadcasting under the name Andrew Howe on University Radio Bath. After graduating Foxy worked for a time selling printed plastic bags, before getting a job on Radio Wyvern (97.6 FM in Herefordshire, 102.8 FM in Worcestershire). In less than a year he had been signed up to work on Radio Luxembourg. From 1987 until 2005 he was a presenter with Capital Radio. He also fronted Channel 5's Pepsi Chart Show from 1998 to 2002, alongside the greatly underrated Liz Eastwood. He is probably best known as the indulgent judge on the TV talent show *Pop Idol*. Fact: He's not really a doctor, but he does have a degree in Business and Marketing. His work's relationship to that of Jean-Paul Sartre remains hotly debated.

On Friday at 12:25 Barney replied:

To quote Merleau-Ponty's *Adventures of the Dialectic*: 'Vous êtes un cul'.

Need a translation?

On Friday at 12:27 Martin replied:

Mme Deganis would be so proud. Only trying to save you from getting hurt, mate.

On Friday at 12:29 Barney replied:

Cheers pal. (Since emails don't always convey tone I should explain that the previous phrase is to be delivered in a tone of withering sarcasm). I think I know exactly what you were trying to 'save' me from.

Last Night

On Friday at 12:30 Sally wrote:

Dear Martin,

I don't think it's a very good idea if you ring me drunk again.
Or indeed at all, if you're going to be like this. I'm not going to
apologise for falling in love with someone else, and I think it's
rather selfish of you to expect me to.

Sally

On Friday at 12:34 Martin replied:

Oh come on now, Sally,

I thought it was easy to apologise but hard to accept an
apology. Try me.

Love

Martin

On Friday at 12:40 Sally replied:

What am I supposed to be apologising for?

On Friday at 12:45 Martin replied:

Oh, I don't know...

Oh yes I do. How about hooking up with the Phantom of the
Pub Theatre behind my back? Several weeks behind my back.
And then leaving me sitting around thinking things were all

my fault and you moving out was something to do with me not cleaning the oven or forgetting your pony's birthday?
Martin

On Friday at 12:50 Sally replied:

Are you still drunk?

On Friday at 12:51 Martin replied:

I may have had a pint at lunch.

On Friday at 12:54 Sally replied:

It's only 12:54.

On Friday at 12:55 Martin replied:

Breakfast, then.

On Friday at 13:04 Sally replied:

Please don't get in touch with me until you're prepared to be reasonable about what has happened. I have bent over backwards to make this whole thing amicable, but you seem determined to make everything as unpleasant as you can. I think, when you look at things soberly, you will realise you are being an ass.

On Friday at 13:09 Martin replied:

Well I have a right to be an ass. I'm an ass and proud. I'm

a cuckolded ass and I'm bad at sex. But I'm a free ass in giddy London.

On Friday at 13:13 Martin wrote:

Hi Laura

Lunch? I've spilled something on my computer and I have to get out of here. Meet me at the Grapes in three minutes. It's Friday! Pub lunch on me! Also meeting up with mates later if you want to come too. Gwyn not invited - planning on getting hammered, but not literally.

Martin the Ass

Wallet

On Saturday at 9:58 Martin wrote:

Hi Chris

Many congratulations again on your big news. I had a great night. I have big news of my own, in fact: I don't suppose you saw what I did with my tie, jacket or indeed wallet? Presumably I had at least one of them in the taxi. Unless I drunkenly blew the driver for a free ride. Again. Couldn't have a fouler tasting mouth this morning if I had.

Yuck.

Martin

P.S. So I assume the obvious...?

P.P.S. Seriously mate, she's a lovely girl. God knows what she sees in you.

On Saturday at 10:45 Chris replied:

Not sure what happened to your stuff, mate. Don't think you left it in the pub. I can assure you we haven't nicked your wallet to defray the cost of the wedding. No, Emily is not with child, if that is 'the obvious'. Cheeky bastard. As it happens we've been on the waiting-list for the chapel for quite a while. They've had an unexpected cancellation for later in the year, so it's all going to be a bit of a rush.

147

On Saturday at 11:00 Martin wrote:

Emily

It's not too late to back out. I'll always wait for you. We can even raise the child as our own, and live in the mountains.

On Saturday at 11:32 Emily replied:

Martin, you know I use this account as well. I hope the offer stands for me too? I think lederhosen would quite suit me, in fact, and I can see you in a little Tiroler hat. Trust me, if Emily really was knocked up, I'd be holding a goat on a glacier before you could say 'yodel-eei-hoo'.

Chris

On Saturday at 11:40 Martin replied:

By the way, I don't suppose you've had a chance to think about potential best men? This is an enquiry, not a hint...

Re: Wallet

Dear Martin 'the Ass'
Didn't make it into work yesterday due to crisis at home.
Sorry to stand you up! Hope the Grapes was OK. Isn't it a bit
grim? Whenever I've been in it's full of shaky old men with
watery eyes. How was the night out with your friends?

Laura

On Saturday at 12:56 Martin replied:

Hi Laura
Yes, it is an extraordinarily depressing place for a solitary
lunchtime pint.
Gosh, I feel terrible. My mates announced their engagement
last night, and the toasting went on into the early hours. I seem
to have lost my jacket and tie. And wallet. But not, for once, my
dignity.
I've had to ring round and cancel all my cards. Waiting for my
flatmate to come home and hopefully buy me some food.

On Saturday at 13:20 Laura replied:

Oh, in that case you are an ass. What did you spill on your
computer?

PS. I don't really think you're an ass. I know worse.

On Saturday at 14:01 Martin replied:

Ribena. I think I was trying to make a cocktail…

I've found my jacket in the kitchen. My wallet was on the sideboard with all cards present and correct. But of course they're all now cancelled so entirely useless. Still, if I get really hungry there's some lettuce and a little fragment of kebab meat in one of the jacket pockets. There's no sign of my tie, though. Or my flatmate.

On Saturday at 14:12 Laura replied:

How annoying. If you can scrape together enough for a travel card you can come over here for dinner later. I might even be persuaded to take you out for a pizza.

On Saturday at 14:15 Martin replied:

Sounds great. But won't Gwyn mind? I would prefer not to be hit with a hammer.

On Saturday at 14:21 Laura replied:

Nah, he's rehearsing tonight and staying with mates afterwards. We had a bit of a row yesterday morning. Would be lovely to see you. Come over. But we must try to figure out where your tie is, using logical deduction from the available evidence. First, eliminate the obvious. Are you wearing it?

On Saturday at 14:22 Martin replied:

Aha!… No.

On Saturday at 14:23 Laura replied:

Nope, it's no good, it's lost. You'll have to hire a psychic. Haven't you got another one you could wear on Monday?

On Saturday at 14:26 Martin replied:

I've got a tie Dad gave me for Christmas, but I don't know if it really projects the right image for work. It's got Homer Simpson on with a can of beer, and he's thinking 'Hmmm Beer'. I don't even think it's official. Homer looks a bit orange and his head is slightly rectangular. Cheers, Pop. Oh God, I'm much too hungover today to start contemplating the sadness of dadness.

On Saturday at 14:31 Laura replied:

Well, it's the thought that counts - although I'm not sure that saying is very reassuring in this context. Wear it on Monday!

On a similar note, last birthday Gwyn gave me a load of cheesy lingerie and a spice rack. Pretty subtle demonstration of how he thinks about me. And he gave me that card with a skinhead saying to an old granny 'Show us yer tits'. And inside the card she lifts up her skirt and there they are, dangling around her knees. That was just before we broke up, in fact ...

On Saturday at 14:35 Martin replied:

Charming. I always wondered in what possible circumstances that card would be appropriate. Guess I'll have to keep on wondering.

I got the birthday tie out to have a look at and it's brought the sadness. It's the thought of Dad seeing it and thinking, 'Martin likes *The Simpsons* and he drinks beer, this is the perfect present'.

On Saturday at 14:37 Laura replied:

I think perhaps we need to get you a new tie ...
Actually, to be fair, it is a bloody nice spice rack.

Change of Plans

On Saturday at 18:02 Laura wrote:

Hi, Martin,
Sorry about this, but can we do the pizza another night? I tried to call you, but the phone was engaged, so I guess you're online. Gwyn has reappeared after all and I get the feeling we're going to have to have yet another discussion about 'us'. I feel rubbish about this, but I hope you'll understand. Hope your flatmate comes back to feed you! So sorry to muck you about, and I would much much rather be having pizza with you. Good luck with the tie hunt, and look forward to seeing you on Monday.
Lots of love

Laura

Re: Fork Is Genius!

Dear Johanna.

Thank you for your lovely email. It was really nice to hear from a fan. But I'm afraid to say Fork have broken up, and we won't be working together any more. Don't worry - we are still great friends and I wish them all the greatest success with their new singer. Although you're right, he's not as good as me!!!

Anyhow, I am working with a new band now, and we will be doing new material as well as favourites from the Fork days. We are rehearsing at the moment and we are called Acklington Stanley. Our first gig is in London in a few weeks and I hope we will be touring Germany soon. Not sure about the Far East but anything is possible!!!

I'll be looking forward to meeting you.

Gwyn

Neglected

On Sunday at 16:01 Martin wrote:

Hello Sis
Remember me? We used to email each other. Presumably
things going well with Sam. Not going home for the holidays?
Lots of Love
Martin
(your brother)

Review

On Sunday at 16:04 Martin wrote:

Hi Sally

Guess what? I'm emailing to apologise. I shouldn't have rung you drunk, and I'm now prepared to act like a human being. I saw the online review - congratulations. By the way, Chris and Emily are getting married. They said they'd love it if we both came to the wedding. I hope that wouldn't be too weird for you. Anyway, look forward to hearing all your news. Regards to David.

Best

Martin

On Sunday at 16:09 Martin wrote:

Hi Laura

I've been reading an online review of *The Lady of Shalott*. Unbelievably, they thought it showed promise. I quote: 'As I crammed into the New Place with the rest of the hipsters and theatre in-crowd I was prepared to dislike David Fauntleroy's new reading of *The Lady of Shalott*. Partly improvised? Live DJ? Dancing onstage? All the signs were there for a thoroughly self-indulgent evening.'

(So far so good, but wait...)

'But I am pleased to report that David Fauntleroy has given this hoariest of ideas new clothes, and they look... pretty fine, actually. With a gifted cast and a willingness to push any envelope he encounters, Fauntleroy conjures a magical evening out of the air with all the confidence and talent of a new Merlin (if that's not mixing my Arthurian legends!).'

And so on, and so on, before concluding: 'In particular the use of mime, particularly at the finale, and the playful use of music made this an evening I would recommend to anyone who is still prepared to believe in theatrical magic. Deserves a bigger space. Five Stars.'

Who is Danny Rodham? Has too much theatre driven him insane? Did he actually go to the play? There's a little box at the bottom of the page where you can add your own opinion. One can only hope that the general public takes full advantage of this opportunity.

Perhaps we are just philistines.

Hope last night was OK. Ross appeared eventually and brought me some chips, and I found a scotch egg in the fridge.
Lots of Love
Martin

On Sunday at 17:12 Laura replied:

Hmmm, mysterious. But it depends how many stars he has to give. Perhaps it's five out of a hundred. What bigger space has he in mind? Perhaps a transfer to the Arctic tundra could be arranged.

What is 'pushing the envelope'? It sounds painful.

So sorry to let you down last night. Gwyn and I managed to have a pretty good talk, though. I let him know my disapproval of his choice in birthday presents. Hope your scotch egg was nice.

Glad to hear we are hipsters.

Lots of love,

Laura

Quick Query

On Sunday at 17:16 Martin wrote:

Hey Barney

Are you still PO'd at me? I don't suppose you know where I could hire a hitman, preferably one who can do a job-lot at discount prices? Axe, garrotte, rifle, I don't mind as long as they're good.

Otherwise, and unless you're busy, pint later?

Martin

On Sunday at 18:19 Barney replied:

Too knackered and drained of essential vitamins to bear a grudge. Not sure about hitmen, but will ask around. Would love to come for pint but can't speak - I think I tore that little piece of skin underneath my tongue. Also can't walk. And I'm typing this with my nose. I may never DJ again.

On Sunday at 18:42 Martin replied:

I'll withhold comment regarding your DJing. No need to rub it in, mate. Glad you're having fun.

On Sunday at 18:45 Barney replied:

It's gone beyond fun, mate. It's either love or at some point soon Ella is going to bite my head off and lay her eggs in my torso.

PS Don't suppose Chris needs a DJ for the wedding?

On Sunday at 18:52 Martin replied:

He didn't mention it, but I'll put in the good word.

PS Barney, by the way, I was joking about the hitman.

Re: Review

On Sunday at 19:14 Ella wrote:

> Martin,
> Have you seen the online review of that awful play of Sally's?
> Ella

On Sunday at 19:16 Martin replied:

> I know, the world has gone mad. Rodham must be another victim of David's drugged bread. The idea that that clown pushes any sort of envelope is an insult to postal workers everywhere.

On Sunday at 19:18 Ella replied:

> I added my own comment to the general melee on the messageboard. At least we're not alone in our opinion. See if you can guess which one was mine. I take it 'My favourite bit was the bloke who wandered in and wanted cigarettes, the rest was mad gay' is your handiwork? I didn't think you were going to take me literally about slagging David off anonymously online. It's so creepy of you. Not that I entirely disapprove.
> Ella

On Sunday at 19:34 Martin replied:

Not actually all my handiwork, surprisingly. I only wrote: 'The Jester was the least ridiculous person involved.' By the way, are you not seeing Barney tonight?

On Sunday at 19:40 Ella replied:

About the play: I believe you. Good luck getting anyone else to.

About Barney: I'm going to have to not see him tonight. In fact, it's possible that that little business may have to be put on hold. Something came up at Church this morning. Or rather, someone.

Ella

On Sunday at 19:43 Martin replied:

Ella!

I will never lend you an idiot again. Stay the hell away from Ross. Although the state of his bedroom should be sufficient deterrent. I knew this would happen. I must admit I wouldn't have predicted the exact circumstances. Church? I thought you started sizzling if you crossed holy ground.

On Sunday at 19:55 Ella replied:

Alpha Course. It's the new supermarket, as far as pulling goes. Should be an article in that somewhere. You should try it.

And I didn't break Barney - you did.

On Sunday at 20:05 Martin replied:

Don't follow.

On Sunday at 20:11 Ella replied:

He spent yesterday afternoon trying to mount his own
critique of Sartre's ontology. Not quite what I had planned for
us, you might say. Also, he kept insisting on leaping out of bed to
play me records. He really is crap at DJing, isn't he?

By the way, my comment was 'As a greengrocer I was
greatly misled by the title of this play. The evening featured no
vegetable's at all. I want my money back.'

Best Man

On Monday at 9:04 Martin wrote:

Hi Mike
Shame you couldn't make it to Chris and Emily's drinks on
Friday. I hear you have been away on a corporate brainwashing
weekend. Ah, the perks of the high-flying young professional.
Have you heard the big news?
Martin

On Monday at 9:08 Mike replied:

Once again, you've got me bang to rights, Martin. The *training*
weekend, as we here refer to it, involved an hour-long lecture
and an all-expenses-paid weekend in a Scottish castle. Damn,
damn, how I regret my life choices. Are they still making you
clock out every time you go to the loo?
Of course I know about Chris and Emily. In fact I've known
they've been planning it for months.

On Monday at 9:11 Martin replied:

I don't suppose Chris has mentioned anything about who he's
asking to be his best man? I did ask but he hasn't got back to me,
and I don't want to seem to be fishing...

On Monday at 9:18 Mike replied:

Actually, Martin, he has. Chris and Emily asked me to do it, a few weeks ago. I said I was sure you wouldn't be upset.

On Monday at 9:21 Martin replied:

Of course I'm not. I am a little bemused, though... Do you know if I made the short-list?

On Monday at 9:24 Mike replied:

Oh, Martin, I'm sure they would have asked you if, say, I was tragically schmoozed to death, Chris's brother disappeared, and Barney died in a freak DJing accident. I think what finally swung it for me was the brief presentation I gave Chris and Emily outlining my vision of what I would bring to the role. After a lot of blue-skying and spit-balling, I went for the simple yet powerful slogan: 'For your Best Man, choose the Best Man'. I used Powerpoint and everything.

Either that, or they simply went with the person they liked and trusted more. I admit it's hard to understand why they wouldn't want a bloke who can manage to lose his wallet and jacket in his own kitchen to be in charge of the rings.

By the way, how are things going with your housemate?

On Monday at 9:30 Martin replied:

Nice segue. I don't know why you think I'm so bothered about it. To be honest, it's a little bit sad that you're making so much of it. It's not like it literally means you're the best man. Or even a better man. Frankly, I wouldn't want all the hassle.

If you're genuinely interested, things with Ross are fine. He's hardly ever there, for one thing. We occasionally cross paths over breakfast or when he knocks on my door to tell me we need more loo-roll. Supposedly he's writing a sitcom, but I haven't seen much evidence of it. I think he's worried about me stealing his ideas, but as he's pitching it as a cross between *Coupling* and *No Logo* I think he can put his mind at rest on that front...

On Monday at 9:30 Mike replied:

Glad you're being so mature about the best man thing. Can't wait to see Ross's sitcom. Has he got a title? How about *Two Pints of Lager, Globalization and its Discontents, and a Packet of Crisps*?

In case you're wondering, Emily's already chosen her bridesmaids. Not that you wouldn't look lovely in a dress...

Re: Re: Review

On Monday at 10:55 Sally wrote:

Hey Martin,

Yes, I heard about the wedding and called to congratulate Chris and Emily. It should be a lovely day. Hope you're not too upset about not making best man. I have to confess I can sort of see their reasoning, though.

I presume the online comments about the play are yours? They will be coming down shortly and I would be grateful if you could restrain yourself. Not funny, just bitter.

Best wishes,

Sally

On Monday at 11:02 Martin replied:

Look forward to seeing you at the wedding then.

I swear to God that the comments aren't mine. I'm sure you know me well enough to know that I'd have gone for something a bit more witty than 'That was no way a real horse.' And come on, the response to that was quite funny.

Martin

On Monday at 11:12 Sally replied:

'Not the only person making a horse's ass of themselves onstage'? It's really sad that people have to snipe from the shadows this way.

166

On Monday at 11:24 Martin replied:

Sniping from the shadows. If only I had thought of that...

On Monday at 11:27 Sally replied:

Pathetic. I hope you aren't going to be like this at the wedding. Seriously, stop it now.

On Monday at 11:35 Martin replied:

Actually, I was referring to the comment that 'The back end of the horse provided a useful clue as to the manner in which this play was created.' But I agree, it's sad and petty. And I assure you it's not me. Not all me, at any rate.

I think the personal attacks on David are unjustified and offensive. I would never stoop to demanding that someone 'stakes him through the heart and burns his corpse at a crossroads, to prevent a repetition of this crime against theatre.' Perhaps it's one of his exes who describes him as 'a loathsome animated voodoo doll' and adds 'I would stab him in the head with a pin, but I don't want to give Malcolm McLaren a headache!!!!' I'd never use that many exclamation marks. I find the whole thing distasteful, and your implication that I am either behind it or revelling in it offensive.

Martin

On Monday at 11:36 Martin wrote:

Hey Lucy

Check out the online reviews of David and Sally's play. The public has shown its thumb, and it is pointing firmly downwards. At last, something to restore my faith in the human spirit!!!!

Love

Martin

P.S. You haven't eloped, have you? REPLY TO ME

Ella

On Monday at 11:52 Barney wrote:

Did you know Ella was going to dump me? I'm absolutely gutted mate. God knows what I did wrong. Did she say anything to you?

On Monday at 11:57 Martin replied:

Of course not. All I heard was what a tiger you are. Women, eh? Ah well, God moves in mysterious ways, mate.

On Monday at 12:04 Barney replied:

Cheers, mate. Knew I could count on you.
Sally and David are pretty upset about the online reviews, by the way.

On Monday at 12:06 Martin replied:

It's not bloody me!
I think I could do a bit better than writing 'My arse ate my trousers it was so bored during this farrago.'
No one seems to be knocking you or Sally personally.

You don't count 'Sally Kendle couldn't convey urgency of emotion if she was shouting "Fire!" in a burning orphanage' as personal?

On Monday at 12:15 Martin replied:

If you scroll down, someone has added 'And I wish she was.' But it really wasn't me.

Re: Neglected

On Monday at 12:25 Lucy wrote:

Hi Martin,

Glad to see the family guilt-trip gene has survived another generation. Staying up here to try to earn a bit of cash for next term. Bloody bar-work. Thinking about applying to be part of one of those medical experiments they pay you cash for. If one more punter tells me to 'Cheer up, love, it may never happen,' I'm signing up. No matter if it's with Dr Frankenstein. Tempted to reply: 'It already has happened. I'm looking glum because I have to serve pints in this alleged funpub to people like you, i.e. the kind of twat who would spend time in this idiot sanctuary without having to be paid to do so.'

I wonder if they take requests for what experiment they do to you? I want a big ear on my back.

By the way, I've seen yourtheatre.com. Been busy? What have you got against Barney?

Lots of love,
Lucy

On Monday at 12:35 Martin wrote:

Nothing.

On Monday at 12:45 Lucy wrote:

I quote: 'I was prepared to salute the bravery and talent of DJ Idiot, but only because I had been misinformed that he has flippers instead of arms.'

On Monday at 13:04 Martin wrote:

That is sick. Possibly Ella.

I swear to God I only wrote one thing on there. Why will no one believe me?

On Monday at 13:07 Lucy wrote:

Because you have the motivation, and it fits your MO. Which is yours, then? The thing about the voodoo doll? Or is it the simple yet damning observation 'I now know I have 246 veins on the inside of my eyelids. I counted twice to check'?

By the way, sorry to hear about your public cuckolding. Bummer.

On Monday at 14:04 Martin replied:

Yeah, tell me about it. I guess Mum told you. Maybe she's behind the internet slander campaign.

I had lunch with Laura, who doesn't believe me about the online messages, either. Dammit, I think she's getting back together with her ex. Actually, come to think of it, when I spoke to Mum the other day, she was asking what Laura's surname was. Bit odd, surely?

On which note, I have been involved with a little internet jiggery-pokery. Let's just say that Acklington Stanley have acquired a new fan who is not all they appear...

On Monday at 14:48 Lucy replied:

Acklington Stanley. Who are they?

On Monday at 14:49 Martin replied:

Exactly.

On Monday at 14:56 Lucy replied:

Glad to hear you are channelling your energies to good effect.
I have an inkling why Mum might be interested in Laura's
surname, but I'll let you work it out for yourself.
Things going well with Sam.

On Monday at 14:57 Martin replied:

Only 'well'?

On Monday at 15:02 Lucy replied:

Yeah, you know, everything's perfect, and everyone thinks
he's lovely, but there's something missing. It's probably me being
overcritical and unable to accept happiness. I can't quite put my
finger on what's odd there. He's charming, he's funny, he's fairly
gorgeous.

On Monday at 15:04 Martin replied:

Has he only got one leg?

On Monday at 15:06 Lucy replied:

No, it's not that. What's Laura's surname?

On Monday at 15:08 Martin replied:

Don't laugh.

On Monday at 15:10 Lucy replied:

No, 'cos you were so understanding when I went out with Charlie Kerton.

On Monday at 15:12 Martin replied:

Charlie Curtain? Are you certain? Didja go steady or were ya just flirtin'? Got to stop - my sides are hurtin'.
Her surname is Mutton.

On Monday at 15:13 Lucy replied:

Oh dear, snorted tea onto my keyboard.
Well, she should be keen to get married.

On Monday at 15:15 Martin replied:

Actually, and bizarrely, she mentioned early on that she wants to keep her name. I should make it clear that we were speaking generally. So, in the unlikely event of our nuptials, she would be Mutton-Sargent.

On Monday at 15:17 Lucy replied:

Or Sargent-Mutton. Who sounds like someone who'd turn up in one of those hideous *Punch* cartoons about the Napoleonic Wars or the Crimea that you used to have to analyse in A-Level History.

On Monday at 15:19 Martin replied:

Man, were they ever funny! Dr Greaves used to crease up at those. Ho ho ho, look at Madame Thames dancing with King Cholera. Tee Hee, look at the Russian Bear being barked at by the British Bulldog. What was Turkey? Can't remember.

On which note, there is a deeply unfunny email entitled 'George's Bush' which I won't bother sending you.

On Monday at 15:21 Lucy replied:

Umm, surely Turkey was a Turkey?

Have seen 'George's Bush'. Mum sent it to me, of all people. She's getting quite web-happy these days.

On Monday at 15:22 Martin replied:

Or perhaps an Ottoman. Oh well, that's milked that one pretty dry.

On Monday at 15:23 Lucy replied:

I'm still laughing at Laura's surname.

Oh, oh, oh, by the way, Miriam is single. Frank dumped her! Right at the start of the holidays, too. You better move fast, though, she's having dinner with sinister Rupert tonight.

But perhaps you don't want fresh meat if you're lusting after mutton? Gotta go - meeting Sam. But what is it that's missing? It's going to really annoy me now.

Can't wait till you figure out why Mum needed to know Laura's surname. It's freaky ...

On Monday at 15:26 Martin replied:

What? What? What? Is there a family secret I don't know about? Do you know why the milkman whistles so gaily round our way?

Re: Re: Re: Review

On Monday at 15:34 Barney wrote:

Flippers, you bastard?

On Monday at 15:35 Martin replied:

Whatcha gonna do? Give me a slap?
IT WASN'T ME

The Mutton Mystery

On Monday at 15:45 Elizabeth Sargent wrote:

Hi, Martin,
So which Laura Mutton is she? The radical cheerleader, the one who breeds Wiemeranas, the one who does watercolours of Stevie Nicks, or the one at goocoveredgirls.com? Don't think I should investigate too closely into the last one.
Lots of love,

Mum

On Monday at 15:46 Martin replied:

MUM! Are you googling people I fancy?

On Monday at 15:56 Elizabeth Sargent replied:

Well, I like to know what's going on. You should try it with Lucy's new boy. I wonder if he's the Sam Bonar who was arrested in Mexico for practising medicine without a licence? Or the Fire Chief of Paradise City, New Jersey? Probably not. He did go on the uni ski trip two years ago - there's a picture. But he has a ski mask on. Still, it's amazing what you can uncover.

On Monday at 15:57 Martin replied:

Hold up. Sam's surname is Bonar? Strangely Lucy neglected to mention that. Very interesting...

I'll check with Laura about her 'hobbies'.

On Monday at 16:00 Elizabeth Sargent replied:

Don't you dare. By the way, I know it's Mummish and you'll roll your eyes, but I've sent you a brochure for an Alpha course. They're very popular nowadays, you know. You can meet all sorts of people you wouldn't expect at that kind of thing. So maybe give it a try.

And by the way I looked at yourtheatre.com when I was online. I don't think some of those are in very good taste, Martin. I do worry about where some of this stuff comes from ...

On Monday at 16:03 Martin replied:

So you google my exes, too? It wasn't bloody me! God, what do people take me for?

As regards Alpha, it might surprise you to know that I've been hearing good things about it myself. I have heard you meet all sorts there. May check it out. Thanks for thinking of me. This doesn't mean I've forgiven you for that Easter camp. Every bloody day singing 'Jesus, Prince of Thieves' and wandering around in the woods.

On Monday at 16:08 Elizabeth Sargent wrote:

I don't know where you get this guilt-tripping streak from. You'll never let me forget that, will you? I thought it would be fun. And as you well know, it's 'Jesus, Prince of Peace'.

On Monday at 16:09 Martin replied:

Not the way we sang it. And whoever catered that hellpit will need to turn the other cheek a fair few times if I ever meet them. There were three hundred hungry teens who would have killed for five loaves and three fishes...

Rainbow Club, my arse.

On Monday at 16:11 Elizabeth Sargent replied:

I think you made your point at the time. I do remember the embarrassment of having to pick up the child who instituted a chant of 'We want Barabbas!' during the closing festivities. One of the counsellors suggested we consider having you exorcised. At the time, we thought it was a silly idea ...

On Monday at 16:13 Martin wrote:

Hi Laura
This may sound like a bit of an odd question, but my mum was wondering if that's you on goocoveredgirls.com? It's kind of hard to tell with all that stuff on your face. Only way to check I suppose is to discover whether you have a flaming skull tattooed on your hip.

On Monday at 16:14 Laura replied:

You're far from the first to ask me that. No, it's not me. Bit odd of your mum to ask, but not as unsettling as when my gran wanted to know. Ewww. I'm not that freaky Stevie Nicks fan, either. I expect another warning from the internet-misuse monitors is winging its way to you as we speak, sicko.

Sam

On Monday at 20:19 Lucy wrote:

I figured out what it is about Sam!

On Tuesday at 9:01 Martin replied:

Is it his surname?

On Tuesday at 9:03 Lucy replied:

I take it you spoke to Mum. No, it's not that. I realised as we were sitting there having dinner, he's really boring. He looks nice, and he talks about quite interesting things, and his voice isn't too bad, but everything he says is ... Readybrek. And then you find yourself being boring, too, because you haven't been paying attention. And then the candles start going in and out of focus. I have forkmarks in my thigh from stabbing myself to stay awake.
Bollocks.

On Tuesday at 9:04 Martin replied:

Surely it's good that you figured it out. Now you can break up and move on.

On Tuesday at 9:05 Lucy replied:

Well, what am I going to tell him?

On Tuesday at 9:06 Martin replied:

Why not say: 'You sap my will to live with your mysterious ability to churn dross out of conversational gold, but don't worry there are probably lots of girls who will like it.'

On Tuesday at 9:07 Lucy replied:

No, the rule is you only tell someone things like that if they can change it. Like if they have a hairy back.

On Tuesday at 9:08 Martin replied:

Or a crap surname.

On Tuesday at 9:10 Lucy replied:

Indeed. I tried to tell him this morning.

On Tuesday at 9:12 Martin replied:

This morning?!?

On Tuesday at 9:14 Lucy replied:

I told you, he's only boring when he talks … Gotta go, he's bringing breakfast in.

Oh, by the way, *is* that Laura on goocoveredgirls.com? Gross … Nice tattoo, though.

Re: Sam

On Tuesday at 14:12 Lucy wrote:

Oops! Sam saw the forkprints on my leg.

On Tuesday at 14:15 Martin replied:

Wow, I thought that was a figure of speech.
So you explained and now you're free/alone (delete according to taste)?

On Tuesday at 14:16 Lucy replied:

Not exactly. He asked me if I was self-harming. He did a course on it and everything. Apparently he had a girlfriend before who did that.

On Tuesday at 14:17 Martin replied:

Did you suggest that he might have driven her to it with his ... zzzz. Sorry, drifted off.

On Tuesday at 14:19 Lucy replied:

The same wicked thought crossed my mind, too. But he was really noble and sweet about it. I made up an excuse, but I don't think he bought it. He put some leaflets in my pigeon-hole earlier.

On Tuesday at 14:21 Martin replied:

I take it that's not an unusually unpleasant double entendre.
What was your excuse?

On Tuesday at 14:23 Lucy replied:

Er, I said a cat did it.

On Tuesday at 14:25 Martin replied:

Presumably a cat hopping up and down your thigh on one
foot?
That's so absurd. So now he's obviously convinced that you
actually are self-harming?

On Tuesday at 14:26 Lucy replied:

Yeah. He was asking all about our family and my childhood.
He was being so sweet.

On Tuesday at 14:28 Martin replied:

Oh God. What did you tell him?

On Tuesday at 14:34 Lucy replied:

I may have mentioned the French Service Station Incident.
And about the Hide and Seek prank. He looked very serious. I
think he was a bit puzzled by the 'Bombardiez' gag.
Anyway, I really upset him by telling him I wasn't going to
ask for help. But now I can't break up with him, you see.

On Tuesday at 14:38 Martin replied:

Don't see at all. Sounds like the perfect excuse. He must be desperate to get away from you. No offence.

On Tuesday at 14:45 Lucy replied:

Weirdly, exactly the opposite. Now we have something to talk about, and he's all excited and protective. And if I break up with him now he'll think it's because he discovered my dark secret and be all worried. He just slipped a card from the Union shop with a smiley lion on it under my door.

On Tuesday at 14:47 Martin replied:

Smiley lion? Dump him. Dump him now.

P.S. Christ, if my kids were going to have the surname Sargent-Bonar, I wouldn't be messing about.

Re: Ross

On Tuesday at 15:03 Mike wrote:

All right, mate,

Still bitter about not being best man? I've had a thought about that. How about if I ask Chris if we could give you an honorary title of some kind? Something like 'Understudy to the Best Man' or 'Assistant Best Man'? Maybe 'Second-Best Man'?

Actually, that's not the chief reason I'm emailing. In fact, I've made a bit of a strange discovery.

Mike

On Tuesday at 15:15 Martin replied:

If this is about goocoveredgirls.com, I know. My mum told me.

On Tuesday at 15:17 Mike replied:

Well, that's one way of explaining about the birds and the bees, I guess. Nothing like breaking it to you gently, is there?

No, seriously, this is properly odd.

On Tuesday at 15:18 Martin replied:

Your financial backstabbing and desperate corporate ladder climbing has left you spiritually empty and paranoid as to who your real friends are? Or if you have any? There are some spiritual vacuums not even paintballing and fantasising about my sister can fill? I have a book that might help - I believe the void you are feeling inside may well be Jesus-shaped, my friend. I hear good things about the Alpha course...

On Tuesday at 15:22 Mike replied:

No, no, not that. Although of course that's true. God, it's unfulfilling being a soulless suit. Why do I do it? Oh yes, money, respect, power, and, most of all, not to be a temp loser like you.

On Tuesday at 15:25 Martin replied:

Actually, I got taken on here permanently last November, so up yours, Gordon Gekko.

On Tuesday at 15:32 Mike replied:

Martin, Martin, Martin. Now *that* was the response of a sad and broken man. Join me, Martin, join me ... you'll like it as one of us ... we're a big happy family ...

On Tuesday at 15:35 Martin replied:

I'd rather die than join the Dark Side.

On Tuesday at 15:40 Mike replied:

Cute, but actually, the entrance procedure here is highly competitive, and you're not really cut from the kind of officer material we're looking for, if you know what I mean. But one of our tea-ladies is off sick.

Do you want to know what I found out or not?

On Tuesday at 15:45 Martin replied:

You're gay?
We all knew that, Mike.

On Tuesday at 15:48 Mike replied:

Martin,
My time is valuable, even if yours is not. I know where your flatmate goes at all hours, and he isn't sitting writing in some café in North Brent and hoping no one throws him out or nicks his laptop.

On Tuesday at 16:12 Martin replied:

I don't live in North Brent. It's easy to distinguish: North Brent is where they do the shooting. Kensal Green is in South Brent, where they dump the bodies.

On Tuesday at 16:15 Mike replied:

Whatever. The point is I met your boy today. I went for a big corporate lunch with people from another firm, and he was there.

On Tuesday at 16:17 Martin replied:

So:
Ross works in Spearmint Rhino?
Ross hands out breathmints in the toilets at a restaurant?

On Tuesday at 16:36 Mike replied:

Your flatmate works for Grimble, Mallet and Spoke. He ain't writing no sitcom.

On Tuesday at 16:38 Martin replied:

I don't follow. What is that?

On Tuesday at 16:45 Mike replied:

Pretty hot consultancy firm. Ross has a fully fledged secret identity - as a management consultant.

On Tuesday at 16:52 Martin replied:

Well, fuck me. I knew that samurai sword was a bad sign.

On Tuesday at 16:57 Mike replied:

By the way, I think you might have gone a bit far with those comments on yourtheatre.com. Some of them made me chuckle, though.

On Tuesday at 16:58 Martin replied:

OH FOR THE LAST TIME IT'S NOT ME.
Anyway, about time for me to be getting home. Only about five more hours for you, eh?

Nah, Tuesday night our Dark Master cashes up early, 'cos he likes to get back for the redecorating programmes on BBC2. I'm about to start helping him load the sacks full of souls into the little train in the basement.

Re: Re: Sam

Crap. Was making tea on the shitty little fucking kettle in my room and managed to scald my wrist. Another typical piece of Sargent-family crapware. Like those bloody calculators.

On Wednesday at 9:04 Martin replied:

Yeah. I could have been Carol Vorderman by now if I hadn't gone through school with a calculator Dad got as a freebie from a Dental Floss company. Cosines? Tangents? Forget it. You had to turn it upside down and press 'multiply' to get it to divide.

But was it really an accident?

On Wednesday at 9:19 Lucy replied:

Don't you start. I had Sam on at me half the night. Although he did reveal that 'Chubby Chris' went through a similar 'phase' at school. Quelle surprise. Sam confirmed that she also had an army surplus bag but couldn't think of anything to write on it. Perhaps 'Pies. Hands Off. For future regurgitation' would have been appropriate. I suggested that if I was Christine I'd be tempted to self-harm as well, but Sam didn't think that was anything to joke about. Did you know that the hardest thing about fighting teenage self-harm is changing attitudes and getting people to take it seriously? Oh my God I'm dating the *Guardian*.

Did you know we use humour as a defence mechanism in our family?

On Wednesday at 9:24 Martin replied:

He's right. Use it as a defence mechanism against him.

P.S. Jokes about Teen Depression are Nut jokes.

On Wednesday at 9:28 Lucy replied:

I'm afraid I accidentally used his smiley lion as an ashtray, too.

On Wednesday at 9:34 Martin replied:

No such thing as an accident. You did it because you are angry and hostile towards yourself and are striking out at him.

On Wednesday at 9:38 Lucy replied:

Uncanny. How did you know? Presumably I am projecting my own inner blankness onto him as well, but I didn't say anything about that. Oh, I didn't mention it before because I knew what your response would be, but he has a beard.

On Wednesday at 9:43 Martin replied:

He's a Jesus-shaped arsehole!

On Wednesday at 9:44 Lucy replied:

He thinks you may have anger issues that you refuse to confront.

On Wednesday at 10:12 Martin replied:

Brilliant diagnosis, Dr Bonar. Come here and say that to my face and I'll show you anger issues with a fucking mallet.

On Wednesday at 10:14 Lucy replied:

Well, he may have a point ...

On Wednesday at 10:20 Martin replied:

What is he? A first-year psychology student?

On Wednesday at 10:21 Lucy replied:

Third-year geographer.

On Wednesday at 10:22 Martin replied:

Jesus, if that's not a bloody great warning I don't know what it. But if he's analysing our family, who's colouring in the map and counting the pebbles?
There's no other option. Do the beard gag on him.

On Wednesday at 10:26 Lucy replied:

I'm saving it for when I really need it. You don't do the beard gag unless you mean it. There's no going back from the beard gag.

Pretty in Pink

On Wednesday at 10:35 Martin wrote:

Hey Ella
Any truth in the rumour that Emily's asked you to be a bridesmaid? This I can't wait to see...

On Wednesday at 10:40 Ella replied:

Don't even start to go there, Sargent. I won't begin to number the ways in which this goes against the grain with me. I'm starting to suspect the whole wedding thing is an elaborate ploy to see me dolled up in pink.

On Wednesday at 10:42 Martin replied:

It does baffle the imagination. I more pictured you appearing at their first christening with a cackle and a puff of smoke. No offence.

On Wednesday at 10:45 Ella replied:

Sure. After all, why would I be offended at being compared to a bitter old witch? To make matters worse, the other bridesmaids are Emily's teenage cousins. I don't know whether we're having a hen-night or a sleepover. On the positive side, though, this is *exactly* how I planned on bumping into Barney again.

On Wednesday at 10:47 Martin replied:

Really? How so?

On Wednesday at 10:51 Ella replied:

Firstly, I don't want to see Barney, full stop. Secondly, if I do have to see him, I seldom look my best done up like Little Bo Peep, taking part in a patriarchal ceremony about which I am at best ambivalent, and surrounded by a bunch of fresh-faced nubiles.

And if you see Mike, tell him if he thinks he can try it on with me because he's best man, he's messing with the wrong fucking bridesmaid.

Acklington Stanley

On Wednesday at 11:05 Laura wrote:

Hello, all,

Writing to let you know that the Wednesday after next my boyfriend's new band, Acklington Stanley, will be playing in Camden (flyer attached). The new songs are really good. Some of them are about me! I think any of you who remember Fork would be advised to remain open-minded (open-eared?). Anyway, the flyer is pretty self-explanatory. The beer is cheap, and the glasses plastic. Indie disco after for those who don't care it's midweek and the floor is sticky.

Lots of love,

Laura

UPSTAIRS AT THE CAMDEN TAVERN
'KEEPING MUSIC LIVE SINCE 1985'

19 OLD GLUE FACTORY LANE.
CAMDEN TOWN TUBE

WEDNESDAY JULY 6

acklington stanley

FEAT. FORMER JAZZBUCKET DRUMMER
JEZ MOORE

SUPPORT FROM

The Lost Cause

Bar from 8. Support Act at 8:30.
£6/£4.50 Students
Disco until 12 (60s/70s/80s/Alternative)
The Camden Tavern operates a zero-tolerance
policy on drugs
R.O.A.R.

On Wednesday at 11:06 Martin wrote:

Hi Laura

I don't have anyone to point out the absurdities of this flyer to except you. I see there is support from The Lost Cause. Please God tell me they are a slightly obscurely-named tribute band. Lovely-looking girls, shame about Jim.

Could you not suggest to your boyfriend that the name Acklington Stanley is perhaps an in-joke too far? I mean, the Rolling Stones took their name from a Muddy Waters tune; Led Zeppelin was originally a joke of Keith Moon's; Steely Dan is the name of a dildo. But a reference to an 80s Milk Marketing Board promotion? If I had to pick one thing and put it in a time capsule to explain the 'spirit' of indie, that name would be it. They must be kicking themselves about John Peel...

Hold on. Gwyn is your boyfriend again?

Martin

On Wednesday at 11:12 Laura replied:

Yes, it all sort of happened over the weekend. I had been meaning to tell you. Hope you're not upset.

On Wednesday at 11:13 Martin replied:

Upset? No, why would I be? See you around, and probably at the gig.

Re: Re: Fork Is Genius!

On Wednesday at 18:01 Johannes Jester wrote:

Dear darling Gwyn

I am hearing you have a new band. I am excited about the Acklington Stanley and hope they play at my home town real soon. It is such a good name - strong, mysterious, evocative. Exactly like your music. One day when my mother dies I would love to visit the hamlet of Camden. Perhaps you could show me around.

But I worry does this mean no more Forkmusic? Please don't say it's true!!!???!!!

Love

Johannes

On Wednesday at 19:35 Gwyn replied:

Hey Johanna,

You heard right. From the ashes of Fork has risen... Acklington Stanley. Well, to be fair, we have all of us been in bands before. Our bass player Johnno was in the Mucky Faces; our drummer Jez was in Herbalessence (known in certain territories as JazzBucket for legal reasons); Mark, our lead guitar, was in Overpass and The Kids. So you can imagine there's a lot of excitement about us all playing together! The *Camden Flyer* has already labelled us a 'supergroup', but that's not really the angle we want to play up. Hopefully people will leave their preconceptions at the door, and judge us on our music. People are ready for something new after all the artificial Crap Idol stuff of the last few years. And Acklington Stanley is it!

I would love to show you around Camden, I hope your mother dies soon. Only kidding!!!

Lotsa love

Gwyn

P.S. It's amazing that we can keep in touch with all our fans through the internet these days. I'm thinking of you reading this all the way in Germany. What are you wearing? Grrrowl.

On Wednesday at 19:48 Johannes Jester replied:

Dear Gwyn

I am wearing solely my pink housecleaning coat and a pointy helmet. What are you wearing?

But does this mean there is no more Fork? Everyone in Dusseldorf will be weeping and wailing. There may be a 'Sad Riot' (to quote one of your song-titles!). I don't believe it.

I am a little upset with you.

Love

Johannes

On Wednesday at 20:15 Gwyn replied:

Dear Johanna,

Sounds pretty sexy! Are you serious? I'm wearing skinny drainpipes and a pair of aviators. I was wearing a vest, but I took it off...

What are you doing now?

Gwyn

On Wednesday at 20:23 Johannes wrote:

Dear Gwyn

I am tearing down all my posters of Fork and screwing them

up in balls and jumping on them. I am SO ANGRY!!! I hope
Acklington Stanley are the big flop and you have to reform
Fork right away. My mother is angry too and she says it is
DISGUSTING how you treat your fans. You are sell-out and
traitor. Even thought of you with no vest is not pleasant to me at
this time.

Love

Johannes

P.S. Put your vest back on. Johannes is a bloke's name,
dickhead.

Part Six

The Worst Play in the World

Milk • Bread • Mr Socky
Issues • The Intervention
The Book • The Old Barney Magic
Names

Milk

On Monday at 13:57 Martin wrote:

Long time no see, flatmate
Listen, I used the last of the milk this morning. I was
wondering if you could pick some up on the way home? Are
you going to be around tonight? I can't remember the last
time we SPOKE. Also I don't want to GRIMBLE, but could
we CONSULT about dividing up the bills sometime? Hope the
'sitcom' is going well.
Martin

On Monday at 14:35 Ross replied:

Oh God. Who told you? Don't suppose you would believe that
I have an evil twin? I swear I really am planning on writing this
sitcom, though.

The Big Questions

On Monday at 15:12 Ella wrote:

Hi, Martin,
I think we need to stage an intervention between Sally and David.
Ella

On Monday at 15:15 Martin replied:

Intervention? I don't follow.

On Monday at 15:18 Ella replied:

I had dinner with them last night. I ran out of excuses not to. He's truly appalling. We need to break them up. I know that sounds cruel but it's for the best.
Ella

On Monday at 15:25 Martin replied:

Ella, I've been saying this for weeks. But why is it all of a sudden for the best? Is Sally unhappy?

On Monday at 15:34 Ella replied:

Sally is completely radiant and bubbly as ever. Boy, you guys really weren't suited, were you? I don't think I've ever seen her this happy. It's not for the benefit of David or Sally, it's for my sake. Another dinner like that and I will lose the will to live.

So! You! Make! Bread! Enough already. 'I love to get my hands doughy, it really puts me in touch with what matters in life'. What? Yeast? Stop the search for the meaning of life everyone, it's in David's kitchen.

And that fucking bread tastes horrible. I nearly chipped a tooth.

No, it's abhorrent how happy they are together. It's all little pecks on the cheek when they think you're not looking. Sally ended up perching on his lap at the end of the evening. They were talking about the future. Like, kids. Like, moving out of London.

On Monday at 15:42 Martin replied:

NO! Well, it does happen, Ella. You know we're all getting to the age when we start thinking about growing up.

It's astonishing I ever open an email from you. Every one is like a hammer blow to the back of the head. I'm glad Sally is happy. I may not be the best person to intervene. We're not really in communication.

On Monday at 15:48 Ella replied:

I'm just trying to stir you into action. By the way, I didn't know you rang Sally up drunk...

On Monday at 16:05 Martin replied:

Yeah, not one of my prouder moments. From a period in my life which isn't exactly throwing up an abundance of them. I mounted a fairly detailed and sustained critique of David then, if I recall correctly, and it didn't get me anywhere.

On Monday at 16:15 Ella replied:

You really are a class act, aren't you? I quote: 'I must still like you, I sat through your shitty play.' 'I'm writing a novel about our relationship.' 'What's it called?' 'I'm thinking of entitling it *I Hate David, and He Smells of Floorboards.*' Oh I almost forgot the piece de la resistance: 'I have to go now. I'm still really angry and I have loads to say, but the room is spinning and I think I'm going to be sick.' Nice work, Cyrano.

On Tuesday at 9:04 Martin replied:

Yes, well there's more than one way to say I love you. I take it she wasn't won back?

On Tuesday at 10:21 Ella replied:

I think not. Baffled, yes. Upset, yes. But not won back. Apparently at one point you put a sock on your hand?

On Tuesday at 10:25 Martin replied:

Yes, I thought I might have done that.

On Tuesday at 10:30 Ella replied:

Pretty pointless over the phone I should have thought.

On Tuesday at 10:34 Martin replied:

It used to be one of our games when we were upset with each other. You know: 'Mrs Socky says she felt you were a bit selfish about Sally's mother coming to stay', 'Mr Socky says have a good time when you're out with the girls and he has to stay home with boring Martin.'

On Tuesday at 10:37 Ella replied:

That is truly sick.

PS Why floorboards, if you don't mind me asking?

On Tuesday at 10:40 Martin replied:

I didn't say I was proud of it. Anyway, Mr Socky let Sally know how he felt about how she treated Martin.

P.S. Because I don't ever get close enough to floorboards to smell them, and I don't ever want to get close enough to David to smell him. It seemed a very obvious connection at the time.
P.P.S. Mr Socky tells me that he is willing to help with the 'intervention'. But what in particular has triggered all this off? I mean, we have agreed in the past that we both think he's a bit of a twat. What's new?

On Tuesday at 10:43 Ella replied:

It struck me when David was talking about his new play. He actually called Sally his 'muse' at one point. And I had a vision that if we don't stop him now it may be too late. And you won't be able to read the paper or listen to the radio or watch the TV without him opining and pontificating. It was around the point when he said 'Today the New Place, tomorrow the world.' And I realised he might very well do it. But to be honest, now I know about Mr and Mrs Socky I'm beginning to think Sally might be better off staying put with him.

PS Are you really writing a novel called *I Hate David, and He Smells of Floorboards*? I'd love to read it.

On Tuesday at 10:48 Martin replied:

No, I'm not. I've given up writing novels about people I know. And I haven't written anything at all since Sally left.

P.S. She's not my muse. She just took all the pens.
P.P.S. So what is David's new play about?

On Tuesday at 11:01 Ella replied:

This is it. I realised as he was talking about the play that somewhere in our society the idiot filter is broken, and there's nothing to stop David unless we do it ourselves.

The new play, as you will recall from the *Chalk Farm Gazette*, is the one where he deals with issues of race, class, gender, sexuality and religion. And love. And war. And history. In 90 minutes.

On Tuesday at 11:06 Martin replied:

Is Sally in it?

On Tuesday at 11:11 Ella replied:

Oh yeah. So he was telling us about it, and believe me my fingers wince and my nails leak blood as I force myself to type this:

Sally is a backpacker in India who falls in love.

On Tuesday at 11:12 Martin replied:

OK. It sounds bad. In fact, it sounds terrible. I trust she falls in love against a background of conflict in a beautiful place...

On Tuesday at 11:15 Ella replied:

She does indeed. Guess what she has in her backpack?

On Tuesday at 11:17 Martin replied:

Imodium? *Rough Guide*? Beedis? Toilet roll?

On Tuesday at 11:21 Ella replied:

Letters her grandmother wrote ...

On Tuesday at 11:25 Martin replied:

... to the maharajah she had a fling with two generations before?
Damn. Now I need to think of a new idea for my next novel. Farewell, Man Booker Prize...

On Tuesday at 11:27 Ella replied:

Now, I know there are a million sound political reasons to object to this kind of pandering exoticising patronising crap. But more to the point: We Are Going to Have to Sit Through It.

On Tuesday at 11:29 Martin replied:

Nah, only you. I've got a sharp pencil and I'm about to pierce my eardrums and put my eyes out.

On Tuesday at 11:34 Ella replied:

Wait until you've read this, and then sharpen one for me too.

Me: So you must know a lot about the political and historical background?

David: I think coming to these things fresh is often an advantage.

Sally: I think we're going over together for a few weeks to soak up the atmosphere.

David: I always think what's most important is not that theatre provides answers, but that theatre asks the questions.

Me: I need a pee.

On Tuesday at 11:37 Martin replied:

Pencil poised. The questions being?

On Tuesday at 11:43 Ella replied:

I dunno. Is love good? Is war bad? Is racism bad? Do the deeds of history echo in the present?

On Tuesday at 11:52 Martin replied:

Oh good, I think I know the answers already. Does that mean I don't have to go/destroy eyesight and hearing? Off to do some research of my own.

On Tuesday at 12:00 Ella replied:

In what way?

On Tuesday at 12:02 Martin replied:

I've got floorboards to sniff.
By the way, I don't think an intervention will be necessary.
The magic of being with David travelling around India for a few
weeks should do the trick.

Re: Ella

On Tuesday at 13:09 Barney wrote:

Mate,
Listen, I need a straight answer. Ella isn't returning my calls or emails. Have you heard from her? I dunno what went wrong. Do you think there's any chance of getting back with her?
Depressed,
Best,
Barney

PS don't suppose Chris got back to you about me DJing at the wedding?

On Tuesday at 14:10 Martin wrote:

Hi Ella
Barney wants to know if you would ever consider getting back with him? What should I say? Any chance?
Martin

On Tuesday at 14:14 Ella replied:

Yeah. I ignore his calls and emails 'cos I'm desperate to rekindle that magic. What do you think?
I have explained this to him. Maybe I should have used shorter words. We. Were. A. Fling. When. I. Think. About. It. I. Feel. No. Nostalgia. Only. Vague. Nausea.
I suppose there is a minuscule chance things could get

rekindled. But there's a similar probability of Atlantis rising off the Isle of Wight, David Icke turning out to be the Messiah, and the new Oasis album genuinely being 'a massive return to form'.

Send him my regards.

Ella

\-

On Tuesday at 14:17 Martin wrote:

Hi Barney

There is a slim possibility of your getting back together. VERY slim.

Martin

\-

On Tuesday at 14:18 Barney replied:

What should I do?

\-

On Tuesday at 14:20 Martin replied:

I'll ask. But if I were you, I'd give up on it. Seriously.

\-

On Tuesday at 14:23 Martin wrote:

Hi Ella

What should Barney do?

Martin

\-

On Tuesday at 14:34 Ella replied:

He should practise DJing. A lot.

\-

On Tuesday at 14:35 Martin replied:

I'll suggest that. Let me rephrase: under what circumstances would you give Barney another try? What could he do to make that a more realistic possibility? I think he's saying he can change...

On Tuesday at 14:40 Ella replied:

Well, I have thought about this quite seriously over the past five minutes. It's sweet of him to offer to change. In a burst of over-generous reciprocity I've come up with a short list of things that he might think about changing.

Barney might possibly become attractive to me again if all the following criteria were fulfilled:

1 He had different hair
2 He had a different face
3 He had a different body
4 His voice was different
5 He behaved differently
6 He had a different name
7 He was a different person
8 He won the lottery
9 I was drunk

But probably not even then.

On Tuesday at 14:45 Martin wrote:

Barney, I think it may be time to let this one go.

On Tuesday at 14:52 Barney replied:

It's because she thinks I'm thick, isn't it?

On Tuesday at 14:54 Martin replied:

Actually, that wasn't something she mentioned.

On Tuesday at 14:57 Ella wrote:

Oh yeah, and he would have to be a lot less thick.

On Tuesday at 15:03 Barney wrote:

Cheers for your advice, mate.
I guess there's not much hope. Let me know if she says anything about me. Well, let her know that there's always someone who'll be lapping up the old Barney magic.
Startin' again, Martin my friend
Barney

On Tuesday at 15:04 Martin wrote:

Bafflingly, that does indeed seem to be the case. Oh, there was one thing she did mention.

On Tuesday at 15:05 Barney wrote:

What was that?

On Tuesday at 15:07 Martin wrote:

Stop doing those godawful rhymed sign-offs. Honestly. Stop it. Now.

Barney

On Tuesday at 15:13 Martin wrote:

Hi Chris

Hope the wedding preparations are all in hand and Emily's bulge isn't showing yet. Mate, have you given any thought to letting Barney DJ for a bit? I know he ain't the best DJ in the world, and may well be among the worst, but he'd really appreciate it. He's not in a very good way at the mo about Ella and I think it would help take his mind off things.

Love to Emily

Martin

On Wednesday at 12:14 Chris wrote:

Hi Martin,

Actually, I have been thinking about it. The other day Emily and I were sitting around and she turned to me and said, 'Do you know what would make our special day that extra-bit special, Chris?'

And I said, 'What, my precious?'

And she said, 'I want us to have the worst DJ we can possibly find.' And I thought of Barney, because the last time I saw him play he managed to slice his thumb open on a 12" record. And he was no worse with one hand than he is with two.

But then Emily and I realised we already know lots of people who DJ. All of whom want to play at the wedding. Some of them are quite good. All of them are better than Barney. My granny is a better DJ than Barney. And she won't be DJing at the wedding, either. Because she's dead.

218

But we had to find some way of choosing a DJ. So Emily said, 'You know, my little fruitplum, what would make our extra-special day even more extra-special than a crap DJ?'

And I said, 'No, my little rosebud, what could that be?'

And Emily said, 'A DJ who's not only crap, but who once described himself to you as an "art-noise-terrorist, messing with people's heads".'

And I said, 'Why, I know the very man you mean.'

But still there was something not quite right. I could see Emily was thinking about something. So I said, 'What is it, shnoozles? What furrows your little brow?'

And Emily said, 'You'll think I'm being silly. But I always wanted a DJ at my wedding who was really depressed and upset with women.'

And I said, 'That's amazing, pookie. It's what I've always dreamed of, too. But where can we possibly find one at such short notice?'

So you see, your email caught me at the perfect time.

Chris

On Wednesday at 12:16 Martin replied:

I take it you're being sarcastic. Couldn't you let him play in the corner, and unplug the speakers? I don't think he'd notice.

On Wednesday at 12:30 Chris replied:

Let me put it plainly. The only possible way we are going to let Barney spin a platter at our wedding is if he is dressed as a waiter and he is revolving a large round silver tray to offer someone a vol-au-vent.

On Wednesday at 12:34 Martin replied:

I'll tell him you already have someone booked.

On Wednesday at 12:40 Chris replied:

You do that.

Also, I think the best man is going to be in touch to ask about suggestions for the stag night. DO NOT suggest anything involving Finnish clowns, avant-garde origami or open-mike poetry. Or, indeed, Barney DJing.

Hi

Hi Sally

Wondering how you are doing. I was thinking last night and I realise I may have taken this break-up thing badly. Really badly. I hope you know how much I treasure our time together, and how much you still mean to me. I think you are a truly amazing person, and I am so proud to see your talent receiving the recognition it deserves. (I don't mean the nasty comments on the website, I mean the good notices). Ella was telling me about the new play and it sounds intriguing. Best of luck with it. I guess when there's a breakup it's pointless to try and apportion the blame. We were something that wasn't meant to be, and the best we can do is to look on it as a learning experience, and both try to grow as people. Like flowers, if you will, out of the manure of our messy past. I have discussed it with Mr Socky and he agrees. I look forward to seeing you at the wedding.

Sincerely

Martin

On Thursday at 10:20 Sally replied:

Dear Martin,

I was moved by your sweet email. That's how I feel, too. It is silly, after all we've been through, to be on bad terms. I do have a lot of happy memories from our time together, and I'm sorry about how it ended. See you at the wedding.

Mrs Socky sends her regards also!

Affectionately,

Sally

On Thursday at 10:28 Martin replied:

Dear Sally
That's great. Now that we're friends again, can I make a
friendly suggestion?
Affectionately
Martin

On Thursday at 10:45 Sally replied:

Of course. But it isn't that creepy thing again about wearing
each other's clothes, is it? That wasn't appropriate then and it
certainly isn't appropriate now.
Sally

On Thursday at 11:22 Martin replied:

Of course not. Jesus, I was joking. You never let it lie, do you?
No this is something different.

On Thursday at 11:27 Sally replied:

Joking is when you suggest something once, Martin …
On a similar note, I've already told you quite definitely that
I'm never going to change my name to 'Busty de Winter'. Even if
it would 'get the punters in'.
So what is this great suggestion?

On Thursday at 11:45 Martin replied:

I say this not as an ex, not because I am jealous, and not
because I hold any hope or even desire to get back together. As a
friend:

222

Dump the creep. Dump him, dump him, dump him.

Take him to the dump like a sofa that doesn't meet fire safety regulations.

Make like Stig, and Dump him.

Next time you have a dump, flush David.

Lots of Love

Martin

P.S. Mr Socky agrees. In fact, he feels even more strongly on the issue than I do.

On Thursday at 12:45 Sally replied:

Twat.

On Thursday at 13:14 Martin wrote:

At least say you'll consider the idea? Glad we're friends again.

Lots of Love

Martin

Congratulations

On Friday at 14:02 Ella wrote:

Good going, Martin. That was exactly what I had in mind.
Ella

On Friday at 14:10 Martin replied:

What? It was worth a try, surely?

On Friday at 14:45 Ella replied:

Twat.
By the way, glad you and Sally have decided to be mates. She
says never to contact her again.

On Friday at 15:02 Martin replied:

She is quite definite about that?

On Friday at 15:15 Ella replied:

I'd certainly give it a few weeks. But she's pretty nice, so
eventually she will no doubt forgive you.
    Christ, if you pulled this kind of crap with me you would be
in so much pain. And I don't mean 'Oh, my heart aches'. I mean
'Please, I can't bear to wait for the ambulance. Shoot me. Death
would be a release.'

Christ, you never think about what you're doing, do you?

On Friday at 15:17 Martin replied:

Oh Ella
I would prefer to be shot before I got involved with you, if it's all the same. Barney sends his love. Again.
Yes, I never think, do I?
I can't see Sally.
I can't talk to Sally.
I can't email Sally.
I'm not welcome at Sally's plays...
Man, I'm good.

On Friday at 15:19 Ella replied:

Dammit. You're a genius. A sick, twisted, bitter kind of genius, but a genius nevertheless.

On Friday at 15:46 Ella wrote:

Hi, Sally
I don't like David, either. He really does smell of floorboards. Damp floorboards with bodies under them in a house with bad feng shui. I abhor him. I don't think I could stand to be in the same room with him. Even if it is a large room with lots of chairs in it. Sorry. See you in a few months.
Lots of love, Ella

On Friday at 16:22 Sally wrote:

Dear Martin and Ella,
You guys are so lame. I expect to see you both at opening

night, where you can both grovel and try to make it up to me. And David.

Jesus, I had to read Martin's book ...

On Friday at 16:30 Ella wrote:

Rumbled!

On Friday at 16:42 Martin replied:

Yeah, she copied me in. Bollocks. Don't suppose you still consider me a genius?

On Friday at 16:46 Ella replied:

No. What is this book whereof she speaks?

On Friday at 16:48 Martin replied:

Nothing. Drop it. Don't mention it to anyone else.

On Friday at 16:56 Ella replied:

Sure. If it's something you're sensitive about I'll leave it alone.

On Friday at 16:57 Ella wrote:

PS Martin wrote a book, Martin wrote a book.
PPS What's it about? Mr and Mrs Socky?

Reading

On Monday at 8:47 Chris wrote:

All right, Mate,
Emily and I were having a chat last night, and we were wondering: would you mind doing a reading at our wedding? Feel free to turn us down.

Chris

On Monday at 9:02 Martin replied:

Sure! Thanks for thinking of me. That would be great. Very flattered. What would you like me to read?
Martin

On Monday at 9:06 Chris wrote:

We were thinking of something from your book?

Re: Reading

On Monday at 9:07 Martin wrote:

Ella!

On Monday at 9:36 Ella replied:

Yes?

On Monday at 9:38 Martin replied:

I asked you not to say anything about my book.

On Monday at 9:39 Ella replied:

I know. I don't have a memory problem.

On Monday at 9:42 Martin replied:

You told Chris!

On Monday at 9:45 Ella replied:

I know. I said I *don't* have a memory problem. Although you do, apparently.

On Monday at 9:47 Martin replied:

But you said you wouldn't tell anyone.

On Monday at 9:50 Ella replied:

No I didn't. Are you sure your memory is OK?

On Monday at 9:55 Martin replied:

I checked. Ha! The magic of email has caught you out. You said 'Sure. If it's something you're sensitive about I'll leave it alone.' You broke your word.

On Monday at 9:59 Ella replied:

Damn, I broke my word. Now I will never be worthy to succeed in my quest for the Holy Grail.

Martin, you forgot emails don't always convey tone. I said 'Sure' sarcastically.

Hope this helps.

Ella

PS What's it about?

On Monday at 10:04 Martin replied:

It's none of your business what it's about.

On Monday at 10:06 Ella replied:

Is it a Mills & Boon?

On Monday at 10:09 Martin replied:

No.

On Monday at 10:13 Ella replied:

Is it a sex book?
i.e. 'Miss Lucy's Punishment', 'She Knew It Was Wrong', not a 'How To …' Obviously.

On Monday at 10:15 Martin wrote:

No. If you must know, it's a children's book. But it was a bit misconceived, so I abandoned it.

On Monday at 10:16 Ella wrote:

Is it a children's sex book?
Can I read it?

On Monday at 10:19 Martin wrote:

To answer your questions in reverse order: No, and No (eww, what is that?).
But I will tell you what it's about if you promise not to tell anyone else anything about it or ever mention it, allude to it, or indeed allude to the existence of children's literature of any kind in my presence ever again.

On Monday at 10:20 Ella replied:

Sure

On Monday at 10:25 Martin replied:

Well, if you're sitting comfortably, then I'll begin...

Dates

On Monday at 13:02 Barney wrote:

Mate,
You didn't tell me you wrote a book! Can I read it?
Best wishes,
Barney

On Monday at 13:10 Martin wrote:

I don't know. Can you? It's aimed at your reading age, but some of it you might have to get someone to help you with. How come you know?
Martin

P.S. If you're going to write 'Best wishes' I think I prefer the rhyming sign-offs. 'Best wishes' is creepy.

On Monday at 13:27 Barney wrote:

Sorry for the long time it took me to reply. I had to look up some of the words from your email in 'My First Dictionary'.
Ella wrote to me! She didn't say much, just told me there was no hope for us, and to ask you about your book. Is it being published?

On Monday at 13:29 Martin wrote:

No, it's not being published. The fact that its existence is a closely guarded embarrassing secret would make publishing it kind of counter-productive.

Why aren't you more upset about Ella? No offence. It's that when you're depressed you lose that bouncy puppy quality that really gets on my nerves.

Martin

On Monday at 13:45 Barney wrote:

Hooked up with someone last night. Someone really nice who I have a lot more in common with. I would have emailed earlier, but she only left a little while ago.

On Monday at 13:52 Martin wrote:

Someone you 'have a lot more in common with'? Barney, I shudder to think where you found this person...

On Monday at 14:00 Barney replied:

DJ'd an office party on Saturday night. She's a great dancer, really funny too. I think you'd like her.

On Monday at 14:01 Martin wrote:

You never cease to amaze me, Barney. You must emit some kind of pheromone. Next time I'm going out I want to rub myself against you for a long time. Oh, can she DJ?

On Monday at 14:05 Barney replied:

No. Why should she?

On Monday at 14:10 Martin wrote:

You sound perfectly suited. What's her name?

On Monday at 14:11 Barney replied:

Kate Staple. Oh, the weirdest coincidence...

On Monday at 14:15 Martin wrote:

Yeah, yeah, I know. Listen, Barney, I don't want to come on like your dad, but be very careful to use protection. Will explain later.

Ella will no doubt be heartbroken.

On Monday at 14:16 Martin wrote:

Ella, I quote: 'I will tell you what the book is about if you promise not to tell anyone else anything about it or ever mention it or allude to it ever again.'

But somehow Barney knows about it. Barney!

However I spoke to Chris last night, who had spoken to Barney, and he told me something that makes me feel a lot better about things.

Martin

On Monday at 14:35 Ella replied:

Martin, I'm not in the mood. Yes, I wrote that. But only knowing that to tell anyone else who cared about your book I would have to make a new friend, introduce them to you, and then tell them.

I can imagine what Barney told Chris and what Chris told you. I don't want to discuss it.

Ella

On Monday at 14:47 Martin replied:

Oh come now, Ella, there's no need to be embarrassed. I think it's sweet you and Barney talked potential kids' names.

On Monday at 15:03 Ella replied:

Martin, seriously, don't.

On Monday at 15:07 Martin replied:

This is a new side to you. And what cute names you suggested!

On Monday at 15:10 Ella replied:

Martin, please, stop.

I think you can tell from the names I suggested that the subtext, at least on my side, was 'Barney, I don't want to reproduce with you.' And that was before he suggested Bradley or Sophia.

On Monday at 15:13 Martin replied:

Oh, really? But I think Robusto, Beef and Bruton are great names for boys. In fact, I may adopt one of them myself in future. And who wouldn't want a daughter called Mercuria, Balthazette or Superia?

Can't wait to tell everyone that the fearsome Ella Tvertko is a BIG SOFTY.

Lots of Love

Robusto Sargent

On Monday at 15:16 Ella replied:

Robusto, I'm not kidding. What is the date today? Is it really the 4th?

On Monday at 15:17 Martin replied:

It is indeed the 4th.

On Monday at 15:18 Ella replied:

Are you sure?

On Monday at 15:20 Martin replied:

Pretty sure. It's written in a little box in the corner of my computer screen. Why?

On Monday at 15:21 Martin replied:

Actually, no need to answer that. Oh shit.

P.S. I'd go with Bruton or Mercuria, if it comes to that.
P.P.S. You'll look great coming down the aisle. Do they do
maternity bridesmaid's dresses? If you need a happy thought,
picture Barney's face.

A Reminder

On Monday at 15:34 Lucy wrote:

Martin, do you know what the date is?

On Monday at 15:44 Martin wrote:

Oh God, not you too. For goodness' sakes, it's written in the corner of your screen.

It's the 4th.

And please, call me Robusto.

On Monday at 15:47 Lucy replied:

Dear Robusto,

What happens every year on the 4th of July? And I don't mean Independence Day.

Love,

Lucy

On Monday at 15:50 Martin wrote:

Oh fuckaroo.

On Monday at 15:57 Martin wrote:

Hi Mum!

Bet you thought I'd forgotten! SURPRISE! I hope the parcel

got there safely. If not, I'm sure it will get there tomorrow. I tried ringing but the phone was engaged. That's what you get for being too popular! I'll try again later. Anyway, hope you're having a lovely day, and hope you didn't think I'd forgotten!
Lots of Love
Martin X X X

On Monday at 16:04 Martin wrote:

Hi Ella
It's definitely the 4th.
Robusto

On Monday at 16:08 Ella wrote:

I know. Fucking hell.

On Monday at 16:10 Martin wrote:

I think the brains tend to come from the mother's side of the family, if that makes you feel better. Don't suppose it's what you want to hear, but I forgot my mum's birthday. I feel crap. Think I covered for it, though.

On Monday at 18:11 Stephen Sargent wrote:

Hi, Martin,
Your mother's off the phone now. I think she'd appreciate a call. Flimsy email, by the way. You forgot, didn't you? You get your memory from your mum's side of the family, if that's any consolation to anyone.
Dad

Re: Acklington Stanley

On Tuesday at 10:12 Laura wrote:

This is to remind everyone that tomorrow is the debut gig by Acklington Stanley. No excuses!
Lots of love,

Laura

PS. This includes you, Martin. Would be great if you could come.

On Tuesday at 10:15 Martin replied:

Dear Laura
Would love to come, but I've stapled my balls to a table leg. Don't think I can make it.
Martin

On Tuesday at 10:23 Laura replied:

How awful!
Have you logged it in the accident book?

Laura

On Tuesday at 10:25 Martin replied:

It was no accident.

Don't be a grouch. Come! I'll dance with you. Bring lots of people, even better. I'll expect to see you there and dancing, even if you have a work-desk in tow ...

Laura

Part Seven
Firkin Hell

A Serious Interlude

Peace and Love

Barney Reveals Some Surprising News

Firkin Hell

On Thursday at 9:15 Emily wrote:

Hope everyone's OK. There were explosions at Edgware Road, King's Cross and Aldgate about half an hour ago. I can't get through to Chris on his mobile.

On Thursday at 9:17 Martin replied:

Jesus, I guess someone really didn't like Acklington Stanley.

On Thursday at 9:46 Chris wrote:

Martin - that's totally inappropriate, mate.
Just got into work due to massive disruption. There was an announcement about a gas leak or something and we all had to get off at Tottenham Court Road. There's a load of ambulances and police cars around the tube opposite where I work.

On Thursday at 9:49 Ella replied:

I'm alright. I'm still in bed, and planning to remain there.

On Thursday at 10:05 Emily wrote:

There's been another explosion. They said something about it being a bus, but I didn't catch where. There are definitely casualties.

On Thursday at 10:12 Martin wrote:

Apologies for earlier insensitivity. Anyone heard from Barney? Is everyone else's phone fucked?

On Thursday at 10:14 Martin wrote:

Sorry, got my email back from Emily's server with a warning about swearing. For FOCK's sake.
Anyone heard from Barney or Ross?
Everyone else's phone PLAYING UP?

On Thursday at 10:15 Ella wrote:

Why would Ross be in the centre?

On Thursday at 10:17 Martin replied:

Long story.

On Thursday at 10:18 Ross wrote:

I'm OK. Phone coming and going - must be everyone ringing around to check people are safe. Oh by the way, Martin, I picked up milk this morning. Not quite on the same operatic scale as everything else that's unfolding, but I knew it would mean a lot to you.

On Thursday at 10:34 Martin wrote:

Hi Sally
Hope you're OK. It sounds pretty serious. Hope David's OK
too.
Martin

On Thursday at 10:36 Sally replied:

Yeah, we're both safe. Glad you're all right.
Lots of love
    Sally

On Thursday at 10:38 Martin wrote:

Hi Mum
I'm OK - in work at the moment. Everyone here seems to be
fine. Phones keep cutting out, if you're trying to get through. It
sounds like there have been four explosions, three on the tube
and one on a bus. Chris can see stuff from his office and it's a hell
of a mess over there. Could you let Dad and Lucy know I'm safe?
Love
Martin

On Thursday at 10:40 Martin wrote:

Barney
When you get this can you reply a.s.a.p. Not sure what's up
with phones – someone says the phone lines have been diverted
to emergency use only. We're getting a bit worried about you.
Martin

On Thursday at 11:45 Chris wrote:

It looks like bloody Baghdad out the window here. They're bringing up bodies and there are people milling around covered in blood. Loads of smoke and mess. There's someone sitting in reception with their fucking nose hanging off. Definitely not a fucking gas leak.

On Thursday at 12:02 Chris wrote:

For Emily, and those others of you whose servers have kindly refused to deliver my message:

'It looks like BALLY Baghdad out the window here. They're bringing up bodies and there are people milling around covered in blood. Loads of smoke and mess. There's someone sitting in reception with their FLIPPING nose hanging off. Definitely not a FREAKING gas leak.'

Re: Firkin Hell

On Thursday at 12:21 Barney wrote:

Hi All,
I'm OK. Wasn't on usual line due to staying at Kate's house last night. Apparently the whole tube service has shut down, so I guess I'll be trying for the repeat tonight.
Barney

On Thursday at 12:22 Martin wrote:

Well, Barney seems to be taking things in his stride.
Anyone else feeling the tiniest bit tense?

On Thursday at 12:34 Emily replied:

I got through to Chris and he sounds like he's in shock. A girl from his office was on one of the trains. She had FRICKING glass in her hair. I think someone had to suggest to her that she could go home if she wanted.
Everyone here is sitting around wondering what to do and checking the news online.

On Thursday at 12:40 Martin replied:

Not quite sure how anyone's going to get home. Not over-keen to hop on a bus right now, even if there are any.

On Thursday at 13:56 Ella wrote:

If anyone is stuck in central London they are welcome to come over to mine. I'm out of bed now. Pictures on the news look fucking atrocious. Literally.

I think under the circumstances it's not too early to unscrew a bottle. If you guys fancy facing sodding Armageddon pissed, the more the merrier.

Ella

PS Barney, this doesn't mean I'm reconsidering shagging you again.

On Thursday at 14:04 Ross wrote:

Cheers, Ella. I think I just want to get back home. About to join the thousands who've had the same idea.

Martin, I have bad news. I went to the fridge at work and someone has used our milk. We seem to be getting through a lot of caffeinated drinks in the office today.

On Thursday at 14:10 Ella wrote:

Oh for goodness sake. To preserve the purity of Emily's eyes and ears I will rephrase my offer:

'If anyone is stuck in central London they are welcome to come over to mine. I'm out of bed now. Pictures on the news look REALLY RATHER atrocious. Literally.

I think under the circumstances it's not too early to unscrew a bottle. If you guys fancy facing SILLY OLD Armageddon pissed, the more the merrier.

Ella

PS. Barney this still doesn't mean I'm reconsidering COPULATING WITH you again.'

Oh, if anyone wants to hear some good news, I'm not pregnant.

Blitz Spirit

On Friday at 10:00 Sally wrote:

I take it we're all back at our desks?

On Friday at 10:02 Emily replied:

Chris got in all right, eventually. He was pretty determined. On home email, so you can swear again.

On Friday at 10:04 Martin replied:

Yeah, I came in. Otherwise I'd have had no excuse not to tidy the flat. Whatcha doing at home, Emily?

On Friday at 10:08 Emily replied:

I have flu. Seriously. Ask Chris.

On Friday at 10:14 Sally wrote:

Must be going around. The office is half empty. Anyone else about?

On Friday at 10:16 Ross wrote:

Yeah, I kind of had to come in. Martin and I have run out of milk at home. Could buy some, but I still have a quarter of a pint I paid for here, so...

On Friday at 10:18 Martin replied:

From anyone else I'd think that was unflappable British pluck. But I suspect you really are that tight, aren't you?

On Friday at 10:32 Sally replied:

Hmm, David seems to have got this flu that's going around. Chicken flu? I guess theatre needs him.

I had a weird conversation with my gran last night. She said it was like the Blitz. Except of course that during the Blitz the tube was where people went to be safe from bombs. Also, I never understand how people made tights out of gravy. Or indeed why? What was that all about?

How was Ella's?

On Friday at 10:35 Martin replied:

Alas, the end-of-the-world orgy I had envisaged didn't come to pass. We did open the Princess Diana Memorial Brandy she'd been treasuring, though.

On Friday at 10:38 Sally replied:

The stuff in the heart-shaped bottle? How was it?

Gone off. Just as well, really, considering we must have been fairly smashed to have even considered it.

Yet another police car with a wailing siren going past at top speed.

Puts it all in perspective, doesn't it?

Not really. You're still a twat. But there aren't that many people around. Pint later?

Suggestions

On Friday at 13:34 Mike wrote:

Hey, guys,
Glad to hear everyone's OK. Don't suppose anyone's in the mood to suggest fun or wacky ways to celebrate our mutual friend's impending nuptials?
Mike

Reassured?

On Friday at 13:45 Martin wrote:

Am I the only one to feel less rather than more safe having learned that the high-level group charged with safeguarding us from terrorism is called COBRA? Who came up with that? Austin Powers?

On Friday at 13:56 Sally replied:

It's scary, but probably not in the way they intended.

On Friday at 14:09 Martin replied:

Where do they meet? Hollow dormant volcano? Do they each step into an ordinary-looking postbox or phone booth, go down a shute and then get driven by golf buggy to the Cobradome or whatever they no doubt call it?

On Friday at 14:26 Sally replied:

Possibly they are hoping that the bomb-makers are laughing too hard at the name to do the fiddly bits...

On Friday at 15:03 Chris wrote:

Sorry to break the 'hilarious' mood. They're still looking for bodies opposite where I'm sitting. And it's COBR, anyway.

Re: Re: Acklington Stanley

On Saturday at 14:08 Lucy wrote:

Glad to hear you're alive. It all sounds pretty scary. Take care of yourself, big bro.

PS: Working in the pub is absolutely knackering. Can't be arsed even to transform the semi-psychotic feelings it produces in me into comedy. I swear to God I'm not leaving bed today. Until four o'clock, when I have to go to work. Damn.

PPS: I've emailed Miriam to ask her to bring me a cup of tea. If this works I may never have to leave my bed again.

On Saturday at 14:11 Martin replied:

I appreciate the sentiment, but 'taking care of myself' isn't really going to help if someone decides to blow me up. I mean, I will take a clean hanky and not go out with wet hair, but that almost certainly won't do much good.

Fucking hell, this hangover's pretty scary too. Definitely not leaving the house today. Toying with the idea of ringing the pizza company and ordering something with a paracetemol topping. My liver must be getting old. I seem to be shedding a lot of hair as well. Either it's time for my summer coat or I'm going bald. In divine compensation, however, I'm sprouting a lot of hair from my nose and ears.

On Saturday at 14:13 Lucy replied:

Who were you out with? What are you up to today?

On Saturday at 14:27 Martin replied:

Well I've spent the last half hour deciding whether or not to clip my nails. The backs of my hands are hairy. How long have the backs of my hands been hairy? I don't want hairy hands. I feel like something is going to happen any moment. It's like an existential sense of dread. Mixed with moments when I want to go out and cuddle a puppy and buy balloons.

On Saturday at 14:30 Lucy replied:

Yes, 'existential dread'. Either that or you're hungover. I've warned you about going drinking with that Jean-Paul Sartre ...

On Saturday at 14:35 Martin replied:

I was out with Sally, of all people. It was quite nice. Didn't even make an insane prick of myself. Or try to pull her. Or put a sock on my hand and berate her. No anecdotes to be recounted, really. We had a lot of pints and went home. Believe I had a conversation about Iraq with the taxi driver and we had pretty much established a plan for the future by the time we got back. Alas, I can't remember it.

On Saturday at 14:37 Lucy replied:

Sock??? I won't even ask.
By the way, how were the Stanley? As 'the kids' aren't calling them. Their debut kind of got pushed off the front pages.

On Saturday at 14:40 Martin replied:

I'm a bit low on bile at the moment, so imagine this a lot more vitriolic:

First, think of U2

On Saturday at 14:41 Lucy replied:

If I must.

On Saturday at 14:43 Martin replied:

Well, Acklington Stanley sound a bit like U2. If U2 were all wasps. Playing in a damp matchbox. I thought I had one of their songs stuck in my head the next day, but it turned out to be that thing when you still have water in your ear from the shower.

On Saturday at 14:45 Lucy replied:

So not great? And what's Gwyn like?

On Saturday at 14:48 Martin replied:

Well, most of all he's fat. Not that I have anything against people being fat, except that they're lazy, greedy and they look a bit shit. But he jiggles around on stage and bounces up and down. Which is fine. Except that when he shakes his hips, he stops shaking a long time before his hips do. And one of his flabby tits fell out of his vest at one point. But it's all about the music, man.

And the music is not so hot?

PS: Am I still meant to be adding extra vitriol and toppings of spite?

I'm getting into my stride now. As alleged 'supergroups' go, they were all right. Better than Dalis Car, not as good as Me Me Me.

Listen, if you say 'It's all about the music', the music better be strong enough to distract you from the sight of a heaving white arse peering out at the audience whenever you bend over to pick up your tambourine. I mean, even Mozart wore a wig onstage, for Christ's sake.

The music. More to the point, the songs for Laura. Which I have a hideous suspicion Gwyn considers a 'suite'.

There's one called 'Laura', which is about how nice Laura is, especially to overlook the singer's many failings. Doesn't mention the fact that he's an ugly biffer with a face like a hospital bag of extracted liposuction fat. Contains the lines 'Laura/ I was so cruel/ But you made it all cool.' Or as I sang along 'Laura/ I am a fool/ I am the biggest tool.'

There's 'The Saddest Eyes'. It's about Laura's eyes. Which are, allegedly, 'the saddest'. Only, perhaps, when she's looking at a lardy talentless wanker?

There is the moving ballad 'I Didn't Know', in which Gwyn alleges 'he didn't know he was hurting you' and bawls about Laura 'loving her better'. I heard the second bit as 'loving her batter', which makes sense. Perhaps he was hurting her by lying on top of her when attempting sexual intercourse. Because he is so fucking fat.

There is a song called, I shit you not, 'Lady'. It is also about Laura. Like all songs called 'Lady' it was asinine, mawkish shite.

At that point I went for a very long slash. Nevertheless, through the damp-beaded walls, unable to block my ears due to my hands being otherwise engaged, I could hear Gwyn laryngically bellowing the couplet 'Lady, lady, lady/ Save me, save me, save me.' Fuckin' Shakespeare.

Actually, by that point, he was finally bellowing an emotion with which I connected. I see why they only use plastic glasses at these events.

I'm not even going to get into the acoustic section. For a band who claim The Fall and The Velvet Underground as key influences, they sound surprisingly like a weedier version of Keane.

Acklington Stanley? Armitage Shanks more like.

Didn't get my dance with Laura either.

Glad to get that off my chest.

Lots of Love
Martin

P.S. The Lost Cause were crap as well. In fact they made Acklington Stanley look good, which requires a certain very special kind of genius. They all look about twelve apart from the drummer, who is about 45, wears a big Russian fur hat, and plays a solo in every song. They have a song called 'Roland Barthes', the only lyric of which I caught was: 'I was sitting in the bath/ reading Roland Barthes'. I may be wrong - the sound was pretty poor. Thank God.

On Saturday at 15:10 Lucy replied:

Phew. Not a big fan, then?

PS: Nice of Gwyn to write a song about our dog, though. On the subject of Lady, I got a long email about her health from Mum. Poor little thing.

PPS: Shame you didn't catch the rest of the lyrics to 'Roland Barthes'. How do you follow that couplet? 'Then the phone rang/ it was Giscard D'Estaing'? Except that actually rhymes ...

PPPS: I know he's not a philosopher, but I think he is French.

PPPPS: Oh, of course - 'Driving in my car/ Reading Jacques Derrida'

PPPPPS: 'Sitting on the loo/ Reading Albert Camus'

PPPPPPS: You can't expect every band to be as good as Me Me Me. It's over. Time to move on. Stop hangin' around, bangin' around.

PPPPPPPS: Where is my cup of tea, Miriam? That's it, there's no choice but to get up.

On Saturday at 15:14 Martin replied:

I notice you are using humour in an increasingly threadbare attempt to avoid mentioning Sam. Please tell me that is because you've jettisoned him.

On Saturday at 15:18 Lucy replied:

Damn, was hoping you wouldn't notice that. Yeah, I've been meaning to get round to letting him go, but I've been really busy. And the streams of presents and lavish attention have made it hard to find the appropriate time. He's away on a field trip. I will do it when he gets back.

On Saturday at 15:30 Martin replied:

Sam's off counting pebbles, eh?

Anyway, it's been lovely and a welcome chance to vent, but I must get back to contemplating the fragility of life. Let me know when you have bade Sam take up his kagoule and crayons and fuck off.

262

Rucksacks

On Wednesday at 9:48 Martin wrote:

Why do they keep talking about the hunt for the 'mastermind' behind the attacks? Does it really take Moriarty to put a bomb in a backpack?

On Wednesday at 10:13 Barney wrote:

Well, I'm not Einstein, but shouldn't they just ban rucksacks from public transport?
They are well sad anyway.

On Wednesday at 10:23 Martin replied:

Thanks, Barney. I think you've penetrated to the heart of the issue.
Although that idea would have the side benefit of keeping bloody backpackers off the tube and preventing them from jamming a load of smelly socks under your nose as they stand on your feet.

On Wednesday at 10:33 Ella replied:

But cheers for clearing up any potential confusion between you and the man who split the atom ...
However, I have been calling for the banning of rucksacks for years, merely on aesthetic grounds.

On Wednesday at 10:45 Barney wrote:

They look shit too.

Joke - Christ guys can you lay off with the 'stupid' comments a bit? I mean I may not be...

Hold on a minute. I'll mail back.

On Wednesday at 10:47 Martin wrote:

Barney?

On Wednesday at 10:48 Ella wrote:

Did he get his finger stuck in the disk drive? Again?

On Wednesday at 10:50 Barney wrote:

Sorry. I couldn't think of any other major intellectual figure that fits the sentence I was trying to write. That was another joke.

Yeah I can - Merleau-Ponty.

There's no need to always be putting me down, just to make yourselves feel better about yourselves. It's not necessary, because I already think you are both smart and funny. Anyway, I may not be the smartest, or even a very good DJ, but I've got a good heart and I'm a loyal friend and that's what matters.

Barney

On Wednesday at 11:02 Ella wrote:

Who told you that? Your mum?

264

On Wednesday at 11:13 Martin wrote:

Hi Ella

I should note that those were the first jokes I think Barney has ever made to me. And, moreover, Barney's first ever use of inverted commas.

Do I detect the hand of the new girlfriend here? Give it two weeks and she'll be ripping the piss with the rest of us.

Martin

On Wednesday at 11:15 Ella replied:

You might mention to him that you don't have to write 'that was a joke' every time. Although the clarification was helpful in those particular cases. I had almost forgotten how glad I am not to be bearing his child.

Peace and Love

On Friday at 10:22 Martin Sergeant wrote:

Dear Colleagues,

As you know, last Thursday London was the target of a terrorist outrage. MediaSolutions takes the safety of our employees very seriously, and you will have noticed that security checks have now been instituted in the reception area.

After much discussion about the proper response to the events of last Thursday, it has been decided to establish a new electronic bulletin board for the benefit of those employees who wish to share their thoughts and feelings in the aftermath of this tragedy. Perhaps you would like to talk about how the attacks affected you, to describe how your life has changed since the bombings, or perhaps to share messages of hope.

Comments may be made anonymously.

Please report any misuse of this board to Martin Sergeant in the IT Department.

Simon Tapper, Head of Security

Martin Sergeant, IT

- I want to say that what happened has shocked me to the core. I never thought anything like this could happen to us. I feel so lucky to be alive. [Sarah H]
- I feel so angry, not only with the terrorists, but with our leaders who misled us and failed to keep us safe [Andy T]
- I never thought I'd feel unsafe walking the streets of London [Luke J]
- You used to feel safe walking the streets of London? You don't live around where I'm from then. [anonymous]
- Anyone want to buy a bike? Good condition, £75 quid o.n.o.

includes pump. [please contact Phil Thornhill in Accounts]
- When I look at pictures of the people who died, I realise what a diverse, talented society we live in. We must all work to cherish that, otherwise the terrorists really have won. [Claire G]
- I'm so proud of how Londoners have pulled together to show the world what we are made of. I think we all deserve a pat on the back. [Ben J]
- Apart from the terrorists, of course, who may well also have been Londoners. [anonymous]
- I still can't believe what is happening. It could have been any one of us. [Matthew B]
- Not Martin Sergeant. He sleeps in the office 'cos his girlfriend chucked him out. [anonymous]
- I feel nervous every time I take a bus or tube. [Mary W]
- I moved carriages twice today because I was suspicious of foreign-looking people. [anonymous]
- I would like to express my deepest sympathies to those who lost their lives, and send my thoughts to their families in this terrible time. What drove these killers was not religion but hate. [Feisal M]
- I think we need to look at the deeper causes behind the actions of last Thursday, and ask ourselves: Were we to blame? [Charlie D]
- Charlie, I think that's nonsense. I think the people who did the bombings were to blame, and we shouldn't seek to excuse them. [Petra V]
- Petra, to understand is not to condone. I think we should ask whether our actions in the Middle East have made the situation better or worse. [Charlie D]
- What, because I didn't go on the anti-war march I deserve to die? Cheers, Charlie [Petra V]
- I think you would have died even if you had, Petra, if you were in the wrong place at the wrong time. These people are sick. [Stuart F]
- I think we need less understanding, not more. I'm sickened when people try to justify these terrible actions. We've been

too understanding for too long. [anonymous]
- Why post anonymously, unless you're embarrassed by what you think? [Hamid A]
- How has anyone's life changed since last Thursday? [Elizabeth J]
- I've started learning Arabic. [anonymous]
- I don't sit next to foreigners on the tube [Pierre S]
- I think he means *other* foreigners. [anonymous]
- I think that attitude is really unhelpful, Pierre. We should all realise that not every Muslim is a terrorist. Lots of them have condemned the attacks and are as horrified as we are. [Sarah G]
- Thank you, Sarah G. The more people learn about Islam the more they will see that it's nothing to do with terrorism. [Hamid A]
- I don't take the tube any more. [Michael B]
- Well, lucky you being able to walk in to work. 'Oh no, I'm not going to die screaming underground with the plebs, 'cos I can afford to live on the edge of Zone One.' And your FIRKIN trainers stink, Michael. Could you start leaving them in reception? Or preferably outside the building? [anonymous]
- What this has taught me is that we need to start taking pride in being British again. It is a privilege to live in this country with its great history. We should be teaching all our kids to be PROUD of being British. God knows, we have given a lot to the world: Shakespeare, democracy, the Industrial Revolution, the Beatles and the flushing toilet, to name but five things. [Barry H]
- Yeah, not to mention the Empire, the package holiday and Pop Idol. Democracy was the Greeks, by the way. [Oli E]
- Just one of their great inventions. [Andrew D]
- Which definitely don't include the modern flushing toilet. Never going back to Corfu again. [Luke G]
- Actually, that is ignorant. There were toilets in the palace at Knossos over three thousand years ago, when the English were wiping their bums with peat. [Aris K]
- I think the toilets in our hotel were older than that, Aris. [Luke G]

- Fascinating. Did they appear to have ever been 'excavated'? [Oli E]
- OK. Has anyone else got anything to say ON THE SUBJECT FOR WHICH THIS NOTICEBOARD WAS SET UP? Anyone made any resolutions or noticed any changes about themselves? [Sarah G]
- I feel like everyone is staring at me on the tube. I've started leaving my rucksack at home, and yesterday I even thought about whether my beard was really necessary. I've never felt like this in England before. [anonymous]
- I've given up drinking. [anonymous]
- I've started drinking again. [Steve B]
- I've started pilfering things from my employers and colleagues. [anonymous]
- Yeah, we noticed, Luke [Laura M].
- I had a wank in the work toilets yesterday. Didn't want to die horny. [anonymous]
- You used to do that before, Luke (again). What was your excuse then? [Laura M]
- I've decided to come out to my family, friends, and colleagues in the IT department. [Martin Sergeant]
- Congratulations! [Andrew D]
- That's really brave of you, Martin. Of course, we all knew. Best wishes for the future. I hope you'll be very happy. But surely you should have mentioned this to Charlotte G first? Do it now - she's on the way to your office looking pretty unimpressed. [Martin Sargent]
- I didn't write that. That message is going to be removed and this noticeboard will shortly be temporarily suspended, due to its misuse at the hands of a few immature people. Any subsequent misuse will result in the messageboard being shut down permanently and without further warning. [Martin Sergeant]
- Also, can people please stop reporting misuses of the board to me? I'm the other Martin Sargent and I'm really not that bothered. To those who congratulated me on coming out, that's the other Martin too. Still, much appreciated. [Martin Sargent]

- 'Misuse at the hands of immature people'? Sounds like a great night out for some. Arf arf. [anonymous]
- Being homosexual has no connection to paedophilia, and is nothing to be ashamed of. [Sarah G]
- Being immature has no connection to age. And you made the connection, Sarah G. Although of course they're both Greek inventions … [anonymous]
- That is another very ignorant comment. [Aris K]
- Nobody mind Aris, he's still upset since he found out about Alexander the Great. [anonymous]
- Oh I know what's changed. What happened to all the articles about 'How to Spot a Chav'? [Laura M]
- They're being rewritten as 'How to Spot a Suicide Bomber' [Oli E]
- I think some people who have posted on this noticeboard are really sick. It's an insult to those who died. [Sarah H]
- Hi, Sarah. I don't think anyone has posted anything that insults the dead, although the usual blend of thinly-veiled homophobia, Islamophobia and racism that infects our society is fully displayed. I think it's important to recognise that humour is the way some people deal with events that they otherwise could not deal with. [Hamid A]
- I agree with Hamid A. I also think it's a tragedy that everyone's refusal to accept Martin's decision has scared him back into the closet. [Martin Sargent]
- I agree with Hamid A. We should remember that the British sense of humour is part of what makes this country GREAT Britain. [Ben J]
- I agree with Ben J and Hamid A. If we stop laughing, the terrorists have won. [Sarah H]
- Umm, no. Surprisingly the British sense of humour has never been mentioned as a target by any terrorist group. I think the terrorists have 'won' if they establish a Global Caliphate based on a strict interpretation of certain aspects of Islamic law. [anonymous]
- Or if we stopped interfering ILLEGALLY in the Middle East, acted to enforce Israel's adherence to UN regulations and used

our global influence to build a better, fairer world. [Charlie D]
- Is anybody in this building planning on doing any work today? [Laura M]

Thursdays

On Thursday at 12:44 Martin wrote:

OK, now I really am terrified.

On Thursday at 13:01 Ella replied:

Damn. Why are they bombing on Thursdays? Thursday is singles' night at my local Sainsbury's.

On Thursday at 13:13 Martin replied:

What happened to the Alpha Course guy?

On Thursday at 13:15 Ella replied:

Oh, he turned out to be trying to save me.
That was not a misspelling.

PS Oh Martin, you're at your desk at lunchtime? Sweet. What is in your sandwiches? Did Ross make them for you?
PPS Sorry, forgot to call you by your new nickname. Mr Prickles.

On Thursday at 13:18 Martin replied:

I've been called worse. But I still prefer Robusto.

On Thursday at 14:25 Barney wrote:

Dear Martin and Ella,
It may surprise you to learn that I have been accepted on an MA course starting in September. Ha!
Now I have to tell my boss...
Best wishes,
Barney

On Thursday at 14:35 Ella replied:

You're right, Barney. That does surprise me.
But congratulations.
Ella

On Thursday at 14:36 Ella wrote:

Well, Mr Prickles, what do you make of that? I guess I unlocked something in the boy.
What happened to Barney's rhyming sign-offs? I rather liked those.
Ella

On Thursday at 14:40 Martin replied:

DJ Idiot, Master of Arts? That's it. The world really has gone mad.

P.S. Don't call me Mr Prickles.

Part Eight
Normal Service Resumes

Stag Night Plans • Hairy Hands
The Saddest Hedgehog
The Beard Gag Explained

Re: Suggestions

On Wednesday at 18:04 Mike wrote:

Dear Mates-of-Chris,

All the suggestions for the stag night are in and have been given due consideration. I got a lot of useful feedback. As well as some that were ... not so helpful. I'm sorry to have to disappoint those who suggested: a watercolouring class; antenatal support sessions for dads; hiring a dead-eyed Latvian 'masseuse' for Chris and watching through a two-way mirror; doing a tour of historical East End crime scenes; or 'putting Chris in a big box and sending him, nude, to Alaska'. Actually, only one person will be disappointed, since all those suggestions were provided by Martin. Luckily I was expecting that.

Various people suggested: go-karting; going to a dry ski slope; going sailing or going paint-balling. I should perhaps have clarified that this event is meant to celebrate/mourn Chris getting married, rather than turning 15.

Karaoke was considered, but Chris was a little worried about one of our number 'doing a repeat of last time', and we weren't sure which karaoke bars he is barred from. (Martin, again).

Throwing convention to the wind, I have asked Chris himself what his ideal evening would involve. With typical adventurousness he replied, 'Pub, curry, pub, club. Not getting tied to anything naked.' I think the nudity bit refers to him, as opposed to our tying a clothed Chris to something or someone in a state of undress.

Anyway, the final, provisional, tentative plan is this: a cruise up the river to admire our magnificent city, dinner, then on to a club. Suggestions for club venues still being considered. I rang around a few places to check they accepted stag nights. A surprising number of people hung up on me.

I've attached a possible schedule and a map to find the meeting place, in case any of you can't find the Thames without one. Mark the date in your diaries in big red letters and dust off your fake plastic breasts.

See you all then,

Mike

PS - Barney, I'm afraid Emily is using the flat that night for her hen night. Sorry, 'bachelorette evening'. Not that I think Chris would be amused if we were to 'bust in, crap on the floor and mess everything up to make it look like he's been burgled'. Chris has, seriously, requested that we keep a lid on the seething homosocial psychosis that characterises the average stag night. Or as the man himself put it: 'If you guys stitch me up, I will hunt you down and make you suffer.'

Re: Re: Re: Acklington Stanley

On Wednesday at 12:02 Gwyn wrote:

Dear Friends and Fans (of Acklington Stanley),

We'd like to extend our apologies to those who managed to struggle across London for our recent show at the Falcon. Unfortunately, as you know, Johnno our bassist was stranded in Greenwich, and Jez our drummer decided not to show up. We hope those who did make it enjoyed the acoustic set. Those people who wanted their money back should contact the box office.

First some bad news: due to events beyond our control, Acklington Stanley have been forced to cancel our series of 'guerrilla gigs' around the capital.

Now for some good news (at last!): we have more shows coming up. Dates and locations to be announced shortly!

Now for some more good news: from a selection of press clippings we have gleaned the following items:

'Acklington Stanley […] have all the makings of a band who are going places' [www.gigsonline.com]

'their sound evokes the glacial majesty of peak period U2' [*Camden Gazette*]

'Could Acklington Stanley be the new new new Coldplay?' [www.jewishherald.com; see the print edition for a rather fetching photo of us in Mark's mum's garden!]

'The lead singer is f*cking sexy' [www.laurasblog.com]

And a big 'fuck off' to the man from the *NME* who never showed up.

Look forward to seeing you all at the upcoming gigs

Gwyn, Johnno, Mark (and Jez, if he can be bothered to show. Drum machines ain't expensive mate)

Hi Laura

Glad to see the Stanley aren't letting the terrorists win. What a blow for freedom they're striking.

I don't know if it was accidental, but Gwyn left out the telling central bit of that quote from www.gigsonline.com, which reads in full: 'Acklington Stanley, *despite being comprised of graduates of third-string no-hopers Fork, Overpass and Mucky Faces, as well as the bald drummer from tuneless jazz-funk noodlers Herbalessence (known round these parts as "Guffbucket")*, have all the makings of a band going places.' Oh yes, and it continues, 'This reviewer hopes that the place they are going is far far away, and that they stay there for ever.'

I wasn't aware that the *Camden Gazette* employed wasps as reviewers.

As for Gwyn being sexy, the mind reels...

Martin

On Thursday at 12:18 Laura wrote:

Wasps???

Re: Pretty in Pink

Hey Ella

How was the fitting session with the bridesmaids? I hear
Emily designed the dresses herself, so they can't be that bad. Can
they?

Martin

Yeah. Unfortunately I suspect she designed them when she
was twelve. I won't be surprised if she arrives at the church
riding My Little Pony. The whole experience was excruciating.
I kept expecting Jeremy Beadle to pop out and reveal it was a
wind-up. Sadly, he didn't.

What can I say without being too mean? Probably nothing.
Ballerina Barbie would be embarrassed to be seen in this get-up.
The dresses turn out to be not just pink, but a variety of pinks.
A variety of pinks that clash not only with each other, but with
the complexion of human skin. I don't know whether this was
intentional. Maybe Emily kept running out of felt-tips when she
was doing the original design. Apparently I look sweet. Great. If
I wanted to look sweet, I'd turn up dressed as Pikachu. Thank
God someone managed to dissuade Emily from the bonnet idea,
but she wouldn't be budged on the ruffles and bows. I look like
Barbara Cartland's truffle-box. And an idiot. The whole thing is
so Freudian.

Stop. Laughing.

PS Obviously this is all strictly *entre nous*. Emily is already cross at me for asking 'Why do I have to be Mr Pink?' in my best Steve Buscemi voice.

On Thursday at 12:32 Martin replied:

Freudian? Well, if nothing else, this explains why Chris is wearing that skin-tight pink bodysuit and the fuzzy shoes.

I wasn't laughing. I was enjoying picturing you dressed as Pikachu.

As it happens, I'm feeling somewhat weirded. I found something odd on the internet while I was googling Laura.

On Thursday at 12:35 Ella replied:

Let me guess. Was it some girls, covered in goo?

On Thursday at 12:40 Martin replied:

No, actually it's much more disturbing than that.

Laurasblog

On Thursday at 12:56 Martin wrote:

I've been reading www.laurasblog.com. She has the same first name as you. Wow, she even works in this building. That's really eerie. God, I don't think much of that M. guy she was thinking about seeing. I quote:

'As you guys know, I don't really go for conventionally handsome.'

'I think M. may be going a bit bald. Noticed the light reflecting off his forehead as he was typing today.'

'Not sure if he's yet another self-obsessed wannabe-hipster.'

'I noticed at lunch today that M. has hairy hands! Gross!!! Have to do something about that.'

'His ex has done a real number on him. Do I really want to hook up with someone with "damaged goods" stamped on his forehead?'

You're holding an online poll on the subject??? And pass on my thanks to Sandra from Texas, who thinks I sound like 'bad news, girl' and then compares me to a boyfriend who ended up in prison for stealing her car drunk. The only sense on the whole site is the recent comment from Johannes Jester: 'I should inform the voters that Gwyn is a talentless tedious whiner who takes the already debased medium of rock and roll to previously unimagined new lows. And Martin is not going bald. Also Laura has slightly protruding googly eyes which under certain circumstances can appear somewhat unnerving.'

I am not a 'wannabe' hipster.

I wash my hairy hands of you.

Martin

P.S. Let me know how the poll turns out. I predict a late surge.

On Thursday at 14:02 Laura replied:

Thanks for ignoring me at lunch.

Sorry about the weblog - I started it before I got to know you. If you scroll back you may notice that I've been interested in you for a long time.

The poll's meant to be a bit of fun, by the way, so you can stop trying to rig it.

On Thursday at 14:04 Martin replied:

Oh, didn't see you at lunch. I have to concentrate because my hairy hands make it a bit difficult to carry my tray. Or perhaps I was dazzled by the reflected glare of the canteen lights coming off my cranium. Or perhaps I thought you were looking at someone else with your enormous distended eyes.

Like I'd stoop to rigging your stupid poll. Don't flatter yourself.

By the way, Acklington Stanley: they look like crap, sound like crap, and probably smell like crap. If I had to think of one word to sum them up, do you know what it would be? Clue: it comes out of your backside. I'm praying for a Jazzbucket reunion. And Gwyn can put that on his next flyer.

I've been meaning to ask if you can shed any light on how Gwyn comes up with his lyrics. Does he write them in some other language (possibly Finnish) and translate them using babelfish.com? That's all I can come up with to explain lines like 'Now it's plunder regency/ Look out pandemonium pandemic' and the grammatically and biologically baffling 'Here we were, I stand/ In my heart and out of my head.' He then announces he has 'something he needs to say to you', which turns out to be 'I can't turn around'. Well, I'm hardly surprised given the circumstances. May I speculate via which orifice he entered his own torso? And if he will insist on partly acting-out his words in bad mime, you might suggest he takes steps to prevent his bingo wings flapping around. Oh, and be sure to mention that 'Cancel my subscription/ To televised affliction', apart from making no sense, doesn't bloody rhyme. Even if delivered with a furrowed brow and in a 'meaningful' voice. So there.

On Thursday at 14:07 Martin wrote:

Hi guys
You can ignore the text about the poll. I've been rumbled.
Martin

On Thursday at 14:11 Sally replied:

Wow, Martin, she realises things about you that I took years to notice. I voted for Gwyn. By the way, thanks for telling her so much about us. You didn't mention Mr Socky, I notice. Or the clothes thing. Or your book.

On Thursday at 14:14 Martin replied:

Sally, would it surprise you to learn that I didn't realise she was going to pass on our conversations to the world at large? Nor indeed to speculate whether my maternal grandfather was 'also a slaphead'.

On Thursday at 14:15 Sally replied:

Reading on.
What the fuck? 'Martin's ex sounds like a real maniac. That fucking play was like being trapped during a riot at an Institution for the Criminally Talentless. Thank God Martin

thought so too, otherwise all bets would be well and truly off. Still, hard to forgive the person responsible for dragging me to that traduction of the very concept of "entertainment". To read more of what I thought, check out www.yourtheatre.com.'

Well, it's hard to act when you are getting blinded by the reflection off someone's bonedome and you can't tell where the girl sitting next to them is looking with her freaky Marty Feldman eyes. When you see her again knock her other contact lens out for me.

PS - Sandra from Texas suggests you 'shave your hands and put it on your head'. Worth thinking about.

On Thursday at 14:18 Laura wrote:

You should be more careful about flinging the personal comments about, if you can't handle it being directed at you.
You're not that tall, by the way.
Or thin.

On Thursday at 14:20 Martin replied:

Yeah, good comeback. That's one in the eye for me. You psycho.

On Thursday at 15:00 Ella wrote:

Martin, out of interest, what upsets you most about this sorry but fascinating affair? Is it
   a)   the invasion of your privacy
   b)   the accurate but ungallant physical observations
   c)   the unsurprising revelation that you obsessively bitch out your supposed 'mates' to a comparative stranger
   d)   the assertion that you are a 'wannabe' hipster

e) the fact that you are trailing in the poll by a considerable margin?

By the way, Laura has updated her readers with the latest news. I suppose the fact she calls herself Laura M (understandably) meant that you didn't pick up on this at an earlier stage, when you no doubt 'googled' her. So to speak.

On Thursday at 15:13 Chris wrote:

Hey, Baldie,

Do you want us to vote in the new poll as well? She's taking suggestions as to what to do now. Willing to write in for you, since I know those hairy hands of yours make it hard to type. Take it easy, Teenwolf.

See you at the stag.

Chris

On Thursday at 15:16 Ross wrote:

Hi Martin,

Glad to see that the readers of www.laurasblog.com have been treated to a hugely exaggerated account of the state of my bedroom and some potentially libellous material about my alleged unwillingness to buy milk.

By the way, I voted for Laura's next move to be 'Get Gwyn to hit you with a hammer.'

Cheers 'mate',

Ross

On Thursday at 15:23 Barney wrote:

'From the invention of the wheel to Barney at the decks, intellectual history has come full circle, if not actually changed direction.' You arrogant wanker.

I voted for Laura to put her recording of you singing 'You Were Always on My Mind' online.
Barney

On Thursday at 15:45 Martin Sergeant wrote:

Hi, Martin,
Hope your day is going well. I've been helping some of the staff get used to using the internet. Of course, most of us have been following things online for months. Wouldn't want to be you during your 'security check' tomorrow. Simon's off to buy some 'special gloves'. I hope he doesn't borrow Benita's rings too. Ouch! Oh yeah, she says to tell you that you can empty your own bin from now on.
Best wishes,
Martin

On Thursday at 16:00 Martin Sargent wrote:

Guys
I think we may be losing sight of who's the victim here.
Martin

P.S. It's me, by the way.
P.P.S. Still time to vote in the poll, unless you want to see me hit with a hammer.

On Thursday at 16:45 Martin Sargent wrote:

I'm serious, guys. Hello? Anyone still speaking to me?

On Thursday at 16:52 Ella replied:

Well, I think you've certainly dispelled those claims that you're 'self-obsessed'...

\----------------------------

Mr Prickles

On Monday at 9:04 Barney wrote:

I'm thinking about forgiving you. On one condition.

On Monday at 9:15 Martin replied:

Barney, for the last time, I will NEVER be DJ Idiot's pet dancing fool. Not even if I do get to dress as a scary clown.
Why not ask Ms Staple?

On Monday at 9:20 Barney replied:

She said no too. Dammit. I need a gimmick to set me apart. Kate's on holiday.

On Monday at 9:23 Martin replied:

Barney, trust me. Your sound is distinctive enough without gimmicks. No one is ever going to forget having experienced a set by DJ Idiot.
Where has she gone?

On Monday at 9:26 Barney replied:

Thanks. I think. Kate says DJ Idiot may give people the wrong impression about me.

She's gone off to Greece with her mate Martin.

On Monday at 9:28 Martin replied:

Martin Sergeant? Barney, you do know about their past, right? What did she suggest as an alternative name? DJ Clever? DJ MA? DJ Holiday Cuckold?

On Monday at 9:34 Barney replied:

Yeah, I know. I'm not exactly over the moon about it. But it was booked weeks ago, and apparently nothing's going to happen. We'll have to wait and see.

On Monday at 9:36 Martin replied:

Bummer for you, but that does mean that at least one of my enemies is going to be out of the way. Hope Simon Tapper goes on holiday soon. Climbing up the fire-escape to get to my desk without a security check in the morning is wearing thin quite quickly.

On Monday at 9:40 Barney replied:

Martin, have you ever considered that you might be a bit paranoid? Perhaps you don't have lots of 'enemies'. Perhaps there are loads of people who go through a whole day without thinking at all about Martin Sargent.

On Monday at 9:42 Martin replied:

Are you trying to make me paranoid about being paranoid?

Trust me, I have considered the possibility that there's no one out to get me, and people to whom my existence is of little or no concern. But then again, that's exactly what you'd want me to think if you were out to get me, isn't it?

Besides, the Laurasblog episode has perhaps unsurprisingly not diminished my paranoia.

On which note, what is this 'condition' on which my forgiveness depends?

On Monday at 9:45 Barney replied:

Tell me what your book is about.

On Monday at 9:52 Martin replied:

I'm afraid I don't value your friendship that much. Sorry. Why do you care?

On Monday at 9:54 Barney replied:

I care because I want to know why you're freaking out about it. Tell me. Is it about me?

On Monday at 9:55 Martin replied:

It's a full-length book, Barney. I think you are pretty much summed up on a flyer saying 'DJ Idiot'.

On Monday at 10:01 Barney replied:

Is it about a gingerbread man who gets left in the pantry and gets so hungry he eats himself?

On Monday at 10:08 Martin replied:

What? Why on earth would it be?

Umm, if Kate told you that's what happened to your gingerbread man, she may not have as high a regard for your intelligence as you think.

On Monday at 10:13 Barney replied:

Because I know your book is a kids' book, and I was trying to think of the kind of thing I'd write if I was trying to make up a story for kids.

On Monday at 10:15 Martin replied:

Remind me when the time comes never to let you babysit my kids.

OK OK OK. If only to stop any more stupid suggestions on those lines, and because no one else has offered to forgive me, I'll tell you. But you have to swear that it goes absolutely no further than you.

On Monday at 10:20 Barney replied:

I swear on my record box that I will not tell anyone what you are about to confide. Now spill the beans. What is your book about?

On Monday at 10:23 Martin replied:

It's about fifty pages.

On Monday at 10:28 Barney replied:

Martin, how many people called you, emailed you or invited you out this weekend? I estimate approximately none. Unless you're enjoying your new status as a hermit, tell me what your book is about.

On Monday at 10:30 Martin replied:

It's about a hedgehog called Mr Prickles.

On Monday at 10:31 Barney replied:

And?

On Monday at 10:34 Martin replied:

And nothing. That's what it's about. He has an adventure. That's it. End of.

On Monday at 10:38 Barney replied:

It sounds rubbish.

On Monday at 10:49 Martin replied:

What, is that a trick to get me pissed off so I tell you?
No, can't be. You didn't write 'This is a trick' after it.
Fine: Mr Prickles is a lonely hedgehog, who lives, obviously, in a hedge.
He goes looking for love, and keeps thinking he has found it. But he is wrong.

Then he dies.

On Monday at 10:54 Barney replied:

Great, sounds perfectly aimed at that 4-7 market. What's the
message?

On Monday at 11:00 Martin replied:

It's shit being a hedgehog.
And by the way, kids, hedgehogs aren't sweet, they're fucking
rats with spikes on and they're crawling with fleas.
I had a lot of fun with the illustrations.

On Monday at 11:03 Barney replied:

It's an important message for us all, I think. How does Mr
Prickles die?

On Monday at 11:07 Martin replied:

He gets squished, but it's a little more complicated than that.
Do you really still want to hear about it?

On Monday at 11:10 Barney replied:

Actually, mate, I lost interest quite a while ago. I think if you
don't mind I'm going to play poker online for a bit. Maybe even
do some work, catch up with my correspondence. Glad we're
mates again.
Oh, go on and tell me, since you're obviously secretly dying to.

Right. Mr Prickles, the lonely hedgehog, gets sick of having no one to play with. So he crawls out of his hedge one night when everyone is asleep, and goes to look for a special hedgehog friend.

On the silvery lawn he sees a bowl of milk the kids have left out for him. And when he goes to investigate, he sees the moon's face reflected in it. He thinks 'What a pretty face', and goes to lick it. The milk ripples and he thinks the face is winking at him, so he goes on licking.

But soon he has licked up all the milk, and the face has gone.

Then he sees a garden gnome fishing in the pond. So he goes and sits next to it. And he quite likes that, and the gnome is smiling and wearing his jaunty hat and everything. Mr Prickles asks him if he's caught anything, but the gnome ignores him. After a while he decides the gnome is pretty boring, so the search goes on.

He goes into the house through the catflap. There's a fridge humming, and he thinks it's talking to him, so he goes over and sits by it. But it doesn't answer any of his questions, so he decides it's only interested in talking to itself, and he goes upstairs.

He goes into the little girl's bedroom, and there, in the moonlight spilling onto the desk, he sees... her! His soulmate! Another hedgehog.

He climbs up onto the desk, and it's a struggle, but after various trials and tribulations he gets there. And she is the most beautiful hedgehog he has ever seen. So he snuggles up to her, but she's all cold and doesn't respond to him. Then it gets a bit lighter and he realises he has fallen in love with a hairbrush.

Bitterly disappointed, he climbs down again, and goes outside. He starts wandering along the road, and he's hanging his head, and thinking about what a sham love is, when suddenly he sees the most gorgeous face in the world, lying there in front of him. He smiles at it, and it smiles back. And he sits there for ages, perfectly happy. Of course, it's really his own reflection in a puddle.

Then a milk-float comes along and runs him over.
THE END

On Monday at 11:49 Barney wrote:

That's beautiful. So it's about how you have to learn to love
yourself before you can love anyone else?

On Monday at 11:50 Martin replied:

No, Barney. It's about a horny hedgehog.
I'm thinking of calling it *It's Hard to Masturbate When You
Have Claws.*

Re: Re: Sam

On Tuesday at 10:12 Elizabeth Sargent wrote:

Dear Martin,

I got a text from Lucy - she's broken up with Sam. I hope she's not too upset, the poor thing. Will ring her when I get out of my meeting.

How was your weekend? Sorry not to call, I was taking Lady to the vet and your dad to the barber, and the weekend just went.

Lots of love,

Mum

PS: What is the 'beard gag'?

On Tuesday at 10:13 Martin wrote:

Hi Lucy

I heard the good news. Hooray! At last.

And it was the beard gag that did it?

Or did you get out an Ordinance Survey and show him where to go?

Lots of Love

Martin

On Tuesday at 10:41 Lucy replied:

Hey Martin,

Yes, I'm free at last. Eventually.

But the beard gag didn't work. Unbelievable, I know.

We were in the pub last night, and the subject came up. OK, I brought it up. And then, of course, I was compelled to do the gag. But all he said was 'Didn't nanny ever tell you personal comments are odious?' And went on with his pint.

He's right, you know.

Lucy

On Tuesday at 10:44 Martin wrote:

The obvious response to that comment would surely be: 'I find you odious, you big patronising beardy Sloane. Take your supposed personality and your hairy back and go and find some traffic to count.' But if that wasn't it, how did you get rid of him? Martin

----

On Tuesday at 11:02 Lucy wrote:

Well, call me crazy, but I decided not to go into a tempest of anger and venom and then subside into self-loathing isolation. I just told him, 'I think we are on different journeys, and this is where our paths have to part. I hope there is no bitterness and that we can still be friends.'

On Tuesday at 11:05 Martin replied:

Have I taught you nothing? And that was that?

On Tuesday at 11:10 Lucy replied:

Not exactly. He responded by saying that he felt I'd been trying to push him away for a long time, and asking why I was afraid of love.

On Tuesday at 11:12 Martin replied:

At which point you hit him with an ashtray?

On Tuesday at 11:14 Lucy replied:

No, at which point I said I thought life was all about learning and helping people to grow, and that I thought we had learned all we were going to learn together and we had to grow apart now.

On Tuesday at 11:16 Martin replied:

At which point he hit you with an ashtray?

On Tuesday at 11:19 Lucy replied:

No. At which point he said he wasn't sure I was strong enough to stand alone yet.
Which was when I hit him with the ashtray. Fucking twat.
But how was your weekend?

On Tuesday at 11:22 Martin replied:

Well, no one's talking to me, because Laura turned out to be keeping an intimate diary of our relationship online and it revealed that I slag people off behind their backs. I don't know why everyone's upset - it's not like I don't slag them off to their faces too.
Anyway, I've been moping around having a long dark weekend of the soul. Welcome to being single. It's completely shit.

On Tuesday at 11:30 Lucy replied:

Yeah, I can see that people might be upset. But don't worry, you're catching up in the poll.

On Tuesday at 11:32 Martin replied:

Oh, you know about that? Thanks for your vote.

On Tuesday at 11:33 Lucy replied:

Yeah, I emailed Sally to say good luck moving house and she mentioned it.

PS: What makes you assume I voted for you?

On Tuesday at 11:35 Martin replied:

Sally's moving house?

On Tuesday at 11:36 Martin wrote:

You email Sally?

On Tuesday at 11:40 Lucy replied:

Well, I assumed you knew that Sally was moving, since you are supposedly friends again. Sally emailed to invite me to the play, and I emailed back, and we've been in touch ever since.

On Tuesday at 11:43 Martin replied:

But she cheated on me!

On Tuesday at 11:55 Lucy replied:

Bloody hell, Martin. 'Rock and Roll Heart'? The sock thing?
I mean, you're my brother and that, but I can kind of see where
she was coming from. You did write a book in which she appears
as a hairbrush. That's pretty mean.

On Tuesday at 12:01 Martin replied:

You didn't think to mention it to me?

On Tuesday at 12:05 Lucy replied:

Surprisingly, I thought you might overreact.

On Tuesday at 12:14 Martin replied:

I'm not overreacting. I'm going to tell Mum Sam dumped you
because you blow sailors for cash and are addicted to smack.
Judas.

On Tuesday at 12:18 Martin wrote:

Hi Mum
Lucy sounds fine. It sounds like it was her idea and all went
reasonably amicably. She may have hit him with an ashtray at
one point, but I'm hoping that was a joke. Did you know she's
in touch with Sally? Who is apparently moving. Not that she

mentioned it to me. I guess David got that job directing Gilbert and Sullivan in Hell.

In response to your queries:

I had a fairly quiet weekend. Everyone seemed to be away. Had a very restful time chilling out in the flat.

The beard gag is a masterpiece of my own devising. Feel free to use it. It's straightforward but effective. You see someone you know who is growing a beard. You point at it and say, 'Beered?' quizzically. They reply, 'Yes.' And you say, 'Yeah, you must have been.' Works a treat, but it doesn't look so good in print...

Lots of Love

Martin

On Tuesday at 14:56 Elizabeth Sargent replied:

What do you do if they just tell you to bugger off?
Sometimes I worry about you, Martin.

Re: Mr Prickles

On Wednesday at 11:24 Barney wrote:

Am I the gnome?

On Wednesday at 11:25 Martin replied:

No, Barney. The gnome never talks. But you could try to be like him if you want...

On Wednesday at 11:26 Barney wrote:

Is Sally the hairbrush?

On Wednesday at 11:27 Martin replied:

Why does everyone think that?

Yes, Barney, you're right. You have intuitively grasped my creative method. I decided to write a book in which my then-girlfriend appears as a hairbrush. Can you see where I got the idea? It's because Sally is made of wood and has thick bristles entirely covering one side of her.

Listen, let me explain something to you about my craft. No one in a book is just someone you know. You take bits and pieces from lots of people and distil them into an imaginary character.

For example, I took your astonishing shallowness, and depicted that as a saucer full of milk.

Do you see what I'm saying?

On Wednesday at 11:29 Barney replied:

I see. So if the milk had been sour and thin-skinned, it would have been a self-portrait?

PS are you the hedgehog?

On Wednesday at 11:31 Martin replied:

Yes, that's right, I am. Because whichever way I turn I'm surrounded by pricks.

The Eyes of Laura Mutton

On Wednesday at 12:01 Martin wrote:

Hi Laura,
Don't suppose you fancy lunch?
Martin

On Wednesday at 12:15 Laura replied:

What is this? Are you planning an ambush? I can see 270 degrees around me you know.

Or am I supposed to go 'Yes' and then you go 'Well have it alone, you bug-eyed freak'?

Laura

On Wednesday at 12:18 Martin replied:

And they all say I'm the paranoid one.

No, I'm not going to ambush you. No one else wants to talk to me 'cos they think I'm a dick for being horrible about you.

But quite apart from that I am genuinely sorry.

On Wednesday at 12:20 Laura replied:

Are you sorry because you were incredibly hurtful (and untruthful), or because you don't want me to write any more stuff about you online?

On Wednesday at 12:24 Martin replied:

Bit of both. Which comments were yours at www.yourtheatre. com? I'll tell you which were mine...

P.S. How am I doing in the poll?

On Wednesday at 12:28 Laura wrote:

Let's put it this way. You've pulled ahead of Gwyn, due to a suspicious number of votes from one 'Johannes Jester'. However, the poll is far from closed.
Good weekend?

On Wednesday at 12:34 Martin replied:

I've had better.

P.S. I'm not taking it back about Acklington Stanley, though. They really do stink.

Part Nine
Pirates

The Stag Night • Captain Claw
Sad News for Acklington Stanley
Words of Warning

Stag Night

On Sunday at 9:31 Elizabeth Sargent wrote:

Hi, Martin,

I didn't want to call too early because I guessed you might be having a 'lie-in' today. How was the stag night? Hope it went OK – no need to give me all the gory details. Lovely weather for the boat trip. I trust you all behaved yourself.

Lots of love,

Mum

On Sunday at 13:45 Martin wrote:

Hullo the mater

It all started so well. We had a bottle of champagne and went along the Thames, and it was a very nice evening. Bit fuzzy about some of the details, but I'll put it together as best I can.

We were all joking away and teasing Chris about tying him to things, setting him up with a ladyboy, jesting about having a hangover the next day, standard pleasantries. It was great to see everyone. Really nice atmosphere.

But as we passed Blackfriars Bridge a sudden and very local fog descended. Strange noises arose all around us, laughter and what sounded like the clink of metal on metal - swords or perhaps loose change.

'Look!' Barney shouted, and he pointed at a pair of tattered black sails suddenly looming out of the fog. Almost before he'd finished speaking he fell, shot through the neck with an antique pistol.

The tour-guide was the next to go, cut from one end to the

other with a rusty cutlass.

Out of the mist more strange figures appeared, some with hooks, some with parrots, some with eyepatches. We were surrounded. Then a tall figure stepped forth, with a polka-dot headscarf and a wooden leg.

'It's your choice, mateys,' he said 'Join me crew or I'll keel-haul ya.'

I stepped forward and shouted, 'I'd rather die than serve you, Captain Claw,' which was when someone bludgeoned me from behind.

At least, that's how I remember it. Certainly explains why my head aches and I have a tattoo of a mermaid on my arm this morning. Then I woke up back at the flat. I thought it was all a dream before I saw the note on the table: 'If you want to see Chris again send 50,000 Gold Doubloons to Captain Claw, c/o Mrs Claw, Spooky Skull Island, the Sea.'

Other than that the evening was fairly uneventful. Tried ringing earlier but I guess you were having lunch in the garden.
Lots of Love
Martin

P.S. I don't really have a tattoo of a mermaid on my arm.
P.P.S. It's on my arse.

On Sunday at 14:32 Emily wrote:

Martin,
Hope you enjoyed the stag. Writing to check Chris didn't get up to any mischief. I will know if you are lying because I have asked more than one person to see if you can keep your stories straight. Mike has already sold you out, and Barney is in the next room tied to a chair and about to crack. So you may as well tell me everything and save your own skin.
Lots of love
Look forward to seeing your tattoo at the Wedding,
        Emily

PS. As long as the tattoo's on your arm, that is.

Dear Stag-Nighters,
Thanks for your candid replies. Your stories check out and
Chris is off the hook.
Wait a minute ...
I thought he was in bed. But there's only a note from someone
called Captain Claw ... Wonder how he holds a pen with
two hooks for hands? (Only Barney noticed that about him.
Surprisingly no one else mentioned it).
If you jokers think I'd pay 50,000 doubloons to get Chris back
you have another think coming.
I can't believe you all collaborated to provide a cover story ...
Lots of love,
     Emily

PS. Chris cracked and told me the whole sordid tale. He would
have made a rubbish pirate.

Good going, Barney. You blew the whole story. We told you to
stick to the facts we all agreed.
Captain Claw has two *eye-patches*, not *hooks*.
Likewise I don't remember anyone mentioning anything about
any *Admiral* Martin. And that bit about you and Mrs Claw was
sheer fantasy.
Still, Emily has only penetrated the *first* cover-story. Hopefully
the robot Chris is going to last till the wedding, and the real
Chris should be on the beach in Buenos Aires with that barmaid
by now ...

On Sunday at 14:51 Mike wrote:

Oops, didn't mean to reply to all with that email. Hope Emily doesn't read it.

Lucky I didn't mention the Polish lap-dancer.

On Sunday at 14:53 Mike wrote:

Oops again. Sorry, Chris.

On Sunday at 15:00 Martin wrote:

I've reread the wedding schedule. What's this? DJ Claw? Hooks for hands and they'd still rather he played than DJ Idiot?

Sweet Thames, Run Softly

All right, Prickles,

How was the stag? Let me make myself very clear: I don't want to read a fucking word about pirates.

Ella

OK OK. Or should that be 'Aye aye, Captain Ella'?

Actually the boat trip was a bit bizarre even without pirates. Although don't tell the others I revealed that there weren't any.

Surprisingly we were the only stag-night boat trip, and we were up topside with two Canadian Goths and their parents, a group of Japanese pensioners, some giggly Italian teenagers, and the tour guide. Of all of them, I think the tour guide knew the least about London. Not just nothing, less than nothing.

I quote: 'All right, everyone speak English?... OK, you won't understand a word I'm saying, but hardly anyone does anyway, so I'll keep going... Sometimes people have a problem understanding my accent. Anyone having any difficulties? [*a forest of hands goes up, including Chris's*]. Well I was born with it and I can't change it now... Right, up ahead we're coming up to London Bridge [*we were approaching Vauxhall Bridge, but anyway*]... The story is some dumb Yank bought that, thinking it was Tower Bridge, which we'll see in a minute [*much laughter from the Canadians and others unaware that they are going under Vauxhall Bridge*]... On your left that's the Houses of Parliament. Not sure what they do in there but they get paid a lot to sit

315

around and do it... And that on your left is the London Eye. It's actually a huge windmill that raises and lowers Tower Bridge [*lots of oohs and aahs*]... Only joking [*some very disappointed looks*]. I tell you if you ever go on a date with a London girl, offer to take her up the London Eye [*some ribaldry at the back of the boat ensues. A boatswain is detached to come up and stand next to us disapprovingly*]... Now, where were we? [*Chris: 'You tell us, mate, you're the tour guide'*]...Oh, here's the Embankment. If you look closely you can see Terry and Julie crossing over the river [*baffled silence*]. Nah, that one never works. You all right love? I wasn't sure whether you were dropping off... This is Blackfriars Bridge, and anyone who had breakfast at the café over there can tell you why that is... Do wave to the people, otherwise they tend to drop bricks on us, or worse. Don't look so worried, sir. It hardly ever happens... On your right now is the Tate Modern. For those of you who don't know English, that's pronounced with a silent "e"... This is the Millennium Bridge, otherwise known as the wobbly bridge, built, as you can tell from the name, over one thousand years ago... Bloody hell, that was a bit close. [*Seagull nearly smacks into guide, to much applause. And not only from us*]... Wave at the people on this bridge now, otherwise they'll think we're being rude [*What they think of us is not clear, as it is a gang of youths who start gobbing down on us. Wisely, several people put up umbrellas or pull up hoods. Barney, unwisely, looks up with his mouth open.*] Little fuckers... Sorry about that, ladies and gentlemen, and please pardon my French... No, love, I don't actually speak French. It was a figure of speech... And coming up now is the famous Tower of London, where the Queen lives. Looks very old, doesn't it? In fact it was built last year...'

There were no pirates, but there was bloody nearly a mutiny.

We had to wait for ages for taxis on to the restaurant, but when we left the Japanese group were still pointing at the Tower of London and bickering, while the Goth teens looked as if they were considering suicide. Even more than Goth teens usually do. Felt bloody proud to be a Londoner after that little display, I can tell you. Didn't tip, and got cussed as a result. Presumably somewhere someone who actually knows and likes London is bound and gagged in a cupboard with a tour guide hat on.

How was the bachelorette thing?

On Sunday at 18:40 Ella replied:

None of your business.

You see, we all agreed to say that. Rather than spending the whole night making up a story about pirates ...

Re: Re: Re: Re: Acklington Stanley

On Monday at 9:36 Laura wrote:

You'll be glad to hear Acklington Stanley broke up. Jez the drummer quit. Or rather, he didn't turn up at the show and when they phoned his folks he'd gone travelling in Bolivia for six months.

I took some of the more offensive stuff off the blog over the weekend. As you'll no doubt have noticed. Mostly the bits about your friends and your hairy hands. Ross threatened to sue. In relation to the bits about his bedroom and speculating where he spends his time, rather than the hairy hands, I should make clear. Oh yeah, he says you need to get milk.

The poll is closed. Sorry to tell you, but you didn't win.

On Monday at 9:40 Martin wrote:

Very surprised to hear that about Jez. I guess they really were a band that was going places.

I'm not at all gloating that the Stanley have split. Not only is it always good for people to express themselves, but in my living room I have a thousand badges saying 'Acklington Stanley Should Shut the Fuck Up' that I had printed and are now entirely useless.

So I guess Gwyn was cheered up by the poll result? These things only mean anything when they're voted for by 'the kids', after all...
Martin

P.S. Sod the hairy hands. Take back the accusation that I am a 'wannabe' hipster. I didn't sit through all those Belgian movies and avant-industrial gigs to be labelled a wannabe. I once had a pee in the ICA next to Steve Mackay. I was showing everyone the splash-stain on my right trainer for weeks. And I know DJ Idiot. So there.

P.P.S. I spotted Victor Lewis-Smith rooting through a bin in Soho once, and wrote in to *Heat*. Although they didn't print it. And come to think of it it may have been a tramp.

On Monday at 9:43 Laura replied:

Have you not seen the poll? There was a late surge in favour of a third option: 'Die alone before considering dating either of these buffoons.' Oh well. Gwyn suspects the interference of disgruntled Fork fans.

On Monday at 9:47 Martin replied:

Well, they're probably right. About the best option for you, I mean, not about wanting to hear more from Fork. How is he taking the break-up?

On Monday at 9:53 Laura replied:

Which one?

On Monday at 9:55 Martin replied:

Sorry?

On Monday at 9:57 Laura replied:

I thought you were referring to my chucking Gwyn out over

the weekend. He's staying with his mum.

On Monday at 10:03 Martin replied:

But surely the poll results weren't in by then?

On Monday at 10:06 Laura replied:

Martin, I don't run my life according to what a bunch of freaks on the internet think. The poll was only meant to be a joke. There was no need to spend the whole week voting under a series of increasingly ludicrous pseudonyms.

On Monday at 10:08 Martin replied:

'Ludicrous pseudonyms'? I think Robusto P. Rickles and D. Umpgwyn would be very upset to hear you say that. So why did you ditch him?

On Monday at 10:13 Laura replied:

Acklington Stanley really were shit, weren't they? And besides, he's fucking fat.

On Monday at 10:15 Martin replied:

I don't suppose this means there's any chance...?

On Monday at 10:18 Laura replied:

I don't think so, baldy.

Kate Staple

On Monday at 11:23 Martin wrote:

I've seen Martin Sergeant and he doesn't look too happy. I take it his holiday with Kate didn't rekindle the old spark?

On Monday at 11:30 Barney replied:

Yeah, it's turned out great. She got back last night and came straight over to mine. Couldn't have planned it better. They spent the whole week in bed.
Barney

On Monday at 11:33 Martin replied:

OK, I've missed something. Reread what you wrote to me, and then send me some sense.

On Monday at 11:40 Barney replied:

I meant exactly what I wrote. They both got food poisoning on the first night. I'm over the moon.
By the way, I've got some pretty blurry memories of the stag. Were we really kidnapped by pirates?

On Monday at 11:41 Barney wrote:

By the way, that was a joke.

On Monday at 11:45 Martin replied:

Barney, sometimes I wish you had been...

Glad to hear Kate was sick. Which is a pretty sick sentiment in itself, but you know what I mean.

Gotta go and jerk Martin around.

On Monday at 11:46 Martin wrote:

Just reread that, and realised it was open to misinterpretation. I meant:

I have to go and ask Martin Sergeant about his holiday. Did he bring back souvenirs, I wonder, or a series of labelled sick-bags?

Wedding

On Friday at 12:32 Sally wrote:

Hi Martin,

Tried my dress on last night and it looks absolutely stunning. Weather forecast looks all right. It should be a really great day.

Enough small talk.

I'm writing to check you're not going to pull anything stupid at the wedding tomorrow. No sock, no drunken rants, no weeping, no dancing on the tables (unless other people are doing it, and even then not during the actual ceremony). OK?

Look forward to seeing you tomorrow,

Sally

PS - Sorry to hear about the poll.

On Friday at 12:40 Martin wrote:

I promise I won't do anything to spoil Chris and Emily's special day. Jesus, what do you take me for?

stops stencilling 'Sally is a cheating hairbrush' on back of dinner jacket

----

On Friday at 12:43 Sally replied:

Uncross your fingers.

On Friday at 12:45 Martin replied:

OK, they're uncrossed. I promise.

On Friday at 12:50 Sally wrote:

And please persuade Barney not to dress as a pirate ...

On Friday at 12:51 Martin replied:

Oh, but he looks so cute.

I wanted him to leap out from behind the altar waving his cutlass when the vicar asks if anyone knows any reason why these two cannot be lawfully joined, then shouting: 'Aarrgh, I know a reason! He's signed up to be my cabin boy in a contract written in blood.'

It would certainly make it a day never to forget.

On Friday at 12:55 Sally replied:

You know of course that Emily's dad is a farmer, and has access to firearms ...

On Friday at 13:01 Martin replied:

I'll have a quiet word with Barney...

A Word of Advice

On Friday at 14:24 Emily wrote:

Hi Martin,

I hope the weather stays nice for tomorrow. We've had the rehearsal and everything went great. The vicar doesn't stutter, the ringbearer has been warned not to eat the ring accidentally (as has Barney), Chris hasn't seen the dress, my uncle hasn't got the best man drunk, our parents aren't engaged in an increasingly elaborate series of misunderstandings, there are no senile but heart-warming aged relatives causing genial chaos, no one has accidentally told my father I'm pregnant (I'm not), and Chris assures me he is neither having last-minute cold feet nor hiding a secret room full of dead ex-wives. According to my extensive research that just about covers everything that can go wrong at a wedding. Except for one thing.

Martin, I swear to God if you fuck things up I will kill you. You will be the first man ever to be beaten to death with a bouquet. Try to pretend for one day that Chris and I are the centre of attention, rather than mere pawns in your own convoluted psychodrama. Try to imagine that when I look back at my wedding day in fifty years' time, I hope my chief memory will not be you wrestling naked with my father, you swinging Sally off on a chandelier, or you falling into the wedding cake. In fact, if I may be blunt, I hope my memories of this momentous day will hardly feature you at all.

Look forward to seeing you.

Love,

      Emily

PS. And I'm holding you personally responsible for Barney as well. If he has as much as an eyepatch or a parrot with him I'll keel-haul you both myself.

PPS. I'm not joking.

Part Ten
The Next Big Thing

The Wedding

The Sunday Times Style
Supplement

Departures • Big Dreams

The End

Re: Wedding

Hi, everyone,

Excuse the group email. This is a quick note to say thanks for coming and making it such a special day for both of us. In particular I'd like to thank Mike for being an excellent best man, Emily would like to thank Ella for making such a lovely bridesmaid, and we'd both like to thank Barney for not coming dressed as a pirate. (Those who know Barney will understand, those who don't have a lot to be grateful for). Look forward to seeing you all when we get back from Sardinia. Be good to each other, and to yourselves.

Mr and Mrs Chris and Emily Fence

On Sunday at 15:01 Mike replied:

Chris and Emily,

It's your honeymoon! Stop bloody emailing and start producing little Fences. So I see Emily has taken your surname?

Congratulations, guys,

Mike

On Sunday at 15:04 Emily replied:

It's under discussion. Christ, you'd think after 26 years of being a farmer's daughter called Emily Lamb I'd be glad to change, but no, I have to fall in love with a Fence ...

On Sunday at 15:06 Barney replied:

Sounds painful! *joke*

On Sunday at 15:08 Ella wrote:

Barney, we have to have a serious talk about this comedy thing. No joke.

Re: Re: Wedding

On Sunday at 15:08 Lucy wrote:

Hi, Martin,

Hope you didn't make a complete flaming tit of yourself at the wedding!

So tell me, without mentioning pirates once:

What was the Bride's dress like? Was she pretty?

What was her mother like?

Did you smooch a bridesmaid?

Did you smooch Sally?

Did ya cry?

Have you seen the papers today?

Who caught the bouquet?

Lots of love,

Lucy

PS: Lady came through all clear at the vet yesterday. In case you were worrying about it during the wedding.

On Sunday at 15:10 Martin replied:

Hi Lucy

Glad to hear about Lady. No, I didn't make a flaming tit of myself. Not completely. In fact, apart from dancing badly and falling over due to slippery shoes, then insisting on showing everyone my shoes and how slippery they were to prove I wasn't drunk, I was perfectly behaved. Although a bit drunk.

Yes, the bride was gorgeous, and from the looks of her mother, she'll age gracefully.

Her dress? It was white. It was a dress. There was a floaty bit and a shiny bit. It was nice.

I was dancing with a bridesmaid when I had the shoe malfunction. You may be surprised to learn there was no smooching.

Didn't smooch Sally either. It was cool. We had a nice chat about her catching the bouquet. Despite a desperate dive to avoid it. I didn't cry, even at that. Although there was something stuck behind one of my contact lenses at one point. Properly. Ah, why would you believe me when no one else does?

I liked the way you snuck the papers in there. Yes, I saw the piece you are referring to.

I'm absolutely ecstatic about it.

Lots of Love

Martin

P.S. To add to my good mood: best man he may have been, but Mike dances like a monkey being teased with a sharp stick. Several sharp sticks, to be exact.

On Sunday at 15:15 Lucy replied:

By 'ecstatic' do you mean 'flabbergasted and planning revenge'? I don't get it. Are we talking about the same thing? I mean the bit in *Style* where they name David Fauntleroy as their 'Next Big Thing'? You're not a teensy bit upset? That's pretty big of you.

On Sunday at 15:17 Martin replied:

My dear Lucy

Let me reassure you I am as bitter and small a person as I have ever been. I am thrilled because being named the *Sunday Times*'s next big thing is as brutal a kiss of death as putting a gun in your mouth and propelling your tonsils through the back of your head. In fact, the latter is almost always preferable, at least in career terms. Remember those posh rockers who were going to be huge? The bloke who was filming a version of *Ulysses* set in downtown Manhattan? That comedy double-act who used to sing at Elton's parties? No? Not even I can remember the names of any of them. Yes, I can, the band was called the Double-Barrels. Being Style's 'Next Big Thing' is the next worst thing to Michael Stipe declaring he likes your band. Concrete Blonde, anyone? Seriously, anyone for Grant Lee Buffalo?

That article is the best news I've heard all year. All at once the world seems to make sense again. And the picture of David is rubbish. Even photographed down a dark stairwell and dressed in black he looks like a good luck troll.

I am utterly jubilant.

Dreams

On Sunday at 15:20 Martin wrote:

Dear Sally
See? I told you I could behave.
I saw the piece on David in the paper. That's great. I'm genuinely pleased for you. So you guys are leaving London?
Lots of Love
Martin

On Sunday at 15:57 Sally wrote:

Hi, Martin,
Yes, it's official. I've got some work at a theatre in Bristol and David's coming with me to finish his new play. It's going to be really exciting. Thanks for saying about the paper, that's sweet of you.
I've been thinking about what you asked me at the wedding, if you still want to know the answer.
Lots of love
Sally

On Sunday at 16:04 Martin replied:

Sally, I think we've left it a bit late to do 'the Timewarp' now.
But leaving London? I know, there's the dirty pigeons, and you can never get a proper taxi on a Saturday night, and it's expensive, and it's full of fakes and freaks, and it's dangerous, and the weather's shit, and the public transport is a joke, and

everyone hates Londoners, and the streets are full of drunks, and there's the constant threat of crime, and no one smiles or says hello, and it's polluted and...

I lost my train of thought. Go on.

On Sunday at 16:08 Sally replied:

I meant when you asked what I'd change about you if there was one thing.

On Sunday at 16:11 Martin replied:

OK, OK, I'm doing something about the hands. Was it that?

On Sunday at 16:14 Sally replied:

Well, there was that. But I thought, actually, people don't ever change. And probably the things that made it so we didn't work out are exactly what someone else will fall in love with you for.

On Sunday at 16:17 Martin replied:

That's so beautiful.
But seriously, you took 24 hours to come up with that?
How was David about the bouquet thing?

On Sunday at 16:25 Sally replied:

Freaked. But tell me honestly, is David really a total wanker?

On Sunday at 16:27 Martin replied:

Well, he can't change if he is.

On Sunday at 16:35 Sally replied:

Maybe people can change. That was quite diplomatic.
So what is next for Martin Sargent?

On Sunday at 16:40 Martin replied:

What, after storming around my room shouting, 'David is a
wanker. David is a wanker'? Again. Possibly one of the reasons
Ross is moving out. I quote: 'Among other things, I want to
experiment living somewhere nice with someone nice.' Trying
not to take it personally.

On Sunday at 16:43 Sally replied:

Or maybe people can't change after all.

On Sunday at 16:45 Martin replied:

Let me tell you, Sally, I have dreams too. Big dreams. I'm not
going to work in that office for ever. Might go travelling for a
year. Maybe do teacher training.

P.S. If you are moving, can I have that book about Jesus back?
My mum keeps asking if I've read it.

Felicitations

Hey Emily

Hope the honeymoon was great. Thanks so much for inviting me to the wedding. It really got me thinking, you know, about love. I guess you heard that Sally's moving down to Bristol. I'm pleased for her. David too, I guess. Did you know it's one of the rainiest cities in Britain? Anyway, I suppose there's not much chance of me and Sally getting back together now. Things are still pretty odd with Laura, too. She's having some time alone. As I guess am I, but she seems to be doing so intentionally. Or at least so her website claims. We aren't speaking that much.

Ross moved out at the weekend. He assures me it's not entirely personal. He's decided to go travelling for a few months, and he's living at home for a bit to save money. He wants to take a break from his job, and I think he's decided that the world isn't quite ready yet for a sitcom that juxtaposes the romantic pratfalls and misadventures of a bunch of eccentric but loveable characters sharing a house in London and a scathing critique of the machinations of global capitalism. He left a bottle of milk, which was sweet of him. I suppose the next couple of months will give me a chance to think about what I really want, and to try and discover who the real Martin Sargent is. Maybe it's time for a change of career. Hope I didn't spoil your big day.

Lots of Love

Martin

Hey Martin,

A change of career sounds exciting. Although Chris and I were talking the other day and we realised we've never been entirely sure what it is that you actually do now.

The honeymoon was amazing, although of course we missed you. Seriously, thanks for coming to the wedding. It was great to have you there, and thank you again for behaving yourself. Although we still haven't got to the bottom of who it was who asked Auntie Claire if she'd ever noticed that her baby girl looks like 'the young Mussolini'. She hadn't in fact noticed, although it certainly does. It's the big bald head, I think, rather than a penchant for giving long dramatic speeches in Italian and making trains run on time. We suspect the culprit was also responsible for persuading Barney to eat the pot-pourri at the hotel. He was very disappointed when Chris told him there's no such thing as 'edible confetti from Japan'.

Yes, I suppose it is unlikely you'll get back with Sally now. Although I can't say I ever thought it was hugely likely. To be perfectly honest neither Chris nor I could quite work out what she saw in you. I had a theory, but Ella dismissed it. 'Rock and Roll Heart' is rubbish. And besides, Chris has it on tape. For obvious reasons.

Are you sure you want to discover the real Martin Sargent? Oh, and of course you won't be entirely alone ...

Emily X

On Friday at 11:20 Martin replied:

Aargh, so you know about that. Yeah, I had a sudden and surprising access of affection for Barney during the reception, and I knew he wanted to change where he was living. I almost instantly regretted it, of course. I think I realised what I'd done when he said 'And I can set my decks up in the living room.' No, it was probably a little later, when he suggested we give one day

338

each week a costumed theme. Well, I suppose I did always want a pet when I was a kid. I must remember to keep the lid down on the loo. On the plus side, I've always wanted to meet Kate Staple. I hear such astonishing things about her.
Martin

P.S. Now I think of it, I was wondering if you could let me have Felicity's number? The cute bridesmaid? We were dancing to ABC and I think I was getting the look of love from her a bit. Until I fell on my arse.

On Friday at 11:32 Emily replied:

Ah, Martin, maybe one day you'll find true love.

Heavens above! It may indeed have been the look of love that Felicity was giving you, although she did tell me later she was having trouble with a contact lens (and by the way no one was fooled by your pathetic excuse for blubbing all the way through the readings). She also commented that she's never seen dancing like yours before. Take that as you will. She didn't tell me not to give you her number, so that's a pretty promising start by your standards. But seriously, mate, have you ever thought of just getting a hobby?

Or is the message of all this that while lovers come and go, mates last for ever?

I'll text you Felicity's number, if you really want it. But before I do, I should probably check you know that Felicity is sixteen years old. How about I give you her number and you call her in a few years' time when the age difference is a little more appropriate?

Furthermore, I'm a little surprised that you would be interested in following that up, considering the cosy little tête-à-tête you and Ella were having at the reception. What was that all about?

On Friday at 11:35 Martin replied:

Hey Emily

Thanks for letting me know about Felicity. It probably would
have been kinder to mention her age before you got my hopes
up, but anyway... I think on reflection I'll leave it. I'm always
available to babysit, though. Not in a creepy way. Crikey,
she's very well-developed for sixteen. I simply mean that as a
compliment.

Now you mention it, I did have a fairly long chat with Ella.
To be honest I'm pretty hazy on most of the details, but I do
seem to recall suggesting that if we're both still single at thirty
we should get married, for the presents. It seemed like a pretty
good idea at the time. That said, I believe we also agreed to go
halves on a racehorse.

On Friday at 11:40 Emily replied:

Thirty? I hate to point it out, but that doesn't leave you much
wiggle-room ...

PS. 'Well-developed'? Stop digging, Martin. I know exactly
how you mean that.

On Friday at 11:43 Martin replied:

Thanks for the crack about my age. Jeez, Emily, I'm only 25.
Even if my hairline does seem to be taking early retirement.

Now, I know this is a little premature, but if you and Chris
are planning on having kids, I'm very much available for
godfathering duties. No pressure, but I thought I'd get in there
with the offer before Mike does.

Oh, since you asked: the message I'm drawing from the past
couple of months is this: if you systematically make a prick of
yourself, you end up living with an idiot. By the way, Barney

wanted me to ask you (and Chris) to dinner on Tuesday. We hope you can come.

It's Pirates Night.

Re: Just a Pint

On Friday at 12:00 Ella wrote:

Hallo, Sargent
How are you doing? Still feel a little weepy?

On Friday at 12:03 Martin replied:

How many times? I. Had. Something. In. My. Eye.

On Friday at 12:04 Ella replied:

Yes, I know that. A load of tears. Anyway, enough badinage.
What about this pint you keep promising me? How are you fixed
for this evening?

On Friday at 12:07 Martin replied:

Tonight I'm free. And God knows I'll be ready for a drink by
then. So that sounds perfect.

On Friday at 12:13 Ella replied:

Great. I assume Felicity has homework to do.

On Friday at 12:15 Martin replied:

Emily had stern words for me on the topic of Felicity. I swear I never would have guessed her age. I've decided not to pursue it any further, and I'm very much regretting having used my work computer to google her earlier in the week.

On Friday at 12:18 Ella replied:

To clear the air, I take it you've forgotten our conversation at the reception.

On Friday at 12:21 Martin replied:

I'm afraid I'm drawing a total blank on it.

On Friday at 12:25 Ella replied:

Me too. I'm glad we understand one another. See you later on. I'll give you a ring when I've decided where we're going.

On Friday at 12:31 Martin replied:

Can I make a suggestion? There's a haunted pub in Newgate Street I've always wanted to check out. Apparently there's a grey monk who lurks around the men's loos and moans ominously. They've also got a good range of regional ales, I'm told.

P.S. I assume that among the things we aren't remembering is your promise to marry me in five years? For the presents, obviously.
P.P.S. Not that I necessarily think there's anything wrong with having a five-year plan...

Thanks for your suggestion, Sargent. I think you've illustrated exactly why I'll be the one choosing the venue.

PS Bingo. To clarify the terms of our pact, it only holds if no one better comes along before then. And that's a way scarier thought than a haunted toilet. Looking on the bright side, the world may have ended before then.

I'd also like to remind you that thirty was a compromise figure: you suggested right away, I said sixty. Not that I can remember actually agreeing to this deal. Verbal contract, mate. It's not worth the paper it's written on.

PPS Now I think about it, though, I do recall you repeatedly requesting 'a go' wearing my bridesmaid's dress …

PPPS What the hell? Five-year plan? You're taking your love-life advice from Josef Stalin now?

What can I say? Mass-murdering tyrant he may have been, but who else's advice am I going to take? Barney's? He mentioned to me the other day that sometimes he likes to practise DJing in the nude. But then I expect you knew that. As if I needed another reason to dread living with him. I still can't figure out what you saw in the guy. However, since his decks are set up in our living room, I may be about to find out.

By the way, if you ever mention the dress thing in public I solemnly swear I'm going to hold you to our little agreement. Verbal contract or no.

See you later, Ms Tvertko.

P.S. Just a thought, but wouldn't it be funny if after all this we ended up together?

On Friday at 12:45 Ella replied:

Don't count your chickens, Sargent. It's amazing how much
more appealing the thought of ending up with you makes the
prospect of dying alone. No offence. I should also mention I'm
having serious second thoughts about the racehorse.

On Friday at 12:47 Martin replied:

Oh, Ella, always trying to get round me with your sweet-talk.
I think we both know I wasn't the only one with something in
my eye at the wedding. Could it be that underneath that frosty
façade, a tender heart waits to be thawed?

On Friday at 12:50 Ella replied:

You're completely right. Martin, it's always been you. Oh how
long these nights have been ...
Wouldn't that be a happy ending to your sad little tale, if it were
true? Unfortunately, though, it's not. People often seem to assume
that because I seem cold and sarcastic, I have a problem expressing
how I really feel. Let me warn you right know that would be a
grievous mistake to make. If I was getting a bit dewy-eyed, it was
because those stupid bridesmaid's shoes were killing my feet. Actually,
my heart is considerably frostier than my façade would suggest.
On the other hand, there's something about a man dressed as
a pirate ...

On Friday at 12:52 Martin wrote:

Hey Barney
This may sound weird, but I'm going to need to borrow a
bandanna ...

Teaching all the children to read

Concentrated language encounter techniques

RICHARD WALKER,
SAOWALAK RATTANAVICH AND
JOHN W. OLLER, Jr

Open University Press
Buckingham · Philadelphia

Open University Press
Celtic Court
22 Ballmoor
Buckingham
MK18 1XW

and
1900 Frost Road, Suite 101
Bristol, PA 19007, USA

First Published 1992

A catalogue record of this book is available
from the British Library

Library of Congress Cataloging-in-Publication Data

Walker, Richard, 1925–
    Teaching all the children to read : concentrated language
encounter techniques / Richard Walker, Saowalak Rattanavich & John
Oller.
        p.   cm. — (Rethinking reading)
    Includes index.
    ISBN 0–335–15729–7   ISBN 0–335–15728–9 (pbk.)
    1. Reading (Elementary)—Developing countries.   2. Literacy—
Developing countries.   3. Classroom management—Developing
countries.   I. Rattanavich, Saowalak, 1951–   .   II. Oller, John W.
III. Title.   IV. Series.
LB1573.W313   1992
372.4′1—dc20   92–8566
                                                                      CIP

Typeset by Inforum, Rowlands Castle, Hants
Printed in Great Britain by St Edmundsbury Press,
Bury St Edmunds, Suffolk

Contents

Acknowledgements

The authors of this book find themselves with two roles. The first is as spokespersons for those who developed what has come to be known as the approach to teaching language and literacy. The second is as recorders for the large and varied group of people in Thailand who, recognizing its potential, embraced the large-scale application of that approach in a nationwide programme.

Foremost among the former is Brian Gray, now senior lecturer in education at the University of Canberra, Australia. Brian was director of the curriculum project, at Traeger Park School, in which the concentrated language encounter (CLE) methodology was developed. He has maintained contact with the work in Thailand by contributing to the training of key personnel; and the Thai project team regard him as a good friend. We know, also, that Brian and those who worked with him at the Traeger Park School would want us to pay tribute to the late Graeme Cooper, former principal of that school. Graeme was the rock on which the Traeger Park CLE project was founded. He was closely involved with Thai key personnel whom he extended hospitality to in Darwin just a few weeks before his untimely death in late 1990.

Others who contributed to the training of key personnel for the Thai CLE work, both in Thailand and Australia, and thereby influenced the directions in which that work developed, were Professor Frances Christie of the University of the Northern Territory, and Dr Nea Stewart-Dore and Dr Brendan Bartlett, of the Brisbane College of Advanced Education (now Griffith University), Australia. The role played by Dr John Chapman, of the Open University, UK, is noted within the pages of this book.

Above all, we should like to acknowledge the work of those from the Srinakharinwirot University, from the Thai Ministry of Education, and the Rotarians of Thailand who took the CLE methodology and from it built a complete programme for primary schools, developed a teacher-training system, and set up the basis from which to disseminate CLE language teaching techniques, nationwide and abroad. No acknowledgement that we could make would adequately reflect our admiration for the vision, the courage and the energy of Dr Chatri Muangnapoe, Rector of the Srinakharinwirot University, Dr Aree Sanhahawee, past principal of the Demonstration School at Prasarnmit Campus of Srinakharinwirot University, or of Associate Professors Hearthai Tandjong and Chari Suvathi who played continuing direct roles in book development, teacher training and assessment.

Much of what is recounted in this book could never have occurred without the cooperation and encouragement of Dr Komel Phuprasert, of the Office of National Primary Education, Ministry of Education in Thailand, and of Mr Phanom Keokamnerd, a former senior officer of that ministry.

Special acknowledgement is due to Rotary District Governor Nominee Mr Noraseth Pathmanand, the Rotary Chairman of the project over its full five years, to Past Rotary Governor Krisda Arunvongse Na Ayuthaya, who began the work and who, with Rotary Director Bhichai Rattakul and Past Governors Praphan Hutasingh and Mom Rachawongsee Ophas Kanchanavijaya, has maintained a special interest throughout.

It is with warmth and affection that we acknowledge the efforts of close friends and colleagues in Thailand who could truly be said to have written this book, because they did what is recorded within it. Among them are Rotarians Thawatchai Sutibongkot, Preecha Klinkaeo, Chaiyasit Kositapai, Rudi Areesorn, Vinai Sachdev and Howard Mirkin. Others who made outstanding contributions to this work include members of the Ministry of Education team, Praphapan Nil-aroon, Surat Jatakul, Aksorn Praserd, Sa-Ard Sasitharamas and Sanan Meekharnmark.

We would especially like to thank Susan Pike, of SCECGS School, Sydney, for her contribution to the CLE English-language project and for her hospitality to the Thai author in Australia during the writing of this book. Finally, we should like to acknowledge the long and enduring involvement of Fay Walker. Whether it was in Thailand or Australia, in visiting schools or in caring for visitors from Thailand, she was always there to help and support.

CHAPTER 1

General introduction

RICHARD WALKER

Introduction

The general expectation is that people who have had six or more years of formal education can read and write; but that is far from the case. Even in countries that have had universal education for generations there are substantial numbers of illiterates[1], and everywhere a worrying number of children leave school each year with reading difficulties that will adversely affect their future. Actual failure rates vary, of course, but figures above 50 per cent are not uncommon in some places.

What people need to be able to read and write, if they are to lead satisfying and satisfactory lives, also varies from place to place. But it is not unrealistic to expect that the great majority of students will finish their school years with the literacy skills they need as they enter adult life. That is surely no more unreasonable than to expect children to learn to speak their language well enough to cope with everyday demands, before they begin school at the age of five or six years. Indeed, one would be hard-put to make the case that the latter is the easier task. However, the failure rate in learning to speak a language at home, is much lower than in learning to read and write at school.

This book is about developing school programmes that will enable virtually all children to learn to read and write. We believe that all schools, everywhere, can and should do that for all its students, whatever their language background or their prior experience with literacy activities.

This first chapter begins with a review of some of the reasons put forward to account for high literacy failure rates in schools. Then it presents glimpses of Mary, a child who would normally fail to learn to read, and whose failure would be attributed to mistaken reasons. Finally, it introduces *concentrated language encounter* (CLE) – literacy teaching techniques that have enabled Mary and a wide range of other children, who faced almost inevitable failure, to succeed in school.

Reasons why many children fail to learn to read

Children from actively literate families have developed all or most of the essential understandings about reading and writing from literacy experiences during their early childhood – many of them to the extent that they have already begun to read before they come to school (Smith and Johnson, 1976: 28). On the other hand, those who begin school with little or no prior experience of written language are faced with an unfamiliar language code. They still have in front of them the full task of puzzling out its nature, its various forms and conventions, and its uses and usefulness. Researchers such as Wells (1981) have shown that these latter children are the more likely to fail to learn to read and write.

High failure rates in learning to read are also found among minority populations, in which case linguistic and other cultural factors are given as causes of failure, as well as literacy background. Children for whom the language of instruction is a second language or second dialect are seen as having the doubly difficulty task of learning to participate in the spoken as well as the written discourse of the classroom.

As is discussed in Chapter 6, multiple difficulties of that kind exist among rural and city slum populations in many developing countries.

It has even been suggested that failure to learn to read and write is merely inabilty 'to meet their parents' or teachers' expectations in reading' (Smith and Johnson, 1976: 33). The view is that a substantial proportion of school reading failures should be accepted because there will always be students who perform at worse than average level. Reading is seen as 'an intellectual activity' that less able children will not be able to cope with until they reach some predetermined stage of intellectual growth. Teachers are urged to use programmes that 'postpone actual reading activities and move children more slowly through the developmental reading process' (Smith and Johnson, 1976: 38). We are reminded of parents who won't let their children enter the water until they can swim.

Whether it be 15 per cent of the population of an industrialized country, a larger proportion of a minority group, or an even larger proportion of the children who live in a remote region of a developing country, it is unacceptable to use family or language background to explain away a high failure rate. Rather, the known likelihood of failure should enliven a search for ways of preventing it.

The authors believe that the basic reasons why so many school children fail to learn to read have more to do with what goes on in schools than

with what the children bring to school. Certainly, there are pupil characteristics that correlate with failure in the kinds of literacy teaching that
currently go on in schools but that ceases to exist when appropriate
changes are made to the school context for learning and teaching. School
learning environments can be created that suit the full range of students,
and not just those whose family backgrounds fit them for what currently
goes on in schools.

The CLE techniques that are described in this book do indeed suit a
much wider range of children than do conventional programmes, and the
authors believe that they offer much to the theory and practice of literacy
teaching.

'Mary', a child who is destined to fail

The fundamental principles of CLE language/literacy teaching were
worked out in a search for solutions to gross failure among Aboriginal
students at Traeger Park School, in the Northern Territory of Australia
(Gray, 1983).

Mary was a beginning student at that school and the following transcripts reveal the contrast between her language behaviour in the kind of
teacher–child language interaction that normally goes on in schools and in
other kinds of contexts, including the kind of classroom interaction that
marks CLE teaching. The transcripts are from recordings of Mary and her
classmates that were made in a language research project, soon after they
began school (Walker, 1981).

Mary is an accomplished linguist in that she speaks a dialect of English
as well as an Aboriginal first language. In English, she can understand what
is said to her and make herself understood but she will almost inevitably fail
in school and her teachers will attribute her failure mainly to inability to
communicate with her in English.

Transcript A is of an interaction between Mary and her classroom
teacher. Mary and her friend Jane are sitting side by side on the classroom
floor, where they have been making things out of coloured rods and 'fit on'
wooden shapes, in a free activity period at the beginning of a school day.

Transcript A

Teacher: What are you making Mary? (No response)
What are you making? (No response)
Very nice (examining Mary's construction).
What's this part? Is that pink? (Mary shakes her head)
No? What is it? (No response) Blue?

Mary: Yeah.

Teacher: Mm. It's blue. What's this one here?
Mary: Blue.
Teacher: Good. That's blue. What's this one? Yellow? (Mary nods her head)
  Can you see another yellow one? (Mary points) Very good.
  (This procedure is repeated for other colours)
  What are you doing now, Mary? (No response) What are you
  doing love? (No response) Are you putting it together? Build-
  ing something? (No response. Mary goes on working)
Mary: (As she works) Making chair.
Teacher: Making a chair? Oh? Who's the chair for?
Mary: Sitting down.
Teacher: For sitting down? Oh. Who's going to sit on it? (No response) Is
  Jane going to sit on the chair or you? (No response) Who's
  going to sit on it?
Mary: Jane.

In that conversation, a teacher is working hard to establish communication with Mary. She tries to teach the names for objects and colours, on
the basis of Mary's own activity, or to test whether Mary already has those
concepts and the English labels for them.

The teacher's first try at a language exchange requires Mary only to
name the object she has been making but Mary does not respond even to a
second trial of that probe. The teacher tries to establish a better interper-
sonal relationship by praising the chair that Mary has built. She then tries
to make her next question a more specific one – the colour of a part of the
chair. The demand on Mary is made as light as possible by naming the
colour and asking only for affirmation or negation. Mary replies with a
shake of her head and on that basis, the teacher tries, more ambitiously, to
get Mary to supply the name of the colour. That fails, and the teacher goes
back to requiring only affirmation or negation.

She now makes some progress because Mary uses her voice for the first
time, to say 'Yeah' and even says the word 'blue' after the teacher has used
it. The teacher then goes back to requiring affirmation only and pointing
out other pieces of the same colour.

Apparently encouraged by this cooperative turn-taking by Mary, the
teacher then goes back to her original gambit of asking what Mary is doing
but that fails entirely, even when the question is reframed to require only
affirmation or negation.

The teacher seems to think that Mary's problem may lie in inability to
understand the verb she is using. Notice that she uses 'making', 'doing',
'putting together', and 'building' for the one process, in her various attempts to elicit a response. Mary understood her first try, as far as termino-
logy was concerned, because a little later, she volunteered 'making chair'.

The picture is of a teacher fighting hard for a basis for language communication with Mary, but being forced to a lower and lower level of demand. The communication she actually achieved resembles that with a child who has virtually no English. Mary seems either unable or unwilling to communicate on a level of complexity above that of the simplest of concepts and language labels.

But Transcript B, which is a record of playground interaction on the same day, reveals that Mary can operate at a level of English language usage far above what she has revealed to the teacher. Mary is sharing a double push-pull swing with Sue. The two girls are sitting on the same seat, one behind the other, with Mary in front and in control of the push-pull bars. Two other girls are sharing a similar swing nearby, and a fifth is dancing around the swings, awaiting a turn.

Transcript B

Mary: On again. On here again. Me push.

(To Sue) Look, you push me. You push.

(To the other pair of girls) We'll go really fast like you.

(To Sue) Like this, eh?

Hey, Marilyn fall down and . . . (Telling the fifth girl to repeat the trick she's just done).

Move back Sue (Mary is slipping off the front of the seat). No. You, no. Hey Sue (annoyed because Sue slipped along the seat). I'll take you really fast. Sue, you thing (annoyed that Sue is wriggling around).

(Both get off the swing). Me turn. Jane and me and Jane now. Me and Jane now. You and me.

(To the other girls) You and Sue at the back. Jane, other side, other side.

In this playground episode, Mary is garrulous and dominant to the extent that no one else has a turn to speak. More significantly, her dominance of the others is achieved and maintained through using English. Clearly, she can use English confidently and powerfully in this kind of context.

At the end of the day, in free classroom time before leaving for home, Mary is playing with large coloured beads on the floor, and we get some additional insights into Mary's ability to interact in English.

Transcript C

Mary: The colours, the colours, colours. (Bill, a classmate, moves over to her and annoys her) I'll tell on you.

Vera: Bill Brown, leave her alone.

Mary: (To Bill) I'll tell on you. (Calling softly, as a threat to Bill) Mrs
Peters! I'll tell on you, Bill. You're making troubles. You're making
troubles, not me. (Continues playing) All the colours, all the
colours.

From Transcript C, we learn that Mary is sufficiently aware of the
dynamics of classroom control to use the teacher's authority as a threat and
to attribute blame for a breach of behavioural requirements. Finally, we are
struck with Mary's almost poetic use of language to express her feelings
about the colours of the beads and it becomes evident, too, that her use of
English is spontaneous and effortless, as she works away alone in the
classroom.

Other occasions were recorded of Mary's teachers making very earnest
attempts to draw Mary into normal teacher–pupil instructional dialogue
but every time, by perfectly logical steps, they fell into dialogue of the
adult–infant type, in which the adult provides the answer that is required
from the child. The teachers received no indication that Mary would ever
participate in classroom discourse in which meaning is negotiated through
language.

In all the transcripts, Mary's teachers seem to be unaware that Mary
can use English at a higher level of functioning. They act always as if Mary is
almost without language. On her part, Mary is unwilling to take risks. She
won't respond to questions put to her by a teacher unless the answer has
already been supplied.

It seems obvious that these teachers will eventually accept Mary's non-
participation, except for sporadic efforts to communicate with her at a level
of sophistication well below that used with non-Aboriginal children. Mary is
well on the way to a permanent role of a non-participant in most of what
goes on in the classroom. She can take a very active role in the games that
are played outside but she cannot play the one that is being played in the
classroom.

But what happens if that classroom game is changed? Transcript D was
recorded on the next morning but it is from a 'concentrated language
encounter' session – one of the first that was devised at Traeger Park
School to bring Aboriginal children into classroom learning. For about the
third time, the children are making toast together in a corner of the school
language unit.

Transcript D

Bill: Can I put some butter?
Teacher: We have to wait first until the toaster is ready to pop up. What
colour do you think the bread will be when it pops up? What
colour?

Bill:	Brown.
Mary:	Brown.
Teacher:	Brown. That's right.
Mary:	It pop up.
Sally:	I can smell it now.
Teacher:	(To the other children) Can you smell it?
Mary:	(Enjoying the smell of toast) Hey!
Teacher:	Does it make you feel hungry, Mary?
Mary:	(Nods her head) My mother got peanut butter.
Teacher:	Your mother's got peanut butter, has she?
Bill:	We got some peanut butter home.
Teacher:	You've got peanut butter at home too?
Bill:	Yeah, and one of these.
Teacher:	And a toaster.
Mary:	And one of these.
Teacher:	(To Mary) What's that called? (Interrupted by the toaster popping) Oh it's popped up.
Mary:	Black now. It's black.
Teacher:	D'you think it's burnt?
Mary:	Yeah.
Teacher:	I think it's probably all right.
Mary:	(Excited) It's black. Black. It's black.
Teacher:	Dinner time. Yes. It's dinner time.
Mary:	Dinner time. Dinner time.
Teacher:	Take the toast out of the toaster now, Bill. (Bill does so) What are we going to do now, Mary?
Mary:	Clean it.
Teacher:	(Surprised) We're going to clean it?
Mary:	(Demonstrating) This way.
Sally:	Scrape it. Scrape it.
Teacher:	Why do we have to scrape it?
Mary:	It's yucky!
Sally:	With the knife.
Teacher:	No, that's all right! (Thinks the toast doesn't need scraping) Then what do you have to do? What are we going to put on it now?
Mary:	Peanut butter.
Teacher:	What are we going to put on it before we put peanut butter?
Mary:	Butter.
Teacher:	Good girl! Come on, then, you spread this – a nice piece of toast. Bill's going to put some butter on the other slice of toast.
Mary:	This one?

Teacher: Yes, good girl! Do you help your mother to butter the toast at home, Mary?

Mary: (Nods)

Teacher: What's happening to the butter?

Lynette: It'll melt.

Teacher: It's melting. That's right, because the toast is hot. This (the butter container) feels nice and cold.

Lynette: I take it. I take it. (Picks up the butter container to feel it)

Teacher: The toast melts the butter.

Mary: It's melting. Look there. It's melting. Look.

Lynette: Mine melting too. (Looking at Mary's toast)

Note how markedly different Mary's language participation is here from what it was in Transcript A, although the same teacher and the same children are involved, and the transcripts were recorded on consecutive days. Not only does Mary now respond confidently to teacher questions, she also initiates interaction. Even more usefully, she is prepared to adopt and argue a point of view about whether or not the toast should be 'scraped'. There is a much more substantive communicative basis for teaching Mary than in Transcript A.

To those who worked with Mary, the reasons for the change gradually became clear. Because she has shared in toast-making on previous mornings, she is familiar with it: the names of things, what is done with them, and the sequence in which things are done.

She also knows what will be demanded of her in the role of toast-maker, because she's seen others take turns as central participants. Finally, she has realized that all the language demands made on her in this session will be based on her role in the toast-making.

In other words, Mary can interpret all that is said and done within the context of toast-making, herself as toast-maker, and the teacher as organizer/supervisor of that activity. And she has no trouble relating language elements and structures to reality, because the toast-making process and the related language have both been repeatedly modelled, one along with the other.

It is interesting to note, too, that Mary makes a dialectal switch during this session. When she volunteers her first pieces of information with 'It pop up' and 'My mother got peanut butter', she uses her 'playground' dialect of English. Those utterances are accepted by the teacher, but Mary is sensitive to dialect change and switches to 'It's black' after the teacher says 'It's popped up' and she continues in the teacher's dialect with 'It's yucky' and 'It's melting'. She does not need to be taught those standard structures – once a variant has been modelled for meaning and function, she can use it for similar purposes. In these circumstances, modelling is effective because the model has full contextual support.

There seems to be no other explanation for the change, from Transcript A to Transcript D, other than differences between concentrated language encounter sessions and 'normal' classroom contexts.

As Gray states, most of the behaviours that cause children like Mary to be labelled as being in some way different from the majority,

> result largely from confusion about what is required from them in the learning task, their low self-esteem as learners, and experiences of the world that do not lead them to the preconceptions necessary for learning . . . in the manner often taught in schools. (Gray, 1980, 1:3)

They cannot join in classroom learning/teaching processes because they just do not understand what is going on or why.

Whether in the developed or developing world, there are children like Mary wherever there are schools. They may not be Aboriginal, and they may not even be in the minority – one has only to visit schools in almost any developing country to realize that this phenomenon of exclusion from classroom learning exists on a gigantic scale.

With children who, like Mary, speak a first language that differs from the language of instruction, a particularly effective recipe for wholesale failure is to allow only teacher-directed language interaction within the classroom, and to 'cover' only the language elements and structures that are set down in some text book, to be drilled. And in some countries, that is the case across whole regions. Literacy teaching in those places begins with the alphabet, phonic drills, individual words and grammatical rules, and reading and writing for useful purposes is postponed. A whole generation of children find themselves expected to engage, for month after month, in puzzling activities that have no apparent purpose – and before long, they give up trying.

Direct teaching of language also discourages students from learning outside the formal lessons – they learn to learn only when and as directed by a teacher. When each student in a class of thirty or forty has only a few turns in the teacher-directed interaction each day, the quantity and scope of their language experience in school is minimal.

The origins of CLE techniques of teaching

Mary was one of the first group of Aboriginal children to benefit from CLE techniques for literacy teaching. Gray and his colleagues at Traeger Park School worked out classroom learning/teaching contexts that would involve all of a group of children in what was going on, and, within that context, they developed activities from which students learnt to read, write and talk in English, while gaining non-language skills and knowledge that had worthwhile applications in real life.

Over a period of some five years, Gray and his colleagues developed a programme for the early grades of the school in which virtually all the students who attended with anything like reasonable regularity became enthusiastic readers and writers – and there was marked improvement in school attendance.

CLE techniques were introduced into Thailand in 1984 from the Brisbane College of Advanced Education (Rattanavich and Walker, 1990). Chapter 6 relates how those techniques were refined and extended to develop a Thai-language programme and implement it in a large number of primary schools in rural provinces of north-east Thailand.

The programme was next implemented in demonstration schools in the southern border provinces of Thailand, where the mother tongue is a Malaysian dialect, and in the northern provinces, where different hill-tribe languages and dialects are spoken. Then, in 1990, the Thai Ministry of Education announced the adoption of CLE language and literacy teaching principles nationwide, as part of the National Plan for 1992–96.

During 1991, CLE demonstration schools were set up in the remaining parts of the nation, in preparation for implementing the 1992–96 National Plan.

CLE techniques were also taken from Thailand to the Indian subcontinent, where a demonstration programme was set up near Hugli, in India and a successful programme in the Bangla language was piloted in several schools near Dhaka, Bangladesh.

Finally, the movement of CLE techniques from language to language came back to the language in which it began, when work commenced, in Thailand, on a CLE programme for teaching English as a second language.

Conclusion

CLE literacy teaching techniques have proved to be effective in involving all children in learning to read, not just those whose home and cultural backgrounds suit the programmes and teaching techniques that are currently being used in schools. And on the basis of their experience with eradicating gross literacy failure rates in a range of educationally difficult circumstances, the authors contend that the problem lies not so much with the family and ethnic background of the children as with the school literacy programme, and, in particular, with the dynamics of classroom interaction.

Chapter 2 presents a description of CLE teaching techniques in Thai primary schools, Chapter 3 is directed at helping readers to visualize how CLE teachers and their students operate within their classrooms, and Chapter 4 describes the process of developing a CLE literacy programme for primary schools.

Chapters 5 and 6 are an account by Dr John Oller Jr of literacy testing. After reviewing the theoretical position that all three authors agree is basic to learning, teaching and testing literacy, Oller states, in Chapter 5, the basic principles that should be followed in testing. Then, in Chapter 6, he exemplifies those principles, and provides guidelines for a testing programme in literacy.

In view of the imperative need for a new approach to teaching literacy that exists in developing countries that are faced with mass literacy problems, Chapter 6 explains the strategies by which large-scale changes in literacy teaching policy and practice have been achieved in one developing country – Thailand.

In Chapter 7, Richard Walker reflects on some of the issues and insights that arise from what has been presented in the book, and on their significance in understanding what is involved in learning and teaching literacy.

Notes

1. For Australia, see Wickert (1989).

Concentrated language encounter teaching techniques

SAOWALAK RATTANAVICH

Introduction

The term 'concentrated language encounters' has been borrowed from Courtney Cazden, who made the point (Cazden, 1977) that children learn language mainly through encounters with others in which the children concentrate intensely on making themselves understood. As he worked with Aboriginal students at Traeger Park School, Gray (1983) noted that the most successful teaching sessions were those in which students were put in situations where they were doing interesting and useful things, but where they had to confront challenging language tasks to achieve those things. This feature underlies all CLE programmes.

A second underlying feature of CLE teaching is 'scaffolding'. The more that what is said relates to and is supported by the context – the other things that are happening, the actions, the gestures and tone of voice of the speakers, and what previous experience the listener has had with all of these – the easier it is to understand what is being said. In the case of language learning, the easier it will be to participate in the language inter-action, and so to learn from it. This applies also to written language, and learning written language, but in this case there can be an additional component to scaffolding, if the learners can already speak the language, in spoken discourse that is related to or even identical to the written discourse. As Oller states in Chapter 5,

> the already established connection between utterances in a particular lan-guage, and the facts of experience . . . will similarly help the pre-literate child to begin to become literate. (p. 58–9)

This chapter presents a description of CLE teaching separately for three 'stages' of primary schooling – the lower, the middle and the upper grades.

Yet, language learning does not occur in distinct stages – precursors of what becomes predominant in later years are present at earlier stages. So the three stages of the programme are not meant to be rigidly compart-mentalized and students who are rapid learners sometimes engage in learning activities that others do not encounter until a later stage of the programme.

Stage 1 of the programme: The lower primary school grades

The overall teaching objective for Stage 1 of a CLE programme is for beginning school students to become enthusiastic readers and writers. At the end of Stage 1, they should be able to read various types of simple texts, and to recall and talk about what is contained in the texts that they read. They should be able to write several kinds of brief texts, observing the conventions of written language. In progressing to that stage, they will have learned to identify, write and spell hundreds of words from their reading and writing, and to bring effective strategies to bear in recognizing and writing words that they have not previously encountered.

A Stage 1 CLE programme usually covers two or three years, depend-ing on whether or not it is used in preschool or kindergarten classes. The programme for each school year is organized into units, each one extend-ing over a number of weeks. For reasons that will be explained later in this chapter, the actual number of units that are covered in a year will vary from class to class, but most Stage 1 classes in Thailand cover ten to fifteen units in a school year.

Within each Stage 1 programme unit, the teacher and students work through five 'phases', in a fixed sequence. Because there are two kinds of Stage 1 programme units, there are two types of Stage 1 teaching sequence, both of which are illustrated in Fig. 2.1. 'Text-based' units start with the shared reading of a starter book and 'activity-based' units begin with a shared experience of some other kind, such as the toast-making session of Mary's Transcript C in Chapter 1.

Other activities in the north-east Thailand programme are making a paper hat, learning to preserve beans, and breeding fish. In published CLE programmes, a 'How To' (procedure genre, see pp. 46–9, where genre is explained in detail) starter book is provided for some activity-based units but the starter book is only a reference book, and a unit might just as easily begin with a practical demonstration by the teacher or a visiting expert.

As can be seen from Fig. 2.1, Phases 3, 4 and 5 are similar for both kinds of programme units.

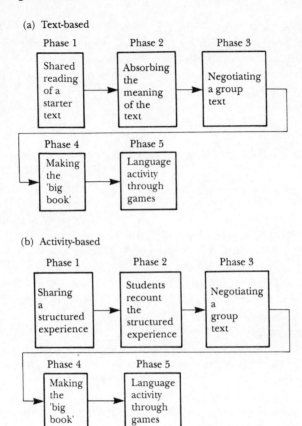

Figure 2.1: Types of Stage 1 CLE units

Phase 1 of an activity-based unit: sharing the experience

In Phase 1 of activity-based units, the teacher demonstrates an activity such as making bread or growing some kind of vegetable. The demonstration can be divided into several sections:

1. discussing what will happen;
2. showing students what materials and equipment are needed;
3. demonstrating, while showing clearly the steps by which the task is carried out; and
4. the students sharing in the activity with the teacher or performing it for themselves.

The teacher and students talk about what they are doing as they do it.

That talk is structured, not in accordance with what is laid down in a programme text, but in accordance with the structure of what is going on: purposeful processes invariably proceed through a series of steps that must occur in a fixed sequence. That being so, the talk that occurs between those who are cooperating in getting the task successfully completed will be structured around and scaffolded by an awareness of those steps. In this case, the children and teacher talk about each step in the process of making toast – what is done, what is used to do it, who are involved in the doing, and how they feel about those things.

Phase 2 of an activity-based unit: reconstructing the experience

Phase 2 is similar for both kinds of programme units in that it concentrates on meaning and recall. In activity-based units, the students list the equipment and materials that are required and tell how to do or make the thing, step by step.

As the students recount a shared activity on repeated occasions, the talk can easily be varied. For example, the teacher can direct attention to different elements of what is going on or the talk can change from simple commentary with action, such as 'I'm planting the bean seeds', while doing that, to more complex language tasks, such as telling what will happen next, what happened to the seed as the days passed, or whether or not something was done properly. Those tasks differ in that they call for different kinds of spoken texts: commentary along with on-going action, a procedural text, a recount text, and a report text, respectively.

Then, as discussed in Chapter 7, the difficulty of the language demand can systematically be increased by gradually separating the talk from the non-language activity and context. Discussion of the activity continues until the students feel that they have expert knowledge of the activity and can confidently talk about it. They are then ready to move across from the spoken to the written language mode in Phase 3, the scaffolds all being in place for written discourse.

Phases 3, 4 and 5 are similar for both types of programme units, but we should first look at Phases 1 and 2 of text-based programme units, as they are shown in Fig. 2.1.

Phase 1 of a text-based unit: shared reading

When the sequence begins with shared reading, the objective in Phase 1 is to have the learners come to a firm understanding of the starter text, from its overall structure down to elements such as what happened, who did what, and the characteristics of people, objects, and events.

The reading should be a leisurely, informal process that involves talking about what is being read, much as parents read a story to their infant children. Teachers bring the whole range of story-telling techniques to bear to make the reading a more exciting and lively experience and, when there are children whose first language is different from the language of instruction, the teacher scaffolds the language in every possible way such as by using pictures from the text, gesturing and using facial expressions. In extreme cases, the teacher may explain essential concepts in the children's first language, though the reading must not become a translation.

However, the substance of the talk, and to a large extent the language needed to talk, have to be supplied and modelled in the shared experience of the reading until at least the more outgoing and confident students, and later the others, can talk with the teacher about what is being read.

Between readings, songs and dances on the same theme can also help children to understand, remember and enjoy the story.

Teachers should be patient with the less confident students, giving them praise for non-language involvement, and waiting for their confidence to build up to the point where they can join in the talk. Once that occurs, they will have permanently left their most serious difficulty behind them.

Phase 2 of a text-based unit: absorbing the meaning of the text

In Phase 2, the main objective is to have the learners recall what they have heard during the Phase 1 readings, making sure that they understand the meaning of what was read.

Phase 2 can follow directly after Phase 1. If not, teachers usually begin by 'warming up' their students with a few simple questions about the story, such as 'What people are in the story?' and 'What happened to (a character)?' The song or dance that was learnt during Phase 1 may also be used in the 'warm up'. The teacher then asks students to retell the story, step by step.

As many students as possible are brought into retelling the story and, at intervals, a student may be allowed to read parts of the book, along with the teacher – perhaps by taking the part of narrator in role-play. But the students should not be made to feel that they have to learn to read or recite the starter book.

When the story has been retold once or twice, role-play is recommended as a means of involving all of the students in recalling the story and in using the language in which it can be told.

The importance of role-play, like some of the other CLE processes, varies according to whether or not the children are operating in their first language. With those for whom the language or dialect is unfamiliar, it provides repeated but enjoyable opportunities to hear the language along with seeing the actual characters and events that the language refers to. If, at first, students are reluctant to role-play individually, several children can role-play the one part, as a group, until one of them becomes confident enough to act alone. Through watching others role-play, shy students develop a sense of participation that usually leads to being able to follow their example. The teacher acts as director of the role-play, helping both the narrators and the players to perform their roles and speak their 'lines' as dramatically as can be. In the next performance, the groups exchange their tasks, the narrators being actors and the actors becoming the narrating group.

Phase 3 of both text-based and experience-based units:
negotiating a group text

During Phases 1 and 2 of a text-based unit, the students absorb the meaning of the story, they then build up an enriched background to the elements and aspects of that story, and, through their own creative thought, they elaborate on what was contained in the story book. By the end of Phase 2, they are able to draw on shared language and experiential resources to tell and talk about their own version of the story. In Phases 1 and 2 of an experience-based unit, the students will have reached a similar stage of being able to recount and talk about the structured experience that they have shared with their teacher and fellow students. In either case, they are now ready to build a written text that conveys what they want to say about what they have read or experienced together.

This first experience focuses primarily on a whole text, not just small elements of it. The teacher asks the students to tell the story or recount the experience again, so that the group can write a book for themselves. She again asks such questions as 'What happened first?', 'Then what happened?' and so on, but this time she writes each sentence on a large sheet of paper, transforming it from the spoken to the written form, before their eyes, to become part of a written text.

Each time she writes a sentence, she will ask the other students if they want to say it a different way and she will change the sentence if another version is preferred. The students thus negotiate an entire written text, sentence by sentence, cooperating to make the text satisfactory in all respects. They read their text many times as it is built up, because the teacher frequently has them chorus read it from the beginning, 'to see what we now have'.

It is preferable to work with groups that are small enough for all the members to make a substantial input to the text, or at least to feel that they have agreed to the wording of all the text. The teacher does not dictate what is written but she modifies sentences as needed to observe accepted language conventions, saying the corrected version as she writes it.

For the first few units of the Stage 1 programme, teachers have to do all the writing. As they write each word, they say it, to enable the students to note the written form of words and parts of words. Some teachers favour having the students chorus the words as they are being written. Later, students will take pleasure in displaying their ability to 'be the teacher' and do some of the writing. For example, they will be able to insert punctuation and (in Thai) tone marks, from a very early stage.

The pages used for writing group texts should be large enough for students to see individual symbols clearly, to chorus read from it, and to check the accuracy of a reading by another student. Spaces are usually left for art work and students draw illustrations at suitable points on each page. To do this, they have to read and think about the overall meaning of that section of the group text.

The negotiating of a group text will not be finished at the one session so it is left in place between sessions, allowing students to read and discuss it at leisure. Before they start work on it again as a group, they chorus read through what has been written, with the teacher pointing to each word as it is read. Again, a student can soon be asked to 'be teacher' and do the pointing as the others read. When the complete text has been written up, teacher and learners go through it together again, discussing whether it can be improved.

If the teacher has proceeded patiently and carefully in negotiating the text with the students, most of them will be able to read the whole text, and to identify any particular word by 'reading up to it'.

Phase 4: making the 'big book'

Then a 'fair copy' is made of the negotiated text, to constitute a 'big book'. After the students have learnt to work in small groups, there can be as many big books made as there will be activity groups in Phase 5. A book that is to be used with the class as one group needs to be as large as a poster or chart. Books for use with smaller groups may be only a quarter of that size.

In some parts of Thailand, the big book was no more than sheets of paper stapled together. At Traeger Park School, elaborate hard-covered big books of intriguing shapes were made. What form the big book takes will vary according to the local circumstances.

The procedures used in making the book will also change as students become better acquainted with book-making and can work with minimal supervision. In any case, the first task is to decide on page layout, and illustrations. That process involves reading the text, discussing what should be in the illustrations and where they should be placed on the page.

When the students work in small groups and print the book for themselves, the more able students help those who are struggling to read the text, so that all can share in the decision-making. The teacher will have prepared for this, while the students were still working in one large group, by modelling helping behaviour and then having prospective leaders 'be teacher'.

To watch students at work in small groups, making their big books, reveals much about their ability to read and write. It is particularly important to monitor how the groups go about editing their book, so that they develop habits of systematic and effective proofreading and self-evaluation.

Phase 5: language games and other group activities

By the time a group of learners have produced their own book, they will be able to chorus read it with ease and most will be able to read it individually, with minimum prompting. As a group exercise, they will be able to identify any word within its context, by 'chorus reading' up to it and they can be brought to do that individually. Some will already be able to identify some of the words in isolation. Most importantly, all will have a firm grasp of the meaning of the text, from its overall structure down to sentences and individual words.

The book now becomes a resource for language activities in which students focus on the smaller elements of the written language, such as sentences, words, letters and phonic correspondences, and sub-skills such as spelling, and parsing. But, as John Oller emphasizes in Chapter 5, behind that, there is always the context of the whole group text and what it represents.

Language games are a way of practising language skills, and of drawing attention to language items and features, without boredom. As a new activity or game is introduced, the students are first trained to take part in the activity and then to manage it by themselves, in small groups.

Teachers take a number of factors into account in deciding what activities to introduce in Phase 5. Level of enjoyment is important, because students learn much faster if they enjoy the games sufficiently to play them in their own time. Secondly, the activities must cover the necessary range of objectives for the unit. Table 2.1 shows the kind of spread that teachers aim for in later units of Stage 1 Thai-language CLE programmes.

Table 2.1 Sample activities for Stage 1, Phase 5

1. *Recognizing words that occur in the group big book:* word card games, such as match-word, bingo, domino, word hunt.
2. *Reading sentences that contain words from the big book:* reading competition games, such as word-matching, pair work, fill in the word.
3. *Writing the words that occur in the big book:* playing competitive games, such as hang man, and dictation competition.
4. *Making up sentences, orally, that include words from the book:* sentence-making competition, a sentence for a picture.
5. *Reading and writing sentences that include words from the book:* reading competition, dictation, pair work in reading and writing sentences.
6. *Spelling words from the book, and making up new words:* crossword puzzle, complete the sentence, homonyms, look-a-like words.
7. *Making up sentences, orally, with new words:* shopping game competition – each group prepares a 'shopping list' of words they can put into sentences, and challenge another group.
8. *Reading and writing new sentences:* jigsaw puzzle, of sentences, pair-work or inter-group competition in dictation, small book writing competition.
9. *Reading new texts:* guessing words or sentences from reading competition – prose or poetry.
10. *Recounting or telling the content of a text from everyday life:* 'interviewing a star' game, telephone conversation, twenty questions, charades.
11. *Responding to new texts:* telling stories, news-reading, master chairman contest, TV announcer contest.
12. *Generating short written texts:* cards for occasions, finish the story, writing competition.

In either type of programme unit, the teacher should not hurry over any of the five phases. Before leaving one phase, the students need to be ready for the demands of the next. For the first few programme units, therefore, progress may seem slow but students are able to move faster as they become accustomed to and understand what happens in each phase.

That speeding up is reinforced by growth of self-reliance in individual learning tasks. As soon as possible, learners are given tasks which require individual initiative and leadership and, in the activities of Phase 5, they learn how to solve for themselves most of the problems they encounter.

Stage 2 of the programme: The middle primary school grades

There are many kinds of texts, each with a different characteristic structure (generic structure). Different kinds of texts are written and read for different purposes and need to be written and read in different ways. The

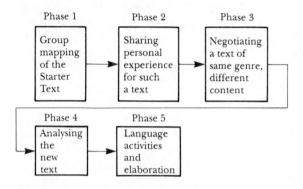

Figure 2.2: CLE unit structures for Stage 2

range of genres encountered in Stage 1 of the programme is necessarily limited so that the central objective at Stage 2 is to widen the students' experience with different kinds of texts (genres), particularly those that are most commonly encountered in everyday life.

In Thailand, starter books are still used in Stage 2. Most of them are examples of one kind of text, such as an instruction manual or a story book but some are collections of different kinds of texts. For example, the one starter book might contain application forms, timetables, posters, letters, invoices, receipts and the like, that are used in everyday life. The Thai starter books for Stage 2 are much larger and have larger print than normal books, to allow the teacher to use them with the whole class as one group.

The overall Stage 2 strategy is to have the students analyse the model text, to come to understand its uses and its characteristics, and then to compose and use a text of that kind for themselves. Within each programme unit, they do that for at least one genre.

Again, there are five phases within each programme unit. Fig. 2.2 shows these five phases.

Phase 1: analysing the model text

The first objective in Phase 1 is for the teacher to model and then help students to use the reading strategies that are appropriate for a particular kind of text. At the same time, the students are also forming a basis for organizing their own ideas into a text of that kind and for improving drafts of their own texts.

In the early weeks of the Stage 2 programme, the teacher will need to use scaffolding techniques to lead the students into talking about the text in a structured and insightful way. Strategies that are commonly used to help students to analyse texts include mapping, note-taking and summarizing.

In general, the teacher asks the students to seek out the main idea and supporting detail for each section or paragraph of a text, and asks questions that guide them towards discovering how the text is organized. To do that the teachers need to have a general understanding of the characteristics of the genres that are to be covered within the programme.

The kinds of questions that teachers ask, and that students should learn to ask themselves as they read a text, will vary between genres but, in general, they are open questions such as:

What are the really important points in this text?
What is the main point in that paragraph?
What is the problem that faces these people?
How can (they) solve the problem, do you think?
Is that a good solution? Why?
What caused that to happen?
What resulted from that?
What are the differences between X and Y?

Phase 2: Linking the text to personal experience

The objective in Phase 2 is to stimulate the students to thought and discussion that leads to their identifying something in their own experience that could just as well be expressed in the same kind of text as the one they examined in Phase 1.

Discussion begins with questions such as:

'How about yourself – has something like that ever happened to you?
    When? What was it?'
'If you were that character, what would you have done?' Why?

These kinds of questions are used to prompt students to bring forward interesting experiences that could appropriately give rise to the kind of text analysed in Phase 1. When that occurs, the shared experiential and language basis for writing texts of this kind is then enlarged and enriched through focused discussion of personal experiences. Readers who are familiar with systemic-functional grammar will realize that the students are substituting a different 'field' component for the context, retaining the same 'tenor' and 'mode' (see Halliday, 1973).

Phase 3: Negotiating a new text

The students now set out to organize and express their own ideas and experience in a text of the same genre as the one that they analysed in Phase 1.

On the first few occasions, the teacher negotiates the text with the whole class in one group, using questions based on the structure that was revealed in analysis of the sample text. The teacher is still modelling and scaffolding, just as in the Stage 1 teaching/learning processes – but she is now modelling the reasoning and decision-making that is involved in producing and polishing a text of this kind.

For the first few programme units, the teacher works with the whole class, but she gradually prepares the students for work in small groups, by introducing such questions as 'What should we ask ourselves next?', and by fostering leadership by the most confident students until they are capable of leading small groups as they conduct their own negotiating of a text.

The whole progression of Phase 3 of Stage 2 is similar to the same phase of Stage 1, except that the negotiating takes place at the level of structure as well as form – direct attention is now being given to the underlying structure of the text, not only to what is being said and how it is being said. The notion of appropriateness of the language for that kind of text, rather than just correctness or attractiveness, also emerges in the discussions.

The ultimate step for Phase 3 is to have the students independently writing their own texts within each of the genres. This will become possible for different students at different times, and it should not be unduly hurried.

Phase 4: Critically analysing the new text

In Phase 4, the students use the procedures that were modelled in Phase 1 to analyse their own text: they determine how the ideas are organized, they examine the language for appropriateness and clarity, and they proofread for accuracy in grammar, spelling and punctuation – always in that order.

Again, the Phase 4 process is modelled and then scaffolded by the teacher with the whole class before it is controlled by student leaders of small groups. And again, the ultimate aim is to have students take individual responsibility for analysing and improving their own texts, although, for most students, it may not be realistic to expect the latter before Stage 3 of the programme.

Phase 5: Language activities and elaboration

In Phase 5, students are given further opportunities to practise working within the various genres that they have examined to that time. Activities are introduced one by one, until the full range of objectives for this stage of

Table 2.2   Phase 5 activities for Stage 2 of the CLE programme

1. Writing new texts of the same kind as the starter books:
   - writing short texts in a set time;
   - 'Lucky Dip': sketch out a text of the particular genre, with a picture or word as stimulus.
2. Analysing and improving written texts:
   - pair work on student texts;
   - mapping texts in small groups;
   - competition in collecting errors from a set of student texts.
3. Finding texts of the same type as the starter books:
   - competition in finding texts of different types;
   - quiz game on characteristics of different kinds of texts.
4. Writing texts of the same type as the starter books:
   - 'Story-writing' and 'letter-writing' contests.
5. Analysing and improving texts of the same type as the starter books:
   - pair work on improving texts;
   - editorial meetings;
   - explaining the main idea and structure of a group text;
   - jig-saw game: reconstituting a text from sentences.
6. Reporting on texts:
   - TV author interview;
   - newscast;
   - board display illustrating different kinds of texts.
7. Grasping the main idea and supporting ideas from new texts:
   - quiz contest, after reading new texts;
   - illustrating the meaning of a text;
   - filling in gaps in a text;
   - supplying missing parts by illustrating.
8. Summarizing texts:
   - taking notes as teacher reads;
   - mapping texts from reading (can be a competition for speed and accuracy).
9. Comparing and contrasting the structure of words and sentences:
   - domino games (for words);
   - finding synonyms and antonyms;
   - replacing words, retaining the same sentence structure;
   - finding sentences with similar structure.
10. Grouping words and phrases by type and structure:
    - hunting for words of one type from dictionary or texts;
    - collecting words of the same part of speech;
    - collecting and grouping clauses of the same tense.

the programme are covered. Table 2.2 shows sets of some of the activities that were suggested by the pilot schools of north-east Thailand.

To mount the Phase 5 activities, supplementary material is needed in all the genres. Some of that material, such as forms and schedules, is readily available from public and commercial sources and many other types of texts may be cut from newspapers and magazines.

A good way of extending first-hand experience with different kinds of texts is to use the present class activity as a basis for writing a number of different kinds of texts. While growing beans, for example the students might: write an account of the project, write an expository text telling how to grow beans, write a personal letter telling about the project, write a fictional narrative with an agricultural setting, keep cultivation, fertilizing and harvesting records for their garden plot, and write a report on vegetable growing in their village. Some teachers have the children assemble an appropriate range of texts for the one activity, to constitute a project folio.

Stage 3 of the programme: the upper primary school grades

The Stage 3 programme is intended to cover the last few years of primary school, and the same methodology could well carry over into secondary school. Literacy teaching does not lessen in importance in these higher grades; indeed, the need to foster effectiveness in and enthusiasm for literacy activities grows in importance with the approach of secondary school or working life.

As students move into higher levels of schooling, and into adult life, they will encounter a wider variety of texts that are directed towards some specific purpose. The prospects that these students will cope successfully with later stages of schooling and with vocational training depend largely on how well they can cope with the range of specialized reading and writing that is involved.

Accordingly, one component of the Stage 3 programme is to broaden further the range of texts that students have learnt to use. The Stage 2 learning/teaching sequence remains appropriate for that component.

An additional dimension of the Stage 3 programme arises from the fact that ability to use written language to generate and structure new knowledge now becomes of major importance, as increasingly, students are expected to learn for themselves. To learn from different kinds of texts, a reader has to be able to bring to bear the appropriate strategy for each particular kind of text. Moreover, because knowledge is arranged, expressed and reported in different ways in different subject fields, students need to learn how to organize knowledge for themselves in ways that are conventional to subject areas.

For that added dimension of the Stage 3 programme, a different learning/teaching sequence is needed to give students experience in:

1. using 'scientific' ways of finding out about a range of subject matter, within their regular school curriculum;
2. reporting what they have found out.

There are six phases within this additional Stage 3 sequence: orientation, reflection, note-taking, synthesis, editing and final copy.

Again, the students first go through the new learning/teaching sequence, under the guidance of the teacher then they do it in small groups and, finally, they learn to work through the sequence unaided, except for group review of what has been achieved. And again, modelling and scaffolding are used to induct students into these new routines.

Phase 1: Orientation

In Phase 1, having been assigned a reading and writing task, the students are asked to survey a relevant text, analyse its content structure, and use the context to work out the meaning of unfamiliar words.

In leading students through this orientation, in the earliest programme units, the teacher may use a chart, or write up the following steps for guidance.

1. Contextualization

In Stages 1 and 2 of the programme, the reading and writing of a text by the students was preceded by either first-hand shared experience or shared exploration of the content and context of a text. In Stage 3, the students are trained to build up for themselves a context for the text that is compatible with that understood by the author. Students need to ask themselves questions such as:

What is this text about?
Why did the author write it?
For what audience was it written and how much did the author expect a reader to know already?
What do I already know about this topic?
What do I know about using this kind of text?

2. Mapping the topic

Having done that, the students will be ready to pool their own knowledge about the topic of the text. Having used mapping strategies for some years now, they should readily be able to discuss and map their ideas.

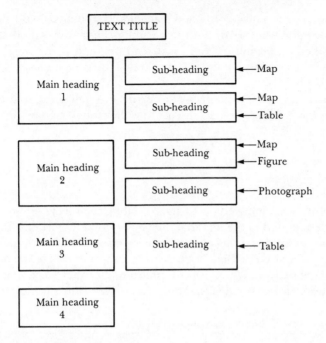

Figure 2.3: A sample graphical outline

3. Surveying the text organization

The students then survey the text for organization of its content, as revealed in headings, sub-headings, illustrations, tables, topic sentences, and summaries.

This survey of the text can result in a graphic outline that predicts the content of the text. A typical graphic outline for a single-chapter text is shown in Fig. 2.3.

4. Establishing the genre of the text being read and the text to be written

From working through Stage 2 of the programme in previous years, the students will readily be able to establish the genre of the text that has been surveyed and remind themselves of the generic characteristics of the text that they are to write.

5. Dealing with unfamiliar vocabulary

The students then deal with unfamiliar vocabulary. There may be words that are unfamiliar because they are part of the technical or semi-technical vocabulary that is associated with the particular topic and genre. There may also be unfamiliar items of general vocabulary.

For the first few programme units, the teacher usually asks the students to locate a few new words, and teacher and students discuss them one by one to decide whether or not the meaning can be worked out from the context, whether the author has provided another way of finding the meaning (such as a glossary or index) or whether it is necessary to consult a reference book.

In later units, the students work on this in small groups, after which the teacher and the whole class discuss how they found out the meaning of unfamiliar words.

Phase 2: Reflection

The students now change their focus to relating their assigned writing task to what is contained in the text that they surveyed in the orientation phase. Their objective at this time is to produce a writing plan from reflecting on both what is required of them in the writing task, and what is available from the text. That plan could well be a graphical outline, like the one in Fig. 2.3 but, this time, it is of the text that they themselves will write.

Table 2.3   Format for a simple writing plan

Introductory paragraph
   Point 1:
   Point 2:
   Point 3:

Paragraph 2
   Major concept:
   Supporting point 1:
   Supporting point 2:
   Supporting point 3

Paragraph 3
   Major concept:
   Supporting point 1:
   Supporting point 2:
   Supporting point 3:

Paragraph 4
   Major concept:
   Supporting point 1:
   Supporting point 2:
   Supporting point 3:

Conclusion
   Point 1:
   Point 2:
   Point 3:

Sometimes, the writing task will be to produce a text of a different genre from the one they have read, in which case their writing plan has to conform to the generic structure that has been specified for them rather than that of the text they have examined.

That writing plan may be a graphical outline, or it may be a simpler construct such as headings and sub-headings. To begin with, the plan may be no more than a simple table, such as that shown in Table 2.3.

The students plan their writing in small groups, which then break up for the individual students to make their own notes for their individual texts, in Phase 3. The teacher does not guide students in this phase unless a difficult new task has been assigned.

When the teacher, or the student group, is satisfied with the writing plans, the students are ready to search out what they need to write a text based on that plan.

Phase 3: Note-taking

The briefing for this step takes place in Phase 2 so that, from the beginning, the students are able to work in small groups for this Phase. Each student fills in an individual writing plan with information that was noted down from reading the text. Then each group reconvenes, to negotiate a common set of notes for the group. The discussion that takes place in this step is among the most highly instructive shared experiences of the Stage 3 CLE processes.

Phase 4: Synthesis

The students now write a first draft of a text that is aimed at realizing the writing task goal.

At first, a group text is written by the negotiating procedures that are familiar from Stages 1 and 2 of the programme. The more capable students may be ready to work alone almost from the beginning, but their presence is valuable in a group that is negotiating a text. Before long, all the students should be able to write their text individually and then come together only to share in a review of their draft texts, in Phase 5. This is a case where a 'small group' may be as small as two students.

In any case, the students are urged, beforehand, to establish:

1. the purposes of the text, and
2. the audience for the text,

and to keep those two firmly in mind as they turn their notes into a continuous text.

Phase 5: Editing

There are three steps for Phase 5: *reviewing, redrafting* and *polishing.*

1. Reviewing
The review is carried out through group discussion and negotiation. The students examine their texts for adequacy and suitability in relation to the task goal. They focus first on whole-text qualities such as completeness, structure and logical progression, and then on appropriateness and accuracy of wording.

2. Redrafting
The students then redraft their texts, in the light of the review. Initially, this involves brain-storming and negotiating, to fill in gaps or improve logical progression, and then rewriting to improve effectiveness and clarity of expression. As the year progresses, students are encouraged to carry out that redrafting step individually, as a conventional step in the authoring process.

3. Polishing
The final step is a thorough polishing of the redraft. For the first few units of the programme, the teacher may lead the whole group in polishing a group text, discussing ways of eliminating surface weaknesses such as errors in grammar, spelling and punctuation. But the students should soon learn to carry them out as a group exercise, and then as an individual exercise.

Phase 6: Final copy and elaboration

Final copy
In this final stage, the students discuss what physical properties are needed for the text to best serve its purposes and they produce a final copy in accordance with their decisions.

The final copy may be made into a book for the classroom or home library, it may be photocopied for distribution to other students, it may be put up on a display board as a poster, and so on, in accordance with the function for which it was designed and written.

Elaboration
In the course of a programme unit, the teacher will have noted that some students or groups of students are having difficulty with a particular process, such as surveying a text or compiling a writing plan and that others are ready to go on to more individualized work.

At the conclusion of this final phase of the unit, the teacher organizes independent activities for groups of students or individuals in some aspect of reading and writing, while she works with those students who need help to strengthen their participation in the next programme unit.

Sets of cloze exercises, semantic mapping exercises, context-clue exercises, jig-saw reading, crossword puzzles, and 'make up the question from the answer' games, are a few of the kinds of activities that strengthen or extend the literacy insights and skills for those involved in a Stage 3 programme. Most modern published programmes have activity books that contain useful ideas for use here. Mount Gravatt Developmental Language Reading Program (BCAE, 1982), and *Learning to Learn from Text* (Morris and Stewart-Dore, 1984) are good examples.

As John Oller states in Chapter 6, exercises like these can be used for evaluation as well as learning, without any change of stance or philosophy. It is in the elaboration step, too, that every student can achieve the reading and writing independence that will be needed in later education or later life. The modelling and scaffolding techniques that persist throughout all levels of the programme, and the progression from class-group, to small-group, to paired and finally to individual learning, support and facilitate the development of independence in reading and writing. Ability to work through a Stage 3 programme unit alone and unaided, is the final goal for every student within the programme and teachers use this final step of each programme unit to monitor and foster the progress of individual students towards that goal.

CLE across the curriculum

Ideally, the Stage 3 programme would spread across all subject areas of the primary school curriculum. However, that possibility is remote when a CLE programme is first introduced and it would probably be unwise, in any case, until teachers are confident of their mastery of the methodology.

In schools where the same person teaches all subjects, the CLE methodology is likely to spread fairly quickly across other subjects. In that case, the students will learn to use the kinds of texts that are used in other school subjects within the time allocated to those subjects. This will allow more room within the language-arts or literacy programme for working with the traditional literary genres.

On the other hand, where students have different teachers for different subject areas in the upper grades, the CLE programme is not likely to spread beyond the 'language' area for some years. This puts pressure on the 'language' programme, because work with all the various kinds of texts has to be done within the time allocated to that strand of the curriculum. It then becomes a priority to introduce the teachers of other subjects to CLE literacy teaching.

It will be obvious from this chapter that CLE teaching necessarily involves fluid classroom groupings. Students sometimes work as a class group, sometimes in a number of small groups, and at other times individually, with changes from one to another often occurring within the one session. For that reason, it has been found that teachers who are accustomed only to teaching their class as one group need to learn new classroom management strategies. This is the topic of Chapter 3.

Classroom management

SAOWALAK RATTANAVICH

Introduction

In traditional classrooms, the interaction between teacher and students is teacher-dominated, virtually all interaction is between the teacher and one child (or a group of children who must answer as one), and the normal procedure is for the teacher to initiate each instance of interaction and then to indicate which child is to respond. Deliberate abandonment by the teacher of domination of the classroom language interaction represents a fundamental change in the teacher's classroom role, requiring a different kind of classroom management. But that is only one difference between a classroom that is managed by a CLE teacher and other, more traditional classrooms. Table 3.1 lists the differences between the CLE and the traditional classroom.

These characteristics of a CLE classroom cannot be brought about without planning and careful management. In the description of CLE teaching techniques in Chapter 2, mention was made of strategies by which some of those changes can be instigated. For example, it was frequently stated that some particular activity is first carried out by the whole class group, under the control of the teacher, and then by small groups each led by a student who has been trained to lead. This chapter presents a more complete and methodical explanation of strategies for managing a CLE classroom.

Rationale

There are compelling reasons for changing the perceived source of motivation and control from the teacher to purposes to do with what students are trying to achieve. The speed with which young children learn to speak their

Table 3.1 A comparison between CLE and traditional classrooms

CLE classroom	*Traditional classroom*
The activities	
Student activities are always related to real-life contexts that have importance to the learners.	The lesson content is usually based on language units, rules and structures.
Students are encouraged to work independently.	Students generally do only what the teacher tells them to do.
Games and songs are used to enliven learning.	Usually not found in the traditional classroom.
Students often read and play language learning games in free time.	Students seldom read or write outside class lessons.
Classroom interaction	
Students learn by interacting among themselves and with the teacher.	The teacher asks questions and selects those who should answer.
There is a great deal of negotiating of meaning by students, with teacher as moderator.	The teacher acts as broker and the students merely receive information, often passively.
The pace of learning is not prescribed. Students can participate in the learning activities, whatever their stage of learning.	A fixed amount of learning is prescribed for each particular period of time.
Classroom management	
Learners often work in small groups, actively discussing and cooperating.	The students usually work seated in rows as a class group, stationary.
Students frequently manage their own activities.	Students await direction from the teacher before speaking or acting.
Discipline is positive. Students are work-oriented.	Discipline is negative. Students are kept under control by prohibitions.
Student attitudes	
Students assume responsibility, with self-confidence and self-actualization. Student leadership is systematically developed and used.	Many of the learners do not participate in learning. They are inclined to lack confidence when asked to communicate.

first language is matched by the earnestness and persistence that they bring to the task. They are prepared to go on trying to use language because they want to get things done. They often take the initiative, and they sometimes persist in trying to make themselves understood in the face of repeated failure.

Similarly, rapid literacy learning occurs when students are enthusiastically and constantly engaged in purposeful activities to do with reading and writing. The success of CLE literacy teaching depends on maintaining that kind of situation within classrooms and the teachers who are most successful with CLE teaching invariably are those who are most adept at managing CLE classroom routines in such a way that all the students enthusiastically participate. That represents a challenge for teachers who have worked only in conventional classrooms, because a different kind of relationship is needed between them and their pupils to achieve maximal conditions for rapid learning.

Management objectives

Within CLE classrooms, there are objectives operating at several levels. Hopefully, all the students and teachers share the common objective of succeeding in the task at hand, whether it be the production of a group big book or the growing of the finest crop of beans in the province. Students are also motivated by personal objectives such as the joy of achievement and the teacher has objectives, to do with the educational process, that are not usually shared by the students.

One important teacher objective is that the learning/teaching activities continue to a successful conclusion, through all the phases of the programme unit, and that they do not break down. Every other aspect of classroom management is subsidiary to this. Experienced CLE teachers work gradually towards having more and more students share that focus, by systematically training their students to participate in each kind of CLE learning/teaching routine and, finally, to manage routines for themselves.

That is not to say that disorder is tolerated for fear of interruption to the learning/teaching sequence. Because CLE activities are directed at practical outcomes that are known and valued by the students, they tend to favour behaviour that contributes to achievement of that purpose and to reject anything that does not. Order is maintained because disorder interferes with prospects of success in the shared activity. Industry and order in the classroom no longer depend on the presence and will of a teacher, alone.

A second concern of a CLE teacher is that all the students participate in the learning activities as often and as continuously as possible, on the reasonable assumption that the more often and more intensely a student is involved, the more rapidly he/she will learn. If the class always works in one large group, not every student can be given an active role in what goes on. The way to bring about maximum student involvement is to have the students working in small groups, in pairs, or, ultimately, as individuals.

These conditions can be achieved only through systematically training the students to work in small groups, and to take more and more responsibility for managing their own group work.

CLE classroom management is facilitated by the fact that the phase structure of programme units remains constant through each of the three stages of the programme. This means that the overall classroom routine becomes increasingly familiar to the students and the teacher needs to devote progressively less time and attention to helping students to participate.

A third objective of CLE classroom management is to foster student personal characteristics such as self-confidence and a willingness to take risks in mastering a new literacy skill. Cooperative attitudes, a willingness to negotiate with others for a better result, and to perceive where there is room for improvement in their own performance, are also fostered. Students develop leadership skills and gain self-confidence through learning to lead a small work group and students learn to get along with others, and to contribute to group decision-making while they are pursuing, with others, the common purpose of writing a group book, for example.

Finally, when most or all of the students are from non-literate families, as is often the case in educationally difficult places, there is a particular need for them to become immersed in book-reading, book-writing and book-making at school.

Keeping all the students actively involved, managing a number of small groups instead of the one class group, encouraging students to cooperate with others and to undertake more and more active and challenging roles within the groups, require classroom management that is characteristically different from that of teacher-dominated classrooms. The remainder of this chapter presents suggestions and ideas for achieving the appropriate kind of classroom management for CLE teaching.

General management techniques

Classroom organization

The most fundamental requirement is that the classroom itself allows for flexibility in student grouping. For sessions in which the teacher models literacy behaviour, or takes the students through a new routine, the children will need to be clustered in the one large group. At other times, the requirement will be for a number of groups of four or five students, working independently. And sometimes, students have to carry out individual tasks, even at the same time as small groups are working.

For Stages 1 and 2, it has been found that a classroom needs to have the following:

1. A clear floor space wide enough for the whole class to sit in a semi-circle for shared reading, negotiating a text, and conference sessions between the teacher and the whole class. That area should be left permanently clear, to allow the teacher to call the whole class together at any time.
2. Clusters of desks or tables that will allow four or five students to work together, or, alternatively, this area can be used for individual work that needs seating or a flat surface.
3. An area for storage of language games and supplementary reading materials. It can also serve as a display and storage area for group big books and word cards. The big books can be placed on display shelves, hung over racks or clamped on to rails along a wall.
4. A quiet reading corner, near the supplementary reading materials.
5. A corner for storage of writing and book-making materials.
6. A wall area with display boards for individual student work, posters and charts that are generated within the literacy programme.

The composition of student work groups

By and large, each small group should contain students with different ability levels. That reflects normal social life and it allows for desirable and productive social behaviours such as helping one another, and taking pride in a personal contribution to a common task while also respecting every other person's contribution. Students will inevitably realize that some of them learn more quickly and easily than others, but they will not feel labelled as they would be if they worked in homogeneous ability groups. Moreover, mixed ability groups present the more able students with the challenge and opportunity of leading the group, as a whole, to a higher level of achievement and satisfaction through more effective cooperation and communication.

It is advisable, too, to change the composition of work groups for different tasks or for different phases of the programme unit, so that students will be given the opportunity to interact with and learn to relate to all of their fellow students. Furthermore, a student who cannot be given a turn as a leader in one group may have a turn at being leader in another.

Flexibility of time limits

Different classes and different class groups will work at somewhat different speeds and, in particular, one group may become particularly enthused with different programme units. Whether the work is being done by the whole class, a small group or by individuals, the students should not be prevented from completing their task to their own satisfaction, because of the importance of generating a sense of responsibility for the quality of their own work. Moreover, the success of the next phase of a programme unit very often rests on the soundness and completeness of what was done in the previous phase. Consequently, rigid time limits should not be imposed on a programme unit or on individual phases of a programme unit.

Moreover, the nature of a CLE programme unit allows for recursion, in that, after generating and using one kind of text, a class group may go back to Phase 3 and generate a second or even a third text, perhaps of different kinds. Consequently, within sensible limits, each class should move through a programme unit at the pace that suits the students and their stage of learning. Within a school year, different class groups may be given equivalent sets of experiences and achieve equivalent gains in literacy learning from a very different number of programme units.

Providing individualized instruction

Within the same class, too, one small group may work at a different speed from another but all should be allowed to complete their task at their own pace. That will require some groups to elaborate their task, or to engage in extension activities of some kind, until other groups are ready to go on to the next phase of the work. That requires teacher ingenuity, but student groups will not remain goal-oriented and self-motivated if the teacher imposes arbitrary limits on what can be achieved. Of course, teachers can unobtrusively give special support to a slow group, and assist them to succeed more quickly. A group that achieves its goals, but at a slower pace, is likely to aim at achieving its next set of goals at a faster pace. Whereas one that is prevented from achieving its goals is likely to be discouraged by failure.

In every class, too, there are differences between individual students in general ability and in progress in learning to read and write. The teacher should be the one who is most aware of those differences, so that she will be ready to assist any student who is having real difficulty. One of the principles of CLE teaching is to have students solve their own problems but they need to be shown how to do that and, above all, they must build up confidence that they can succeed. For that to be the case, the teacher needs to be alert to instances in which students of lower ability are faced with possible failure, and to provide whatever support the student needs to struggle through to a solution of the problem.

That is much easier to do when other students can work in independent small groups. While other groups carry on with their tasks, the teacher can join a group that is having trouble and she can prevent the occurrence of difficulties for individual students by helping them with appropriate scaffolding. An important part of literacy learning is learning how to solve problems.

It is not usually necessary to form special remedial groups within a CLE programme. Nor has it been found necessary to devise a special programme for very able students. In a programme where students generate, illustrate and use texts of various kinds, there is no limit to the difficulty of the tasks that able students can attempt. They can pursue those challenges to whatever level of excellence, while the teacher helps other students to consolidate and strengthen their grasp of what they have learnt to do to that time.

A balance should be kept, for able students, between working on challenging tasks and helping others to solve less difficult problems. And teachers should remember that their very able students will also need individual attention and assistance to achieve what they are capable of. Sometimes all that is needed is to note and appreciate what these students have achieved. At other times, they may need to share their thoughts on some original project they want to undertake or on aspects of language that have not yet interested the other students.

Trends in class management

CLE classroom management should never be static – it should develop throughout each year and from year to year. That development becomes possible because of the additional things that students learn to do: they learn to participate successfully in more demanding types of classroom procedures, and to take greater responsibility for their own learning so that management techniques that require more of the students' initiative and self-reliance may be introduced. Of course, teachers need to train their students to undertake and participate in each new routine, as part of their classroom management.

In respect to basic classroom routines, development can occur on the following dimensions.

1. Greater demands can progressively be made on the students for participation in existing CLE routines.
2. As management problems diminish with greater student mastery of existing CLE routines, further, more demanding types of routines may be introduced.
3. Students will learn to act as leader of a CLE activity group, thus freeing the teacher to help other sub-groups.

4. The students will progressively be expected to solve more and more of their own problems, and make more of their own decisions.

Teachers should ensure that students come to understand what is required of them, within every new type of learning activity, and help them to take control over the activity until, eventually, they can carry it out unsupervised. That is a central principle of CLE classroom management, because it is essential to producing students who are independent readers and writers and who will improve their literacy through independent learning, outside school and beyond their school years.

Classroom management for Stage 1

General principles

1. Begin with sound training in the basic CLE routines and systematically add to the number and variety of routines, unit after unit.
2. At the beginning, work with the one large group but train a few confident students to lead small groups in an activity that they have learnt with you.
3. Begin small group work with one activity at a time then work towards having several groups working simultaneously on different tasks.

Working with texts

1. Begin by negotiating one text with the whole class, work towards having small groups negotiate their own texts, and, finally, individual students will write short texts for themselves.
2. Not all texts need be made into books of the conventional type, sheets of paper can be collated to make chart-like books.
3. Progressively increase the variety of the book formats, types of illustrations, and types of script.

Classroom management for Stage 2

General principles

Accustom the students to a classroom procedure based on the following steps:

1. a briefing by the teacher on what is to be done and how;

2. the students work on the task, in small groups;
3. the class reassembles to review the work, with the teacher leading.

As the students master the demands of this routine, work gradually towards:

1. having students take individual responsibility for part of the group task and;
2. having a group of students review their work, for themselves, before the teacher conducts a review.

Working with texts

1. At this stage, the students will work with many non-literary texts, such as brochures, instruction manuals, telephone books, commercial and public documents, and notices and advertisements. These should be used, where possible, as part of a real project.
2. Only special, selected texts will be made into books of the conventional type.
3. Instead of negotiating the wording of texts, the group will very often negotiate change on one dimension of an existing text (e.g. use an owner-manual for a camera as a model for writing an owner-manual for a cassette player or change a report on growing mushrooms into an instruction manual for growing mushrooms).

Overall

1. Move always towards self-reliance and independence in learning. For that to happen, students must be shown how to overcome their own difficulties, while learning.
2. Strive to have every student continually thinking about or participating in the work.

Classroom management for Stage 3

Organization

Accustom the students to an additional learning routine which follows the following steps:

1. identification of a problem or task;

2. a conference to decide on how to solve the problem or carry out the task;
2. individual effort towards fulfilling the requirements of the task;
4. review of the outcomes.

As the students progress through these final years, work towards the more strictly scientific process:

'analysis of problem → solution → evaluation
of outcome → further response'

Working with texts

1. Students will usually work alone with a text but use paired-learning where appropriate.
2. One major emphasis in reading will be on learning from texts.
3. In writing, the students will discuss the structure of the text – with reference to task requirements – before they work on the wording.
4. The other major emphasis, will be on reviewing texts. This should involve thinking and talking about texts, thinking about the processes involved in reading and writing, finding out about the public uses of various kinds of texts, and discussing how to improve the effectiveness of functional texts.

Summary

The simplicity of the structure of CLE programme units and the use of many well-known teaching techniques can mislead casual observers. The differences between CLE and most other teaching methodologies lie deeper than what casual observation of a CLE classroom will reveal. At the level of classroom dynamics, of development within each programme unit, and of teacher–student interaction, the CLE teaching techniques that are described in Chapter 2 represent a fundamental change from what happens in most conventional classrooms, and their success requires a very different type of learning environment.

Not all of that difference can be described in terms of what a classroom looks like or what is done within it. The most significant differences are attitudinal, with enthusiasm replacing boredom, and with happy and purposeful activity replacing the apathy of hopelessness.

Moreover, there is not just one type of CLE classroom management. The nature of the classroom as a learning environment, and therefore the role of the teacher as classroom manager, changes from one stage of the programme to the next.

In Stage 1, while the emphasis is on deriving sound basic understandings about reading, writing and written language, the classroom is primarily an activity centre, where students participate in group and individual literacy activities.

In Stage 2, where there is a widening of experience with texts and with reading and writing texts differently for different purposes, the classroom is primarily a workshop, where students get things done.

In Stage 3, the classroom may be seen as primarily a laboratory for life, where students learn the literacy skills and procedures that they will need in later life.

That is not to say that Stage 1 students do not 'get things done' as a result of their 'participating', or that Stage 2 students do not learn how to 'seek out information' while they 'get things done'. All three activities: participating, getting things done, seeking out information, are achieved at every stage, but, from stage to stage, there is a change of emphasis and that change of emphasis necessitates a change in how teachers manage their classrooms.

In Chapters 2 and 3, we examined CLE teaching and the management of CLE learning within classrooms. However, a CLE programme needs to be developed where it is to be used and Chapter 4 describes how that may be done.

Developing a CLE primary school literacy programme

RICHARD WALKER

Introduction

To develop a new literacy programme requires time and considerable human and material resources (and, as will be discussed in Chapter 7, those resources are not always readily available in developing countries). Account must be taken, too, of what level of provision is available to continue the programme after it has been implemented. It is not sensible, for example, to set up a highly complex programme in a place where there are few trained teachers, poor technical support or, in a poorly resourced school, to develop a programme that requires large recurrent expenditure.

Even in more affluent places, there is a tendency to underestimate the time, personnel and other resources that are needed to build a literacy programme firmly and well. It takes a year to trial each year of a programme so the minimum time for developing a literacy programme for the primary school is six to eight years.

On the other hand, there is a simplistic view that increased expenditure is all that is needed to alleviate a literacy problem and a complementary view is that a low-cost programme is an inferior one. Neither view is sound. Literacy problems within special situations in affluent communities may prove particularly intractable, for the very reason that elaborate and expensive efforts have already been made to solve them.

The failure of repeated expensive efforts to improve a poor situation brings about the worst kind of hopelessness. In those circumstances, it becomes all the more desirable to develop the programme where it is to be used and to involve those who will use the programme in developing it, from the earliest possible stage. It is probably better not to begin programme development in these kinds of situations until that level of local participation is assured.

Assuming that these kinds of general factors will be taken into account, the remainder of this chapter is devoted to techniques for developing CLE literacy programmes. The same basic principles apply whether the programme be for an industrialized country or for a developing country. However, the scale of operations when the work is in a developing country causes additional difficulties that are covered in Chapter 7.

Programme objectives

The first step in developing a CLE programme, like any other, is to set down its objectives after which comes the task of devising the content and structure of a programme through which those objectives may be achieved.

CLE programmes are not based on objectives to do with lists of language items, functions and structures, or on the development of abilities or skills that are assumed to be involved in reading and writing. Instead the central focus is on the real-life needs of the learners. In respect to literacy, those needs may be stated in terms of the kinds of texts (written genres, see pp. 46–9) that students will need to deal with, and what they will need to be able to do with those texts. In other words, CLE programming is based on the principle that literacy learning is essentially becoming able to read and write more kinds of texts, and to use them more effectively.

Ability to read and write has value not so much in itself as in what it gives access to. Being able to compose effective notices, advertisements, and other persuasive or instructional texts, increase power to influence what others do. Ability to read travel books, history books, science magazines, hobby books, brochures, novels, and poems, to mention just a few, enables people to learn more about and reflect on the world and what goes on within it. And so we could go on across the full range of written genres, showing that learning to use each genre constitutes an increase in power to get things done.

So, programme developers need to decide

1. what kinds of texts (written genres) will be encompassed by each stage of their programme and
2. what students should learn to do with those texts.

Because one of the major reasons for reading and writing texts is to gain knowledge and/or skills, it would be as well to consider, also,

3. what non-language knowledge and skills would be useful to learners at the various stages.

Texts and genres

Following Halliday and Hasan (1985), a text, whether spoken or written, is defined as 'language that is functional': a cohesive body of language that is used to get something done.

There is usually more than one step involved in getting something done, so that most texts have structure. Texts that are oriented towards the same goal, are said to be of the same genre, and they tend to have a similar (generic) structure. Besides the recognized literary genres, there are the spoken and written genres of everyday life, such as letters, speeches, advertisements, service encounters, notices, instruction manuals, and interviews.

The text types that are listed as examples in this chapter are for north-east Thailand and differ somewhat from those for other regions of the country or other countries, because the usefulness of some genres depends on aspects of everyday life. For example, bus and train schedules are included in the Stage 2 curriculum for these north-east provinces, but that is not so for hill-tribe schools in the northern provinces. In contrast, bus schedules would probably be listed for Grade 1 in a school in Bangkok.

What students read and write about (non-language content) also varies from place to place. The procedural texts that are listed for the north-east provinces, for example, deal with how to breed fish, maintain a garden and store drinking water – matters of vital urgency in the dry rural north-east, but of little importance in the wet southern provinces or in Bangkok city.

Overall, it has been found in Thailand that about three-quarters of the starter books are suitable for use in all regions of the country. They are called 'core' starter books to distinguish them from 'regional' starter books that are written for use in some particular part of the country.

In practice, the genre coverage of the programme is not limited by the range of starter books. Rather it depends on what students do within the learning/teaching activities that follow from the starter books because the possibility is there for students to go on to write two or even more different kinds of texts within the one programme unit and Level 1 students, for example, may go on to write letters, advertisements, and other kinds of texts in some of their programme units, in spite of the fact that only story, information and procedural ('How To') starter books are provided at that level.

In Thailand, sufficient starter texts were provided to allow teachers to have some choice, because conditions, and therefore needs, vary there between schools even in the same region. Teachers are encouraged, too, to develop additional programme units that are based on activities of local importance.

One class may read and write the same number of books and cover the same number of genres as another, while working through considerably fewer programme units. That happens when students become exceptionally engrossed in a particular topic and they go on to write several different kinds of texts. CLE literacy programmes are meant to have that kind of flexibility.

Stage 1

In the course of the Stage 1 programme, students usually write and use the following kinds of texts:

1. Story books, such as
    (a) single-episode narratives, telling of legends or carrying a moral and;
    (b) recounts, telling the sequence of events of a student project (e.g. 'Planting Our Rice').
2. Procedural texts (called 'How To' books) such as, 'How To Make a Paper Hat' or 'How to Bottle Beans'.
3. Expository texts (called 'Information Books'):
    (a) descriptions of a place, thing, or people (e.g. 'This is Surin', 'My Home' or 'The Frog Family') and
    (b) books about a class of things (e.g. 'Our Book of Birds').
4. Incidental letters, notices, messages and display texts of various kinds.

Stage 2

By the time students complete Stage 1, they typically have become independent readers and writers of simple texts within some genres and they already have implicit understandings of differences between those kinds of texts. Some of those differences will also have been given incidental explicit attention, but students now deepen and systematize their understandings of the differences between the different types of texts, and how to use texts for different purposes. Accordingly, the starter books for Stage 2 include examples of 'public' texts, such as advertisements and bus timetables, that are used in everyday life, different kinds of letters, and the like, as well as narrative, procedural, and expository texts.

In the genres that are continued from Level 1, the starter texts become more complex and more sophisticated in both structure and content. The following is a general description of that trend for a Stage 2 programme:

1. Stories with a more complex structure than in Stage 1, including:

    (a) Longer episodical narratives set in some other time ('Once upon a time . . .') or some other place ('In a far-off country . . .').

    (b) Stories with a recountal embedded within them and stories with a recurrent structure (like, 'The Boy Who Cried Wolf').

    (c) True narratives (with a setting–complication–resolution structure).
        In general, the students progress from writing 'recount' to writing 'reports', and then to true narratives.

2. Procedural and expository books that have practical uses – the focus is on the content – and the students tend to write more than one kind of text in the course of the programme unit.

3. Brochures and pamphlets, are good models for using within the particular community.

4. Letters for personal communication.

5. Newspaper items such as reports of local events, advertisements and cartoons.

6. Verse, jingles, fun with language.

Stage 3

The genres that students deal with in this final stage of elementary schooling encompass as complete a coverage as possible of what they will need in later life. Students who are going on to secondary education should encounter the types of texts that they will be required to study and write at secondary school and all the students should learn to deal with the kinds of texts that they are likely to encounter in private and commercial life.

    Level 3 students are concerned with such genres as:

1. newspaper articles and reports;
2. short stories of literary quality (fictional narrative);
3. biographies, travel tales (factual narrative);
4. plays and films;
5. radio scripts (including advertisements);
6. commercial and public documents, such as user manuals, government forms, commercial documents, business letters, invoices, receipts and accounts, timetables, catalogues;
7. reference books, e.g. dictionaries, encyclopaedias.
8. texts used in formal business, minutes of meetings, annual reports of community bodies, and speeches.

    In these final years of the elementary school, it is neither possible nor desirable to provide models of some of the genres, such as novels, plays, reference books, application forms, schedules, reports and films within the reading programme itself – examples exist and are used in the wider community or in other subject areas of the school curriculum. But examples can be provided of particularly important types of public and commercial texts and the typical structure for others can be given, for students to use in examining authentic texts, including their own.

In some cases, too, it is not desirable to prescribe additional reading within the literacy programme, because that would tend to be restrictive rather than facilitative. Instead, schools need to widen the range of genres that are available to students in the school library. With classroom reading and writing activities becoming more and more individual, the need for a good school library becomes ever more urgent.

Genres should not be thought of apart from operational and referential context, as those concepts are explained in Chapter 8. A genre is associated with a particular kind of social process and generic structure arises from the nature of that social process. It follows that learning to read and write a particular genre involves learning to read and write appropriately within particular kinds of operational contexts.

Focus

Focus refers to what students will learn to do with the types of texts that are listed for that Stage of the programme.

Stage 1

In the Stage 1 programme, the overt emphasis is on enjoyment from finding meaning and making meaning in print. But the educational purposes include a consolidation and enrichment of basic understandings about reading, writing, and written language as well as a demonstration of the usefulness of reading and writing in enabling people to do interesting, enjoyable and satisfying things. That was the focus of these same children as they set out to learn to speak their mother tongue and the focus must remain the same in their first formal acquaintanceship with written discourse, because we want them to continue to use the same language-learning strategies, with similar enthusiasm and persistence.

Stage 2

In Stage 2, there is a widening of the variety of the texts and the fields of knowledge that they treat, and the focus is on using different reading and writing strategies for different purposes.

Stage 3

In Stage 3, the focus moves to using reading and writing to learn and to cope with demands on their literacy that they will meet in the immediate future.

Non-language content

'Relevancy' is an overused word but it is an important one to keep in mind when framing a reading/writing programme for those who as yet do not see anything like the full extent to which reading and writing can be of value in their daily lives. If the knowledge and skills that students acquire while learning to read and write are immediately useful in their daily lives, they are likely to be convinced of the value of literacy, and their literacy is likely to go on growing and improving, through continued use.

The non-language content of a literacy programme will change, of course, as students move up through the grades. But there should also be differences between programmes for different school populations. What is a valuable piece of knowledge or an essential skill in northern Cornwall may be completely irrelevant in Brixton or Leeds. And what are essential knowledge and skills for children in rural Tennessee may have only curiosity value in down-town Memphis.

Choice of the non-language content of the reading programme is crucially important when, through poverty, people necessarily place a high priority on individual and community welfare and material needs. Anything that is irrelevant to those urgent needs is likely to have a low community priority so that the topics of the reading, writing, and talking should include some that are of high importance to the learners' immediate welfare and happiness. For that reason, at least some of the decisions for content should be made locally.

For the poor rural areas of north-east provinces of Thailand, for example, units of the literacy programme were written around hygiene, immunization against preventable diseases, and clean water storage and where malnutrition is a problem, children are likely to learn how to set up and maintain a school fish and poultry farm, and a vegetable garden, in the course of reading and writing about that. Whether or not students learn how to set up and maintain a fish farm, for example, depends on whether or not one is in operation at their school.

Programme materials

The classroom kit

In the Thai-language CLE programmes, a classroom kit contains the following:

Starter texts for use by the teacher in introducing the programme units. For example, fifteen such texts were supplied in the initial north-east Thailand programme. Students do not read the published starter books. Instead, they 'write' for themselves the group and/or individual texts that they use within the programme.

There is a *teacher's guide* for each stage of the programme, and *teacher's notes* for each programme unit. In Thailand, there are usually two volumes of teacher's notes: one for the core starter texts, and one for the starter texts for the particular region.

The classroom kit also contains *equipment that is needed to teach* that grade level for the first time but is not otherwise likely to be available in a classroom. For Stage 1 classes, that includes a 'pocket' chart, a supply of large sheets of cheap paper, sheets of white card, sets of wick pens, scissors and glue. Most of those are reusable or refillable in subsequent years.

Supplementary reading material is needed for each grade beyond the first, because of the rapid growth of enthusiasm for reading and writing. And children must, of course, handle and use published books, as well as those that they and their fellow students write. In developing countries, that becomes a difficulty, albeit a positive one, because there are seldom adequate school libraries.

Teacher inservice training

The success of programmes as innovative as these depend on effective inservice training of teachers. And in places where there has been long-term serious educational failure, those teachers who will use the programme need to see, first-hand, that the programme will work with students like theirs.

The setting up of 'pilot' schools and classes is a first priority as a CLE programme is developed in a new region, because of the need to trial programme materials as part of the programme developmental process.

The training of teachers is not usually done at the 'pilot' schools nor are 'pilot' classes used to demonstrate the methodology. Instead, the first step towards introducing the programme into a group of schools is to have a member of the CLE programme development team demonstrate each step of a Stage 1 CLE unit, with children from one of the target schools. This is usually done in three or four sessions, over a period of several days.

It has been found that this is a far more effective introduction to the methodology than any amount of talking, showing of videos, slide presentations, and the like. Teachers will see someone else teaching their pupils much more than they themselves could hope to do and, in particular, see students like their own becoming enthusiastically involved in learning.

After such a demonstration, teachers are usually ready to volunteer for a week-long seminar/workshop. They return from that seminar with the materials and information they need to teach several programme units. After the teachers begin to implement the programme, periodic teachers' meetings are held to allow them to discuss problems with members of the CLE project team, and to share ideas and experiences with one another. The more complex procedures that are needed for large-scale programme implementation are discussed in Chapter 7.

Inservice teacher-training materials

In any case, inservice training kits are needed. An introductory kit is usually needed for administrators who do not have the time to witness a teaching demonstration that is necessarily spread over two or three days. The kit usually includes a video that covers all levels of the programme.

Members of the project team need a separate teacher-training kit for each of the three stages of the programme. A kit usually includes such things as a video and a slide set, the teacher's manual, a few starter books, teacher's notes, and a set of overhead transparencies. In Thailand, the kit is used in conjunction with demonstration teaching, during four- or five-day teacher-training seminars.

Teacher-training kits assume importance only when dealing with large populations. In single-school situations, more can be done by demonstration and working with teachers than by talking and showing videos and slides.

The programme development schedule

In general, the literacy programme for each school grade is developed over a period of three years, in accordance with the following schedule.

First year
1. Outline of the programme for that grade level.
2. Development and trial of programme elements.

Second year

3. Writers' workshop for that grade.
4. Prototype version of the teacher's manual and training materials.
5. Piloting of the grade programme in schools.

Third year

6. Programme review.
7. Revision and printing of the starter books.
8. Revision and piloting of the teacher's manual.
9. Compilation of teacher's notes.
10. Revision and piloting of the training materials.

Fourth year

11. Printing of the starter books and teacher's manual.
12. Printing of the teacher's notes.
13. General implementation of the year's programme (in projects over 100 classrooms in size).

Conclusion

Whether it be a text, a teaching process, a video, a teacher's manual, or the entire programme for a year, every item goes through the four consecutive steps of developing, trialling, piloting, and implementing. The first three of these steps each take one year, and it is followed by revision of the item. For the developmental and pilot years only low-cost prototype versions of the programme materials are used. Finished versions are produced only in time for the general implementation phase in the fourth year.

The authors have learnt to adopt this unhurried approach to programme development for the very reason that they have been working in situations where there has been gross failure, so that fundamental changes have to be made in teacher and student behaviours. The fact that no published pupil materials are produced make possible further progressive development of the programme, even after the fourth year. If a programme unit or a starter book ought to be withdrawn because a better one may be devised, only the teacher's notes and/or the starter book for that one unit become obsolete. It should be reasonably easy, therefore, to prevent the programme from ossifying if the educational administrators remember that they have adopted CLE techniques for programme development, not a particular CLE programme.

Chapters 2 and 3 described the nature of CLE literacy teaching and of how teachers and students work together within CLE classroom activities; and Chapter 4 outlined a CLE programme for elementary schools, across several major dimensions. One further programme dimension – the assessment of learning and teaching – remains; and it is essential that assessment be based on the same understandings of language and learning if they are not to conflict with, and thereby mar, both the teaching and the programme building. In Chapters 5 and 6, Dr John Oller Jr deals with that remaining dimension of literacy teaching and programming.

CHAPTER 5

Testing literacy and related language skills: Part I, Review of theory

JOHN W. OLLER, Jr

Introduction

Tests are important because they define what the curriculum is about and what is expected of the curriculum, of the students, and of the teachers. In fact, tests probably define the objectives of schooling more exactly and with more binding power than any other sort of activity that takes place in a school context. The fact is that, just as a liquid seeks its own level, teaching will rise or fall to the level of the testing. If the expectations set by testing are high the teaching and learning will tend to rise to the challenge. If the level defined by the tests is mediocre or low, teaching will tend to sink to that level. Therefore, an approach to testing ought to be based on the best possible theory because it will tend to define curricular objectives in addition to most of what happens in the classroom. Part of the need for theory will be fulfilled by a clear idea of what the curriculum should consist of. Previous chapters of this book are about theory, curriculum, and its implementation in classroom activities. Now, in this chapter, we come to testing the sort of activity that can provide the practical milestones for the curriculum and its implementation. Teaching always tends toward the activities defined by tests. The tests define the ends in view throughout the educational process. These facts about the relation between theory, curriculum, teaching, and testing are shown in Fig. 5.1.

This chapter sums up and reviews theory in anticipation of the next, which gives examples of tests. The discussion of theory is consistent with that of previous chapters, although language is viewed from, perhaps, a slightly different perspective. It then presents five basic principles to be followed in testing (and in the curriculum at large). To exemplify the principles and show how they might work in hypothetical cases, a number of example tests that illustrate requirements laid down in the theory are

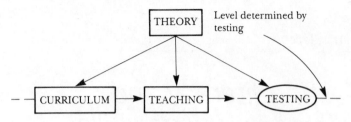

Figure 5.1: Curriculum and teaching will rise or fall to the level of the testing

discussed. Finally, the chapter concludes with some guidelines for teachers and educators to follow in implementing an integrated testing programme.

A review of theory

Language plays a central role in nearly any classroom. Language is even important to programmes aimed at athletics, dance, music, and art where movement, gesture, pictures, sculpture and action enjoy great importance as communicative devices. In fact, almost any educator will admit that literacy is at the heart of any well-rounded educational experience. Success in education depends largely on the degree to which children in schools are enabled to understand the connection between what the teacher says, what is written in the books, and what takes place in the world of experience. Success at school means understanding classroom discourse whether it is spoken or written, that is, it means understanding the curriculum, by linking it appropriately with the facts of experience. It might well be said that being educated is a matter of being able to negotiate many kinds of discourse relative to the world of experience.

In helping children to grow into mature, well-educated persons, schools are obliged to place a special emphasis on various forms of written discourse. Literacy means being able to understand and, in some cases, to produce, a fairly wide range of written materials. In the modern world of the 1990s, as we look towards the beginning of the third millennium AD, the technological revolution has transformed itself into an increasingly abstract information processing revolution. In addition to being able to read, write, and handle numbers, literacy today increasingly means being able to find your way around a CRT (cathode ray tube), or a liquid-crystal screen, via a keyboard or 'mouse', and knowing the ins and outs of various kinds of computer software. Language plays a central role in all of this as well. However, our purpose is not merely to understand and appreciate the special role played by language in the modern world, but to get some notion about how to assess or measure those skills and abilities that being literate requires.

In testing literacy and the language skills that support and sustain it, two questions, as Richard Walker and Saowalak Rattanavich have stressed in earlier chapters, are critical: (1) What kinds of discourse must children learn to read, write, and use in other ways? And, (2) What range of uses must children become able to perform with the various kinds of discourse? The answers to these two questions, as pointed out in earlier chapters, will set the limits not only of the curriculum for literacy, but also of the tests that ought to be used in assessing its implementation.

From the curricular point of view, the teacher needs to know what kinds of things literate people are expected to be able to do and with what kinds of discourse. This will enable teachers to determine what kinds of situations to orchestrate in the classroom so that the children will learn to do those things with those kinds of discourse. For instance, in addition to being able to read and understand the writing seen on signs on doors, streets, and product labels, children need to be able to understand and talk about, as well as read and write, stories, descriptions, letters, resumés, summaries and the like. In addition to these standard forms of texts, as children grow and mature within and beyond their school experience, they should become able to handle many other kinds of texts such as news articles, editorials, advertisements, menus, price lists, catalogues, product guarantees, research reports, directions on medicine bottles, timetables (for buses, trains, and aeroplanes), invoices, sales agreements, contracts, maths problems, proofs, written instructions for assembling or using consumer goods, and so on. The question is how all of this growth and development can be brought about in school contexts.

Now, it is a fact that every literate person started out being non-literate and every language-user just as certainly began as an infant that could no more understand a particular language than any illiterate can read. So, how do infants become able to understand and speak a particular language and how do youngsters, who cannot read at first, become able to do so? The problem in both instances is summed up in Fig. 5.2.

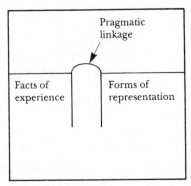

Figure 5.2: The process of making sense of discourse (pragmatic mapping)

The pre-linguistic infant becomes a language user by relating the conventional forms of a particular language (meaningful representations of a certain kind) to the facts of that infant's experience. By the same token, the pre-literate child who learns to read relates meaningful representations of a certain kind (visual representations of words or meanings in a particular language) to the facts of that child's experience. In both cases representations and facts are involved. In each instance, in order for the needed advance to be made, previously unknown and therefore incomprehensible representations must be related to more or less familiar facts. That is, the meanings of the representations (the special class of forms in a language or writing system, or both) must be determined relative to facts of experience.

The connections of the spoken or written forms to the relevant facts of experience must be unpacked. Names have to be linked to persons. Referring phrases must be linked to their objects that is, the things or abstract entities referred to. Predications must be associated with their particular meanings. Events must be identified and placed in their appropriate time frames. Whether an event, process, or state of being is perceived as ongoing or completed must be understood. Meanings intended by a particular person must be distinguished from ones not intended or possibly intended or understood by someone else. Meanings addressed to a particular consumer must be distinguished from those directed elsewhere. What is understood must be kept separate from what is meant. The problem of understanding discourse produced by someone else is to figure out what that person meant in constructing that discourse. What the producer means, however, in writing a text must be judged by that same producer according to what someone else is likely to understand from the text. In addition to all this, the person producing or interpreting discourse must assess it with respect to the facts of experience. It is necessary to make some sort of judgement about whether it is true of those facts (factual), merely resembles them (fictional), or is some sort of fantasy, play with words, irony, sarcasm, lie, joke, and so on.

What makes the unpacking problem solvable, difficult though it is, is that the facts to which representations at least purport to relate are already understood to some extent before we ever come to the problem of unpacking any particular discourse or other representation. The persons, objects, events, and relations of experience are already known in part through *sensory* impressions and in part through prior knowledge whether it is like the innate expectation that visible objects will be tangible or the sort of knowledge acquired from previous understandings of discourse. For example, in the case of the normal pre-lingual child it is the context of experience that helps the child to begin to understand utterances (and gestures) of others (or their writings) and eventually to begin to produce similar utterances (gestures, and writings). By the same token, the already established connection between utterances in a particular language and the facts of experience of, say, a normal post-lingual (talking) but pre-literate (not yet reading) child, will similarly help the pre-literate child to begin to become literate. The child first understands certain facts of experience through sensory impressions (sight, hearing, touch, smell, and taste) and later begins to connect these sensory representations with significant gestures and intonations patterns. Becoming able to return a smile, or to recognize a wave, or to react to pointing by looking in the right direction, to a certain intonation with an appropriate other intonation, would each qualify as growth in the gestural, paralinguistic, or *kinesic*, system. A little later still, the particular bodily gestures we call speech (the elements of the *linguistic* system) will come more and more to have special significance and begin to be unravelled in their special relations to facts. Even later still, written representations of speech gestures will come into view and begin to be unpacked by the child who is moving from pre-literacy into what Smith (1982) has called 'the literacy club'.

All of this is summed up in Fig. 5.3. The first kind of representation we learn to handle is sensory. We learn to recognize objects and events that we see, hear, touch, taste, and smell. Secondarily, we are aided very early in our development by significant movements, especially by the gestures of other persons around us. They point to particular objects and to ourselves. They show approval or disapproval in ways that mark objects and events as acceptable or unacceptable. They move or direct us through our environment. These significant gestures and movements of others have value mainly in guiding us in the way we manage and negotiate relations with things, events, and persons in our environment. At a third remove, and at a substantially higher level of abstraction, other persons use speech (assuming we can hear, or manual signs if we cannot). At a fourth remove from the facts, these significant linguistic forms may be spoken by someone else and only heard by us. Or at a fifth remove, they may eventually be spoken by us. At the sixth level of the diagram (and it must be noted that the levels are somewhat arbitrarily arranged and distinguished here) we come to the writings of others, and finally, at level seven, we come to writings that we ourselves produce. In Fig. 5.3, tape-recorded forms are not pictured, but all the representational forms that are shown serve to represent the facts of experience in abstract ways.

With linguistic forms aided by gestures and sensory information, for example, we can name or describe objects pointed to: 'See that small lizard, there, on the wall?' We can designate their attributes: 'He's so quick.' We can describe their actions: 'See how fast he moves?' We can call attention to characters: 'He has a long tail and stripes on his belly.' And so on. We can refer to facts through specifying subject–predicate relations: '[The lizard] subject [runs into the bushes] predicate.' We can negate such

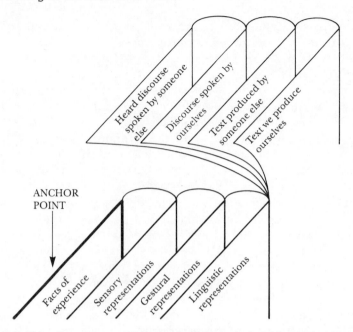

Figure 5.3: Expanding the pragmatic mapping of the facts of experience relative to representations of them (and vice versa – representations to facts)

relations: '[The lizard] $_{subject}$ [does [not] $_{negation}$ like to be approached by people] $_{predicate}$.' We may also string such relations together through conjunction (e.g. by words like 'and') or we may subordinate one subject–predicate relation to another in a hierarchical way: '[[When] $_{subordinator}$ [the lizard [[that] $_{subordinator}$ is on the wall] $_{subordinate\ clause}$ sees me standing here] $_{subordinate\ clause}$ [he immediately runs away] $_{main\ clause}$].' Referring to Fig. 5.3 again, facts are connected first to sensory experience, subsequently to gestures, and finally to language. In interpreting discourse in a linguistic form, therefore, the problem of comprehension is to determine the practical connections of the discourse forms with the facts of experience. Or, in producing discourse, the problem is to arrange forms in such a way that connections with facts which we choose to represent can be correctly determined by someone else.

What does such a theory teach us about a curriculum for literacy and about the kinds of classroom activities and tests that will help children to become literate? One lesson is that the interpreting of linguistic forms is aided by the construction of sensory and gestural representations. In keeping with all that Richard Walker and Saowalak Rattanavich have said in earlier chapters, this may be called the principle of *scaffolding*. It says that the richer the sensory and gestural information about the factual basis of any given discourse (whether spoken, signed, or written) the easier it will be for the consumer (learner, listener, reader) to determine the meanings of that discourse. Scaffolding, especially relevant when it comes to unfamiliar representations such as written ones are for anyone who is still preliterate. In the early stages of becoming literate, supplementary context supplied through still or moving pictures, audio recordings, dramatization, games related to the textual meanings, manipulable illustrations, hands-on experimental activities, all will help the learner to be able to solve the closely related language and literacy problems, that is to link the unfamiliar forms with their respective meanings. Linguistic comprehension (whether in listening or reading activities) means unpacking the meanings intended by the producer(s) of the discourse as well as any additional meanings that are suggested by the facts of experience in relation to the forms of the discourse itself. All of this depends on correctly linking linguistic forms with facts of experience. For such a determination of meanings to be possible, there must *be* some determinate facts. Surprisingly, many educators (and theoreticians too, especially linguists), sad to say, are apt to omit this last and crucial step of connecting forms of representations with facts. They are apt to stress sounds, words, and discourse structures, or sound and letter correspondences (phonics), but forget about the facts of experience that those discourse elements represent. Without connection to such facts, discourse elements are empty. A nearly certain recipe for failure in any kind of language instruction is to try to get children to process linguistic forms that are essentially unrelated to any factual basis. The tendency is to err on the discourse side of the formula to emphasize surface forms of representations – sounds, letters, words, sentences, structures, functions of speech acts (the right-hand side of Fig. 5.2) at the expense of the factual side of the equation (the left-hand side of Fig. 5.2).

Teachers and curriculum writers are apt to assume that because they themselves have reached the stage where the abstract, universal, and virtual aspects of spoken and written discourse are accessible to them, this is an appropriate place for children (or other beginners) to start. Their assumption is false. Such educators have forgotten, because their learning took place mostly at a subconscious level, all the scaffolding they used in order to attain the abstract understanding they have of the meanings of words, written symbols, and so on. Therefore, they are inclined to throw away any scaffolding that would lead learners from facts in the real world to the highest forms of abstract reasoning. Instead these misguided educators, unaware of how they actually learnt and ever cognizant of how they have been taught to think people ought to learn, begin at some remote level. Often they dispense with the facts of experience and even the whole world itself in which those facts have meaning. Phonics approaches to reading, of course, are a classic case in point.

It is about as easy for a foreign language student to acquire an additional language, for a child to acquire the mechanics of written discourse, or for an illiterate to become literate by such methods as it would be to understand what is going on in a film where the utterances of the script are scrambled and the pictures, sound effects, and other supporting elements have been removed. The fact is that we really need to refer to particular facts of the world of experience and to the rich connections between such actual facts and the discourse that relates to those facts in order to solve difficult discourse processing problems such as acquiring a language or becoming literate. Even the acquisition of so-called 'mechanical' aspects of written discourse such as punctuation and spelling will benefit greatly from attention to tasks that take particular facts of the world of experience into consideration.

A handful of recommendations for testing (and teaching)

In keeping with the foregoing theory, here are five recommendations for the testing of language skills (and for teaching them) in relation to literacy programmes:

1. Always use a well-determined and preferably a well-motivated factual basis (i.e. use meaningful discourse or textual material that makes sense relative to a factual basis that is self-contained and is itself motivated, that is *don't use nonsense or pieces of text whose meanings cannot be determined*). For example, use a story, game, activity, dialogue, description, or any discourse that has a beginning and an end and that makes sense as a unit, i.e., that is determinately related to some known or demonstrable experiential basis. In ordinary experience sufficient motivation for discourse is usually supplied by a meaningful conflict or disequilibrium (one that interferes with the attainment of some desired goal), or in general a change that has surprise value relative to the execution of some on-going plan. Select motivated materials that are related in known ways to facts that are or can be made known to learners by some means other than the discourse forms per se. Remember that the learners need scaffolding to help them in unpacking the discourse elements. For instance, do not ever test (or try to teach) a single discourse element separated from the factual context that makes it meaningful. Do not test any isolated sound–symbol relation, vocabulary item, sentence out of the blue sky, or even a paragraph, an apology, a request, or a dialogue out of the blue. Do not (in the early stages) use a text that is abstract and difficult to illustrate with pictures, dramatization, and so on. If you want these kinds of linguistic devices to appear in your test, be sure to embed

them in a meaningful context where sufficient scaffolding is available to learners. *Never try to test bits and pieces of language without linking them to determinate facts of experience.* In other words, *never try to test single items of linguistic form in isolation from some particular, meaningful, demonstrable, factual context.*

2. Respect the facts (what's happening, who's involved, when, where, for what purposes, and so on) *don't ignore the real world.* Every teaching activity, question asked, or test item should relate to facts that are known or that can reasonably be inferred from ones that are known. *Never ask students to manipulate meaningless surface forms of language or text.* On the contrary, ask them about what happened, who was involved, when it happened, where, why George was in such a hurry, why the lizard runs when we approach it, and so on. If elements of surface form (particular sounds, words, structures, functions) need to be considered, they should be examined *in their respective factual contexts* but never in total isolation from such facts. For instance, if the name of a certain symptom relative to a medical prescription is in doubt, for example, say the word 'fever', for instance, then it might make sense to test that word, but only in relation to a fully developed and appropriate factual context. (A certain child in our story is sick. Mother feels his forehead and discovers he is burning up with fever. She takes his temperature, and so on.) These things can be pictured and dramatized. We can even harmlessly create the illusion of a fever by holding a hot wet cloth to our own or a child's forehead. Relative to such facts the term 'fever' can be given a determinate meaning and can be legitimately tested, but merely to say that 'temperature' is a synonym for 'fever' is of little use to anyone who does not yet know the connection of one or both of these terms with the facts of experience.

3. The performance assessed must involve the actual comprehension or expression of meaning relative to known facts: *we should never settle for surface-processing alone.* Never ask students merely to 'use a word in a sentence', or 'ask me a question using "if"', or 'find a word that rhymes with "time"', or 'ask me permission for three things you would like to do', 'give five different ways to apologize for missing an appointment', 'explain how you would ask someone to stop bothering you at the airport', and so on. Of course, it may be important to find out if a language user knows the meaning of a particular word, or even how that word sounds if it is uttered. It may be necessary to find out if a user understands a particular syntactic structure, or whether to take a particular statement as a request, order, suggestion, and so on. However, meanings, sounds, syntactic categories, morphological devices, connective relations, indirect speech acts, and the like, are important precisely because they may be used to determine different facts. There-

fore, nothing whatever will be lost of the sounds, words, phrases, structures, functions, and so on, if we refer always to determinate facts in a well-developed meaningful context. On the contrary, much will be gained.

4. Aim for processing under normal time constraints: *do not teach or test indefinitely shrunken down or expanded half-second segments of reading.* Very rapid tachistoscopic presentations of words may be interesting to certain experimental psychologists, but they generally make a poor basis for a reading curriculum or almost any sort of reading test. Also, at the other end of the time-scale, avoid using activities or tests that allow unrealistically large amounts of time to complete a task. For instance, allowing examinees sufficient time in reading a text to look up every word in a bilingual dictionary would rarely qualify as normal language processing. Nor is writing single words from dictation (as in a traditional spelling test), with long pauses between items, a normal listening task. Normal language processing usually involves a rate of discourse presentation that is at least equal to (or sometimes faster than) a normal rate of speech. A better way of testing spelling, and a great deal of discourse processing capability as well, would be to give a dictation at a normal rate of speech with pauses between natural phrase or clause boundaries. (See below for more about how to give dictation.) Reading silently can proceed, normally, even more rapidly than speech. Writing takes more time, but even here there are limits. A friendly letter that takes more than a year of concentrated energy to write will probably never get written. While in teaching there may be cases where allowing large amounts of time is desirable, in testing this should generally be avoided. Language processing should be expected to occur at a reasonable, normal, rate.

5. The questions or discourse-processing performances asked of the students in a test (or in a teaching activity) should aim at the central elements of the text or discourse the kinds of things that intelligent, normal people would be expected to notice or talk about. For instance, in a narrative where there is a dog-fight and one of the dogs ends up dead on the pavement, it would be odd to ask whether or not there was a yellow cat lurking in the shadows nearby, or how many taxis passed while the dog-fight was in progress, if a fly buzzed past Sam's ear, if one of the on-lookers spoke Chinese, how much time elapsed between the honking of a car horn and the miaowing of the cat while the battle raged, and so on. On the other hand, details that have some bearing on the story (that the German shepherd's thick collar helped him to overcome the fierce Doberman) or actions that might be understood as relevant to the facts depicted (e.g. the need for dog owners to keep their animals off the street) are fair game for test questions.

Exemplifying tests

This section defines testing, discusses its foundational grounding in the facts of experience, sets the limits of what can be legitimately tested, and offers some examples of ways to approach testing, especially in the classroom. It is important to bear in mind that the example tests to be given here are merely for the sake of illustration. The examples themselves are not intended as particular tests to be applied in any actual classroom setting. Rather, they are intended to illustrate *kinds of tests* as well as *kinds of testing activities* that can be *developed from and applied to any factual discourse basis that meets the requirements laid down in our theory*. The purpose here is to illustrate applications of the theory and the five caveats (derived from that theory) which were just stated in the previous section.

The starting point for test construction (on any curricular activity, for that matter), according to our theory, is to select a suitable, factual, discourse basis. In previous chapters these have been referred to as 'concentrated language encounters'. Such a factual basis might come directly from the experience of a single child in the classroom, or it might be supplied by the teacher (or taken from a book or videotape or other source). It might involve an event or series of events that the child shares with other children in the classroom. For instance, in a certain classroom context a first-grader told about a burglar breaking into her house over the weekend, by climbing through a window, right across her sleeping baby brother's crib, and taking out the TV and stereo through the front door. The little girl was concerned for her baby brother's safety, but fortunately he was unharmed. Such a story, recounted by the child could form the (factual) basis for a 'big book' and a great many spin-off activities including a host of tests drawing upon that factual context.

Alternatively, the discourse basis might be a story, game, activity, experiment, field-trip, or some other element of the curriculum. The story could be one provided by the teacher, or taken from a book. The important thing in choosing a discourse basis for teaching and testing is that any given choice should be one of a suitable difficulty level, not too easy or too difficult, and that it be interesting, based on facts that are easy to illustrate, dramatize, and thus, to communicate about and learn from. Further, the factual basis is what will largely determine the validity of our testing activities. Selecting a suitable discourse basis for testing (and, of course, for teaching) may be more a matter of art than science, but there is no way around the choice. The test writer (or teacher) must face up to the task of selecting from the myriad activities, materials, and incidentals that go to make up the curriculum, the sort of factual basis that will provide a grounding for testing activities. Here some intelligent, sensitive, subjective judgement is called for. The decisions required are essentially the same as those that go into the making of a big book, or the selection of a site for a field-trip, or the choice of a game, experiment, or activity to use or foster in the classroom or on the playground.

In addition to considering factors such as interest, dramatizability, level of difficulty, motivation, and the like, the test writer also needs to take into consideration the purpose of the testing. According to the theory advocated in this book there ought not be any testing whatever that does not contribute in a positive way to the clarification (the very definition) of what the curriculum and the whole school experience is about. Only tests and testing activities that help learners and teachers alike to define their objectives should be used. In other words, the tests ought always to be integral parts of the curriculum. They ought to be good teaching tools. Further, if the caveats listed in the immediately preceding section are taken seriously, since the tests are to be based on discourse forms that have been systematically linked to actual facts in the experience of the children to be tested, the test itself *is a teaching device*. It helps learners to understand both the discourse and its relation to the known facts. For this reason, it will do no harm for teachers to use tests as tests per se and at the same time to use them as teaching tools.

CHAPTER 6

Testing literacy and related language skills: Part II, Examples of testing procedures and activities

JOHN W. OLLER, Jr

Introduction

Before giving examples of actual testing activities that might be developed it will be useful to define the term 'test'. What is to count as a test? In fact, any discourse processing performance that can be judged as better or worse relative to some normative standard can be qualified as a test. All that is required is that the rater (the tester, teacher, or whatever rater or group of raters are involved) have a reliable notion of what a better or worse performance on the task in question consists of. A task that meets this minimal testing requirement may be called a *scalable* test. That is to say, performances can be rated on a scale ranging from better to worse. Most language processing tasks, where the factual basis (as discussed in the preceding chapter) is known, will qualify as tests in this minimal sense. Examples would include such things as telling a story, summarizing an argument, recounting a conversation, explaining a process, describing a scene, giving a speech, taking part in a drama, and so on.

A more stringent requirement for a test is that it be *scorable*, in other words, it must be possible to reduce a performance of the task to a number that represents right or wrong answers, or some determinable quantity. Not all scalable tasks tasks meet this more stringent requirement, though all scorable tasks must, in principle, always be scalable. Of the class of scorable tasks, a still smaller set of so-called 'objective' tests exist which can be reduced to marks on an answer sheet or other device (e.g. a keyboard or computer screen) that can be mechanically scored. Further, there probably are tasks which are so indeterminate (usually because no factual basis for them can be determined) as to be unscalable. In general, when the facts to which a given discourse performance relates are unknown or cannot be determined, the performance itself will not be reliably scalable or scorable. It will not serve as an adequate basis for a test.

The kinds of tasks that might qualify as tests can be summed up in Fig. 6.1. Discourse tasks can be divided, loosely, into

1. indeterminate ones (which are unsuitable as tests or as teaching activities);
2. those that are determinate and therefore at least scalable (which minimally qualify as potential tests or as teaching activities);
3. those that are sufficiently determinate to be both scalable and scorable (i.e. ones that are especially useful for classroom purposes);
4. those that are machine-scorable (those most commonly used in widescale institutional testing).

Generally, at the national, provincial, district, or even school-wide levels, only machine scorable tests will be applied, while individual classroom teachers will generally prefer tests that fall into categories (2) and (3), that is that are determinate enough at least to be scalable and in many cases also scorable.

Admittedly, for some institutional purposes, it will occasionally be necessary to use screening procedures that are not machine-scorable. Some test specialists see this as a disadvantage owing to the fact that a 'subjective' element of judgement enters the rating of any non-mechanical scoring procedure. However, what such specialists overlook is that the same sort of 'subjective' judgement enters any scoring or rating whatever including the kind that ultimately depends on an optical scanner or other mechanical device. The fact is that someone (or some group) must decide in advance of any machine scoring what the correct answers are to the test items. At the point where those decisions are made, a machine-scorable test is no more 'objective' than any merely scalable task is.

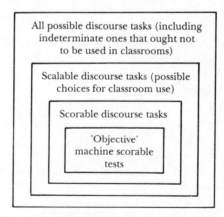

Figure 6.1: Kinds of discourse tasks viewed and classified as kinds of tests

In fact, there is no guarantee whatever that a machine-scorable test will even be more *reliable* (much less that it will be more *valid*) than any test which is not machine scorable. Of course, *reliability* is defined merely as the degree to which a test tends to produce the same results under the same conditions on different occasions, while *validity* is a more stringent requirement. The degree of validity is the extent to which the test actually measures whatever it purports to measure. Now, as to *scorer reliability*, it is true that a machine will usually make fewer errors in scoring than a human scorer might make, but even this is not guaranteed. For instance, certain items in the key used by the machine can be marked incorrectly and result in inaccuracies throughout all the test scores. Or, a given test-taker or any number of them may correctly mark the answer sheets but in ways that the machine does not recognize, for example by using too light a pencil, or making an 'X' through wrong answers, or by using ink instead of graphite, or by getting off by one number and giving all the right answers but to questions numbered 2 through 101 instead of 1 through 100, by crossing out wrongly marked answers instead of erasing them completely, by not filling in the machine-scored bubbles completely, and so on. Human scorers would be apt to spot some of these sources of unreliability and, in such cases, could generate more accurate scores than any current mechanical optical-scanner would be apt to. At any rate, it is inaccurate to suppose that all the subjectivity (i.e. human judgement) has been removed from any machine-scorable 'objective' test.

With the foregoing definitions in mind, we are ready to consider what can be tested in a fact-based discourse. A little later we will go on to consider some examples of actual testing activities that might be applied to a wide range of discourse types. The objective cannot be to illustrate all possible techniques, as that would be impossible, but we can set certain definite limits to the kinds of fact-based items that can be included in the kinds of tests that are recommended. Suppose we use the following narrative about the burglary the first-grader reported. This narrative, or one not very different from it, might form the basis for a big book and the various activities related to its construction, illustration, and mastery by a group of children who are in the process of becoming literate.

The Burglary

Hi. My name is Suzie. On Saturday night, a burglar broke into our apartment. He came through a window. He stepped right across my baby brother's crib. My brother was asleep. He didn't wake up. Everyone else was asleep too. I was asleep. My grandmother was asleep. My mother was asleep. The burglar took the TV and stereo and went right out the front door. Nobody saw him, but we figured out what happened the next morning.

Supposing the children in the classroom (or whatever children are to be tested) already know the language in which the narrative is told, this text may not be too difficult even for fairly early beginners.

Fortunately, even if they do not know the language, much can be done to simplify its presentation and thus to enable the children to acquire the language while they are developing an understanding of the facts of the story. For instance, the events can be acted out. The facts can be portrayed, partially at least, through pictures and illustrations. One of the great advantages of narratives, or in fact of any coherent text (as contrasted with nonsense or less coherent material), is that it is potentially infinitely rich in logical connectedness. A coherent discourse can always be simplified through summarization or it can be expanded. The expansion can be developed either by reading between the lines or by inferring what probably came before or what followed after the facts expressed in the narrative. For instance, the text might be condensed into a single sentence: 'A thief broke into Suzie's house on Saturday night.' Or, it might be expanded. For instance, we may assume that the thief had the intention to steal before he broke into the house and that after doing so he intended to sell the stolen goods. Maybe he did so to support a drug habit. Probably, he did not harm the sleeping infant because his purpose was to steal something of value that he could sell in order to get money. Harming the infant would not have served the thief's purpose – and so forth.

The same sorts of logical manipulations are possible with any coherent text. They are possible because textual structure is such that it sustains certain kinds of inference. It can be proved rigorously that all kinds of discourse comprehension (and production as well) are based on inference. From this it follows that all tests or test items (as well as curricular materials) must ultimately depend on inference. Further, we have seen in the previous chapter why it is that *only* fact-based discourse processing activities ought to be used in assessing (or teaching) literacy and language skills. Any approach to testing (or teaching) which depends on discourse forms separated from their connection to a factual basis is an approach that lacks the necessary basis for determining the meanings of those discourse forms. The scaffolding that is essential to learners in order for them to reach the highest levels of abstraction and generalization (the heights of inferencing) will be absent. Therefore, only fact-based discourse (not excluding plausible fictions that can be illustrated or dramatized with actual facts) should be used in any teaching or testing activity.

It remains to illustrate a sufficiently wide range of fact-based testing activities to adequately cover the broad scope of discourse genres and uses of them that a thorough-going curriculum ought to include. In order to illustrate the kinds of test activities that might be used in, say, a first-grade classroom (or other school context) we will refer to the narrative about the burglary as told by Suzie on p. 69. Let us suppose that the curriculum is organized (as recommended throughout this book) so that the facts of the discourse (absolutely any discourse) introduced into the classroom are first made known to students through drama, realia, pictures, illustrations, and other methods that are more or less directly accessible to the senses.

Suppose, for instance, that the narrative about the burglary is told and acted out by Suzie, or is dramatized with the help of the teacher and class members, for example one who plays the sleeping infant, another who plays the burglar, and so on. Or alternatively, imagine that a very similar story is actually presented in a cartoon form on videotape. The facts of the narrative, in either of these cases, can be known abductively to such an extent that the knowledge of the facts becomes a substantial foundation together with the sort of inferential scaffolding described above upon which to build a rich and deep comprehension of the spoken discourse, written forms of it, and all of the associated language and literacy skills that may be required. For instance, after the facts have been established through drama or film, names, phrases, and whole sentences can be attached to the dramatized or pictured events. At first, this ought to be done with spoken forms and soon after with written ones. For instance, the child (or cartoon character) who plays the part of the burglar can wear an appropriate label printed on a card, 'The burglar', as can all of the other objects and characters of the story. Even the events can be labelled with captions in a cartoon style book. As comprehension deepens as a result of multiple passes through the story, and as the language forms are enriched at each phase of development and on each successive pass through the story, more written elements may be introduced. Eventually all of it is put down in a 'big book' that is illustrated by drawings done by the children themselves.

Yes/No questions

Testing activities are worked into the curriculum all along the way. For instance, the first testing the teacher needs to do is to determine if the children have understood the facts. To begin with, a series of 'yes/no' questions are appropriate. These are pragmatically the simplest sorts of questions and if they focus on facts that can be known abductively from happenings that the children have actually experienced through the drama or cartoon film, the answers to such questions can be largely determined by the most basic sort of ground-level abductive reasoning. For instance, here is a series of 'yes/no' questions that covers the basic facts in the burglar narrative. Questions such as these would be appropriate in a first-grade class where the children are not yet really comfortable in the language of the classroom (e.g. in a classroom where the teacher speaks Thai, say, and the children speak Mandarin, or some other language):

Yes/No questions for 'The Burglar' narrative

[Teacher points to Suzie or a picture of Suzie and asks] 'Is this Suzie?'
[Teacher points to a picture of the burglar and asks] 'Is this Suzie's brother?'
[Pointing to the baby's crib] 'Is this grandmother's bed?'

The questions asked ought to cover the full range of facts in the story starting with the most obvious, central facts, and working up to details that are less easily understood. The questions suggested as examples would actually be quite difficult for children who are trying to become literate in a language they do not yet know. The list of such questions that are possible on the basis of any coherent fact-based discourse can be expanded indefinitely. A good rule would be to begin with questions requiring only the most obvious abductive inferences and then to move through the story without expecting the children to express any inductions or any abstract deductive inferences at all. Although noting that a burglar is a thief is a simple thing for someone who speaks English, for a child who is in the process of acquiring a language, that sort of inference (which depends on abstract syntactic and semantic relations between words) may be beyond reach. A lot of scaffolding will be required in order for the child to be able to get up to such a rarefied atmosphere of abstraction. Even the inductive generalization that the burglar is apt to sell the TV and stereo is way beyond the sort of thing a beginning language learner could be expected to say or even to understand. Of course, such an inductive inference, or other inferences of a deductive sort, would be possible from the very start for children who already know the language of instruction.

'Wh-' questions

At a slightly higher remove, after the second or third pass through the story (e.g. two or three screenings of the film), or even sooner if the children already know the language in question, 'wh-' questions may be introduced. At first, the questions should be answerable in single words. Later, whole phrases may be required. Later still, entire sentences may be within reach. Again, the earliest questions, especially with children who are working in a second language situation, ought to focus on the sorts of facts that are central to the story and also obviously portrayed in pictures or dramatization. Here are a few 'wh-' questions.

'Wh-' questions for 'The Burglar' narrative

[Teacher points to a picture of Suzie] 'Who is this?' *Suzie.*
[Pointing to a picture of the burglar] 'Who is this?' *(the) burglar.*
[Pointing to the window over the baby's crib] 'What is this?' *(the) window.*

'How did the burglar get in?' *Through the window.*
'Who was in the crib?' *Suzie's baby brother.*

So far, the answers to all of the questions asked have been contained in the facts and actual statements in the text. Nevertheless, it is relatively easy in constructing such questions to generate a list in each case that involves a progression from the simplest and most obvious facts to more complex and/or less obvious ones. However, in getting children to really master a text a great deal more work is possible within the limits of the statements actually made in the narrative version of the story.

Elicited imitation

For instance, children might be expected to be able to repeat the story, line by line. This sounds extremely simple (perhaps even too simple) but it will present some special challenges to children who are not native speakers of the language in question, or who may not have progressed even in their first language acquisition as far as the teacher may believe them to have progressed. Even for children who already know the language of the narrative, this task will probably not be performed quite flawlessly by all of the children. Research shows that children adjust discourse forms to fit the level of their own developing grammar. As a result, repetitions are often far from exact.

An elicited imitation task for 'The Burglar' narrative

[Teacher says] 'Hi. My name is Suzie.' [Students repeat] *Hi. My name is Suzie.*
'On Saturday night, a burglar broke into our apartment.' *On Saturday night, a burglar broke into our apartment.*

Obviously, the preceding question tasks (yes/no and 'wh-' types) are scorable. We may simply count the number of correct responses to each question. If those tasks were used as teaching activities, and if the children understood the narrative as well as we would expect them to, the scores should all be nearly perfect. That is, in each such task we should expect mastery of the material up to that level. However, when it comes to the elicited imitation task (a sentence repetition task), scoring is not so obvious and straightforward. If the task is tape-recorded it can be meticulously scored for every phoneme (or distinctive sound segment), syllable, morpheme (distinctive unit of meaning or grammatical function), word, phrase, or sentence used in the elicitation task. Even suprasegmental elements such as intonations and stress patterns may be examined for conformity to those used in the text.

The question usually asked concerning each unit of a given type, words being the most commonly scored element, is whether the unit in question is a recognizable reproduction of the one that was supposed to be produced at that juncture in the sequence of elements. If extraneous elements are inserted, or if necessary elements are left out, the score is accordingly reduced by the number of omitted or added elements. Otherwise the total score on the whole task is the number of elements of a given type (e.g. words) that are correctly produced and in the right order. The total possible score is the number of elements of the type scored appearing in the sentences or other sequences presented for repetition. Since words are, in most languages, the most obvious bundles of meanings, they are generally selected as the units to be scored. For instance, in the first sentence in the example given above, there are five words. In the next there are nine. In all, if the whole narrative were used in the form given above (p. 69), the total possible word score would be seventy-seven (treating as separate words items written between spaces or separated by a hyphen). If phonemes were used as the scored units the total possible score would be much higher. The total number of syllables would be about a third the number of phonemes. The number of phrases would be fewer than the words. And the number of sentences only eleven (counting the first string, 'Hi. My name is Suzie.' as only one sentence).

Moreover, since words and higher structures are made up of phonemes and syllables, and since words constitute the phrases and sentences, scoring for almost any single unit amounts to a partial accounting for the other units. Because words are the units of language that users are probably most conscious of as they speak, perhaps they are the best choice for scoring. However, there is no argument against scoring for other units as well. If sentences are chosen as the unit for scoring, a scale where 3 represents a perfect reproduction, 2, a recognizable but imperfect reproduction, 1, a reproduction that contains at least some recognizable element, and 0, a completely unrecognizable attempt or mere silence, will work very well and can, with just a little practice, be applied without the necessity of tape-recording the responses of each examinee. Or, an even rougher scale may be used if the teacher is using the task as a teaching device in which case the only distinction may be between perfect and nearly perfect reproductions of the elicited material. For teaching purposes, where mastery or nearly perfect performance is the goal, in the early stages it may be useful to cut the discourse up into smaller segments and then later join them into larger sequences. For example, 'Hi. My name is Suzie,' might be broken up into three items: (1) 'Hi.' (2) 'My name' (3) 'is Suzie.' If this is done, whether or not for teaching purposes, the breaks in discourse segments should be inserted only at phrasal boundaries and the stress and intonation patterns on the segmented items should be retained. They should not be presented as items in a list, but rather as segments of the larger discourse with which students are already familiar.

Some educators react negatively to elicited imitation on account of it being 'a purely rote task based only on short-term memory', or so they argue. It is easy to prove that this objection does not hold. If the discourse material has been presented in the manner prescribed in this chapter, and throughout this book, the discourse meanings have already achieved representation at deeper levels of processing that is, beyond short-term memory. The learner knows what the facts are. These are represented in long-term memory and in forms such as visual images and sequences of them, accompanying gestures, and abstract inferences, and so on.

All these are distinct from the surface elements of the original narrative. Those surface elements have become associated with actions, persons, events, and so on. Therefore, any element of surface form (a phoneme, syllable, word, phrase, or sentence) that is presented in the sort of elicited imitation task recommended here will have already been linked to abstract conceptualizations (semantic and syntactic categories) and to concrete meanings (facts) that are far removed from the surface-forms of the discourse and that cannot possibly be accessed at all without doing some of the kinds of pragmatic mapping described above in Figs 5.1, 5.2, and 5.3.

Now, the sort of 'rote memorization' that can be based exclusively on surface forms, say, sounds and syllables (held in short-term memory) cannot involve the deeper pragmatic connections our procedure guarantees. If it did involve them, the objection to 'rote memory' would evaporate instantly. In fact, any sequence of elements that exceeds short-term memory, if it is understood, assures us that the representational form in question has been linked to other representational forms that were not presented recently enough to have been provided to short-term memory. Imagine trying to repeat a sequence of words in a language you do not know that says something as complex as any five-to-fifteen-word segment of 'The Burglary' text. Even if some individual segment, or even all the segments of the discourse, could be managed by rote, the whole discourse could hardly be understood without going far beyond mere storage and recall of surface elements from short-term memory.

Furthermore, in the sort of application of elicited imitation recommended here, the teacher has already assured deeper levels of processing by preceding any elicited imitation task with the sorts of dramatization of the facts, followed by the question-asking procedures described earlier. In addition, the kinds of tasks (including scorable tests) to be introduced subsequently (in this chapter) will virtually remove all possibility of the discourse being understood only at the level of surface elements. Short-term memory will invariably be (as it always necessarily is) an important part of the processing of the elicited segments of the discourse, but it will certainly not be the only basis. It will not even be an adequate basis, by itself, to support comprehension of the dramatization of the discourse, or the cartoon-style film. Nor will it sustain correct answers to the question tasks described earlier, much less the more complex tasks yet to follow (see below).

Reading aloud

As soon as the children have understood the discourse well enough to reproduce it in a spoken form, they are ready to go on to more complex processing activities. Whether these tasks are to be regarded as teaching exercises or as tests is mainly a matter of preference and whatever immediate purpose the task best serves. Assuming the purpose includes instilling literacy skills in children who have not yet acquired those skills, we need to go on to tasks that introduce or expand upon previously introduced written versions of the discourse we are working with. Suppose that a 'big book' has been constructed containing the very sentences given above (p. 69). A variant of the elicited imitation task would be one where the segments are presented in a written form and the problem for the student is to read the segment aloud. By adding the written form into the curriculum at this point we invite the child to make the connections not only between the written form and the spoken version (the latter of which we have already shown that the child knows through the elicited imitation task), but we rely, as always, on all of the deeper levels of scaffolding already established through other pragmatic mapping activities. The facts are known. The sequence of events, persons involved, setting, and outcome are all established. The spoken forms of the utterances have been correctly linked up with the facts, and the child can produce those spoken forms in segment lengths that exceed the limits of short-term memory.

As a result we have (deliberately, with the child's interest at heart) reduced the difficulty of the task of reading the printed elements to a manageable level even for a child who is just barely beginning to move towards membership in the literacy club. The task can be made just a little easier by the teacher (tester) providing prompts, for example a partial or full spoken variant of the written forms just before asking the child to read the given segment aloud. Or, supposing we need to make the task more challenging, the prompts can be omitted and the segments to be read aloud can be lengthened until the children are actually fluently reading aloud the entire big book. In a test situation, the segments to be read aloud can be presented on large cards, one segment at a time, or on an overhead projector, or with a slide projector. Making up the cards, transparencies, or slides could also easily be converted into a teaching activity in which the children participate. The scoring of such tasks can be done in essentially the same ways that elicited imitation tasks are scored.

Copying written discourse

As soon as the children are reading the big book, or even some portion of it, they are in a position to begin writing it as well. There is no reason to postpone writing until the second grade. On the contrary, there are many reasons that reading and writing tasks need to be closely linked with each other and with listening and speaking tasks. If we want the children to succeed at the tasks we set (and on our tests), it should always be our goal (but especially in the early phases) to provide as much scaffolding as we can to enable that success. Listening to another child or to the teacher producing a spoken version of a certain discourse about facts that the child readily understands from a drama or other illustration, provides an additional level of representation that is linked to the facts. As soon as that heard form of representation has been understood (to whatever degree it is understood), this understanding becomes a level of scaffolding which will help in the comprehension and production of the corresponding spoken form (see Fig. 5.3). Similarly, the elicited spoken form, once it is mastered, constitutes a level of scaffolding from which yet other forms can be reached and subsequently mastered.

In the initial phases of writing, segments of the big book can be presented for short durations, as in the manner of presenting segments on cards, transparencies, or slides, for reading aloud. Only here, at an early phase of writing, the task set the examinee (learner) is to read the presented segment and then write it down. In the earliest phase of this sort of writing activity, the problem of forming the letters will be sufficiently challenging that even single words from the big book will exceed the limits of the child's capacity to hold the material in short-term memory. However, as the child becomes more familiar with the shapes of letters and with larger written segments of the discourse, it will be useful to present sequences of words or even whole sentences. At first it may be necessary for children to refer to the written version of a given word repeatedly in order to create a recognizable written variant of it. As the written forms become still more familiar, longer segments can be presented and for even shorter durations. These productions, as in the case of spoken-forms produced by elicited imitation or reading aloud, can be scored in similar ways. An added element will be the legibility of the written forms. Legibility in writing parallels pronunciation (clear and distinct articulation) in speaking. Elements present in the scoring of written productions that are not present in spoken-forms would include the so-called mechanics of spelling, capitalization, and punctuation.

Provided our testing (and teaching) never relates to anything other than fact-based, whole discourse, the full richness of the mechanics of written forms will be assured. In addition, the entire complex of the known facts and the previously mastered spoken and written forms will help the child in solving the special problems associated with the mechanics of writing. In such a rich context of fact-based discourse, supported by multiple levels of scaffolding from dramatization and illustration of meanings, the child will be at an optimal advantage to understand the abstract meanings of such mechanical aspects of writing as spelling, capitalization, and punctuation. But, remove such scaffolding and these aspects of written discourse will continue to baffle the children about as much as they do many present-day curriculum specialists.

Taking dictation

So far, the children have observed and understood the facts of the discourse from its dramatization. They have heard and understood its spoken form. They have listened to and reproduced the spoken form sentence-by-sentence. They have seen the written forms associated with the familiar discourse. They have heard these forms associated with spoken versions of the discourse. They have read the written forms aloud and they have learnt to write those written forms. They are now ready, owing to the scaffolding now in place, to write from dictation. A spoken version of the text may be presented segment-by-segment for children to write down. They have already linked the teacher's speech forms to speech forms they themselves produce. They have linked those same speech forms to written ones the teacher produced. They linked those written forms the teacher produced back to the speech forms of the teacher. Subsequently they linked the written forms produced by the teacher to spoken forms the children themselves produced (reading aloud). Later, they linked the written forms produced by the teacher to written forms they themselves produced. Dictation as a testing (or teaching) task simply takes the last representational form (a written version produced by the student) and links it back to the teacher's spoken version of the familiar discourse.

As in the case of all the other elicitation devices designed to assess (or to instil) familiarity with one or another form of the fact-based discourse, dictation too is an elicitation device. The teacher (or someone else, either live or on a tape-recording of some sort) presents a segment of the discourse in a spoken version and the task set the children is to write down the segment that they have just heard. As in all such tasks, the difficulty may be adjusted upward or downward by giving longer or shorter segments of text respectively, or by slowing down the rate of speech, repeating the segment one or more times, providing prompts, and so on. In a test situation, though we want children to succeed, we also want to challenge them to ever higher levels of achievement and to assure that the kind of processing we ask them to do in the test situation really moves them towards the kind of processing the whole curriculum aims to enable them to perform. Therefore, we would ordinarily not dictate single words. We would want to use segments of, say, five or more words, so as to challenge short-term memory.

In the version of 'The Burglary' discourse that follows, each slash inserted in the text, marks a segment boundary, or pause point. At each of these indicated junctures, the person giving the dictation must allow sufficient time for the children to write down what they have just heard. The amount of time needed here will vary with the level of literacy of the children being tested. A simple way of creating a pause that corresponds to the length and complexity of the segment just uttered is for the person giving the dictation to repeat the segment sub-vocally and to spell it out (silently) one, two, or more times.

The Burglary

Hi. My name is Suzie./On Saturday night,/a burglar broke into our apartment./He came through a window./He stepped right across/my baby brother's crib./My brother was asleep./He didn't wake up./Everyone else was asleep too./I was asleep./My grandmother was asleep./My mother was asleep./The burglar took the TV and stereo/and went right out the front door./Nobody saw him,/but we figured out what happened the next morning./

The objective is to present a segment that is comprehensible, bounded by natural syntactic and/or other junctures, and challenging enough that the child must comprehend the meaning of that segment by working-up a representation of the facts referred to by it. We want dictated segments to be associated with the facts of the discourse as well as with its surface forms both spoken and written. We do not want it to be possible for the child to link the surface form of speech directly with the surface forms of writing without understanding the meaning of either one. In general, this is not possible if we work with significant segments of a whole, fact-based discourse. A direct, short-circuited association between spoken and written surface forms can only occur in something like a traditional spelling test where some of the meanings of at least some of the words are not known to the child but the surface forms (both spoken and written) are known. Such a short circuit cannot obtain if we are using significant multi-syllabic words and phrases of a whole, fact-based discourse. There are many assurances from other tests (teaching activities) that the children really do know the meanings of the surface forms in question. Furthermore, by presenting long enough segments of speech between pauses, we can be certain that short-circuit surface linkages are impossible even for any single segment. If the segment is too long to manage in short-term memory without deep level comprehension a direct association between mere surface-forms cannot be effected by the child. The meaning of both the spoken and written forms must be understood in order to associate them with each other.

Scoring of dictation can proceed exactly as the scoring of the other elicitation procedures described above, so no more needs to be said on that account. Instead, it is time to move on to consider kinds of processing tasks that will ensure still deeper levels of processing. So far, the question-based tests as well as the elicitation devices discussed (imitation, reading aloud, copying, and dictation) all depend fairly exclusively either on specific facts already referred to in the discourse and their connection to particular surface forms (which have also already been provided) or they depend on connections between different surface-forms (e.g. spoken versus written ones) which are deeply interrelated with each other at the level of the facts (see Fig. 5.3 and its explanation). It is time now in our testing (or teaching) activities to go on to consider tasks that more directly demand inferences of an inductive sort, or the production of forms not directly provided in any prior discourse sustained by short-term memory. It is time to move on also to deductively based semantic and syntactic relations as well as inferences that reach inductively beyond what is stated in the discourse.

Cloze exercises

An open-ended cloze exercise is the sort of test (or teaching device) that omits words from a discourse, usually a written text, and requires examinees to guess the missing words. Even if the discourse is a familiar one, such guesses are generally sustained by deductive and inductive inferences that reach beyond the particular facts that can be abductively inferred from the discourse. Such cloze exercises can be done orally or in written form. Here is an example of such an exercise where every fifth word has been deleted from 'The Burglary' discourse.

(I)   Hi. My name is (1) ——. On Saturday night, a (2) —— broke into our apartment. (3) —— came through a window. (4) —— stepped right across my (5) —— brother's crib. My brother (6) —— asleep. He didn't wake (7) ——. Everyone else was asleep (8) ——. I was asleep. My (9) —— was asleep. My mother (10) —— asleep. The burglar took (11) —— TV and stereo and (12) —— right out the front (13) ——. Nobody saw him, but (14) —— figured out what happened (15) —— next morning.

An oral version of this exercise could be given where the teacher would read the narrative in as normal an intonation as possible but pausing at each blank. The task set the listeners would be to supply the missing words. Supposing the written version of the text was not before them at the time, examinees would have to base their guesses on their prior acquaintance with the specific facts of the story (abductive inferences), plus expectations based on previously supplied information (inductive inference), as well as whatever semantic and syntactic information the text provides concerning the requirements of surface forms (deductive inferences), and or, of course, combinations of these. In an oral cloze task, usually the teacher confirms or supplies the correct answers as she goes along, while in a written task, examinees only have the written context plus their previous guesses to help them figure out what goes in any subsequent blank.

Consider the cloze exercise given above. Assuming the examinees know the facts of the story, they should be able to guess 'Suzie' for item (1). The main support for this inferential choice is the fact known abductively (from previous experience) that the story is told by Suzie. This choice also gains some deductive support from the fact that the story-teller is a little girl and 'Suzie' is typically a name for a girl and the diminutive '-ie', an affectionate designation for a small child. However, as soon as the correct answer is known abductively, such deductive additions (from the semantics of the name) support it redundantly.

The solution to item (2) is aided by the deduction that someone who breaks and enters is some sort of criminal, but this deduction, though necessarily correct as far as it goes, is not specific enough to determine that the criminal in question was a burglar and not some other sort of criminal. Prior memory of the facts provide a complete solution to the item on an abductive basis: we remember the word 'burglar' and its previous interpretations relative to the actual facts of the story. Further, that solution is sustained by inductive inference from the rest of the story, for example that a TV and stereo are stolen supports the expectation that burglars typically are thieves. But, as noted already, as soon as the correct abductive inference is attained, we already know more than we needed to know in order to determine it sufficiently.

Item (3) is deductively linked (via syntax and semantics) to the burglar of item (2) and to the pronoun 'him' which appears as the second word before item (14), but can only be determined sufficiently by memory or by the inductive inference apparently made by Suzie that burglars are usually males. The fact that Suzie inferred that this particular burglar, entered alone, is sustained only by deduction from the use of 'him' in this cloze exercise. What her basis for such an inference might be is hardly germane to the text at hand. It can only be guessed at in any event. However, the determination of the correct answer 'he' (for item 3) will probably be based on the recollection (abductively understood) that Suzie only referred to one burglar in telling her story and that she actually referred to him with the pronouns 'he' and 'him'. And so it goes throughout the task.

It is easy to see that if we moved our starting point (the position of item 1) one word to the left, we would get a whole new set of cloze items, a different cloze exercise:

> (II)   Hi. My name (1) —— Suzie. On Saturday night, (2) —— burglar broke into our (3) ——. He came through a (4) ——. He stepped right across (5) —— baby brother's crib. My (6) —— was asleep. He didn't (7) —— up. Everyone else was (8) —— too. I was asleep. (9) —— grandmother was asleep. My (10) —— was asleep. The burglar (11) —— the TV and stereo (12) —— went right out the (13) —— door. Nobody saw him, (14) —— we figured out what (15) —— the next morning.

By moving the starting point again one word to the left, we get still another cloze exercise:

> (III)   Hi. My (1) —— is Suzie. On Saturday (2) ——, a burglar broke into (3) —— apartment. He came through (4) —— window. He stepped right (5) —— my baby brother's crib. (6) —— brother was asleep. He (7) —— wake up. Everyone else (8) —— asleep too. I was (9) ——. My grandmother was asleep. (10) —— mother was asleep. The (11) —— took the TV and (12) —— and went right out (13) —— front door. Nobody saw (14) ——, but we figured out (15) —— happened the next morning.

Since we started with an every fifth word deletion technique in constructing our first cloze exercise, two more exercises are possible:

> (IV)   Hi. (1) —— name is Suzie. On (2) —— night, a burglar broke (3) —— our apartment. He came (4) —— a window. He stepped (5) —— across my baby brother's (6) ——. My brother was asleep. (7) —— didn't wake up. Everyone (8) —— was asleep too. I (9) —— asleep. My grandmother was (10) ——. My mother was asleep. (11) —— burglar took the TV (12) —— stereo and went right (13) —— the front door. Nobody (14) —— him, but we figured (15) —— what happened the next (16) ——.
>
> (V)   (1) ——. My name is Suzie. (2) —— Saturday night, a burglar (3) —— into our apartment. He (4) —— through a window. He (5) —— right across my baby (6) —— crib. My brother was (7) ——. He didn't wake up. (8) —— else was asleep too. (9) —— was asleep. My grandmother (10) —— asleep. My mother was (11) ——. The burglar took the (12) —— and stereo and went (13) —— out the front door. (14) —— saw him, but we (15) —— out what happened the (16) —— morning.

It will become obvious to anyone who works through such a series of cloze exercises that individual items in them may differ markedly in difficulty. It will be equally apparent that the sort of preparatory experience that can be provided in a classroom setting can help to even out some of these differences across items from exercise to exercise. Prior experience with the facts and with the text on which the cloze exercises are based will make some of the more difficult items manageable (e.g. item 8 of cloze exercise I, 'too', and item 8 of IV, 'else'). The word 'too' is difficult to guess because it redundantly marks the agreement of the fact that other people were asleep with the fact that Suzie's baby brother was also asleep. Because of its redundancy, that is that the information it expresses can be deduced from other explicit statements of the text, 'too' could be omitted with little loss in information. Redundant elements of this sort are sometimes very difficult to guess because they express facts already obvious and are therefore not needed. The text may seem complete without such an addition. The word 'else' (item 8 of exercise IV) is also a difficult one to guess for essentially the same reasons. However, it is syntactically required by the appearance of 'too' later in the same sentence. Therefore, it can be inferred deductively by any examinee who is sufficiently sensitive to this subtle requirement of English syntax. However, few first-graders are apt to be that sensitive and probably no non-native speakers of English (at the first grade level) who are also trying to learn to read can be expected to know this connection by deduction. Hence, for them item (8) of exercise IV will be next to impossible unless they are given some experience with the text beforehand. In that case, if appropriate experience is provided, they may remember the use of the words 'else' and 'too' and they may be able to figure out their pragmatic connections with the facts of the story and later their syntactic/semantic relations to each other.

Cloze exercises like I–V are called open-ended because the examinee must supply the missing words, and the ones illustrated here are the most commonly used type of fixed-ratio exercises. In the examples provided, the ratio is one to five. That is, out of every five words, the fifth must be guessed by the examinee. It is also possible to delete the words on a variable ratio basis. Many such exercises could be derived from 'The Burglary' discourse in the form we have been working with. For instance, in exercise VI, the words that are omitted are all nouns.

(VI)   Hi. My (1) —— is Suzie. On Saturday night, a (2) —— broke into our (3) ——. He went through a (4) ——. He stepped right across my baby brother's (5) ——. My (6) —— was asleep. He didn't wake up. Everyone else was asleep too. I was asleep. My (7) —— was asleep. My (8) —— was asleep. The (9) —— took the (10) —— and (11) —— and went right out the front (12) ——. Nobody saw him, but we figured out what happened the next (13) ——.

Many other exercises of the variable ratio type are possible, but all of them together can add little or nothing to the full range of exercises of the fixed ratio type for any given fixed ratio.

Two basic methods for scoring open-ended cloze tests are commonly used. The simplest method is to count as correct only those answers that are identical to the words actually deleted in the construction of the task. This method is called *exact word* scoring. Another approach is to count any word as correct that fits the entire context. For instance, in exercise VI, for item (5), the word omitted was actually 'crib', but 'cot', 'bed', 'basket', or 'bassinet' would all be appropriate to the textual context and even to the facts as we understand them. The method of scoring just described is called *appropriate word* scoring. Both methods require some judgement. By the exact word method the response of each examinee must be compared with the original word. Usually spelling errors are ignored in most testing applications, but changes that result in a grammatically or lexically unacceptable variation are generally marked wrong. By the appropriate word method, the offered response, must be judged against the scorer's understanding of the intended meaning of the entire context. While the strictest variant of exact word scoring can be done by computer software, provided the answers are typed into an appropriate medium, appropriate word scoring generally requires a human scorer.

One way around the scoring difficulties of open-ended cloze items is to replace each blank with a list of alternatives in a multiple-choice format, as shown in VII below.

(VII)

Hi. My (1) —— is Suzie. On Saturday (2) ——

| A. sister |
| B. name |
| C. mother |
| D. granny |
| E. baby |

a burglar broke into (3) —— apartment. He

A. afternoon		A. his
B. morning		B. its
C. night		C. their
D. at noon		D. her
E. at daybreak		E. our

came through a (4) ——   He stepped right across (5) ——

A. tree		A. his
B. hallway		B. its
C. wall		C. my
D. window		D. her
E. mirror.		E. our

baby brother's crib. . . .

While multiple-choice cloze exercises require much more work to prepare, research shows that they measure many of the same kinds of abilities as the open-ended variety of tests. Their usefulness in large-scale testing is well established. However, because of the extra effort involved in the construction of such tests, they are less useful as day-to-day classroom activities.

More complex translation or translation-related tasks

In order to assess the more abstract kinds of deductive inference, open-ended questions (to be answered either orally or in writing), multiple-choice questions requiring inferences of a deductive or inductive sort (reading between or beyond the lines), summary tasks, or other interpretative tasks are required. All of these – including the tasks recommended above – it turns out, end up requiring some form of translation-type activity. We have already seen how the foregoing tasks involve the mapping of one form of representation (e.g. one uttered by the teacher) into a different form (e.g. one written by the student) by passing through a potential series of translations from the first surface form to any one of several underlying representations (e.g. sensory images, gestures, and abstract meanings) and eventually back to a different surface form.

It is equally apparent that paraphrase involves translation between distinct representational forms. For instance, in paraphrasing the sentence 'On Saturday night, a burglar broke into our apartment' Suzie might say 'Late on Saturday, while it was dark, someone jemmied the lock on a window of our apartment and broke in'. The new version of Suzie's statement would convey much of the same information as the former version. It is a paraphrase of the former statement because both of them, at the surface, end up in the same language. Both are statements uttered in English. For this reason, many theorists hesitate to speak of paraphrase as involving translation. Yet, it clearly does in terms of the theory laid out in Figs 5.2 and 5.3 see pages 57 and 60. Suzie must begin by interpreting the surface form of the sentence 'On Saturday night, a burglar broke into our apartment' into a deeper logical representation corresponding to the facts. This factual representation is then interpreted back into a surface form in English distinct from the one with which Suzie began. Certainly, this process may occur in stages, even phrase by phrase perhaps, but even so it must still involve translation in just the sense defined. If some deeper logical representation constituting the likeness in meaning of the two surface forms were not posited, it is difficult to imagine how we could judge the one to be a paraphrase of the other at all.

All such interpretative processes that reach beyond mere rote memory (according to the theory advocated here, see Figs 5.2 and 5.3) involve translation across distinct representational systems in the sense just illustrated. For instance, if Suzie could draw a very good captioned series of pictures showing what happened, there might be a good correspondence in meaning between the pictures (together with their captions) and the two paraphrase statements of the previous paragraph. However, the pictures could not be said to be merely a paraphrase of either or both of the statements. The series of pictures would rather be a translation of those statements insofar as the pictures would represent essentially the same meanings (somewhat more richly) and in a distinct form. Note further that because of the peculiar character of icons (which pictures are), unless some symbolic captions are provided (e.g. in a linguistic form), the pictures will not determine any particular interpretation with respect to the narrative. For instance, we will have no way of knowing when the events occurred relative to our own or to Suzie's experience. Pictures (icons in general) do not come with determined dates or connections to persons or times other than the ones pictured. The actual dates of occurrence, times, and connections with unpictured elements, remain unspecified by the pictures.

A more difficult variety of translation would be for Suzie to tell her story in Spanish, or some other language, just as she told it in English. This we would call a *translation proper*. If Suzie also knew American Sign Language (or some other sign system of a deaf community), she might be able to more or less simultaneously interpret (translate) her narrative into a signed version while speaking English, Spanish, or some other language. However, 'simultaneous translation' (also known as 'interpretation') is perhaps the most difficult sort since it requires a fluent switching between distinct languages in addition to all the other normal interpretative (translation) processes that must accompany the production or comprehension of discourse in any single language. Apparently simultaneous translation, and production in the second language, is actually done in the natural pauses of the producer of the original discourse. For this reason, the shorter the pauses and the more fluent the original discourse, the more difficult the translation task. It is probably the case that, in ordinary interpretation of any kind, working up the scaffolding necessary to the interpretation or production of discourse requires time. It can never be quite instantaneous.

It follows from strict logic that coming up with images (visual, auditory, tactile, olfactory, or gustatory), actual or imagined kinesic forms (e.g. bodily and facial gestures), imagined written forms, inferences, or any sort of judgements of discourse at all, must take time. No matter how fluent we are, we cannot generate speech (much less writing) instantly in correspondence to an observed series of events or any other form of meaning. Even the interpretation of sensory-motor images cannot occur instantaneously. In inventing a story (as opposed to retelling one, or recounting actual experience), the person producing the story must conjure up not only the images and inferences necessary to its interpretation but also must plan the very sequence of events itself, their integration, their reason for being (i.e. the motivation for the story), and probably a great deal more. Otherwise, if the story were merely a string of grammatical sentences invented off the top of someone's head, it could not be expected to make much sense, or even if it did make any sense, it would not likely be sufficiently well-motivated to capture the interest of many would-be listeners or readers. At any rate, because meaningful interpretations always involve the conversion of some form of representation into some other, every interpretation *is* an act of translation in the sense argued by our theory.

Open-ended tasks can be made easier (from the examinee's point of view) by putting them into a multiple-choice form where the examinee does not have to construct the discourse forms but merely to choose from several alternatives the one that best fits the fact(s). For instance, multiple-choice questions based on 'The Burglary' narrative might include the following:

(VIII) 1. The person telling the story is ——.
  (a) a little girl
  (b) an old woman
  (c) a small boy
  (d) a grown man
  (e) a busy housewife

 2. The story is mainly about a ——.
  (a) broken window
  (b) sleepness night
  (c) Saturday night party
  (d) baby in his crib
  (e) theft late at night

 3. The burglar in the story did *not* ——.
  (a) harm the sleeping infant
  (b) steal the television
  (c) take the stereo set
  (d) go out the front door
  (e) come in through a window

Each of the foregoing questions concerns facts actually known through abduction or deduction. Here are a couple of questions that can be answered from inductions based on linking the facts of the narrative with prior and possible future experience:

 4. The burglar will probably —— the TV and stereo.
  (a) keep
  (b) throw away
  (c) sell
  (d) take apart
  (e) return

 5. Suzie and her family were probably —— by what happened.
  (a) very pleased
  (b) pained
  (c) puzzled
  (d) annoyed
  (e) unsettled

Obviously, all such questions could be made easier or more difficult in a variety of ways. In general, however, all else being equal, deductive inferences determined by the semantics or syntax of the discourse will probably be more difficult for persons who do not know the language while inductive inferences will be more difficult for persons who do know the language. For persons who do not know the language, and therefore, who may have trouble understanding any question and its connection to facts, inductive inferences will be next to impossible. Provided adequate exposure to the facts is given via comprehensible representations, abductive inferences ought to be easier than deductive or inductive ones both for native speakers and for non-natives. However, the abductive connections between discourse and experience will be easier for persons who already know the language (and its various surface forms in speech and writing) than for persons who do not. In fact, persons who know the language and its various forms (spoken and written) very well will be able to access facts fluently and with relative ease from discourse alone without other scaffolding. However, in language and literacy programmes we are usually working with children who have not yet attained such an advanced stage of learning. As a result, scaffolding is critical.

In addition to multiple-choice tasks of the types just illustrated in items (1)–(5) of exercise VIII, a great multitude of tasks requiring more or less production of discourse (whether spoken, written, or some combination of these) can be conceived. In all such cases, ranging from open-ended questions at one end, through short-essay or (orally answered) questions, to creative writing and other interpretative tasks, according to the theory advocated here, the starting point for all such activities must be the actual facts of someone's experience. Leave out this element and the task, no matter what it might be, will tend towards meaninglessness. As a result, if the facts are left out or insufficiently determined, the performance of the task in question will be difficult to grade (whether by scaling or by scoring). It will, in short, be both unreliable and also invalid. Validity (according to the theory advocated here) depends on the linking of the discourse task to some relatively well-determined factual basis.

Under numeral IX several test types are listed roughly in an order of increasing difficulty:

(IX)   1. Open-ended questions presented orally for oral response.
      2. The same as (1) but with a written response.
      3. Same as (1) or (2) except that questions are in written form for short-essay type response.
      4. An oral summary of a fact-based discourse.
      5. A written summary.
      6. Expansion of the discourse in oral or written form (for instance,

telling what came before, after, or expanding the detail of some element in the fact-based discourse).

7. Paraphrasing or re-telling (oral or written).
8. Inventing a similar discourse based on one's own experience.
9. Writing such a discourse.

Some might object that the foregoing descriptions of tests must be based in a particular (simple) narrative, or at best a narrative-type task. This is no criticism. The fact is that all meaningful discourses of any type, to the extent that they are the least bit comprehensible or meaningful, relate ultimately to the ongoing stream of experience which is exactly like a narrative. For instance, consider a particularly abstract sort of discourse that is removed from ordinary experience. Consider a mathematical proof such as the proof of the Pythagorean theorem (that the sum of the squares of the sides of a right-angle triangle are equal to the square of the hypotenuse), or the proof that the square root of 2 is an irrational number. If these proofs or any other had no connection whatever to conceptions pertaining to practical experience (e.g. to our perceptions of triangles, their sides, and so on, our ideas about lines and squares and points on lines), it would merely be incomprehensible. In fact any mathematical proof, to the extent that it is understood at all, must be related to conceptions that in some degree relate to conceptions, objects, and events in ordinary experience.

Take another non-narrative sort of text such as a dictionary definition of a word. Say the word is an esoteric word such as 'otiose'. From the dictionary we determine that it may mean (1) 'at leisure, indolent, idle', or (2) 'ineffective or futile', or (3) 'superfluous or useless'. Someone might ask how such a dictionary entry (which we might well want to test at some point) can be related to any narrative. But suppose the word is encountered in the course of reading a certain book by a certain author. It is read on a particular occasion while riding a train from Albuquerque, New Mexico to Barstow, California, in the context of a certain essay by John Dewey on the character of intelligence which is said not to be 'an otiose affair'. As soon as some of the details of the experience that make the dictionary entry useful are added into the picture, we see that any such discourse genre (if a dictionary entry may be considered such) must always relate to some stream of experience with many connections that are exactly like those of a narrative. There is no difference with an encyclopedia entry, or a description in a catalogue, a parts manual, and so on. All such elements of discourse are utterly useless (and meaningless) except for their connections to the experience of persons who construct and use such reference materials in respect to actual experience. All such discourse elements have a narrative basis or they have no basis at all.

Therefore, it must be the case that every conceivable type of fact-based discourse (plausible fictions included) is more or less testable with essentially the same techniques as we have described above relative to our simple narrative about the burglar. If other genres of discourse are introduced in factual settings that are relevant to the experience of the children or are made relevant through some experience that the children in the classroom can identify with and understand, there is no limit to the kinds of language and literacy tasks that can be tested (and taught). Advertisements, menus, product labels, manufacturer warranties, and so on, can all be introduced within the fact-based contexts of meaningful experience. In such contexts, many of the above test-types can easily be extended to such discourse genres and no imaginable discourse-type (with any sort of experiential connections) will be even partly excluded from the kinds of tests recommended above.

Consider, for example, some of the kinds of spin-off activities and discourse genres that might be developed from the simple example narrative in our hypothetical 'big book', 'The Burglary'. What, for instance, would Suzie's mother and grandmother be likely to do after their apartment has been burgled? This question could itself be put to the children. (It requires an inductive generalization.) Suzie's family might well call the police and later file a report concerning the burglary. The telephone conversation (a dialogue) and the subsequent taking down of the facts for the written report would relate precisely to the facts of the burglary. The phone call, the subsequent interview between the mother (possibly grandmother), and the police might be dramatized, written down, and used as a dialogue (conversational) basis for a whole series of teaching and testing activities. The written report, of which a facsimile might be constructed as an addition to our big book, would itself provide a new discourse genre for expanding the literacy curriculum. It would have to contain detailed descriptions of the stolen items. We would need to find out the brand names, the manufacturers, and the approximate value of the TV and stereo.

Here, the question of whether the family or the landlord are covered by insurance might be raised. Such a question could lead Suzie's mother to call the landlord that owns the building to report the break-in and to urge him to repair the broken window and to improve the security of the building. Again this new dialogue could be used as a supplement to the curriculum already developed so far. It might be dramatized, written down, illustrated, taught, tested, and so on. But suppose the landlord is uncooperative? Should Suzie and her folks consider moving? They might want to check newspaper advertisements to see about other apartments. Did they have any insurance coverage to replace the stolen items? If so, a call to their insurance agent would be in order and could again expand the available discourse. A claim would have to be filed with the insurance company. But suppose that moving would be too expensive for them even to consider it. Maybe they ought to form a neighbourhood watch programme. This could lead into matters concerning laws that protect the property of citizens, how those laws are made, what crime costs, and so on. Many other genres of discourse might be introduced. Relative to the insurance claim, the replacement value of the stolen goods would have to be determined. The whole economic question could be brought into the picture along with countless other discourse possibilities. Moreover, because all of these potential expansions of the starting discourse relate to actual facts of experience (or plausible fictions that have such ties), all of the above recommendations concerning tests apply to all such forms of discourse.

Generally, for classroom purposes, when tasks of the sort described above in exercise IX are used, some general scale of adequacy supplemented by specific scales or diagnostic treatments of test performances will be preferred over a strict scoring procedure. For instance, the sort of scale recommended above (p. 74) might be used though it would have to be made a little more general in certain respects and more specific in others. Imagine, for example, that the task set (the test or teaching exercise) involves playing the role of Suzie's mother and responding orally to questions put by the police officer (a role, say, played by the teacher) taking a report about the burglary. Suppose further (just for the sake of the discussion here) that it has been previously determined that the date of the robbery was 2 November 1991, the TV was a 24-inch Sony worth about $450, and the stereo was a Panasonic that cost $650 when it was new. Imagine further that the children have read aloud, written from dictation, and participated in other activities in the classroom that would assure that the task at hand is not beyond what they might be expected to do with some success. Any unfamiliar information, or facts the children might not be expected to remember could be written on the board to be referred to as appropriate during the exercise. For instance, Suzie's address and telephone number might be put on the board along with the specific date of the crime, and the estimated cost of the TV and stereo. Suppose, finally, that the children are to write their responses to each of the following questions put by the teacher (acting in the role of the police officer):

(X) Now, Ms Doe, I understand that someone broke into your apartment and took some things. What is your address here?
What is your phone number?
Exactly when did this happen?
Okay. How did the person get in?
What things did he take?
I see. And about how much would you say the stolen items were worth?
Did he take anything else? Or was anyone harmed?

Notice that the questions asked in X (and in all tests or teaching activities that conform to the theory recommended here) must focus on the actual facts of the discourse activity. We do not ask about anything unrelated to what actually occurred. We do not invite students to invent sentences or any other sort of discourse detached from the facts of experience. We might want to include activities in the curriculum and in our testing where children give their own addresses or write their own stories, but in all such cases, the setting-up of such discourse events would pertain to particular well-determined facts. Also, the questions to elicit the various addresses and phone numbers of the several children, for instance, would be different in critical respects from the ones asked here. In exercise X, question (1) concerns the address where the burglary occurred. Just any old address or telephone number will not do. Similarly, question (3) concerns when the burglary occurred. Therefore, 12 October 1985, is not a correct answer. And so on, throughout. It is only because there are some determined facts upon which the discourse is based that the discourse itself has any particular meaning and that meaning is the only sufficient basis for the valid scalability (or scorability in other cases) of the task in question. Because the task pertains to relatively well-determined facts, responses *can be* scaled.

That is, responses can be judged for different degrees of accuracy to any desired level of detail. For instance, all the questions might be judged on a single five-point scale where, say, '5' means that all the requested information was provided and in a correct form, '4' means that nearly all the facts were conveyed in a correct or nearly correct form, '3' means that most of the facts were conveyed but with several errors in form, '2' means that some of the facts were conveyed but with some multiple errors, and '1' means that little or none of the facts were correctly conveyed. Such a scale could be applied in a rough and ready manner to the questions under numeral X, or almost any of those listed above under IX. Or, the formal aspects of the discourse task (e.g. pronunciation or legibility, spelling, punctuation, word-usage, grammar) might be separated, to some degree, from each other and from the comprehensibility and factual accuracy with which the examinee conveys the intended or desired information concerning the known facts. (Remove the known facts, incidentally, and any performance whatever will become difficult or impossible to scale or to score in any way.)

Distinct scales for factual content and formal accuracy (e.g. spelling, punctuation, vocabulary) of the spoken or written discourse forms can easily be imagined along the lines of the general scale just exemplified. However, in almost any classroom situation separate ratings assigned to all of the conceivable components of any given discourse task would make no sense at all. The trouble is that there are too many components. Imagine assigning separate ratings for content, organization, comprehensibility, spelling, punctuation, capitalization, word choice, morphological form, and syntax. (Also, notice that any one of these categories can be split up into a number of sub-categories that might be graded separately.) So many ratings would hardly be manageable from any teacher's point of view and neither would they be interpretable from the child's perspective (or the parent's or anyone else's, for that matter). Whatever grades, ratings, or scores are assigned, they must be interpretable and relatively simple. Therefore, specific diagnostic feedback on performances is best provided in terms of the correct answers (whether the correction involves a change in the conveyed fact, or in the form in which it is conveyed) relative to the facts. This feedback can be as specific as the particular problems that arise in any given child's performance and will have far greater potential benefit for the child than any number of distinct ratings that require an advanced college degree to construct or interpret in the first place.

For example, suppose the child were to write his or her own address in response to the question about where the crime occurred. The tester (teacher) might point out that the child is on the right track, an address is required, but that it needs to be Suzie's rather than the respondent's: 'not your address, *Suzie's address*'. Such feedback will be interpretable by the child exactly in proportion to the degree that the facts of the discourse in question have been determined by the teaching and, more particularly, by that child. Remove those facts and any such feedback will itself become relatively meaningless. Spelling errors, punctuation errors, problems in syntax, morphology, or whatever, can all be satisfactorily dealt with on a case-by-case basis provided the discourse activity is based on sufficiently determinate facts. Furthermore, it should be clear that if the recommendations contained here are judiciously understood and followed, at any given juncture in the negotiation of the curriculum, success is so very nearly guaranteed that children will generally be getting things right on the first or second attempt at any given activity (test or teaching exercise). There will not be very many errors of any sort. We will be teaching and testing for mastery, relatively complete understanding and ability to manage each phase of discourse processing as we go along. Each aspect of processing will be secured in order to provide a scaffolding for the next aspect prior to our getting to it. Therefore, we will generally be expecting (and getting) nearly perfect performances as we advance towards mature literacy and all its benefits.

Concluding observations

In the final analysis, we will teach and test all of the discrete-point surface elements of phonology, graphology (spelling), morphology, lexicon (capitalization), syntax (punctuation), semantics (word meanings), pragmatics (communicative forms and functions of all sorts), and so on, but always in richly developed factual contexts where sufficient scaffolding is provided so as to ensure success. If the starting guidelines (see above) are strictly observed throughout all phases of teaching and testing, as Richard Walker and Saowalak Rattanavich have argued throughout this book, success in attaining literacy is virtually guaranteed for all the children. Some traditionalists will object that the bits and pieces of language should be separated at the start and provided in tiny bites apart from any particular facts of experience. These persons do not understand the character of discourse. However, all that they seek to achieve by breaking things down into tiny bits and pieces *can and will be achieved by the methods recommended here* and they cannot in principle be achieved at all by strict discrete-point approaches.

Instead of discrete-point tests of phonemic contrasts, sound-symbol correspondences, spelling, punctuation, and so on, we recommend pragmatic tests that are fully and determinately grounded in known facts of experience. Pragmatic tests, of the sort exemplified throughout this chapter, together with the kinds of teaching activities recommended throughout the book, are robust. Unlike discrete-point tasks that divorce linguistic forms from their experiential connections, pragmatic tests are not susceptible to spurious training effects. If scores or ratings improve on a rich pragmatic task, these improvements will generally reflect real growth in relevant proficiencies. The same is not guaranteed for any discrete-point test where improvement is often related only to that specific test and no other. Also, teaching to pragmatic tests has no bad consequences at all. In fact, it is almost guaranteed to have a positive impact on the curriculum. To improve scores on pragmatic tests, it is necessary to advance the actual proficiencies in question.

CHAPTER 7

Improving literacy teaching in developing countries

RICHARD WALKER and SAOWALAK RATTANAVICH

The size and nature of the problem

The figure most commonly given for the number of illiterates in the developing world is one billion. But the true figure must be much higher because reported literacy rates are usually just the percentage of the population that receives elementary schooling, and not all who attend primary school become literate. Whatever the true figure, the problem is an immense one.

The highest incidence of illiteracy is to be found in some of the most populous of the developing countries, such as Pakistan, Bangladesh, and India and the number of illiterates is actually rising. There is no sign of a solution to the problem.

Many of the developing countries have put a high priority on the achievement of universal literacy, with primary education their first priority and some of them have achieved a large increase in school enrolments. But very often, the degree to which increased enrolments have translated into a higher literacy rate has proved disappointing. Thousands of new schools, with many thousands of children attending them, are tangible evidence of progress towards universal education but the elimination of mass illiteracy is much more difficult and problematic than the achievement of universal school enrolment.

An obvious area of difficulty in expanding the provision for education is teacher training but there are also some countries, such as Thailand, that have reasonably well trained teachers in all parts of the nation and yet have whole regions where both the school retention rate and the literacy success rate are intolerably low.

It seems that countries with a large culturally diverse and predominantly rural population have a particularly difficult task. Over and above the obvious difficulties of building, staffing and maintaining schools, such countries usually have exceptional trouble in achieving a satisfactory success rate in literacy teaching. First-year drop-out rates of up to 75 per cent are reported in some South American countries. The proportion of pupils who, having begun school, stay there and succeed in learning to read and write is intolerably low across whole regions and among some particular segments of their population.

Then there are the 'invisible' drop-outs – those who stay at school, but give up on learning to read and write. Very low success rates are found in almost every country, in isolated rural areas, in city slums, and among groups with a first language or dialect different from the language of instruction.

Overall, something like half of the world's population is illiterate. Three-quarters of those illiterates are to be found in south and east Asia, and there are very large illiterate populations in other parts of the world. For these countries to achieve universal primary education will involve massive expenditure, but funding alone will not solve the problem. There is a need for some kind of educational breakthrough by which the success rate of literacy teaching is greatly increased.

A literacy programme for developing countries

Ideally, a literacy programme for schools in educationally difficult regions of developing countries should have the following characteristics:

1. *It should be inexpensive.* With assistance from international agencies, it may be possible to find the extraordinary short-term funding needed to build and equip schools, but the recurrent cost per student of books and other materials must be low enough to be affordable when very few parents can contribute to the costs of schooling.
2. *The teaching methodology should suit the widest possible range of children,* and the programme itself should be easily modified to suit different regions and minority populations.
3. *The teaching methodology should be uncomplicated.* In a developing country, a sizeable proportion of the teachers who are brought into new schools during a large-scale literacy campaign, will inevitably have minimal training but the methodology should be such that they can master it.
4. *The reading programme should relate strongly to everyday life.* Where there is widespread poverty, survival has a much higher priority than education and neither the authorities nor parents will be inclined to expend a large portion of scarce resources on literacy education, unless it will help to supply primary needs. Even in developing countries, educators often do not realize how much that consideration affects attitudes towards learning and teaching.

Moreover, when learning to read and write make little or no immediate difference to standard of living or life prospects, the school and the community find it easy to accept teaching and learning failure. On the other hand, if literacy brings immediate and obvious benefits, few will be content with a low success rate, as the social climate supports educational improvement.

5. Finally, *the literacy programme should bring rapid results.* Teachers who have seen the failure of repeated attempts to improve a poor success rate, come to believe that what they are doing is all that can be done. That acceptance of failure has to be quickly replaced by expectation of success and for that, proof will be required that the new programme is undoubtedly better than the old.

Some factors to be considered

Programme planning in developing countries must go beyond the normal bounds of programme development. It should certainly encompass teacher training and programme dissemination.

Besides the immensity of the task of upgrading teacher competence, administrators in developing countries face other difficulties that would seem insuperable to administrators in more affluent countries. The number of teachers for whom places can be found in institutions of higher education may be hopelessly small, and neither the teachers nor the government may be able to pay the fees to fill what places are available. Moreover, it is probably impossible to withdraw teachers from the schools for inservice courses, because of teacher shortage.

Inservice teacher training seminars and workshops may be conducted in local centres during school vacations but that is usually expensive and difficult to organize, because of isolation and lack of transport. The best that most teachers can hope for is 'on-the-job' training, with a great deal of the responsibility for teacher inservice education being placed on local supervisors or advisers. The information that these people bring to teachers is likely to be specific to a programme or to a project and it usually has an administrative rather than an educational focus. As such, it does very little to deepen understandings of teaching or to encourage initiative.

When a new and very different literacy programme is to be instituted in schools, these factors restrict what can be done within the implementation plan. The nature of the existing school programmes, the degree to which the teaching and testing is centrally prescribed, the extent of cooperation that is available from local educationists and administrators, and what arrangements may be made with them for teacher inservice training all have to be explored, and current support and supervision systems need to be exploited to the full.

If there is to be the required level of systematic support and supervision, the new programme and methodology should be disseminated at all levels in the educational structure: from officials in the central office of education to individual teachers in the schools. And when a programme is being spread from one educational region to another, a choice has to be made as to whether indoctrination will begin with classroom teachers and work up to senior administrators or the reverse, or even to work from top down and bottom up, at the same time.

Because the Thailand operation was so large and diverse, covering the disparate regions of a large nation, what worked there should be well worth considering for at least some other developing countries. Because of this, here we present an account of programme development, teacher training and programme dissemination for CLE reading programmes in Thailand.

Developing a CLE literacy programme

The first systematic trial of a Thai-language CLE programme was carried out in 1987, in two isolated schools in Surin province, near the Kampuchean border. Some 60 per cent of the people of Surin province speak Khmer, 20 per cent speak Lao, 15 per cent speak other minority languages or dialects and only 3 per cent speak standard Thai, as their first language. Language difference and poverty are the reasons most often given for the fact that the literacy teaching success rate is low.

Two Grade 1 teachers in each of the two trial schools were inducted into CLE teaching over a period of four days after which they began teaching a Grade 1 CLE programme, using prototype teacher and pupil materials that the project team had brought with them. Further programme units were developed in subsequent weeks, and they were delivered and explained to the teachers as members of the project team made periodic follow-up visits to the schools.

After six months, an on-site evaluation of the pilot project was carried out by Dr John Chapman, of the Open University, UK. He concluded that the experimental programme was undoubtedly achieving superior results and he recommended that the work be continued and greatly extended (Chapman, 1987). He confirmed the finding of Rattanavich and Walker (1990), a month earlier, that almost all the children in the CLE groups were already reading and writing.

A grant was then obtained from the Rotary Foundation of Rotary International 'to develop and implement an effective primary school literacy programme for Surin, Buriram, Srisaket and Chaiyaphum provinces, and to evolve a plan for disseminating it throughout Thailand' (Rotary International, 1987).

It is necessary to carry out a trial of this kind wherever introduction of a CLE programme is contemplated. It is more than just a means by which a central team trials programme units under field conditions: it brings local people into the decision-making, it assists the development of sound strategies for programme development, teacher training, and teacher support, and it provides a realistic basis for costing future work. When large-scale work is envisaged, as in this case, the employment of an external consultant and an external evaluator, also seems highly worthwhile.

The project schedule

Table 7.1 shows the schedule for the project in the four north-east provinces. The plan was to develop the programme for each grade level over one or two years, to trial its major elements in a small number of classrooms during the next year, to pilot the full grade-level programme in 100 classrooms during the following year, and then to help the provincial education authorities to spread it more widely in subsequent years.

Table 7.1 Schedule for programme development and dissemination: Srisaket, Surin, Chaiyaphum and Buriram. (Cumulative numbers of class groups in the programme.)

Year	Grade 1	Grade 2	Grade 3	Grade 4	Grade 5	Grade 6
1988	100	7	Develop	Develop		
1989	400	100	7	programme	Develop	
1990	800	400	100	7	programme	Develop
1991	1600	800	400	100	7	programme
1992	2000	1600	800	400	100	7

To enable students to remain in the CLE programme, once they had entered it, programme development would move up by one school grade level each year. On that basis, programme units for Grade 6, the final year of the primary school, would be trialled in the final (fifth) year of the project.

So the two 'experimental' schools in Surin became 'trial' schools for the large-scale project and a third trial school in the same school district was added. Programme units for each successive school grade continued to be trialled in those three schools for the next five years, one year ahead of their use in forty 'pilot' schools.

As the work moved up the school grades and out to a greater number of schools, its complexity increased. A comparison of the work schedules for 1988 and 1991 reveals something of that increase.

In 1988, the first of the five years of the main project, the schedule for the year was as follows:

1. decide upon the procedures and range of materials for Grade 3, and write programme units;
2. trial the Grade 2 programme in seven classrooms in the one province;
3. pilot the Grade 1 programme in 100 classrooms, in four provinces.

By 1991, the second last year of the project, the work schedule for both the Central project team and the Ministry's provincial offices of education had greatly expanded.

The Central Project team was scheduled to:

1. determine the procedures and materials for the Grade 6 programme and write a range of the programme units;
2. trial units of the Grade 5 programme in seven classrooms in the one province;
3. prepare prototype teacher-training materials for Grade 5;
4. pilot the Grade 4 programme in 100 classrooms in four provinces;
5. revise the Grade 4 teacher-training materials;
6. train forty regional trainers in four provinces for Stage 2 (Grades 3 and 4);
7. print the Grade 3 classroom and teacher-training materials.

The provincial offices of the Ministry were to:

1. conduct 'extension teacher training' for 800 additional Grade 1 teachers, 400 additional Grade 2 teachers, and 300 additional Grade 3 teachers in four provinces;
2. provide year-long supervision and conduct periodic follow-up seminars for newly trained teachers in the four provinces.

Programme costs

The low cost of implementing and maintaining the Thai CLE programme undoubtedly contributed to the rapidity of its spread. A classroom kit that supplied the needs of some thirty students for a year cost US$50 (£25.90) and most of the kit was reusable. Consequently, the replacement cost was approximately US$15 (£8) per class group per year, a figure that was within the Ministry's budget for the existing programme.

Project leadership

Unreserved commitment and perseverance is required at all levels of leadership in any major curriculum project. As can be seen from the increase in the yearly work schedule for the Thai project, however, comparatively few leaders were needed to begin with, and there was time for a structured leadership development scheme to take effect as the workload increased. For the Thai project, there was a pre-planned leadership training system that worked very well.

As the main project began, three leadership groups emerged: a National Coordinating Committee, a Central Project team, and four Provincial Project teams. The National Coordinating Committee consisted of senior representatives of Rotary, of the Ministry of Education, of the Srinakharinwirot University, and of the Central Project team. It met annually, at the time when programme expansion for the next year was being planned. Between those meetings, it did not have an operational role.

The Central Project team consisted of University staff, officers from the Ministry of Education, and Rotary leaders in Thailand. Throughout the five years, this team carried immediate responsibility for coordination of all aspects of the project.

Key personnel from provincial offices of the Ministry of Education managed the project within their own provinces. That included making local arrangements for training and follow-up seminars, and for week-to-week administration and supervision of the work in the schools. When extension training began in the third year of the project, Regional teacher trainers also became available in each province.

Members of the Central team and of provincial teams received training, as part of the project schedule. Members of the Central team were given training in Australia, as well as in Thailand. Through that training they became familiar with current theory and practice in literacy teaching and literacy programme development.

Project leaders at the regional and provincial levels were trained in Thailand by members of the Central Project team, with the assistance of resource persons who were invited from other countries. Other regional and provincial key personnel, including the regional teacher trainers, were trained by members of the Central Project team.

As the programme spread to further regions of the country, officers who had been appointed by the Ministry of Education to oversee the work in each major region were given training within the project leadership training scheme and they were able to use the training materials and procedures that had been developed by the Central Project Team within the main project.

An external chief consultant, Richard Walker, worked mainly with the

Central Project team. He made annual visits to Thailand, and maintained communication with the Project Coordinator and the Rotary Project Chairman between those visits. He also organized the training of project leaders who were brought to Australia for that purpose. The need for his guidance progressively narrowed as the Central team put teacher training and materials development systems in place, and as the programme moved up through the school grades.

No member of any of the Thai Central Project team worked full-time on the project – even the Project Coordinator retained a reduced but still sizeable University teaching load. Consequently, the two contacts with the external consultant each year facilitated regular intensive reviews of progress and attention to emerging problems that may otherwise have been over-shadowed by other professional responsibilities. In particular, they were occasions for firming up procedures and planning the work for the year ahead.

The Project Coordinator, Saowalak Rattanavich, remained directly responsible for programme development throughout the project. She also had direct control of materials development and 'core' teacher training. Regional teacher trainers carried out the 'extension teacher training' (beyond the 100 'pilot' classes for each grade level) but they were prepared for that work by the Central Project team.

One of the consequences of that personal oversight by the Project Coordinator and other members of the Central Project team was control of the programme 'dilution' that often occurs during large-scale programme dissemination.

As extension teacher training grew in volume, the weight of responsibility for programme dissemination moved more and more towards the Ministry of Education, and the Provincial Offices of Education were able to work more autonomously because they now had competent regional teacher trainers.

The schedule that is shown in Table 7.1 laid down what had to be achieved each year in materials development, teacher inservice training, and programme dissemination.

Materials development

As the project began in February 1988, the Grade 1 programme was nearing the end of its 'trial' year. The Grade 1 programme materials were revised on the basis of that trial, and 100 copies of the starter books and the same number of classroom kits were assembled for the Grade 1 classes in the 'pilot' schools.

An instructional video was made from footage obtained in one of the trial schools and a prototype Stage 1 Teacher's Manual was prepared during the early months of 1988. These were reviewed later in the year, and they were heavily revised before they were produced in quantity for the third year. The same process was followed for Stages 2 and 3, in subsequent years.

A writers' workshop was held, in parallel with the last five days of the ten-day orientation seminar, to develop starter books for Grade 2. The people who were chosen to participate in that workshop were educators with known writing expertise, who had attended the orientation seminar during the previous five days in order to become familiar with principles behind the CLE programme. However, the books did not prove to be as satisfactory as was hoped, and the writers' workshops that were held in later years had a different format: the later workshops focused on instruction in book writing and on the specifications for the starter books. The books were then written in the writers' own time.

In every year after the first, the teacher's notes for the year of the programme that had been piloted were reviewed and revised by regional trainers as a part of their training. These notes were then copied in sufficient number for 'extension' training purposes.

The final version of the teacher training materials for Stage 3 (Grade 5 and 6) training was timed for production in the fifth year of the project, in time for use in other regions of the nation.

Strategies for teacher training

By the end of the fourth year, over 20,000 teachers had been trained in various parts of Thailand. This was achieved through what was called the 'multiplier strategy':

1. the Central Project team trained 200 teachers in pilot schools for each of the three stages of the programme;
2. in their second year of teaching, the most effective forty or so of these teachers were trained to operate as regional teacher trainers; and
3. from the third year, these regional teacher trainers staffed the teacher training seminars and follow-up sessions for hundreds of other teachers each year.

When regional trainers trained teachers, that was called 'extension training' as opposed to 'core' teacher training – the training of teachers in pilot schools, by the Central Project team. The materials for extension training were provided by the Central Project team but the Regional trainers played their part in developing those materials. For example, they reviewed and revised the teacher's manual and teacher's notes for their level of the programme, in the course of their training. Because extension teacher training seminars occurred in vacation time, regional trainers did not have to be withdrawn from their own (pilot) schools.

After the decision to spread the programme nationwide, the regional trainers also took part in spreading it to other regions, by special arrangement.

As the CLE programme was introduced into each province, a ten-day seminar was conducted to familiarize provincial and district administrators, provincial supervisors and district supervisors with the project, the programme, and the methodology, before the first teacher training began. At this seminar, these senior participants actually went through the teacher training sequence for the Grade 1 CLE programme shown in Fig. 7.1, before they planned the teacher-training and supervision programmes for their own province. The principals of pilot schools were also given an orientation seminar before the actual teacher training workshops took place.

There were several reasons for giving these senior people first-hand experience with the CLE teaching and teacher training before their teachers became involved. In these isolated areas of the country, it was highly desirable that the normal provincial, district and school support and supervision systems operate for the CLE programme and that they operate efficiently. Moreover, it was considered that the provincial administrators were most likely to develop a sense of ownership of the programme, and make better judgements for its further dissemination if they had a key leadership role, from the very beginning.

In the case of the original four north-east provinces, that leadership role was taken up immediately, as they went on to set up the training workshops for the Grade 1 teachers in their pilot schools straightaway. The teachers themselves were trained in separate nine-day seminars, at their own provincial centres. These teachers left the seminars equipped with the starter books, the classroom equipment, and the materials that they needed to teach for at least a month.

The teacher training strategy that is shown in Fig. 7.1 remained virtually unchanged throughout the term of the project in Thailand.

The training workshop begins with an introduction to the CLE programme and principles. The teaching of the first phase of a programme unit is then demonstrated with a group of children, and reviewed in group discussion. Then, those that are being trained teach that phase of a different programme unit to groups of other children, after which they reassemble to review their teaching of that phase. This procedure is repeated for each of the phases of the CLE teaching sequence, in turn.

Phase 4, which is the making of a 'big book' and preparing word cards, can be done overnight and Phases 1 and 2 may be combined, thereby

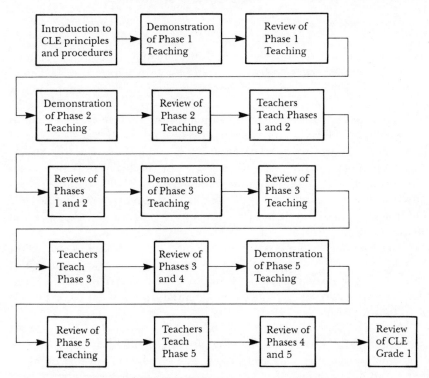

Figure 7.1: The Grade 1 CLE teacher-training sequence

reducing the number of demonstration and practice teaching sessions to three. Accordingly, the minimum length for a teacher-training seminar is three days but it was found desirable to use four days if that were possible. That minimum is set more by the needs of the students than of the teachers, because the groups of students must spend sufficient time on each phase to be able to participate adequately in the teaching of the next phase.

As was stated at the beginning of this section, the most successful Stage 1 teachers and supervisors were given additional training to enable them to act as regional trainers. In their first year of operation, the Stage 1 Regional trainers trained 300 Grade 1 teachers, with members of the Central Project team present, but not taking an active role. Over the next few years, regional trainers for each of the three Stages of the programme trained thousands of teachers, unaided by the Central team except for the supply of basic teacher and pupil materials.

Each year, however, the Central Project team trained and equipped 120 'core' teachers, who piloted the next higher grade level of the programme.

Programme dissemination

With the schedule for the five-year project being maintained, regional trainers trained 800 Grade 1 teachers, 400 Grade 2 teachers, and 300 Grade 3 teachers in 1991. By the end of that year, the Grade 1 programme was being taught in 1600 classrooms in the north-east provinces and some 650 classes in other parts of the land the Grade 2 programme was being taught in more than 1000 classes and the Grade 3 programme in over 400 classes.

Beginning two weeks after Grade 1 teaching began in the 'pilot' classes, members of the Central Project team visited every pilot school. They brought with them additional Grade 1 starter books, and they discussed with the teachers how they had handled the first programme unit and how they might implement the remaining programme units over the weeks ahead.

These initial follow-up visits to schools were regarded as important because they gave an early indication of how effective the first teacher-training workshops had been, and they enabled the project team to find out what was occurring as the programme was introduced across that range of school situations.

After that, the Central Project team revisited these schools at intervals of two months, and half-yearly meetings were held with participating teachers and administrators, to review progress and to discuss possible improvements and modifications. Follow-up visits to the Grade 2 trial classes were continued along with the school visitation programme for Grade 1.

The first end-of-year review, and a comparison of the test scores of the CLE students and a similar number of students still on the old programme, revealed that

1. the CLE Grade 1 programme was clearly producing better results than was the old programme, but that
2. future training workshops should lay greater stress on organizing a classroom for CLE work, and how to move towards teaching a class in small groups.

After 1988, the pattern for bi-monthly follow-up visits was changed so that all of the CLE teachers and supervisors of a province gathered at the provincial centre for a half-day discussion with members of the Central Project team twice each year. Following each of those meetings, Central Project team members visited schools that had been chosen by the provincial key personnel. The schools that Central Project team members visited were chosen as schools needing special help, schools where exceptionally interesting work was being done, and schools that had not been visited for some time. In addition, members of the Central Project team continued to visit the three trial schools.

This procedure was found to be more productive, now that the project team had become familiar with the environment of all the schools. Some advantages of the new system were that it:

1. facilitated administration of the whole project;
2. contributed to teacher morale through the sharing of ideas and experiences;
3. allowed wide-ranging discussion of important matters and an unhurried question and answer session; and
4. saved the project team a great deal of time that would otherwise have been spent in travelling to and from schools, repeatedly giving the same information.

The second year also saw the first 'follow-up meetings' for Grade 1 'extension' teachers that had been trained by Regional trainers. Members of the Central team who attended these first meetings as observers found them highly encouraging in that these teachers seemed in no way inferior to those who were teaching Grade 1 in the pilot schools.

As the CLE programme reached Grade 2 in the pilot schools, teachers began to feel pressure from provincial tests, because the province-wide examinations begin in that grade. Teachers sought reassurance that the results of their students in the provincial examination would not be lower than those who were using the conventional programme, which was designed to prepare them for that examination. Some teachers even tried to teach elements of the conventional programme as well as the CLE programme – a procedure that would certainly confuse their students.

This will commonly become a source of concern in the early stages of substituting a functionally oriented programme for one that is built on traditional sub-skills principles if the students still have to undergo testing that has a discrete-point, sub-skills orientation.

The trialling of the Grade 2 programme had shown that pupils who go through Grades 1 and 2 of the CLE programme develop sub-skills to a high level as well as being much more competent in higher-order literacy skills. That information was given to the Grade 2 teachers but they were also told that any doubt that their students would score well on sub-skills test could be dispelled by adding to Phase 5 of each programme unit games that were oriented towards the particular sub-skills.

To substantiate that advice, the project team administered both conventional and 'pragmatic' literacy tests to 25 per cent of the Grade 1 students and 48 per cent of the Grade 2 students who were in the CLE programme, and compared their results with those from testing a similar number of students from matched class groups outside the programme.

On the 'pragmatic' test items, the scores of CLE students were very much superior indeed – a high proportion of the 'control' group children failed absolutely to cope with many of those items. However, the main concern of the teachers was with scores on the standardized 'Thai language performance test', provided by the Thai Ministry of Education. On that test, the scores of the CLE student groups were also superior for both Grade 1 and Grade 2, with differences that were significant at the 0.001 level of confidence. These results on tests by which literacy achievement would be assessed in provincial examinations provided very welcome support for the reassurance that the project team had so often to give.

However, the use of discrete-point provincial examinations in literacy placed unnecessary stress on the Grade 2 CLE teachers and a request that students within the CLE programme not be required to sit for the current provincial literacy tests was endorsed by the Central Office of the Ministry of Primary Education and the problem was solved for that year.

However, the quality of literacy testing is of central importance in improving literacy curricula and literacy teaching because, as John Oller points out in Chapter 5, 'Curriculum and teaching will rise or fall to the level of the testing'. With an urgent need to improve literacy testing before the CLE programme was adopted nationwide, the Ministry of Education and the project team cooperatively mounted a national seminar and workshop on language testing, headed by John Oller. In the workshop, new schemes for language testing and new test instruments were planned and reports indicate that many of the provinces are continuing that work by setting up local training seminars in literacy testing.

Formative testing continued to reveal that rapid improvement in learning to read, write and speak Thai was occurring, in all areas where the programme was introduced. That kind of evidence remained strong after the Stage 2 programme was introduced – almost all Grade 3 and Grade 4 students could write lengthy reports, stories, poems, and others kinds of texts. This was a crucial outcome because everywhere, the real incidence of failure to learn to read and write seems to become evident at that stage of schooling.

In the fourth year, too, questionnaires were widely used to collect information on such things as student attitudes to school, to reading and to writing, and on teacher perceptions about the adequacy of CLE training, CLE teacher materials, and follow-up support. The data that was collected revealed clear gains in all these affective areas, even more so in the southern and northern provinces than in the north-east, where the project began.

Extension beyond the main project

Towards the end of the second year, 1990, it was decided to investigate whether the CLE programme should be introduced in the south of Thailand. Members of the literacy team visited the south of Thailand to see the educational conditions that existed there, and to prepare teachers in each province to teach the first three units of the Grade 1 programme, as a test of its effectiveness with children of these strongly Muslim communities where Yawee (a Malaysia dialect) is spoken as first language. It was found that:

1. in some schools, very few of the students, at any grade level, could speak standard Thai;
2. there was an appearance of severe poverty in rural families, though not so extreme as in the north-east provinces;
3. school attendance was poor;
4. particularly in rural schools, the majority of the students were failing to learn to read or write;
5. all the supervisors, principals, and teachers were enthusiastic at the prospect of using the CLE programme.

The trial with three Grade 1 programme units was highly successful, and all thirty-seven trial schools were equipped and trained to continue with the programme, as demonstration schools. The results from end-of-year testing in these schools are particularly interesting. Table 7.2 gives a comparison of the scores – on a 'cloze' test of reading, a writing task, and a dictation test – of the thirty-seven class groups that were on the CLE programme and an equal number of matched class groups that were on the conventional literacy programme. The performance of the students on the CLE programme was clearly superior on all three tests – at the 0.001 level of confidence.

Late in the same year, the Thai Ministry of Education informed the

Table 7.2 A comparison of Thai language scores of Grade 1 CLE programme students in the five southern border provinces and those in control classes for the 1990 academic year

Comparison of pilot and control Grade 1 classes Southern provinces 1990	CLE schools (37 classes)		Control school (37 classes)		
	X	SD	X	SD	t
Scores on cloze test of reading	9.99	7.87	5.28	6.37	13.64
Scores on writing task	13.90	10.16	9.79	10.63	8.17
Scores on dictation task	30.37	15.44	23.85	16.77	8.36
Total scores	54.26	25.45	38.92	25.62	12.39

p <0.001

project team that the CLE methodology for language and literacy teaching had been adopted for the nation in the Plan for National Economic and Social Development (1992–96). At the same time, the Ministry requested cooperation in quickly establishing a CLE programme in schools of the northern hill-tribe provinces, and in setting up demonstration schools in all other provinces, before 1992.

With the spread of CLE teaching to all regions of the land, the writing of 'regional' starter books became a priority. A book development workshop was held to produce starter books for use with hill-tribe students. More than thirty Grade 1 and Grade 2 books were produced for trial in those northern schools.

By the middle of the 1991 school year, some 350 hill-tribe schools were using the CLE programme in Chieng Mai, Mae Hong Sorn and Chieng Rai provinces. The programme was introduced simultaneously into Grade 1 and Grade 2 classes, to save a year in taking the programme up through the grades. That strategy involved using a condensed Grade 1/Grade 2 programme with the first Grade 2 groups, but that can be done because the learning–teaching strategies do not change substantially between those two grades.

Follow-up visits revealed that, unlike in the past, these students were now purposefully engaged in school learning at a rate comparable to students in other parts of Thailand, and they were speaking, reading and writing standard Thai in the course of their learning activities.

Further training seminars in six northern provinces catered for another 650 teachers before the end of 1991. It seemed that the number of schools that could begin CLE teaching was limited by the supply of classroom kits rather than by ability to provide teacher training or any lack of schools willing to change to the new programme.

Finally, thirty people who had proved to be highly successful in CLE teaching and teacher training were selected from all regions of Thailand to undertake a special role in the large-scale inservice teacher training that was planned for all regions of the country during the following and subsequent years. They received additional training in a six-day seminar/workshop.

Unrelated to preparation for the 1992–96 National Plan for Education, Thai-language preschool CLE work sprang up in preschool centres, ranging from centres in Bangkok slums to private preschool centres. The latter marked the first use of the CLE method by teachers in private schools.

Work with English-language CLE programmes

CLE teaching of English began on a small scale in primary schools in several provinces where the Thai-language CLE programme had been introduced. Teachers there used materials that had been developed by graduate students of Srinakharinwirot University during their practicum in teaching English. The results of the trial were encouraging, but it became clear that teachers needed much greater support if they were to teach English in English, rather than attempting to teach it in Thai.

During 1990, a CLE-training workshop was conducted for 120 teachers of English in Buriram and Chaiyaphum to explore further the possibility of teaching English as a foreign language, using CLE techniques. Some forty of those teachers abandoned the conventional Grade 5 English programme in favour of a CLE programme.

After these teachers had trialled CLE techniques for a year, the Ministry of Education decided to explore more widely the possibility of using CLE techniques in the teaching of English. The Central Project team, reinforced by a teacher from Australia, staffed a Ministry of Education seminar for 100 teachers of English from all provinces of Thailand. English-language starter books for Grade 5, with cassette audiotapes, and prototype 'English for CLE teachers' booklets, with accompanying audiotapes, were produced for the occasion.

Following that workshop, it was proposed that a complete programme and teacher-training materials for teaching English as a foreign language should be developed in Thailand for use there and in neighbouring countries. This project is still being formulated at the time of writing.

Conclusion

There is no doubt that CLE techniques are exceptionally effective for teaching literacy to children whose mother tongue differs from the language of instruction. Some CLE schools in Buriram province, for example, have only Khmer-speaking children, in other schools in Surin and Srisaket, there are both Khmer- and Lao-speaking students, and in still other schools, Lao is the predominant first language. In south Thailand, the mother tongue of almost all the children is a language that is a dialect of Bahasa Malaysia, a very different language from Thai.

But the most convincing evidence came from the northern provinces of Thailand. The schools of Chieng Mai province, for example, range from those where all the students speak an easily understood northern regional dialect of Thai to schools where all the students speak one or another of the hill-tribe languages that are incomprehensible to Thai speakers. After trialling the CLE programme across those differing situations, the Chieng Mai Office of Primary Education is now spreading the CLE programme through all its schools, as rapidly as resources allow.

Add to that the use of the CLE methodology with Australian Aboriginal children and with children in India and Bangladesh, and it can be said that the methodology has been tested across a wide range of language situations.

It is significant, too, that many of these children were from totally illiterate family backgrounds. The Australian Aboriginal children, most of the children in the rural areas of north-east Thailand, and all the hill-tribe children, came from homes that did not contain a single item of written material in any language.

The system for inservice teacher training that was developed in Thailand also appears to be a highly effective one for developing countries and, as such, it could prove very useful in other countries. The teacher inservice training task that faced the Thai Ministry of Education in changing their national literacy curriculum, seemed to be a huge barrier to instituting a better literacy programme.

But the procedures had been developed, the teacher training materials had been produced, and large numbers of teachers had been trained in every region even before the five-year plan was to take effect. And there seems to have been remarkably few teacher-training failures, even when teachers trained other teachers.

A third significant factor was the use of writers' workshops to adapt the programme to a new region. It was found that teachers and others could quickly be trained to write CLE starter books and unit outlines that were suited to the needs and characteristics of students in a particular region of the country.

An account of the rapid spread of a programme necessarily emphasizes mass teacher training and the mass production of materials. In doing that, it may give an impression that every CLE teacher, everywhere in Thailand, is teaching in exactly the same way, following the same teaching plans, and completing each programme unit in the same length of time. That impression is misleading, because no two classrooms are the same. In one classroom, there may be an atmosphere of noisy competition, with cheer squads in full cry while, in another, there will be quiet, concentrated activity, as small groups of students cooperate in pursuing their allotted tasks. Very different classroom practices have developed from an understanding of the same basic principles CLE teaching. Teachers realize that, as long as they keep to the CLE teaching sequence, there is more than ample scope for variation in teaching style, in group activities and in content.

There is ample room, too for teachers to be pedantic about spelling and good handwriting if they see that as necessary, provided that the sub-skills teaching is done in the final phase, using CLE procedures, and as long as competent students are not being unduly delayed or becoming bored.

Moreover, the range of games and other activities that have been invented by Thai teachers for the final phase of Stage 1 and Stage 2 CLE teaching is somewhat overwhelming to those who visit many schools because different ones are to be seen everywhere. What goes on in classrooms that are truly student- and activity-centred can be as varied as are the students themselves, and what they and their teachers enjoy doing.

Then there are the kinds of differences that occurred between the CLE programme units that were developed in Alice Springs for Aboriginal students, and those produced in Thailand. In the Alice Springs programme, for example, every programme unit tended to continue for a number of weeks or even months. The student texts there were more elaborately produced, with photographs and even drawings by professional artists, and with heavy, well-designed covers. In Thailand, although the orthography in the group texts tended to be more beautiful and exact, the students did all the illustrating, and after the first few months, they also wrote the script for their group texts.

Those differences stem from the local culture, from what technology is available, from different notions as to what students get from making a text, and from what further use will be made of it. Group texts are used continuously in areas of Thailand where there are few other reading materials, so that they fall apart by the end of the year. In contrast, the Alice Springs texts were preserved almost as show pieces. No doubt the group texts being produced by the children in India and in Bangladesh are different again.

To reiterate what was stated in Chapter 4: a CLE programme cannot be transported from place to place. Instead, every CLE programme should be developed where it is to be used, and, as far as possible, by those who will use it. That being so, CLE programmes will look different in the classrooms of different countries and peoples.

Finally, CLE programmes can be very inexpensive, once they have been fully developed so that they promise a timely breakthrough to achieving the cost-effectiveness that is needed if universal literacy is to become more than a dream in many of the developing countries. It is true that such an educational breakthrough is only a beginning to a full solution of mass literacy problems, hopeful though that is. For example, when Thailand has successful CLE school literacy programmes operating in all parts of the country, it will have created a further problem for itself: the schools will need well-stocked libraries for use by their actively literate students. To have reached this problem, however, is to have gone a long way down the road to alleviating mass illiteracy.

CHAPTER 8

Reflecting on the contexts of reading

RICHARD WALKER

Introduction

The central message of this book is that there is no need for so many children to fail to become active readers and writers – in either industrialized or developing countries. It was asserted in Chapter 1 that we should cease explaining away the sizeable proportion of children who fail to learn to read and write and, instead, devise school programmes through which *all* the students learn to read, not just those who have some particular kind of family and experiential background.

It follows that we should also critically examine all compensatory programmes. It is the nature of compensatory programmes that they require children, who are perceived to be different in some way, to travel by a different and usually longer road to literacy than do other children. This being so, we have to be quite sure that a compensatory programme is not just an attempt to change children so that they fit into the existing programme rather than to change the school programme so that it suits all the children.

To judge by a recent front-page report in the Australian national newspaper (*The Australian*, 29–30 June 1991), there are some who even want the compensatory programmes to include the whole family. Under the headline 'Illiteracy may be inherited' this feature article reports on a research finding that a high proportion of school children who are having reading difficulties have at least one parent who cannot read or write; and it goes on to state,

> There is strong evidence that illiteracy is an inherited trait, and some educationists believe it is a contagious disorder best cured by treating the whole family.

The article also reports that

> 30 per cent of the families admitted or were strongly suspected of at least two generations of illiteracy

but it does not suggest that the treatment extend back beyond the living.

People who reason from that philosophical basis would surely have recommended a compensatory language programme for Mary, the little Aboriginal girl who was described in Chapter 1; but Mary's later performance within the Traeger Park CLE programme proved that no compensatory programme was needed. She was a child of more than average potential, who did not need to be changed in any way before she was ready to learn to read and write. The fact that the CLE approach has subsequently succeeded with many thousands of children in many situations, where there had been a history of gross failure, indicates that Mary's is not an isolated case; and that there are many Marys in many places who are failing to learn to read and write only because the school literacy programme is failing them.

A note about contexts

Associated with that central message, and with how the number of failures may be reduced, several major sub-themes permeate what all three authors have written. One such sub-theme is a need to abandon language-reading programmes that focus only on the phonological and the syntactic levels of language, apart from context and purpose. To quote John Oller from Chapter 7, 'A certain recipe for failure in any kind of language instruction is to get children to process linguistic forms that are essentially unrelated to any factual data.' It is from the context of reality – of human needs and daily life – that the meaning, power and usefulness of language is derived; and to try to teach language as if it can be isolated from context is a nonsense.

This chapter presents a closer examination of that sub-theme; and its implications for literacy teaching.

There are two types of context:

1. the context to which the language refers; and
2. the context in which the students are operating.

For convenience, we shall refer to the first of these as the *referential context,* the context to which the language refers; and the second kind as the *operational context,* the situation within which the language users are operating. As quoted above, Oller is referring to both of those kinds of contexts, but some elaboration is still needed.

When a class in a school in England is talking about hunting deer in the Appalachian Mountains of the United States of America, their operational context is their English classroom, its occupants and what is going on there. At the same time, their referential context – what they are talking about – is hunters, deer, the terrain of the Appalachian Mountains, and what goes on there.

In CLE teaching, there is an exceptionally strong focus on the operational context, because, in difficult educational circumstances, the first priority is to develop learning/teaching environments that enable all the students to become actively involved. Only when that has been done, can the teacher focus on managing those environments in ways that enable the students to engage in discourse, and thereby to learn to use language.

The process of 'scaffolding', that has often been mentioned in previous chapters, depends on context – it amounts to contextual support. When discourse relates to and is supported by non-linguistic cues, and when it relates to what Oller refers to in Chapter 5 as 'facts of experience', it is said to be *scaffolded*.

Those facts of experience have to do with the referential context as defined above. However, discourse has structure and function on a deeper level than the meaning of linguistic items. In real life, discourse occurs in the course of and is intermeshed with interactive non-language activity. All important types of interactive activity has structure and real-life purposes; and participants need to understand what is going on, and how what is being said relates to other aspects of what is going on, if they are to manage their part in the discourse. This has to do with the operational context of the discourse.

Fig. 8.1 shows spoken discourse as being related to both a referential context and an operational context. It could be said that the language used in the discourse derives its meaning from its referential context, and its function and purpose from its relationship to the operational context. Those two contexts may or may not be the same.

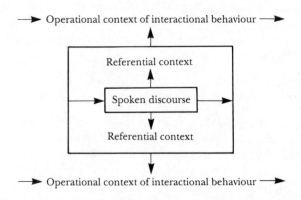

Figure 8.1: Spoken discourse related to both a referential and an operational context

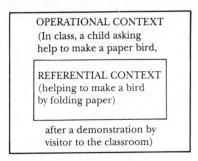

Figure 8.2: Coincidence of referential context and operational context

The task of language users is easiest when the referential context and the operational context coincide, so that they are talking about what is going on around them.

Fig. 8.2 illustrates this kind of situation. A Japanese visitor has shown a class of children how to fold paper to make a bird and flap its wings; and a student is asking another for help to make such a bird. Under these circumstances, the amount of information that has to be included in the child's request is minimal, because the referents (the task, the paper, the bird that the visitor has made, and the child who is addressed) are visible to both children, and both have witnessed a demonstration of the required process (folding the paper). The child would say something like, 'Help me to make my bird.'

When the referential context coincides with the operational context, the chances of being misunderstood are close to zero – so much so, that the request would very likely be understood even if the second child could not speak the language, the more so if facial expression, intonation and gesture are taken into account.

Another way of looking at this is shown in Fig. 8.3. The language behaviour is interwoven with and is interpretable against non-language behaviour, and, at the same time, the talk is about objects and people that are present and visible. In these circumstances, learners can easily and confidently relate language elements to corresponding elements and rela-

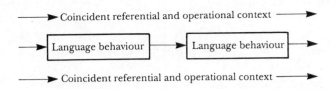

Figure 8.3: Language behaviour related to a context of non-language behaviour

tionships of the reality being spoken or written about – the language inter-action is heavily scaffolded – and they also know what speakers are trying to achieve by their talk, and how the language interaction fits into what else is going on. The resemblance to what is happening as an infant begins to understand and speak its mother tongue is obvious.

Let us suppose, however, that a day has passed and the child who made a paper bird has to recount that event to the class (still within the class-room). The child's language task would now be more difficult; and more complex language will be needed to carry it out. But the increase is not great because the paper bird is still there, and the listeners have also witnessed the events that are being recounted. The child might say some-thing like, 'Harry and I made that paper bird, yesterday, after the Japanese lady showed us how.' That would be enough to recall the experience, together with memories of associated circumstances and events; and fur-ther talk about what happened, who did what, and personal reactions to all and any of those things could readily flow.

However, let us imagine that the recounting took place away from the classroom. In the absence of what is being spoken about, there is a greater possibility of misinterpretation, so more information has to be given and the language task becomes more difficult again. The child would have to say something like, 'Did you see the paper bird that Harry and I made at school yesterday, after the Japanese lady showed us how?' Nevertheless, it would not be difficult for the listeners to relate that to the actual events.

But suppose, instead, that the child is recounting that same event to her mother, who did not witness the paper-folding event. Now the task is considerably more difficult and the language has to convey considerably more information about the referential context. With all efforts, the refer-ential 'reality' that the mother builds up in her mind will differ from what actually occurred, the more so if she has never personally experienced such an event.

The child may have to say something like, 'A Japanese lady came to school yesterday, and she showed us how to make a bird out of paper. Harry and I made one, and we could even make it flap its wings like hers did.'

In the circumstances that are illustrated in Fig. 8.4, the mother has to draw inferences from her own experience of school-room situations and paper-folding to fill out a picture from what the child is saying. And com-plex discourse skills and relatively complex language may be called upon, in questions and answers, before the participants are satisfied that they fully understand each other.

The gradation in difficulty that we have sketched out for spoken dis-course applies also to written language tasks, revealing an important di-mension of what makes some reading and writing tasks harder than others.

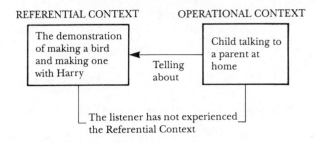

Figure 8.4: Referential context unrelated to the context of operation

The task for readers and writers is least demanding when the referential context coincides with the operational context, as in Fig. 8.2. In those circumstances, what is being written or read is readily interpretable against the reality to which it refers, whereas, in the circumstances that are shown in Fig. 8.4, the task may well be impossible if the reader has not had experience with the referential context.

A child's first encounters with written language should be amidst a context of shared experience, with the written language being open to clear interpretation and discussion because it refers to that shared context. To a considerable extent that explains why the strategies that are used in Phases 1 and 2 of the Stage 1 CLE programmes enable all the students to participate in the learning. If, on the other hand, the first experience that children have with reading resembles the situation shown in Fig. 8.4, the chances are high that some of the children will not be able to understand what is going on, in the absence of strong contextual support for the language.

When the language of instruction is a second language or second dialect

Another sub-theme of this book has been that children can learn to speak a second dialect or second language along with learning to read and write. The more general policy has been to introduce the students to the written mode of a language only after they have a reasonable grasp of the spoken mode; so that instruction in the speaking of the language of instruction precedes learning to read and write. As was pointed out in the conclusion to Chapter 7, experience with CLE programmes casts serious doubt on the necessity for that. It seems very likely that young children are more capable language learners that they are given credit for by those who see a need for teaching only one language mode at a time.

If we continue our examination of scaffolding, in terms of contextual support for language, we can see why that may be so.

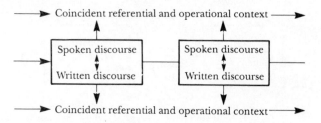

Figure 8.5: Spoken and written discourse, related to each other and to the same contexts

Fig. 8.5 shows corresponding spoken and written language being used along with the non-language contexts behaviour that they refer to, as happens in Phase 3 of the Stage 1 CLE programme. Both the spoken and the written discourse are supported by the context; and, moreover, they support each other. These conditions are favourable for learning to discourse in both modes of the language at the same time. The demand is low, for both modes, because both the spoken and the written language are heavily scaffolded. Moreover, the teacher can reinforce that scaffolding, by gesture, by using the spoken language to help understanding of the written text, and so on, enabling all the students to participate, whether or not they are familiar with the language of instruction.

Conclusion

When teachers with a traditional orientation first witness good CLE teaching the most frequent reaction is amazement at what the students read and write. To some, it is unbelievable that Grade 3 students in a Khmer-speaking, Buriram school, for example, write copiously in standard Thai, including writing beautiful poetry. Probably the most valuable lesson of all, to be learnt from this extensive field experience with CLE techniques in educationally difficult regions, is that the placing of limits on what children should learn and when they should learn it is destructive of learning.

In the past, texts were graded for difficulty in regard to such things as the length of words, the number of words per sentence, and the type, length and complexity of sentences and paragraphs. In addition, the difficulty level of texts that students encountered within reading programmes was carefully controlled. The great error was that teachers then came to believe that students of a particular age were not capable of more than that, and that ability to read and write had to be developed in the sequence that was set down by these arbitrarily imposed limitations.

CLE teaching places no such limits on the difficulty of what a child is allowed to read or write. While children are learning to speak their mother tongue, within the home, they learn to do amazingly difficult and complex things with language, in a very short time. No one places limits there on what they should try to learn. Once children are placed within circumstances where they become enthusiastic readers and writers, they will learn to do things that are similarly amazing, if we do not place limits on what they are allowed to do. In that case, the discrepancy between failure rates in learning to use the spoken and written modes of language that was referred to in Chapter 1 may well diminish – in the best possible way.

References

Brisbane College of Advanced Education (BCAE) (1982) *The Mount Gravatt Developmental Language Reading Program.* Syndey: Addison-Wesley.

Cazden, C.B. (1977) Concentrated versus contrived encounters: suggestions for language assessment in early childhood education. In A. Davies (ed.) *Language Learning in Early Childhood.* London: Heinemann.

Chapman, L.J. (1987) 'Report to Rotary International on the Thailand Pilot Literacy Project'. Manuscript.

Gray, B. (1980) *Developing Language and Literacy with Urban Aboriginal Children.* A first report on the Traeger Park Project presented at Conference 80/2. Darwin: Northern Territory, Department of Education.

Gray, B. (1983) *Helping Children become Language Learners in the Classroom.* A paper delivered at the annual conference of the Meanjin Reading Council, Brisbane, May.

Halliday, M.A.K. (1973) *Explorations in the Functions of Language.* London: Edward Arnold.

Halliday, M.A.K. and Hasan, R. (1985) *Language, Context and Text: A Social Semiotic Perspective.* Geelong: Deakin University Press.

Morris, A. and Stewart-Dore, N. (1984) *Learning to Learn from Text.* Sydney: Addison-Wesley.

Mount Gravatt Developmental Language Reading Program (1982) *Language at Work, Level 5 and Level 6.* Sydney: Addison-Wesley.

Rattanavich, S. and Walker, R.F. (1990) The Rotary Literacy in Thailand Project. *Education for All: Report of the UNESCO South East Asia and South Pacific Regional Conference.* Darwin: Northern Territory Department of Education.

Rotary International (1987) 3-H Literacy Project in Thailand. *Project Application to the Rotary Foundation of Rotary International.* Evanston: The Rotary Foundation of Rotary International.

Smith, F.C. (1982) *Writing and the Writer.* New York: Holt.

Smith, R.J. and Johnson, D.D. (1976) *Teaching Children to Read.* Reading: Addison-Wesley.

Walker, R.F. (1981) *The Language of Entering Children at Traeger Park School.* Occasional Paper No. 11. Canberra: The Australian Curriculum Development Centre.

Walker, R.F. and Rattanavich, S. (1987) *The Concentrated Language Encounter Programme at Srinakharinwirot University.* A paper presented at the Regional English Language Centre Seminar: The Role of Language Education in Human Resource Development. Singapore, 13–16 April.

Wells, G. (1981) *Learning through Interaction: The Study of Language Development.* Cambridge: Cambridge University Press.

Wickert, R. (1989) *No Single Measure: A Survey of Australian Adult Literacy.* Canberra: Commonwealth Department of Employment, Education and Training.

Index